Stuart lives in Tauranga, New Zealand. Up until the beginning of 2020, international work, recreational travel, children and grandchildren occupied the bulk of his time. Then COVID-19 lockdown arrived to New Zealand in March 2020. This gave him the necessary breathing space to write his first novel. It was something that had been parked for a long time. He is especially interested in the scientific world including its diverse geology, fauna and flora. During his travels, Stuart has silently observed how people interact on a personal and group level, and has embraced the amazing diversity of global cultures experienced.

Stuart Duff

RETURN TO HUNTERVILLE AND
THE MĀNUKA HONEY SHOP

AUSTIN MACAULEY PUBLISHERS™
LONDON * CAMBRIDGE * NEW YORK * SHARJAH

Copyright © Stuart Duff 2022

The right of Stuart Duff to be identified as author of this work has been asserted by the author in accordance with sections 77 and 78 of the Copyright, Designs and Patents Act 1988.

All rights reserved. No part of this publication may be reproduced, stored in a retrieval system, or transmitted in any form or by any means, electronic, mechanical, photocopying, recording, or otherwise, without the prior permission of the publishers.

Any person who commits any unauthorised act in relation to this publication may be liable to criminal prosecution and civil claims for damages.

This is a work of fiction. Names, characters, businesses, places, events, locales, and incidents are either the products of the author's imagination or used in a fictitious manner. Any resemblance to actual persons, living or dead, or actual events is purely coincidental.

A CIP catalogue record for this title is available from the British Library.

ISBN 9781398478459 (Paperback)
ISBN 9781398478466 (Hardback)
ISBN 9781398478480 (ePub e-book)
ISBN 9781398478473 (Audiobook)

www.austinmacauley.com

First Published 2022
Austin Macauley Publishers Ltd®
1 Canada Square
Canary Wharf
London
E14 5AA

Thanks to Austin Macauley Publishers for supporting a first time author. Thanks for helping make the impossible dream, possible.

Thanks to Kristal and Larissa for their ongoing support, enthusiasm and encouragement whilst Dad wrote his first novel.

Thanks to the people of Naples, Italy and Hunterville, New Zealand for embracing where they live and for giving countless treasured memories to the author.

Thanks for the magnificence that is Naples, and the unpretentious beauty that is Hunterville and its surrounding district. Both are inspiring.

Table of Contents

Aoife in Galway, Ireland	10
Aoife and Kieran	13
Aoife and Mr Ryan O'Leary	20
William in Hunterville, New Zealand	26
William's World	30
Hunterville Township	33
William and Ram	35
Aoife Arrives and Settles into Naples, Italy	41
William Arrives and Settles into Naples, Italy	47
Nonna Russo's Cooking Class	53
Piazza Bellini and the National Archaeological Museum	61
Sansevero Chapel and the Veiled Christ	73
Herculaneum Ruins and Horse-Riding on Mount Vesuvius	83
Lazy Sunday Around the Waterfront	96
Funicular Railway to San Martino Castle	111
Subterranean Naples and the Palaeontology Museum	127
Churches in the Old City Area and the Vintage Clothing Shop	139
Dinner at Aoife's Apartment	154
Friday Night at the Opera	168
Farewell to Naples	189

Return to Galway and the Surprising Development	194
Return to Hunterville and the Mānuka Honey Shop	200
William and Aoife Make Plans to Reunite	210
Reunited	225
William and Aoife Settle into Life on the Farm	234
Visit to the Café and Mānuka Honey Shop	239
William Scores a Try	247
Celebration at the Mānuka Honey Shop	252
Wedding Plans	267
Wedding Day and Celebration at Simpsons Reserve	281
William Loses His Father	287
Funeral at Hunterville Cemetery	290
The Old Woman by the Giant Macrocarpa Tree	293

How difficult we find it to smile at each other, but that smile is the beginning of love...so let us always meet each other with a smile.

Mother Teresa/Noble Peace Prize acceptance speech, 11 December 1979

Aoife in Galway, Ireland

"Aoife, can you please pull me another glass of beer?"

"Of course," replied Aoife as she had one eye firmly fixed on the clock on the wall, and one eye fixed on her favourite and most loyal customer, Mr Ryan O'Leary. The clock was showing 6 pm.

Although he was her favourite customer at the King Brian Pub, she actually knew very little about him. He was seventy years old, retired, travelled a lot, lived alone and never talked about family. That much she had gleaned from him over the past six months. She wasn't even sure if he had a family. When she did converse with him, it was a case of the proverbial "like getting water out of a stone". He always came to the pub alone, sat alone and left alone. He rarely spoke to anybody and it took a long time before he communicated with Aoife. But the one thing that she did know once conversation between the two of them was a bit more natural, was that he was polite, conservative, friendly, quiet and reliable. She definitely had a soft spot for him. It was hard to say exactly why, but every time she talked to him, even though they were just for short periods, it was reassuring and comforting. Aoife felt she could trust him even though there was a pronounced generational difference.

The pub scene in the city centre of Galway was lively. The setting of the King Brian Pub was both historical and picture perfect sitting close to the right bank of the River Corrib a few hundred meters before it flowed out into Galway Bay. Its clientele was a hotchpotch of interesting and not so interesting types. The arty farty, the fashionistas, the wannabes, the never-will-bes, the hardworking, the artisan foodies, the depressed, the depressing, the optimistic and the musical. The bar food was good and hearty and affordable. The coddle and collar and cabbage were the real deal.

Aoife O'Brien had been working at the King Brian Pub for just over twelve months since she had moved to Galway from the family farm in Ballinrobe.

Ballinrobe was a small rural town on the banks of the River Robe some two kilometres from Lake Mask, and some forty kilometres north of Galway.

The family farm which was a modest 20 hectares (50 acres) was a specialist sheep farm with minor intensive cropping. The sheep were bred for both meat and wool. It was getting harder to make a living from the farm so her parents had opened a small self-contained one-bedroom holiday cottage on the farm, and her brother had started a honey operation. The artisan wool from the farm was starting to get an international following thanks to some clever Irish marketing from Aoife's mother, and her brother's honey was also developing a strong consumer base following the same Irish marketing. Things were improving financially for the family run farm.

Scenically, the area around Ballinrobe and Lake Mask was quintessential Irish countryside. It was lush and green and rolling and had a mystical air to it. The type of countryside where you'd half expect a mischievous Leprechaun or a Pixie Queen to appear from behind a huge rock and wish you 'a long life and a merry one'.

Working at the King Brian Pub wasn't a career choice for Aoife but more of a temporary job while she figured out the forward plan. The past twelve months had flashed by and she had made very little progress sorting out the forward plan.

Life on the O'Brien family farm near Ballinrobe was pleasant enough but for Aoife at 24 years old, the option of simply staying on the farm was limited. Aoife's parents were always supportive but with her elder brother destined to take over the running of the family farm in the next year or two, Aoife felt it was time to head out into the big wide world and explore her place in the world. So that's what she did. Not too far away to start with. Somewhere close enough that she could visit family regularly and without too much difficulty. She didn't have a car largely due to economic reasons, so whenever she wanted to get back to the family farm, either her brother or father collected her, or she used the public transport bus which travelled between Galway and Ballinrobe four times a day seven days a week. Bussing was her preferred method of travelling to and from the family farm.

Galway was close enough to Ballinrobe to enable her to head to the farm and ride her beloved horse when the opportunity arrived. It was close enough to go home and mentally and physically reinvigorate the body and mind when the occasion arose. Although she had a healthy curiosity for everything going on in the world, she was also happy and contented with the simple pleasures of life. Although she had social media accounts she very rarely used them.

The clock on the wall of the pub indicated 7 pm and that meant 'going home time' for Aoife. Her daily shift started at 11 am. For most people, 'going home time' would be received with relief and excitement that the hard graft was over for another day, but for Aoife, going home time was becoming more and more difficult, and it was often fraught with anguish and sadness.

It hadn't always been like this.

Aoife and Kieran

It was twelve months earlier that Aoife had met Kieran at an exhibition at a local art gallery. He was an invited exhibitor and she was an interested passing by attendee. The Riverside Gallery was well known both locally and nationally as a supporter of up and coming regional artists. Artists that would quite often be assigned as not being of the mainstream types. The exhibition title was "Galway Uncensored" with the one covet being that the gallery managers had the right to decline to show any artwork that was extremely or blatantly offensive to Galway City, or offensive to various minority groups, or any named individuals. Times had changed significantly over the previous ten years and all presenting artists were expected to be socially sensitive and accountable, but at the same time, the exhibition subject was "Galway Uncensored" which in itself evoked certain degree of leniency in subject matter. It was a balancing act.

Kieran's work was titled "Beneath the Surface". The title didn't give a lot of clues as to what the subject matter actually was, however, the accompanying notes briefly stated that the artwork explored 16th and 17th century historical objects lost and lying forgotten beneath the surface of the River Corrib.

That gave Aoife very few clues as to what the painting might actually represent. She wondered if it might mean treasure or artefacts, or if was it something else completely.

The painting itself was an expansive 2 m × 2 m oil comprising a dark blue black background with human skeletons seemingly floating in various positions. The skeletons varied infant to adult, male to female, and although most were intact, some indicated lost limbs and a few even appeared headless.

Aoife moved in for a closer look. Nothing was ringing a bell in her head.

She was immediately greeted with "*Dia dhuit, tadhg is ainm dom.* I'm Kieran, welcome and thank you for dropping by."

Aoife's beauty hadn't gone unnoticed by Kieran.

"Hello, I'm Aoife. I'm on my way to work which is just down near the Riverside Walkway. I'm a bit early so thought I'd drop in and take a look."

She continued to look and ponder at the artwork in front of her. Tilting her head at various angles while looking at the artwork didn't help make it any clearer.

"It's a kind of non-specific exhibition title so I was curious as to what the various artists would present. I'm not sure what your painting represents. No, sorry, that's not true. Apologies, but to be totally honest, I haven't got a clue what your painting represents."

"Well, this place has history Aoife. I know what you're thinking, everywhere has history. Galway hasn't always been as near perfect and tranquil as it is now. Maybe I can explain it to you over a cup of coffee sometime, just if and when you're not so busy?"

Kieran was captivated by Aoife's natural beauty and Irish charm. A true 'colleen' if ever there was. Her blonde locks flowing freely over her shoulders, her clear blue eyes, the flawless pale skin, the perpetual smile and the healthy feminine form didn't go unnoticed. Kieran loved her broad Irish accent. It was the type of Irish accent that makes normal men go wobbly at the knees. Every word that came out of her mouth flowed forth as if she was singing an Irish folk song.

Similarly, Aoife was intrigued by the Irish man that presented in front of her. She liked his smile. It was the type of smile that was infectious and comforting. Kieran was tall and slim and had dark brooding features, piercing dark green eyes, unruly medium length dark hair and a boldness that caught her off guard.

"I usually work from 11 am to 7 pm so any day mid-morning around 10 am would work for me. Does that work for you? How about the Secret Garden Café on William Street West over on the other side of the river. It is nice and quiet there. I quite often go there for a morning pick me up and then slowly stroll back over the Wolfe Tonne Bridge to work."

"Perfect," replied Kieran "I can meet you there tomorrow morning just before 10 am. Do you want to exchange mobile phone numbers?"

"No need. I'll be there and if you're not there I'll just enjoy the peaceful courtyard garden over a drink. It's always picture perfect in early summer."

"OK, no pressure. See you tomorrow."

At that point, Aoife made a beeline for the door and disappeared into the early summer sunshine. The days were beginning to warm up slightly now that it was officially summertime. The need to wear heavy winter coats and jackets had gone. In places, the trees lining the banks of the river were all fully green leaved and the varicoloured ceramic flower pots outside the front of pubs and cafes and restaurants and businesses were in early summer flower. The grass strip on the left side of the riverbank was now being used by people to sit and relax, to gossip and plan, to discuss and debate, and to snooze and sunbathe.

The following morning, Aoife arrived at the Secret Garden Café at around 9.45 am thinking she'd have time to look through and send a few texts to family and friends before Kieran's arrival. That was even if he turned up. She was surprised to find Kieran already there and waiting out in the courtyard garden.

Aoife underestimated just how attractive and appealing people found her personality. This included both men and women. Sometimes she was clueless of people trying to connect with her. She had been the subject of many advances in the King Brian Pub but rarely, if ever, responded in the way the suitors had wanted or wished for.

"Morning Aoife, please have a seat. You're right. It's very tranquil and rustic here in this courtyard garden. Are you a tea or coffee person?"

"Morning Kieran. Occasionally tea, but I usually have coffee in the morning. You beat me here! I wasn't expecting that."

"Sorry, just keen. I've tea sometimes with breakfast, but mostly coffee at cafés. What would you like? I'm having a cappuccino with chocolate on top."

"Easy, I'm having exactly the same thanks."

As they sipped their coffees, the conversation turned to Kieran's artwork which she had tried to figure out the proceeding morning at the art gallery.

"I'm sorry, and I don't mean to be offensive, but I still don't know the significance or interpretation of your painting and I'm not going to pretend I do."

"It's OK," reassured Kieran, "in a nutshell, Galway had a history in the 16th and 17th centuries which involved cruel and macabre rivalries and killings and power struggles. It hasn't been proven, but I'm sure that the river bed silts and sands in the Old City Centre contain some of the skeletal remains resulting from those events. They were very cruel and ruthless times."

"That's a bit dark and depressing," was Aoife's response, "and it's hard to imagine that sitting here today. The present day setting where the river flows through the city centre seems so peaceful and tranquil."

The conversation then switched back and forth between Aoife and Kieran. Both were having a good time learning about each other. There was definitely some chemistry going on between them.

Aoife glanced at her mobile phone to check the time. It was showing almost 11 am. Work commenced at 11 am.

"Sorry, but I've got to dash, Kieran. I'm going to be late for work. Thanks for the coffee and chat. If I run, I'll be there in less than ten minutes. Here's my mobile number, text me sometime if you'd like."

And with that she disappeared out of the café courtyard and into the street.

Kieran was besotted. He wanted to text her mobile number straight away but was fearful that he might come across as desperate or too stalker-like. No, he'd wait a day or two and then send a text to Aoife. Two days passed and on Friday morning, he sent his text.

Morning Aoife. Thanks for company at Secret Garden Wed am. Really enjoyed it. Like to catch up again sometime? Kieran.

Aoife hadn't yet left for work and replied immediately.

Ditto Kieran. I'm visiting family farm this weekend. But free next weekend?

Great, I'll contact you late next week. Enjoy the family visit.....Kieran

One week passed. For both Aoife and Kieran it was a case of 'absence makes the heart grow fonder'. Kieran was impatient to send a text to Aoife, and Aoife was checking every text to see who had sent it. Then early on Friday morning, she received the text she had been patiently waiting for.

Morning Aoife. Suggest a picnic in Merlin Park Woods Sunday 11 am. Would that work? If yes, can meet you at Merlin Castle. I'll bring savoury if you bring sweet? Kieran.

Sounds good, Kieran. I'll bring sweet. C you then. Thanks, Aoife.

It was Sunday, 25th June 2018. Aoife arrived at the Merlin Castle ruins ten minutes before 11 am. He had done it again. Kieran was already there waiting with a picnic basket and a drinks cooler in hands. The greeting this time was friendlier than it had been two weeks earlier at the Secret Garden Café. A warm embrace, was followed by a kiss on the cheek and then they walked side by side along a limestone cobbled pathway leading to an area of pretty wildflower meadow at the edge of a stand of ash trees. Kieran spread out the picnic rug.

The conversation was easy, the food was perfect, and the wine flowed. As his 'savoury' contribution to the picnic, Kieran had brought a pork and fennel pie and a jar of blackberry relish, while Aoife's 'sweet' contribution comprised a container of bite sized, new season apple tarts and a small bowl of clotted cream.

Kieran was doing everything in his power to constrain himself physically and verbally since it was only the second time they had met face-to-face. He could sense that Aoife was not as uninhibited as he was. Subconsciously, he worked it over in his mind and elected to proceed with care and caution.

Aoife had told Kieran that she was from a small rural farming town forty km north of Galway and had lived there all of her life with her older brother and parents. Her parents were conservative, she had enjoyed a happy upbringing, and was a devoted Christian who went to church most Sundays. Kieran could see that she was beautiful, innocent, caring and kind, and all those things that people wished they were, or aspired to be.

He told her that he was from Dublin and had endured and survived a difficult upbringing. His father had been abusive to his mother and two younger brothers. He was 29 years old.

Although the details he shared with Aoife were sparse, he did reveal that he didn't like school, didn't like boundaries, didn't like routine and didn't like convention. He had left school at fifteen and floated around Dublin doing several different low skilled jobs while experimenting with life. Since his early 20s he had embraced artistic pursuits like painting, music and poetry. It was for that reason he had decided to leave Dublin for a more peaceful part of Ireland. He had considered Cork and Donegal and Killarney, but in the end decided that due west was his calling. Hence he ended up in Galway in 2016. He was very vague about exactly what his current fulltime job was, but suggested he sold enough artwork to make a survivable living.

Aoife enjoyed Kieran's company. It was liberating. It was something new to her. He seemed to be carefree and relaxed, worldly and interesting. He was also smart and cheeky and confident. He had an opinion about most things. He talked about a lot of things which Aoife knew very little, or nothing about.

She liked everything about him, however, the warning signs were there at their second meeting. Aoife was largely oblivious to them. Even if she did notice that he had quickly and almost single handled finished off the two bottles of the wine he brought. She was caught in the excitement of the moment - the scent of early summer flowers in the meadow, the midday sun glistening and dancing through the canopy of ash trees, the perfect picnic lunch and Kieran's cheeky smiling face. Kieran seemed to know a lot, seemed to have experienced a lot, and seemed to be in control of his life. It was a case of what she wanted to see, and not what she should have seen. In reality, Kieran was far from being in control of his life.

The Sunday picnic was followed by several weeks, and then several months of regular dates. None of the dates included friend or group situations, and this was another sign that Aoife didn't notice or hadn't reflected upon.

By the end of the year, Aoife was smitten with Kieran.

Christmas 2018 had been spent apart despite Aoife desperately wanting Kieran to come and meet her family at Ballinrobe, and stay to enjoy a traditional Irish Christmas. It would have been separate rooms of course since Aoife's parents and older brother were conservative Catholic Irish. There was no way they would have been able to stay in the same bedroom at the family farm. That would have been totally unacceptable.

This was her first significant relationship and she had wanted to share it with her family and small circle of male and female friends she'd grown up with in and around Ballinrobe. They were keen to meet this man she was gushing over. Everybody who knew Aoife trusted her judgement implicitly so there were no concerns that Kieran might be anything other than a decent and loving man who would treat her kindly and respectfully. Being conservative, Aoife's parents were nervous, bordering on worried, but they decided to try and accept and embrace modernist generational thinking.

Kieran had told Aoife that he had to return to Dublin for Christmas with his family. The details of how he would be spending Christmas were vague, and he didn't at any stage suggest that she might go with him and possibly meet his family, even though she understood there were significant constraints.

Although Aoife had enjoyed the six-day Christmas break back home in Ballinrobe with her family, she was very excited to be heading back to Galway and meeting up with Kieran.

Kieran and Aoife meet up at the Secret Garden Café once they were both back in town after the Christmas break. It was now their 'special' meeting place. They usually sat outside and had the garden courtyard to themselves, however, weather constraints in January which was the coldest month of the year in Galway and rarely exceeded 10 degrees C, meant they were forced to sit inside.

Aoife gushed about the wonderful Christmas she had with family and friends while Kieran virtually said nothing about his Christmas. It was a very one sided discussion. It didn't matter to Aoife because she was more focussed on the forward plan. She was very excited about the prospect of moving in to live with Kieran on a permanent basis. By mid-January 2019, they had settled into a one-bedroom apartment only ten minutes' walk from Aoife's work.

Life together started off blissfully.

Aoife and Mr Ryan O'Leary

It was now June 2019 and almost one year since Aoife had first meet Kieran, and six months since they had been living together.

"Afternoon Mr O'Leary, you don't normally come into the pub at this time of the day."

"I know I'm old enough to be your grandad, Aoife, but please can you call me Ryan? Seriously, it's OK."

It was 2 pm and the busy lunchtime session had now finished. Time to take a breather before the pub got busy again from around 4 pm. The period between 2 pm to 4 pm was time allocated for the clean-up, wipe up and straighten up of everything in the pub. Ryan O'Leary usually visited the pub at lunchtime for a feed and beer, or for an hour between 6 pm to 7 pm for a jug of beer, but he had never previously visited the pub at 2 pm.

"You're right, Aoife, I don't usually come in at this hour but there's a reason."

"Oh, I hope nothing's wrong."

"Well, actually, I do want to talk to you. Any chance you can take a short break and we can go over to the corner table and chat?"

"Yes, of course. Now is good."

They sat down at the corner table. Aoife was becoming visibly nervous. What was this all about she wondered. Was there something wrong with Mr O'Leary? Was there something terrible going on in his life and he had nobody to turn to? Please don't let there be something medically wrong with him, she subconsciously thought. Other than that, she was clueless because she knew very little about him on a personal level.

Yes, they had chatted, but the conversations were always general discussions about things happening in the local community or nationally, and occasionally internationally. The conversations were mostly short due to customers wanting and needing to be served. They chatted about all sorts of things. What did she think of the #Me Too movement and the unaffordable cost of housing for young people? What did she think of President Trump, what did she think of the drama unfolding in the Royal Household over in England, about climate change, and the Palestinian-Israeli issue, and veganism?

Aoife who had limited exposure to the big world, was happy to be learning from the experiences of somebody who had been immersed in it. She learnt a lot. She enjoyed their conversations because it meant she had to respond and give an opinion about topics she very rarely thought about. Ryan O'Leary was always interesting to talk to and she enjoyed the verbal exchange when time allowed. The discussions were never about personal matters. She sensed that this was about to change.

"I don't think I've ever told you this Aoife but I used to be married and had one daughter. She brought so much joy to me and my wife's lives. She made our lives full and complete. Her name was Catherine. She was pretty, smart, and a primary school teacher in Dublin. Everybody loved her. I used to think to myself how I could be so lucky, and what I did to deserve such a caring and sharing daughter. All she seemed to do was to give and support others."

Aoife was listening, but she hadn't listened carefully enough to what Ryan had just said about his daughter. She hadn't picked up that he said "was", not "is".

"She sounds lovely. Where is she now? Not in Dublin anymore?"

Aoife could see the tears swelling in Ryan O'Leary's eyes and his voice started to quiver. She was both embarrassed and uncomfortable somehow knowing that the next sentence that was going to come out of Ryan's mouth would not be good.

"She's no longer with us. If she was still alive, she would be forty years old this week. I know the world is full of tragedy every day and everywhere and many, many people are suffering, but that doesn't make it any easier."

"Please tell me more but only if you want to. I'll understand if it's too painful to talk about."

So, Ryan continued.

"About ten years ago, she met a man over east in Dublin. He was a lawyer. The first time I meet him he was very charming. He was very pleasant to be sure. And he was super friendly. He was the perfect gentleman to Catherine when in my presence. Catherine was besotted and it wasn't long before they were significantly partnered and living together. After a few months she stopped visiting us, and then she stopped taking our phone calls and then people started contacting us saying her behaviour was getting strange and that she was becoming reclusive."

Aoife was now listening carefully to every word Ryan was saying.

"Of course, I went to see her immediately but she insisted that nothing was wrong and that she was just tired with the pressures of teaching. Do you think I didn't see how she had tried to hide the signs of physical abuse? How she avoided meeting me face-to-face for that very reason. As any father would be, I was concerned beyond belief. I was enraged and angered."

Aoife was fixated and listened intently because she sensed that something major was about to be revealed.

Ryan stopped talking to wipe his eyes with a white handkerchief as the tears flooded down both his cheeks. He appeared distraught and Aoife was unsure what to do. After he quickly composed himself he continued.

"Sorry Aoife. I promised myself that I'd be brave as I told you this. Two days later, she was dead. She was strangled to death by a psychotic and hedonistic man. He was meant to be her protector."

Suddenly a strange and uncomfortable feeling came over Aoife. Why was Ryan telling her this? Did he know her secret? She had been very, very careful to try and hide the physical signs of the torment she had been going through each and every day for the past three months.

"I won't burden you with the details of her passing but I'm going to make sure that if it's within my powers, a similar event will never happen again. Not if I know about it and can do anything to stop it."

"What do you mean, Ryan? I don't understand."

Of course, she understood.

"Do you trust me?"

"Of course, I do," confirmed Aoife.

"I know I just sit alone and rarely talk to anybody. But I do observe and listen to what others around me are saying and doing. I've noticed how over the past six months since you moved in with Kieran, a natural Irish girl who radiates physical and personality beauty has taken to wearing more and more makeup at work. I've noticed how you avoid all brightly lit areas of the bar and restaurant. I notice how when you do mistakenly walk under well-lit areas, darker patches are visible under the makeup. I've even seen droplets of blood coming from your nose."

Aoife was becoming very uncomfortable. She was both angry and thankful. Angry because she had let down her guard, but mostly, she was thankful. Not because Mr O'Leary was telling any mistruth, but rather, because he had exposed the truth and she now had somebody to confide with.

She was almost at breaking point and didn't think she could hang on much longer. For the past two months especially, all sorts of bad thoughts had been going through her mind. Was it her fault, was there something wrong with her, what would her family say if they knew the truth, what would friends say, what was the point of anything?

"I can see the signs. Aoife, are you being physically and mentally abused by Kieran?"

Aoife went silent and was about to say no, but she paused for a little bit longer and then replied, "Yes, but I think it's going to be OK and get better. He's promised me he will change. He said he loves me. He said he'll get help."

"Aoife, I had a daughter who was a bit older than you and who went through what you're going through now, and I won't stand by and let it happen again. I can't. If I do, it will be a case of deja vu. Kieran won't change unless he goes and gets serious help. He won't change unless he wants to get serious help. I know you've heard the saying…sometimes you have to be cruel to be kind…Aoife please take a meaningful break away from it all. I don't just mean a break from work, or a break from Kieran or a break back home to the family. I mean, a serious break to detox from all the negativity in your life at the moment. Go somewhere different and clear your mind. Explore new sites and experience new things."

Aoife was listening intently and although deep down it sounded like a good idea for her overall sanity and general physical, mental and spiritual wellbeing, she had serious reservations.

"I don't think I'm brave enough to go somewhere different and somewhere new by myself. I've never been out of Ireland before. Not even across the Irish Sea to England. I suppose London would be exciting and interesting even if just for a couple of weeks."

"Yes, you are brave enough. And secondly, I don't mean London. And I'm not meaning the other side of the world like Australia or New Zealand. Is there anywhere in Europe that you've read about or seen on TV and thought to yourself, you'd like to go there someday?"

"There is one place I'd like to go."

"Where?"

"Well, I love Italian food, cafés and markets. I even love Italian cooking but Kieran is never interested. I've seen that old school movie *Journey to Italy* made in the 1950s and set in Naples. I loved it. So if I was to go somewhere really different for me then Naples in Italy would be a dream come true."

"If you could see yourself in a mirror right now, Aoife, you'd be blinded by the sparkle in your eyes and the smile on your face. The passion in your voice as you talk about Naples and the excitement expressed in your body language. I'm not kidding. It's like the Aoife of six months ago has returned."

Aoife sensed it herself. She hadn't been this animated and excited about anything for quite a while.

"But I don't know how to do it."

"Don't worry. I'll help you. I know I haven't mentioned it previously to you, but in my job as an engineer, I have travelled and worked and lived all over the world. I'm not an expert but I've got a pretty good idea of how things work, and what would likely work best for you."

"You don't mind helping me? If I leave home alone for anything but work, Kieran goes nuts."

"I understand. I'll be here during your mid-afternoon breaks at work and we'll organise it then. Nobody else need know."

Over the next two weeks, and with Mr Ryan O'Leary's selfless, efficient and confidential help, Aoife organised a trip to Naples, Italy. Flights going Galway to Dublin and then onwards direct from Dublin to Naples were booked for departure on Sunday 30th June and returning back to Ireland on Sunday 14th July. This would give Aoife a full two-week break in Naples. Airbnb accommodation was booked in the Naples central city area, and necessary accessories like spending cash in euros and mobile phone international roaming were organised.

Aoife didn't have wads of spare cash but she had saved enough and was able to get budget airline flights, reasonably priced accommodation in a 1-bedroom Airbnb apartment, and she still had enough left over to cover the expenses of a trip for Naples for two weeks. She had heard that Naples was one of the more affordable parts of Italy for international tourists. It was not the cheapest city in Italy to travel to, but definitely much more affordable than cities like Milan, Rome, Florence and Venice.

This was the make or break point. It would give Kieran time to deal with his demons and decide if he wanted to continue on the basis of a caring and equal relationship. It would take her away from the physical and mental abuse which was becoming dangerous for Aoife's wellbeing. It was a chance to try something new and exciting in a place very different to what she was used to, and it was also a chance to fulfil a long-time dream of spending time in Naples.

The 30th June couldn't come soon enough for Aoife.

"Ryan, how will I ever thank you? I was totally lost and in a worrying downwards spiral. I urgently needed somebody to help me but I wasn't expecting that help to come from you."

"Aoife, I'm beyond ecstatic. To know that I can help you and make a difference is thanks enough. I'm doing it both for my deceased daughter Catherine, and for you. Just go and embrace the opportunity."

"I seriously needed help. Thanks again."

They embraced and Ryan departed the King Brian Pub a happy man.

Two weeks later on the morning of Sunday, 30 June 2019, Aoife was on her way in a taxi to Galway Airport. Her expected arrival time to Naples Airport would be the evening of the same day. She had explained the situation to Kieran. Needless to say, he was not happy and used every verbal and emotional trick in the book to try and make her stay. When that failed, he was very close to physically lashing out. His hand was raised and his fist clenched but this time Aoife escaped his furious rage. What made him stop this time was uncertain but the tears in Aoife's eye and the smile on her face saying "you can't hurt me anymore" would be compelling and confronting to any sane man.

William in Hunterville, New Zealand

As per his usual daily routine, William jumped out of bed half enthusiastically and half reluctantly, and did his twenty push-ups on the sheepskin floor rug at the end of the bed. It was nearly 6 am. Now that he was fully awake, he went to the kitchen and made himself a strong coffee and two pieces of wholemeal toast with marmalade which he had bought from the local church spring fair six months earlier. Maybe it was his Scottish heritage but marmalade on toast for breakfast worked big time for William. So much so that he had purchased all six jars of marmalade which were for sale at the Hunterville Church Fair back in the spring. Buying up jars of jam at the church fair was something he did every year and just one of the many reasons William was very well liked in the community.

"William, you need to get yourself a wife and then you won't have to buy so many jars of jam," always came with a maternal smile from Mrs Duncan at the church fair.

William was contented with his life overall. He felt he was privileged and lucky to live where he did, and to be doing a job he liked. But it was not a perfect life. Is there such a thing as a perfect life? William had been asking himself this question more and more frequently over the past couple of years. Is it fair to live or want to live the perfect life when so many people in the world are hurting and unhappy, struggling and abused?

There were several things missing in William's life. He knew what they were, but was afraid to admit them or to discuss them with anybody, including his best friend Joseph, colloquially known as Ram to most people in the local community.

There's getting to be a bit of a nip in the air, he thought to himself. It might be time to start wearing boxers and a t shirt to bed at night time? Although he was still a youngish man who was nine months away from his 30th birthday, he wasn't feeling as studly and tough as he used to.

It was the end of May and the season was changing from autumn to early winter. Officially, the 1st May was the start of winter in New Zealand, but it wasn't until the beginning of June that the real signs of winter appeared in the local landscape. Compared to the busy spring and summer periods on the farm, winter was a lot quieter and presented an opportunity for a well-earned respite from the relentless farm tasks such as drenching, worming, lamb docking, and shearing which were typical of the period from spring through to autumn. After breakfast, a quick shower and dressing, it was time for William to get out on the farm.

William was the only permanent person based at the farm. He had two local farmhands who both lived off farm. They were both very reliable and routinely turned up to the farm at around 7 am weekdays. George was in his late 50s and had a lot of farming experience. William valued his patience and stock management input. Cathy who was in her mid-20s was a farm cadet who had recently graduated from the agricultural university in Palmerston North.

It was 7 am. Was this the first real frost of the winter? He stepped outside and observed that the landscape had changed from the vivid green of yesterday, to a uniform greenish white overnight, and that icy grass seemed to crunch under his boots. Every breath of air he exhaled was steamy and dispersed into the crisp morning air like a puff of smoke. However, the sun was rising and it promised to be a sunny, clear, finger snapping crisp kind of a day.

He could already see that the first warming rays of the morning sun were melting the frost on the ground and the nearby hillslopes which were more exposed to the sun were already back to displaying their usual vivid green colour. By 8.30 am all signs of the early winter frost had disappeared. William knew that it wouldn't be long, maybe another two or three weeks, before the hard winter frosts arrived to the farm. Winter was just bearable when the sun was shining, but a real drudge when it was a cloudy, rainy day.

It was a big undertaking for a man in his late twenties, to part own and operate such a large farm. Although he operated the farm and was solely responsible for its day to day management, his elderly parents still owned fifty percent of it. Due to his father having had an unexpected and severe stoke the previous year, just after his seventy first birthday, his mother had decided to relocate to nearby Palmerston North which was seventy kilometres away. It was bigger and had all the necessary medical, hospital and therapy facilities which his father now required. It saddened William that his dad hadn't been able to come back and visit the farm for over twelve months, but he regularly went online and sent his parents photos and local news snippets so they could see what was happening. They both appreciated that.

William loved his parents dearly. He was an only child and had been born when his father was forty three and his mother forty. He was too embarrassed to ask them why they had been married for twelve years before they had decided to have a child. He considered that would be a step too far.

His father was a quiet, reflective man but a very skilled farmer. Not stoic, but controlled in what he said out aloud. Maybe it was a generational thing but William could never recall his father complaining about anything that wasn't livestock related. He was supportive and kind, and loved to cuddle and encourage William as a young boy. On a personal father and son level, William had received a very happy childhood. His mother was a loving, kind and caring person. She was a 'domestic goddess' and her baking was legendary in the district.

She had an intelligence and curiosity that never had a chance to be fully realised while she was on the farm. She had often had discussions with William about art, history, travel and literature.

Whereas some of his mates had complained and totally rubbished their parents with cussing and swearing, he never ever wished he had different parents. William was a dutiful and respectful son.

It saddened William that his parents were now trapped in Palmerston North, away from their beloved farm. It was unlikely that they'd return to live there. William wanted the final years for his parents to be happy ones. He knew what he needed to do, but struggled with how he would achieve that. This tormented him from time to time.

The Thomson Farm was 97 hectares (240 acres). It was classified as a mixed beef and sheep grazing and fattening farm similar to most of the other farms in the district. Forestry, dairy farming and deer farming were also operational in the district but beef and especially sheep farming were its life blood.

The Thomson Farm was located off the main State Highway 1 in a broad valley up Murimotu Road just past the Hunterville Cemetery. It was around a ten minute drive from the farm gate to Hunterville township. The farm had been in the family for four generations.

William's great grandfather had arrived there in the late 1800s as a Scottish immigrant.

Part of the farm was flat to very gently sloping abandoned river terraces, while the remainder was gentle to moderately rolling hilly country. It was good soil especially in the river terrace areas. With the ideal amount of yearly sunshine and rainfall, the grass was virtually green all year round and extended from the valley floors right up to the crest of the surrounding hill tops. There was climatic variation in the area, but not pronounced extremes. It was very rare to have snow lying on the ground in winter, and very rare to have periods of drought in summer.

It was ideal farmland for intensive grazing.

William's World

Although several of his male friends in the district were keen hunters and fishermen, William was happy in his free time to just get out in the wilderness and explore without gun or fishing rod. Given his farming background he was a bit of a misfit. While that annoyed a few people, to others, it was an enduring quality. He had often asked his mates to go with him to explore the local geology and the landforms, the history at the cemeteries, historical ruins and the district's fauna and flora. Responses varied from "fuck off mate" to "sorry I'm busy this weekend", but William went forth regardless. He wasn't offended, but often wondered about the negative responses he invariably got. He sometimes felt hurt.

The Hunterville and nearby Mangaweka Districts are rated scenically as very beautiful parts of New Zealand but not the most scenic parts because they were mostly considered to be down in the South Island.

The landforms and landscapes created in William's backyard had resulted from the Rangitikei River having incised down into the regional cover of Pliocene age geological rocks. River terrace flats were surrounded by low to medium sized hills. The hills mostly sloped gradual to moderate and were rarely steep and extreme. They were variably grassed and forested, but because this was primarily a grazing and beef and sheep fattening farming area, grass ruled supreme.

One very visible feature of the grassed hill slopes on William's farm was roughly parallel terraces which followed the contours of the hillsides. William had been told that the official scientific name for them was '*terracettes*' but he simply referred to them as 'sheep grazing tracks'. William used to laugh to himself that China and Japan might have their rice terraces, but we've got our sheep terraces. He couldn't understand how there was debate about how '*terracettes*' were formed because he'd seen them being created with his own eyes. They were formed by grazing sheep taking the easier route around a hill, rather than expending more energy going vertically up or down. End of story.

Isolated but well developed stands of original and regenerated native bush were intermingled with patches of exotic bush and trees. The early European settlers in the mid to late 1800s had cleared most of the original native bush cover in order to exploit the land for farming. This resulted in extensive erosion on the hill slopes and valleys so slower growing native trees were replanted in valley areas and fast growing exotics such as pinus radiata and eucalyptus planted out on hill slopes and hill tops.

In early winter it was relatively easy to differentiate the two vegetation types even from a distance.

The native bush was mostly evergreen. It was dense and varied and had a primeval appearance. William enjoyed walking through the small stands of native bush which were well developed in places in the district despite the extensive farming. He always felt like a more natural man, and a freer and more spiritual man when he walked through any stands of native bush. He enjoyed interacting with the fearless and trusting native birds and observing how everything worked together.

There had been several occasions when he sensed somebody else was there with him in the bush. He felt as if somebody was looking at him and observing his actions and reactions to nature. He would suddenly look ahead, or turn around, but there was never anybody else there. It was a strange eerie feeling which had happened more than once. And even a couple of times he thought he had heard somebody whisper and call his name.

William. William.

He had brushed it off as just the sound of the wind moving through the trees. Seriously, what else could it be?

The exotic introduced vegetation was quite different to the native bush. The stands of poplar and willow trees on hill slopes and hill tops were totally denuded of their leaves by the end of May and looked like skeletal soldiers standing to attention through the winter period. In the valleys and river flats, the large solitary oak trees and oak groves planted around homestead areas were now showing late autumnal colourations of deep purple and crimson red, yellow and orange, brown and tan. Where they were densely planted, they reminded William of an artist's palate where the primary rainbow colours of red, orange and yellow and been variously mixed and experimented with to produce an eye pleasing result.

William could see and appreciate the beauty in both the native and introduced bush and tree vegetation in the district no matter what the time of the year was. It was not unusual for him to head out on a Sunday morning to go explore his backyard. He loved to explore up all the backroads and tracks to find out 'what was at the end of the road'.

On his Sunday exploration trip the week before, along the Manawatu Scenic Route which branched eastwards and inland at Mangaweka township, he was in awe at the beautiful display of dark green leaved bushes with their clusters of pea sized bright red berries. Theses bushes were growing prolifically along the roadside, and up and down exposed rock faces and riverside bluffs. At the time he didn't know the name of the plant, so did a successful online search when he returned home. He found out that the bush he had been admiring was called Bright Bead Cotoneaster (*Cotoneaster glaucophyllus*). It was a frost tolerant invasive plant species that was a member of the rose family. It hindered native bush regeneration but was a nutritional food source for birds. Its berries were mildly toxic to humans. Despite these constraints, he thought it was a very visually pleasing bush.

William was a very good farmer and good at doing practical things on the farm, but he also had a very curious mind and enjoyed learning about nature and science, especially earth science.

For a long time, William had always gone alone on his Sunday jaunts. He'd often wished that somebody else would be keen enough to accompany him, but nobody else he knew showed any interest so he was resolved to doing it alone for the foreseeable future.

Hunterville Township

William considered himself to be part of the Hunterville township community even though he lived rurally and not in the town itself.

Hunterville township is in the Rangitikei District of the lower North Island, New Zealand. With its population of just over 400 permanent residents it is referred to as a small rural town. The town straddles main State Highway 1 which is the main arterial road down the middle of the North Island from Auckland to Wellington. Although Hunterville is located on a major highway, there is very little reason for the majority of people to make a stop there. Those that do however, are pleasantly surprised at how picturesque and charming the town is.

Hunterville services the local and wider farming communities and enables them to get together for social and civic events, celebrations and memorial days. Apart from life on the farm and visiting his parents in Palmerston North, Hunterville was where William did most of his socialising. Not that he had an extensive portfolio of social events to attend or participate in. In fact, his social calendar was rather lean.

Apart from visiting his favourite café, the local honey shop, the gift and postal shop, the rugby club during the playing season, and stops for petrol and the odd grocery items, he didn't visit Hunterville a lot. Although when he did visit, he enjoyed it.

His favourite café was on the main road passing through Hunterville. With its white painted façade, black canvas shade awnings and window frames, it was a mandatory pit-stop when he visited town. The coffee was as good as he had been served in many big cities where café culture thrives, the home baked food was great, and the service was typically very friendly and down-to-earth. He counted the two ladies that owned the café as his good friends.

William had a sweet tooth and enjoyed every single item that came out of the small productive kitchen onsite. The café in Hunterville worked big time for

William especially since he could have a bit of a chat and a bit of a laugh with the ladies. It was a break from talking to the animals down on the farm.

The town's side streets running perpendicular and parallel to the main State Highway were generously wide, tidy, and uncluttered. It was rare to see any cars parked in the side streets which gave the small town a very spacious appearance, and sometimes an eerily quiet feeling.

There was an assortment of essential shops in town. William's favourite was the Hunterville Village Bookshop. He went there to buy birthday and Christmas gifts for his parents. It was clean and spacious and had a great assortment of gifts for young and old of all sexes. Rarely did he go into the shop and not come out with a purchase. It also had a postal counter which came in handy for sending gifts by post, especially to his parents.

There were two churches in town both pretty from the outside, and even prettier on the inside. William's parents were regular church goers before they had moved to Palmerston North. When they had been living in the Hunterville area, church services were not held weekly but fortnightly or whenever there was an additional need such as for a christening, marriage or death. William was not a 'true believer' and politely excused himself from going to church with his parents. Despite this, he was a spiritual man and still open minded and searching for an answer, but so far, his spiritualty had been focussed on mother earth. He wondered more about the flowing rivers, the native bush and birds, the rocks and landforms, and how they all comingled and complimented each other and how they were reliant on each other.

One of William's favourite stops when he did visit town was the Mānuka Honey Shop just along from the café. It was where he could buy artisan honey, and especially good quality UMF 10+ Mānuka honey sourced from hives set in the district. He also counted Mr Bates who owned the honey shop as one of his good friends.

William had a passion for cooking and he was very good at it. It's not something he advertised and very few people knew he was very handy in the kitchen, but it was something he was proud of. When his parents were living on the farm, he would give his mum a break by cooking for them once a fortnight. He could turn his hand to any style of cuisine but his favourite was Italian. He had done quite a lot of online research about regional Italian cooking and food products and was quite knowledgeable about Italy in general from all the internet research and reading. It was somewhere he dreamed about visiting.

William and Ram

William's life was focussed on the farm and its daily operations, however, he had no desire to be a hermit or cut himself off from the world at large, and for that reason, he played rugby each season for the Hunterville District team. Biweekly practice and training sessions starting in April, and Saturday matches played through the winter period, were a chance to socialise with other people even if they were all testosterone charged men around his own age.

Opportunities for socialising with the opposite sex around Hunterville town were very limited. He could go online for a looksee but had heard horror stories about catfishing, sexting and gold diggers looking for a well off bloke, that he considered it all too hard. It wasn't his thing. It's not that he was a prude, but he was at the stage of life where he was looking for, and ready for, a meaningful and lifetime relationship.

William was physically very fit from all his work on the farm, from his weekend trips exploring the countryside in and around the Hunterville District, and from training for and playing rugby in the winter. He had a naturally athletic physique. His 5'11", 75 kg frame was perfectly muscled and well suited to playing in the wing position for his local rugby team.

He didn't consider himself a good looking man. Just a very average looking man, but he did have a nice smile which was accentuated by his pearly white teeth. He had been complimented on his smile by many people. In the past couple of years, he had noticed slight balding on the crown of his head. His dad was 72 years old and only lightly balding, so he was hoping he might end up the same, hopefully not worse.

He ate healthy most of the time, didn't smoke and was a light to moderate drinker. Wine or beer it didn't matter, he liked both, especially with food. His wine of choice was white. Try as he might, he just couldn't get into drinking red wine.

It was the end of May and William had just played the first rugby game of the season. Hunterville versus Mangaweka. The Hunterville team had been beaten but it was a close game and the following week they would be all out to win.

"Good game mate, we'll get a win next weekend I reckon" said Joseph as he handed William a bottle of cold beer in the rugby dressing room after the game. Everybody called Joseph by his nickname Ram. He was called Ram for obvious reasons. Ram was William's best friend.

"I'm only having one bottle Ram, I've got to drive home and all that."

"Come on mate don't be a bloody woofer. Are you OK William? I don't know but you just don't seem to be your normal self?"

Ram was known in the district as a bit of a larrikin who swore too much, chased skirt too much, drank too much and was very politically incorrect most of the time. Idiot and moron were terms some people used to describe him. Despite those supposed negative traits, he was a good mate to William. It seemed to defy the odds that they were actually best mates. Ram was a conscientious worker and very skilled at his job, but his social skills and behaviour were marginal at best. For some reason he really liked William and valued his friendship. It was probably because William was never judgemental and always managed to say something positive and supportive to him.

"What you got on tomorrow mate? Going on one of your back country jaunts Mr Explorer?"

"Don't think I'll go tomorrow, Ram. I might just have the day off at home."

"Why don't I come around and you can cook me one of those Italian meals you make. I'm heading out with Suzie later in the day and I'll be needing lots of stamina for the night ahead if you know what I mean?"

"Yeah, I know what you mean, but um, I'm not really in the mood for company."

With this response from William he knew something wasn't right.

"We'll I'm coming over anyway mate so be prepared. Be there around 11 am. Beer or wine? No doesn't matter, I'll bring both."

In reality, Ram was incredibly perceptive and knew exactly what was going on around him. He was also thick skinned so no matter what people said about him, whether it was good or bad, it was like water off a duck's back. He was in total control of his own fate.

Sunday morning arrived and it was another sunny crisp early winter's day in the Rangitikei District. It was exactly the kind of day which William would usually take off and be out and about exploring. Ram arrived to William's farm house around 11 am. Although William wasn't enthused about having company, he had made the effort for his friend. After Ram went inside he could smell something pretty good being cooked in the kitchen. It wasn't a food smell he was normally used to, but it was promising. Ram's palate wasn't restricted to just meat pies and roast meals.

"Ok mate sit down, what's this all about?" he enquired as he cracked open a couple of ice cold beers.

William took a deep breath and then it all came out. Apart from Ram there wasn't anybody else he could easily discuss it with. He was finding being home alone as the milestone of being thirty years old approached, more and more difficult.

"Mate, I don't know what's happening. I feel lost. I feel alone and lonely. I feel like what's the point. Where am I heading and what am I doing?"

Upon hearing this Ram was nervous and was taken aback, especially as he saw William's eyes swell up with tears. William was the last person he expected to be having this type of meltdown. William continued.

"I work my butt off day after day for what. I'm Mr Nice Guy big deal. I've got dreams just like everybody else. I want to be married, I want kids, I want to explore the world with somebody significant, I want to do exciting and unexpected things, and occasionally even maybe…even bad-boy things. But it's never going to happen. Not to me."

At this point Ram felt very close to William. Not in a physical way, but in an emotional close brotherly kind of way. Even he was feeling a little bit teary eyed himself. He had to suggest something credible to get William back on track. This was serious and he needed to act accordingly.

He quickly composed himself and took control of his emotions in order to stop the tears being expelled from his eyes. This needs action he thought to himself. He was a lot more worldly and wise than people gave him credit for. There's no way he was going to let his best mate down. He needed to formulate a plan in his subconscious, and then suddenly, it came to him.

"Why don't you just take some time off William and go do something you've wanted to do but haven't done for whatever reason. Not just a day or two, but I'm meaning for several weeks."

"Yeah right" replied William.

"No I'm serious mate. You're always talking about Italy. You seem to have a love affair with the place. Go to Italy for a couple of weeks, explore it and caress it, make love to it. Let it make love to you. You might even find a squeeze while you're there. I'll help you sort things so you can make it happen."

"Who'd look after the farm? You're a good friend Ram but no, it's not possible."

"Nuh, it is possible mate. You know that June and especially July is a much quieter time on the farm. Nothing major happens. Get somebody in to locum for two or three weeks while you go to Italy. Lots of retired farming guys in the district would love to get their boots dirty for few weeks. I'm going to make it happen for you William. It's my gift to you for being a bloody good mate. Actually, you're a bloody fantastic and non-judgemental best friend and if you tell anybody I said that, I'll twist your nuts."

Ram had an unusual way of mixing intelligent thoughtful words, with crass down to earth words.

"You think it's really possible?"

Already William's composure had changed. He was now smiling and seemed a lot more positive. The thought of two weeks in Italy was very appealing. Where in Italy would he go?

It would be summertime in Italy during June and July so the choices were endless. Milan and Lake Como, Florence and Venice, Naples and the Amalfi Coast, Palermo and the Sicily interior, Sardinia and it's beautiful coastline or Rome, or maybe the beaching areas of Puglia. Too much choice he thought. Wherever he went he knew the history, art and food would be great and the cafés seductive.

"Ok Ram come and sit and try this pasta dish I've made. Please be brutally honest. It's OK if you don't like it."

Ram was very impressed with the prawn risotto dish and the lemon ricotta cake served up by William.

"That ricotta cake is made with 10+ Mānuka honey from the honey shop in Hunterville and lemons from my lemon tree outside."

"Delicious mate and thanks for a great meal."

The meal was over and Ram was thankful he'd been able to help William lift his spirits. It was his job over the next few weeks to make sure that William would jet off at the end of the month to the other side of the world.

"Hey Ram, please be nice to Suzie tonight. You know what I mean. I'm serious. And thanks for helping me feel good about myself."

And as quickly as he arrived, Ram was gone.

Over the next few weeks Ram organised locum relief through the local Federated Farmers chapter. It was easy once word got out that it was on the Thomson Farm up Murimotu Road. Jim O'Connor was a retired sheep farmer who had lived and farmed in the district all his life and was well known in the area. He was very excited to be looking after William's farm for a couple of weeks. It was a chance to dust off his old farm work boots. His wife insisted that she also go to help out at the farm. William's parents were well known and the Thomson Family were respected it the community.

William had passed everything by his parents down in Palmerston North because they still owned half of the farm. They were conservative thinking in many ways, but also very modern thinking in others. They sensed that being alone on the farm was not healthy for their son. He was their only child, and their only son. Happiness was the one thing they wanted for William.

Once William had received his parent's blessing for a two to three week holiday break, he had to make the big decision of whereabouts to go in Italy. He was beside himself with excitement. Did he visit several places over a two week period, or did he concentrate on just one or two areas and do them thoroughly? He whittled it down to two options. Either Venice, Milan and Lake Como in the north, or Naples and maybe the Amalfi Coast in the southwest.

He had read previously that the industrial city of Milan in the north was the centre in Italy for modern industrial and furniture design which he was hugely interested in. How cool would it be to bring a modernist light fixture or to ship a piece of modern furniture back home. Lake Como was only fifty kilometres north of Milan and an easy train commute. It was said to be extraordinarily beautiful with deep dark blue waters, its huge lakeside villas and superbly manicured terraced gardens some of which were several hundred years old. While Venice with its water cannels was noted to be a centre for Renaissance art, architecture and sculpture in the 16th century. Given global warming and the potential for sea levels rises who knew how long Venice might be around for. He wondered if he should make an effort to see it before it slipped under the advancing waters.

Ever since he was a young boy he had been interested in archaeology including the famous eruption of Mount Vesuvius which resulted in the destruction of Pompeii. How cool would it be to see that he thought. Plus they invented pizza in Naples didn't they? Maybe he could get a few tips and make a pizza oven when he got back home. He had read that there were fantastic museums and galleries and places of antiquity to visit in Naples. On the negative side, he noted that Naples was said to be dirty and grimy and an impoverished part of Italy, while the people were unfriendly and crime was a serious problem. He wondered if that was really true or just a bad rap.

It was difficult to decide, but no, he had made his decision.

Naples and the surrounding area would be his travel destination in Italy. He would decide for himself what kind of a city and experience Naples offered, after he had been there for two weeks. He would base himself in the Old City Centre of Naples in a one-bedroom Airbnb apartment, and from there, he would consider doing day trips to the Amalfi Coast, Mount Vesuvius and the ancient ruins of Pompeii and Herculaneum, Ischia Island and Sorrento, and anywhere else that seemed worth visiting.

Ram made sure that William organised flights and accommodation and all the other logistics associated with a two week holiday over the other side of the world. There was a premium to be paid for the flights due to the short lead-in booking time but William wasn't too worried about that.

By the end of June, all the arrangements were in place. Ram's support had been stellar. Mr and Mrs O'Connor were installed at the farm for the next two to three weeks and he had visited and said goodbye to his parents. Ram was going to give him a lift to Palmerston North Airport to start his journey to Naples via Auckland and Dubai. A tiring journey of 36 hours total travel time was ahead of him.

Saturday 29th June arrived and William departed Palmerston North on an early morning flight. His expected arrival time to Naples would be the evening of Sunday, 30th June 2019.

Aoife Arrives and Settles into Naples, Italy

Aoife's flight to Naples was uneventful. She was both excited and nervous. She had gone over the plan several times in her mind. Once she had landed in Naples and successfully made her way through immigration and customs, the first priority would be getting to her Airbnb accommodation safely by taxi.

Her flight landed at 6 pm local time in Naples and the airport was very busy. Her first encounter with a Neapolitan person was at the immigration arrivals desk.

"Buona sera signorina, benvenuta a Napoli. Parli Italiano?"

Aoife was instantly overwhelmed. She had definitely arrived in Italy. Aoife knew a little bit of basic Italian which she had picked up from her long held interest in Italian movies and cooking, and from the general searching of all things Italian on the internet. Not enough to speak fluently, but enough to know the basic greetings. She responded to the immigration officer as best she could.

"Scusa signore, parlo solo un po' di Italiano. Lei parla Inglese?"

The immigration officer, although he had only meet her two minutes prior, was captivated with Aoife's natural charm and beauty, and her valiant attempt to speak Italian, albeit with a pronounced Irish accent.

"Si, parlo Inglese," he responded with a broad friendly smile on his face "are you coming to Italy as a tourist? Are you travelling alone?"

"Yes sir I am a tourist, and yes I am travelling alone."

"I see you are planning on staying two weeks. Have a great holiday miss. But please, a word of caution. Italian men can be extraordinarily friendly and very cheeky. It's in their blood. It's in their DNA. It's even more so when a pretty girl is involved. Mostly it's harmless bravado, but please do not go out alone at night time and take care."

"Thank you for the advice sir."

Aoife moved through the immigration area to the arrival baggage carousel assigned for her flight. She collected her bag and moved outside the airport terminal to the official taxi stand. She had read that it's best for a tourist at the airport to negotiate and confirm the taxi fare before actually hopping in a taxi, so that's what she did.

"Where going miss?"

"To this address here sir. It's in a small side street just off Via Toledo, and very close to the Dante Metro station. How much would that be?"

"Forty euros miss. Is that OK?"

Aoife had read that the usual fare to the central city in the evening was forty five to maximum fifty euro's, so she was pleased. All the warnings that she'd get ripped off as soon as she arrived to Naples weren't true.

The taxi driver was a very pleasant, middle aged man who suggested some of the sites she should visit while she was in Naples. In fact, he seemed very proud of the fact that she had elected to visit just Naples for a full two weeks, and not go to other parts of Italy.

By 8 pm she had arrived and was using the coded key pad to let herself into the apartment building where she had booked a one-bedroom apartment for two weeks. She opened the large wooden door. It was a clear night and had only just started to go dark. The air was warm and dry and very pleasant. She took a quick look on her phone and the air temperature was reading 23 degrees C.

The streets were full of people, from the very young to the very old. She could see lots of elderly persons, lots of mums and dads, lots of youths, and lots of toddlers. She was especially surprised that so many young children and babies were out with parents at that time of the night. That was a big difference to back home in Galway where children were usually well and true tucked into bed by 7 pm.

Aoife walked up the three stories to her apartment # 3–10. It was an old 19th century building and didn't have a lift. It was a bit of a struggle with her full twenty kg luggage bag, but the staircase was wide so she took a few shorts rest-stops on her way up. She had been told that the key to her apartment would be placed under the front door mat just before her expected time of arrival. And yes thankfully, it was there.

She unlocked the door and entered what would be her home for the next two weeks. She was very surprised since it far exceeded her expectations. It had tall ceilings, a small but well equipped kitchen, a small but nicely furnished bedroom with crisp white linen, and a bathroom with both bath and free standing shower. She immediately logged onto and tried the internet. The Wi-Fi strength was good. As an added bonus, there was a small balcony off the lounge area. Not big enough to hold a party, but big enough to sit outside in the morning with coffee, or in the evening with a glass of wine and observe everyday life in Naples passing by in the street below.

As another added bonus, the apartment host had left fresh milk, bread, cheese and tomatoes in the fridge, together with a bowl of fresh fruit on the table.

Aoife was very happy to be settled in Naples. All the drama she had endured back home in Galway over the past few months wasn't even on the radar. For now, it was all forgotten.

There was only a one hour time difference between Galway and Naples so she wasn't expecting her usual sleep routine to be affected. She showered, sent her parents and brother a text to let them know that she'd arrived safely to her apartment in Naples. She made a cup of tea and sat out on the balcony for an hour not really believing how things had evolved over the past few weeks, or realising how things would change over the next two weeks. She hadn't felt this free, or relaxed, or at inner peace for several months.

She retired to bed at 9 pm and drifted off to sleep quickly.

The following morning, Monday the 1st July, she woke up at 6 am feeling very contented. She was happy that she had arrived safely to both Naples and her accommodation. There was a list of things she wanted to see and do in Naples but the first day would just be spent exploring around the local nearby area, and making bookings for several different activities and must-do's on her hit-list.

The top priorities on her hit-list were and to go to an authentic cooking class so she could learn how to make proper fresh pasta, and to go horse riding and trekking on the slopes of Mount Vesuvius, if that was possible. These were things which she needed to be part of an organised grouping for, but the rest of the activities she wanted to do, and sites she wanted to explore, were things she could manage by herself.

Aoife went out to the small balcony with coffee and mobile phone in hand. Out on the balcony there was a small round wrought iron table, two chairs to match and some scattered pot plants which looked like they were seriously struggling due to a lack of watering. The first thing she did was to water the pot plants. By the time she departed in two weeks, she was determined that they would have their health restored by her daily care and attention. Once the pot plants were attended to, and with the first coffee of the morning in hand, she searched online cooking classes and horse riding trips. A confirmed booking was received almost instantly for a cooking class on Wednesday. Aoife was very happy and very excited.

As the start of a new week commenced in Naples, the streets below gradually came to life. Initially it was just the sound of garbage trucks collecting the weekend's refuse, but as dawn appeared and the sun rose by 7.30 am, the streets below became visibly busier. There were merchants and traders taking their goods to the nearby market, office workers heading to work, some smaller cafes and shops opening, parents delivering their children to school, and the first tourists taking to the streets.

Aoife hadn't even stepped out of the apartment but already she was enjoying sipping the moka pot coffee she had made, and absorbing the Italian experience provided by the unfolding scene in the street below.

By 9 am she was stepping out the front door of her apartment building onto the cobbled street. As per recommendations she had read online and in her travel guide, she stepped out onto the street with the bare minimum of personal items and nothing of extreme value on her person.

She had her mobile phone, a small amount of cash, personal ID, the address of where she was staying and a map of Naples city centre.

Her first stop would be Mercato Pignasecca an old and very well-known fresh produce, bakery and deli market very close to her apartment. On the way to the market, which was only a seven minute walk away from her apartment, she noted the location of a good mini supermarket, several cafés, a chemist shop and a wine shop.

When Aoife arrived to the Mercato Pignasecca and commenced slowly walking pass the various food stall holders the excitement level built. She was instantly overwhelmed by the range of produce available, how reasonable the prices were, how fresh everything seemed, and how loud and demonstrative both the shop keepers and the customers were. She smiled to herself. She loved it. It was hard not to get carried away and buy a bit of everything on offer.

Aoife arrived at a fresh fruit stall and was amazed at how many different types of fresh fruit were available even though it was still early summer. Life around the Mediterranean had a lot of positives she thought. The peaches looked especially inviting. She picked up a peach to look more closely, but was immediately confronted by the stall holder who shouted to her with flailing arms.

"*No, no, no signorina……..non puoi farlo.*"

Aoife was taken aback but somebody, realising she was a tourist, instantly came to her aid.

"Miss, you're not allowed to touch the produce. Only the shopkeepers can do that."

"Please tell him I'm very sorry. I didn't know."

Aoife explained that back home in Galway they do have fresh produce farmers markets but they operate in the weekends only. Not every day of the week. People often pick up produce to check for blemishes and to smell for freshness.

The young man told the stall holder that Aoife was very sorry and didn't know the correct protocol. The stall holder obviously held no grudge because he ran straight to Aoife, smiled at her, hugged her a little too warmly and kissed her on both cheeks.

"My name is Lorenzo" said the young man who had helped Aoife.

He was olive skinned, dark haired, was wearing more jewellery that she'd seen on a man before, and wore tight jeans. Those jeans are far too tight she thought.

"What are you doing today? I've got the rest of the day free. Would you like some company? I can show you around and make sure you have a good time."

Aoife had wondered how long it would be before she'd encounter one of Napoli's young lothario's. Nice try, and although she was truly appreciative of his help back at the fruit stall, she had just extricated herself from a difficult man situation back in Galway and wasn't looking for a repeat so soon. She told Lorenzo that she was heading away on a group tour in one hours' time so had to dash soon.

He headed off looking for the next 'young lady in distress'.

As she continued walking around the market Aoife was determined to control her buying and restrict it to just a few selective fresh food items. If she needed other things, or wanted to try something different, the market was only seven minutes' walk away from her apartment and open every day. Too easy she thought.

Aoife spent two hours exploring around the market, and all the ancillary deli's and bakeries and homewares shops. As she headed back towards her apartment she was trying to remember the important landmarks on the way so that it would be easier to find her way back to the market on her next visit.

Her jute shopping bag was filled with some crusty grainy bread, a small box of summer berries, two pottles of garlic and herb infused olives, a selection of assorted cold meats, a ready-made roasted aubergine and red capsicum salad, and a bottle of rosé wine.

As she walked back to her apartment at around 11 am, she unknowingly passed by a man walking in the other direction towards the market who would change her life forever over the course of the next two weeks.

The rest of Aoife's first day in Naples was spent exploring the shopping, parks, piazzas and apartment areas along Via Toledo right to its end at the waterfront.

By 7 pm she was out on her apartment balcony again, absorbing the sounds and actions of local passers-by, observing how they interacted with each other, and also assessing her first full day in Naples. It was enlightening and very different to life back in Galway. She loved it. She had done a lot of walking throughout the day and was sure that she'd manage another good night's sleep.

William Arrives and Settles into Naples, Italy

William had a travel time of just over thirty six hours from the moment he left the farm in Hunterville to arrival in Naples. When he did arrive in Naples on the evening of Sunday the 30th June he was physically exhausted with only one thing on his mind. That was bed. His flight arrived at 8 pm local time which was 6 am the following day back home in New Zealand. He knew that his body clock was going to be shot for a few days so he planned to take it easy for the first forty eight hours or so after arriving in Naples.

Half dazed, William joined the long queue in the arrivals hall. The worst part of long distance travel he thought to himself, had to be the flights and airport logistics. Finally he reached one of the immigration booths and the officer addressed him.

"*Buona sera signore. Benvenuta a Napoli. Parli Italiano?*"

William was too tired to respond back to the immigration officer in Italian even though he knew how to speak some of the language. Not fluently, but definitely enough to get by on a day to day basis. He responded back to the immigration officer.

"Sorry sir, I only speak English."

The immigration officer looked at William's passport.

"You have come all the way from New Zealand to Naples? Where else in Italy will you be travelling? Rome, Venice, Florence, Milano?"

"Nowhere else sir, only Naples. I'm going to be exploring Naples and the surrounding area for two weeks and then going back home to New Zealand. I'm very excited. It seems like there is so much to see and do here."

The immigration officer was very impressed with the friendly demeanour of the young man standing in front of him. He had a nice broad smile, a respectful attitude and looked at him directly in the eyes when he spoke. He was also very proud as a Neapolitan, that somebody from so far away on the other side of the world would want to come and visit his city for two weeks. Naples was often maligned as being dirty and disorganised, economically poor and crime ridden, which might be partially true, but it was also a city of fantastic museums, parks and history, and a food culture that would rival any. The people were alert and lively and strived to *'vivi la bella vita'* irrespective of the obstacles that confronted them.

"*Buone vacanze William. Goditi Napoli.*"
"*Grazie signore. Sono molto eccitato.*"

The immigration officer laughed when he realised that William could in fact speak some Italian, and with that, William proceeded on through immigration to the arrivals hall to collect his baggage. There was no problem identifying his bag from it's attached 'kiwiana' name tag, and he made his way outside to the airport approved taxi stand, ignoring the numerous taxi touts which approached him whispering 'hey sir, want a cheap taxi to city'. The evening air at 9.30 pm was still pleasantly warm. There was only one thing on William's mind. He wanted to be in bed asleep.

William negotiated a fare of forty five euros to travel by taxi to his apartment address in the Old City area. His apartment was located on Calata Trinita Maggiore and the taxi driver indicated that he knew where that was. Because it was later in the evening and the busy evening traffic period was over, it was only a twenty minute drive from the international airport to his Airbnb apartment. He checked that he was at the right street number, and that he could access the building's main front door, before he let the taxi driver depart.

Upon opening the front door of the apartment building he was confronted with the steepest stairs he'd ever seen. One of the constraints of modifying old 19th century buildings into modern day apartment buildings he thought. William thanked his lucky stars that he was only going to the first floor because as well as being very steep, the staircase was very narrow. It was less than one metre wide. He struggled up the stairs with his bags to apartment # 1–3, and a promised door key was located under the front door matt. He opened the apartment door and had a quick glance around. It seemed a bit smaller than the listing on Airbnb had indicated, but it would be good enough for the two week period ahead because he was a sole traveller. He logged onto and checked out the Wi-Fi and confirmed that it was in good working order. The small kitchen, bathroom and laundry facilities all looked adequate. The fridge had a few basic foodstuffs in it, courtesy of the apartment host. He was appreciative of that.

There was a small balcony. He opened the door which faced directly out onto Calata Trinita Maggiore and immediately the noise of people having a good time inside and outside the bars and restaurants just a short distance along the street, was evident. Upon going back inside and shutting the balcony door and drawing the thick curtains, he noted that the outside noise had virtually disappeared thanks primarily to double glazing on all the windows and balcony door facing the street.

By now it was almost 10.30 pm and he was ready to sleep. He was even too tired to think about a quick shower after the long journey. William's bedroom was a compact loft type arrangement but the double bed looked really comfortable. No need for the aircon he thought, so he undressed neatly placing his clothes on a side table. He slide into bed and his naked body felt very relaxed rubbing against the clean crisp white sheets. Within a few minutes he was in a deep sleep.

He slept for eleven hours straight and didn't wake up until 9.30 am the following morning Monday 1st July.

Once he was awake he jumped out of bed both thirsty and hungry. He wasn't one of those people that hang around in bed for an hour or two before getting up. Back on the farm in Hunterville there was nobody to stay in bed for, and there were countless jobs to be done and completed out on the farm. For a brief moment he wondered how Mr and Mrs O'Connor were managing back on the farm, but he decided not to enquire for they knew his contact phone number and email address, and had promised to contact him immediately if there were any problems. Additionally, Ram had promised him that he'd keep an eye on things also.

Shower, coffee and food in that order, he told himself. He must have had a good night's sleep because he was feeling very revved up in the shower. He dealt with that, dried off, wrapped the towel around himself, made a coffee and croissant, and went out onto the balcony. It was 10 am.

In the street below all the bars and restaurants were closed. There was a steady stream of mostly locals entering and exiting the café across the street. He would check that café out for sure, but not today. He could see tourists walking the cobbled pavement below towards the numerous museums, churches and piazzas in the Old City area. They were easy to spot with maps in hand, too many accessories in their back packs, and languages which he could hear, but not assign as either Italian or English.

His apartment balcony on the first floor of the building was semi-private it that it would be hard for people in the street below to get a clear view looking up at him, but he had a good clear view looking down on them. The outside air temperature was a warm 24 degrees C and there was a gentle breeze blowing down the street, so he dried off almost immediately. He went inside and changed into a pair of white jocks, and then went back out onto the balcony to finish his coffee and croissant. First coffee of the day is always the best he thought.

Suddenly he had this feeling that he was being watched. On scanning up and across, and left and right he realised that several people, mostly *'nonne e nonni'* in the nearby apartment buildings, were staring in his direction and smiling. The *'nonne'* especially, were none too disappointed by the fine physical specimen of a man they were viewing on the balcony of apartment # 1–3.

He instantly felt embarrassed that several grandmas and grandpas were seeing his scantily clad body. He bowed his head slightly and lifted his hand to try and indicate that he was sorry. He quickly went inside to put on more modest attire. Lesson learnt for the rest of his stay.

By now it was 10.30 am and it was time to do something productive. He gathered his thoughts. He needed to get some food supplies and wine, do a reconnaissance of the immediate area, do an internet search of 'top 10' places to explore, and make some activity bookings. There was plenty to do to fill the remainder of the day.

His trusty travel guide said that the nearby Mercato Pignasecca was one of the best in fresh produce markets in Naples. Since it was only a five minute walk away from his apartment, that's where he would go first. There was also a good conventional supermarket another five minute walk away in the opposite direction, so he'd check that out also.

On his way to the market, William took some time looking in shop windows. William noted that the men's and women's fashion and homewares and home décor shops all looked very trendy and contemporary compared to what he was used to back home. He had read that Italians were noted for excellent design sense and affordable luxury, and now he could see it before his very eyes. It was true. Glancing around the streets, he observed that the locals seemed to be very fashion conscious. Not something he was in to, or used to, down on the farm.

As he walked up the side street leading to Mercato Pignasecca, he unknowingly passed by a woman walking in the other direction away from the market who would change his life forever over the course of the next two weeks.

William arrived to the food market just after 11 am and wandered up and down Pignasecca Market street trying to decide what fresh produce items he would buy. The fish stalls looked very appealing with so many different types of fish and shellfish on offer. All the seafood items were either still alive in tanks, or dead but still glistening with obvious freshness. Living in a rural inland town community back in New Zealand, fresh fish was not on the menu very often back home. Everything looked appealing, but in the end, he decided to get items which didn't need a lot of cooking or were pre-prepared. He was on holiday so wanted to keep it simple, at least initially.

William liked to be as environmentally sensitive as possible so he had already packed a few 'biodegradable and combustible' carry bags into his luggage before leaving home. He had to do something to try and cancel the negative carbon footprint his journey to and from New Zealand to Naples had chalked up. That worried him. He also promised himself that after he returned home he would plant one thousand native tree seedlings annually out on the farm to compensate for the long flight.

On his way back to the apartment, having acquired all the fresh food supplies he wanted, William stopped at a wine shop. He wasn't a wine connoisseur but just liked a single glass of wine or a couple of beers with dinner, or pre-dinner. He entered the wine shop and was immediately surprised by the huge choice of wines and beers. Not only was the choice extensive, but some of the prices were very low compared to what he was used to. He walked out with a bottle each of rosé and white wine, and half a dozen bottles of Italian pilsner beer.

The rest of the day was spent going to the nearby supermarket for ancillary supplies, exploring some of the side streets around his apartment, and planning ahead some of the activities he'd like to do. His first significant activity booking was a traditional Napoli fresh pasta and dessert cooking class with lunch provided. It was scheduled for mid-morning Wednesday 3rd June.

By 7 pm he was back out on his balcony enjoying a cold beer and antipasto salad plate he had put together. It had been a great first full day in Naples. Everything was positive.

Nothing was really negative. Yes, there was too much graffiti showing on the building walls on some of the side streets, and yes there were too many discarded cigarette butts lodged in the cracks between cobbles on some of the streets, and yes some people seemed less than friendly, but it was real and it was not pretentious. It came with the territory and he liked that.

The sun was just going down. The restaurants and bars along from his apartment were filling up with mainly younger people and there were still plenty of tourists milling around. Considering it was a Monday night, he was surprised how busy the street below was. He looked up and across to the other balconies and could see numerous, mainly elderly people also looking down onto the street scene below. He was glad they weren't all focussed in his direction after the morning's faux par.

By 8 pm his body clock was going into meltdown due to the time difference between New Zealand and Italy. 8 pm Italy time was 6 am New Zealand time and he had only been away from New Zealand for two and a half days. Not enough time yet for his body to have readjusted. He was struggling to keep his eyes open. He resisted for another half hour but then gave in. He went back inside, drew the curtains, brushed his teeth, went upstairs, undressed and five minutes later he was fast asleep.

Nonna Russo's Cooking Class

Independently, both Aoife and William had booked to attend Nonna Russo's Cooking Class on Wednesday 3rd July. It would be the day that Aoife and William met face-to-face for the first time.

The meeting time and place for the cooking class was given as "we will meet at 10.30 am in front of the grand horse statue in the small open area on Via Toledo, at the Toledo Metro Station. I will be identified by my red apron." For both Aoife and William, this meeting point was a leisurely fifteen minute walk from their respective apartments.

Both had a real interest in Italian cuisine and both were looking forward to it. William arrived first and then Aoife. And then just before 10.30 am, a young married couple arrived. It didn't take long for them to establish that they were all attending Nonna Russo's Cooking Class.

Right on 10.30 am an elderly lady with a huge smile and wearing a red apron arrived to the horse statue.

"*Buongiorno, Buongiorno, pia cere. Mi chiamo Generosa Russo.* Good morning, good morning and welcome. My name is Generosa Russo. Do we have Aoife, William, Ben and Cathy? Excuse me miss, do you pronounce your name a-o-fee?"

"No not quite Nonna Russo, Irish pronunciation is difficult sometimes. For my name you ignore the first two letters and then pronounce it as EE-fa."

"Ok I understand. Please follow me everybody. My apartment is in the historical Quartieri Spagnoli area. It's about a five minute walk from here. It's on the 6th floor but there is a lift."

The group arrived to the apartment building which was non-descript on the outside, but tidy and clean. The lift took them up to the 6th floor together and they entered Nonna Russo's apartment which lead them straight to the kitchen area. It was surprisingly large and had obviously undergone some renovations to accommodate the cooking classes. There was a very large island in the centre of the kitchen with a solid wooden top. At one end of the kitchen there was a wooden table which could easily accommodate eight dining guests.

It was time for introductions.

"I have a world map on my kitchen wall over there which records where all my cooking students live. Please take a coloured drawing pin and place it where you come from and tell us all your name."

"My name is Aoife. I'm from Galway which is a small town on the west coast of Ireland."

There were a lot of pins indicating students that had attended the cooking class from Dublin in Ireland, but Aoife's was the first from Galway.

"My name is William. I'm from a very small rural town called Hunterville which is in the lower part of the North Island of New Zealand."

"We have a lot of people attending the cooking class from Australia, especially Melbourne where there are many Italian immigrants and their families, but you're my first student from New Zealand. Thank you for coming to Naples."

Nonna Russo seemed very proud that she had a student attending her class from the other side of the world. It was even further away than Melbourne, Australia.

"We're Ben and Cathy and we live in London. We were married a few weeks ago and are here on our honeymoon. We have three days in Naples and then we're flying to Rome."

With introductions over, it was time to commence the cooking class.

"Today we'll each be making fresh pasta around the kitchen island, and then I'll show you how to cook it with a pork and fennel tomato sauce. Then for dessert, we'll make baked pears with amaretti stuffing. I bought all the ingredients fresh from the market earlier this morning. I hope you will like. Just to make it more enjoyable I have a bottle of chilled pinot grigio white wine for us."

"Like it, I think we'll love it. It sounds delicious," replied Aoife.

They all agreed, and set to work carefully following Generosa's step by step instructions for making the pasta. Her instructions were to make a flour mound using best quality "00" flour, crack a fresh egg in the centre, add a tablespoon of fresh virgin olive oil and a tablespoon of chilled water. Then to mix all the ingredients and work it well and then knead, knead, knead.

Nonna Russo made it look very easy. They were all apprehensive that what they had just individually made, would be anywhere near as good as hers. Once each of the student's pasta dough was completed, it was wrapped in clear cling film and placed in the fridge to chill for half an hour.

"When did you arrive in Naples?" Aoife asked William.

"On Sunday night," he replied with his trademark beaming smile "this is only my 3rd day here."

"That's exactly the same as me. I arrived on Sunday night also. It's all been great so far. On Monday I went to Mercato Pignasecca and explored around a little bit, bought some fresh produce supplies, and yesterday I did more exploring and scoped a few activities."

"That's funny. I've pretty much done the same."

"When did you go to Mercato Pignasecca?" asked Aoife.

"Monday late morning."

"Me too."

Aoife and William continued the general chit chat while the young newly married couple from London mostly just looked on and listened. Nonna Russo made them all a coffee and handed around a plate of homemade biscuits while they waited for the pasta to chill in the fridge.

Aoife and William continued the conversation. Privately, she was surprised how friendly, genuine and down-to-earth this man from New Zealand seemed. His kiwi accent was pretty strong. She didn't think he was a handsome man like Kieran back in Galway, but if they were giving out prizes for 'the best smile', surely he would win hands down she thought to herself.

As he conversed with Aoife, William was trying not to stare too much at this beautiful Irish girl in front of him. He also thought she was very down-to-earth and genuine. And her Irish accent made him go a bit wobbly at the knees. He'd always loved hearing an Irish accent whether it was a man's or a woman's.

The cooking lesson continued.

Each student rolled out their chilled pasta ball firstly with rolling pin, and then they passed the rectangular shaped sheet of pasta several times through a pasta machine to get the pasta thinner and thinner.

"That's enough," signalled Nonna Russo "would you like to make linguine or fettucine or tagliatelle? The only difference is the width of the ribbons you will cut."

The consensus was to make fettucine, so she showed them the correct five millimetre width to cut. At the conclusion of the fresh pasta making part of the cooking class, they were all a bit surprised and proud of what they had achieved.

"It looks like the real thing," said the newly married young lady from London.

Nonna Russo moved over to the gas stove and the students gathered around. Not too close, but close enough to see clearly what was going on. To hot extra virgin olive oil in her large cooking pan, she added garlic and finally diced onions and sautéed them off. Then she squeezed out the meat from the casings of six large pork sausages she had also purchased from the market earlier that day. A teaspoon of fennel seeds was added, together with little bit of salt and a liberal amount of pepper.

"The sausages must be fresh, of good quality meat and coarse textured" she explained.

She used a large wooden spoon to break the sausages up into fingernail sized bits, and moved it all around in the pan until she was satisfied that the meat was almost but not completely cooked through, and that all the ingredients were mixed properly. To this mixture she added one kilogram of the reddest, juiciest tomatoes which had been chopped coarsely. After five minutes of further cooking, a handful of chopped Italian parsley and the zest from one lemon was added and stirred around.

"*Finito*. Now let's cook your pasta."

Nonna Russo had obviously done this many times before because she was very efficient and made the whole process look too easy. To several small pots of salted boiling water she had on the gas stove burners, she added each student's uncooked pasta.

"Don't overcook the pasta. Only three or four minutes cooking is required. You must not overcook otherwise the pasta will be too soft and have no bite. Al dente, it's got to be al dente. Firm to the bite."

She drained the water from each pot very quickly, and then emptied the cooked fettucine pasta into glistening white Italian ceramic pasta bowls lined up on the benchtop. All four of the students were visibly impressed. To each bowl of fettucine pasta she added a generous ladle of the pork and tomato sauce mixture.

"Does everybody want a glass of white wine?"

The yes nods were immediate and unanimous. They sat around the table eating the lunch they had partly made. It was enjoyed by all. William turned to Generosa and spoke.

"*E'delizioso Nonna Russo. Grazie.*"

That's a nice thing to say, and he seems like such a nice guy, Aoife thought to herself. The main course was finished and the cooking class continued.

"Today we will make pears with amaretti stuffing. The preparation is easy and cooking time is only twenty minutes at a temperature of 170 degrees C. Does everybody like almond flavour?"

She liked the students in her class today because they keep nodding yes to everything she said or asked which made things easy. Sometimes she had students with allergies and food dislikes and that was a bit more difficult. It made things more difficult but not impossible. Over the years and with a lot of experience, she knew exactly what to substitute for various allergy causing ingredients.

Nonna Russo halved and cored the pears. In a separate bowl she added a cup of coarsely crushed amaretti biscuits to a generous knob of softened butter, a generous splash of masala and half a cup of sugar. A teaspoon of vanilla extract and the zest of a lemon were also added. She mixed the ingredients together and spooned the resulting mix into the cored cavities of the pears, arranged on a baking dish, and then placed the dish in the oven.

Again, the students were all surprised at how simple the whole process seemed.

Twenty minutes later dessert was served. The smell was very enticing. It was sweet and fruity and almondy. Aoife and William, Ben and Cathy enjoyed the dessert served with thick Italian cream, and an additional glass of the chilled white wine.

It was now 2.30 pm and the cooking class at Nonna Russo's apartment was coming to an end. It had been a great success. They all said they'd try and replicate her dishes, and variations of those dishes, when they got back home.

Although Generosa offered to walk them back to the Toledo Metro Station pickup point, they were all confident they could find their way back there by themselves. After goodbye hugs and sincere thanks to Nonna Russo for the great cooking class and lunch, they all went down in the lift together and walked back to Toledo Metro Station.

"Enjoy the rest of your honeymoon and very nice to meet you," Aoife said to the young couple, who waved goodbye and then disappeared into the mid-afternoon crowd.

"I've got a few things to do back at the apartment," Aoife said to William "I'm staying up Via Toledo near Dante Metro Station. Where are you staying?"

"In the same general area, but my apartment is more over by the Monteoliveto Fountain landmark. Do you know it?"

"I do. Do you want to walk back that way together up Via Toledo?" Aoife asked William.

So off they went. Twenty minutes later, after strolling back slowly and chatting about what they planned to do while in Naples, gazing into various shopfront windows, and talking a little bit about their home towns, they reached Dante Metro Station. William liked Aoife and didn't like the idea of them departing and going their respective ways never to cross paths again. He had to think of something quickly and sensed that the 'ghost of Ram', who would have already made his move long ago, was sitting on his left shoulder speaking.

"For duck sake mate, don't be a wuss, man up and ask her if she'd like to do something together tomorrow, or the next day, or any day!"

William wasn't a loud mouthed extrovert or a painfully shy introvert, rather he was measured in everything he said and did, erring on the conservative side. He was a bit slow when it came to making a connection with the opposite sex. He took a deep breath and looked Aoife straight in the eyes.

"What have you got planned for the next few days? I'm heading to the Naples National Museum tomorrow. It's quite close to here. Would you like to join me? I hear that there's a really interesting café at Piazza Bellini which is kind of on the way there from where I'm staying. I could meet you there for a coffee first if you're interested."

Aoife did want to go to the Naples National Museum since it was highly rated in her travel guide, and thought it would be great to go with somebody else to see and enjoy what was there. She didn't have anything firm planned for the following day, so being in the company of a friendly and genuine man who was obviously a foreign tourist, would save her the hassle of dealing with the advances of the local lotharios which was seemingly harmless, but was becoming a bit tedious.

"Sure that would be great. Thanks for asking William. I know where Piazza Bellini is located. Anyway it's easy to find my way there using my mobile phone and map app. Meet you there at 10 am?"

"Perfect," said William hardly believing his luck "see you tomorrow morning."

They lightly hugged farewell and Aoife disappeared down one side of the main street towards her apartment. William passed over the main street and walked down a side street on the other side, towards his apartment.

William was very excited as he walked the remaining short distance back towards to his apartment, and as if it even seemed possible, his trademark beaming smile became even more pronounced. By now it was 3.30 pm. He thought that was a little bit early to go for aperitivo and decided to leave that until the weekend. Instead he'd head back to his apartment to do a little bit of reading about the National Museum. He wanted to know just enough to speak with a little bit of authority when he got to the museum with Aoife. As soon as he got back to his apartment the plan was to have a couple of cold beers out on his balcony and to make an antipasto plate with the fresh market produce remaining in the fridge.

By 6 pm he was sitting out on his small balcony with a couple of cold beers and a delicious looking antipasto plate. Droplets of moisture appeared almost instantly on the outside of his beer bottles and trickled down the side forming small puddles of water on his glass topped table. Cold beer and a warm evening, almost perfect he thought to himself. The sun was just starting to set but it wasn't fully dark yet.

Across the street and two floors further up, he could see an elderly woman leaning over her apartment's balcony railing taking in the street scene below. The throngs of people appearing in the street below mostly seemed to be of the younger age demographic, likely heading out for drinks and food with partners and friends. Suddenly the elderly woman flashed a smile and waved enthusiastically across in William's general direction. He wondered if perhaps she was waving to a friend of hers in an apartment close by his. He looked left and right, and up and down, to the apartments on his side of the street. No, she was definitely trying to get his attention and the wave was directed to him. Then he remembered back to a couple of days ago when he was sitting out on the balcony in his jocks. It was the same nonna that had waved and smiled to him then. He chuckled privately to himself, and gave a polite wave back. But sorry, the "jocks faux par" of a couple of days ago was not going to be repeated.

It was almost five days ago that he had departed from Hunterville. He was feeling a bit guilty that "life on the farm" was the furthest thing from his mind at the present moment. He felt relaxed and recharged. But most of all, he was very excited about meeting up again with Aoife for coffee at Piazza Bellini the following morning.

It was 9 pm and although his body clock was slowly readjusting, he was still feeling physically tired. He retired inside, shut the balcony door and drew the curtains, showered, sent an email to his parents back in Palmerston North, went up to his loft bedroom, stripped and slide into bed. He lay there wide awake and feeling contented that he'd had a great day. He was hopeful that the next day, Thursday 4th July would be an even better day. A few minutes later he had drifted off to sleep.

Piazza Bellini and the National Archaeological Museum

William nearly always slept well and on Thursday morning at 6.30 am, he woke up feeling alive and thankful. Very alive after nine hours of deep sleep, and thankful that several people back home had enabled him to make this trip to Italy to ponder his future and to take a little bit of time out for himself. He lay in bed for an additional half hour and then sprung out of bed and walked down from his loft bedroom to make himself a cup of coffee.

At 7 am he opened his balcony doors. The air was warm and a little bit humid and he could feel beads of sweat forming on his brow. He boiled himself a moka coffee on the gas top stove and took it out to the balcony. As always, the first coffee of the day was by far the best coffee of the day. His fridge was getting a little bit low on supplies, so if time allowed, a revisit to the Mercato Pignasecca was necessary. This morning's breakfast food offering was the last of the cold meats and olives.

Over at Aoife's apartment a similar scene was unfolding. By 7 am she was sitting out on her small private balcony dressed in faded jeans and a loose t shirt with her voluminous fair curly hair bundled up with a rubber band on top of her head. Despite no makeup her natural beauty was evident. Her personal beauty wasn't something she often thought about. She was not a mirror gazer. A person's personality and morals and opinions, which didn't have to be the same as hers, were more important to her. Prior to coming to Naples, and over the previous six months, her ability to judge a person on those attributes had been questionable.

Out on the balcony she was also sipping a moka coffee, and enjoying it with an egg croissant. A simple start to the day but it seemed right. Aoife was logged onto the internet searching for any horse-riding treks she could do at some stage over the weekend. The one that keep appearing in all the search engines with good reviews was horse trekking on the slopes of Mount Vesuvius. Aoife was very excited by this prospect and was determined to book herself on a tour as soon as she got back to her apartment later in the day. Since it was operating twice a day in the weekend with one trek starting late morning and the other late afternoon, she would try and combine it with a half day trip of either the Pompeii or Herculaneum ruins. She had read that although the Pompeii ruins were the more extensive, the Herculaneum ruins were considered to be the much better preserved.

Piazza Bellini was a five minute walk away from Aoife's apartment. She arrived there at 10 am exactly. It was closer to a ten minute walk from William's apartment and he had arrived there ten minutes early, not because he was desperate, but because he didn't want Aoife to arrive there and have to wait by herself in case there were any petty thieves, pickpockets or annoying lotharios milling around. That's the sort of considerate man he was.

"Morning Aoife, it's nice to see you again. Thanks for coming."

"All good William, it's nice to see you again also. The National Museum is meant to be really good. My travel guidebook says they have some incredible marble sculptures there."

"Let's have a coffee first. That café over there is highly rated. It's meant to be a bit bohemian and good for people watching. Apparently many well-known Napoli artists, writers, poets and fashion designers frequent there. Not that I'd know or recognise any of them. They could serve me a coffee and I'd be totally oblivious."

They both smiled at each other. It was a café scene very different to what they were used to in their respective towns back home. It seemed more interesting. It had that something about it which was hard to define. The French would say it had 'je ne sais quoi'.

"Inside or outside?" asked William.

"Outside looks nicer. It looks too dark inside," replied Aoife.

They sat down at an outside two person table in the shaded, cobbled open courtyard area. Baskets of flowering red petunia were hanging from wooden beams. The waiters were semi formally dressed. One headed in their direction.

"Hope you don't mind Aoife, but I'm going to try and order in Italian. No pain, no gain. It is very unlikely to be perfect but I want to try. What sort of coffee would you like?"

"I usually have a cappuccino with a chocolate dusting on top."

"Me too."

"I'll listen and see if I can translate your Italian to English as you speak, so don't talk too fast."

"Ok. I'll order two cappuccinos and a plate of those mini sized apricot and cherry biscuits. I had some the other day and they were good. Here goes."

William took a deep breath, concentrated and spoke to the waiter while flashing his usual beaming smile.

"*Buongiorno signore. Possiamo per favour due cappuccini e un piatto di biscottini all'albicocca e amarene. Grazie.*"

The young waiter smiled back and replied in English. He was impressed with William's attempt to order in Italian.

"Yes sir, I understand your order. Your Italian is good. Where do you come from? Are you husband and wife?"

William was a bit embarrassed at the waiter's questions, whereas Aoife seemed unfazed.

"I come from New Zealand, and my friend Aoife is from Ireland."

"Do you play rugby?" he asked William.

The waiter seemed very excited. He said that his cousin in Milan plays rugby and that they knew the New Zealand All Black rugby team well.

"Yes I do, every Saturday through winter. If I was in New Zealand now I'd be playing in my rugby team because it's wintertime there."

"Yes, now it's opposite season to here in Napoli. What position do you play sir?"

"On the wing. I'm not a big solid man. I'm more speedy than powerful."

The waiter was super excited by William's response.

"New Zealand is a long way. You make a nice couple," the waiter replied.

This made William even more embarrassed and insecure, for he was in the presence of a beautiful girl. He could see people looking directly over towards them and talking. Were they talking about her, or about him. He considered the latter highly unlikely.

It wasn't long before their coffees and a plate of mini biscuits arrived. Aoife and William sipped, munched, and chatted while they absorbed the ambience of Piazza Bellini. It was mid-morning and the tourists were starting to appear on the street bordering the piazza. The shops in and around Piazza Bellini looked interesting and inviting, and they all seemed to ooze Italian style and quality. While walking on his way to the café rendezvous William had noted a leather goods shop, a scarf shop, a ceramics shop, an antique map and book shop, a men's tailor shop. The list went on. This was definitely an area he'd return to at some later stage to explore further especially since Italian contemporary design was a real interest of his.

It was 11 am and the café stop had been a great success. William and Aoife had both learnt a lot more about each other. They were both surprised to find out that they had rural farming backgrounds in common.

William called for the bill. Their waiter came over with bill in hand and William paid cash including a two euro tip for the waiter's excellent attention. Tipping was something that William was not used to back home in New Zealand. It was very rarely done by anybody. However, in this case he felt it was appropriate. He was so happy that he didn't really care. Aoife had wanted to split the bill but William insisted it was his 'shout'. He had invited her so he would pay the bill.

As they prepared to leave, the young waiter unexpectedly gave Aoife a light hug and kissed both cheeks, and then turned to William and shook his hand vigorously. He said that he had just texted his cousin in Milan and told him he was serving a New Zealand rugby player.

William was hoping that he wasn't going to ask him for his autograph. He was just a low grade provincial weekend rugby player back home. He was nothing more than that.

The café experience had been a good one. Both Aoife and William were starting to feel very comfortable in each other's company. It was only twenty four hours ago that they had first met at the cooking class. Aoife and William walked out of the café and Piazza Bellini onto Via Santa Maria di Constantinopoli. It was only a few hundred meters walk up the street to the renowned National Archaeological Museum of Naples, usually referred to as the Naples National Museum.

After several minutes' walk up Via Santa Maria di Constantinopoli, and then across the busy Piazza Museo street, they had arrived at the dusky pink façade of the National Museum.

William had read that the museum was initially a cavalry barracks and then the administration building for the city's university. It wasn't until the late 1700s that the Bourbon King Charles V11 established the museum, primarily to safely house the collection of Greek-Roman artefacts and antiquities and sculptures he had inherited from his mother Elisabetta Farnese. The museum also housed a collection of treasures and mosaics looted and ambiguously acquired from the ruins of Pompeii and Herculaneum. He was excited to be visiting it.

They walked up the front steps of the museum and waited in a small line to buy their entrance tickets. After buying their tickets and confirming that it was acceptable to take pics as they walked around, they entered the large foyer area. Already they were both impressed with what was on display in the foyer area and the exploring hadn't really even started yet.

"Shall we get an audio guide?" asked Aoife.

"I'm happy to just go and explore and take it as it presents. I think they have information panels in both English and Italian to help out."

"Ok let's do that. Sounds good."

"Let's start off on the ground floor. I seriously want to see the Farnese Collection and especially the Farnese Bull and Hercules sculptures. Are you OK with that, or would you rather start off with something else first?"

"No that's good William. It all looks and seems so fantastic that I'm happy to start anywhere."

They walked down a wide corridor lined on either side with impressive life sized and larger marble sculptures of ancient males and females and some animals, primarily dogs. William hadn't yet grasped why the male sculptures were mostly completely naked, whereas the female sculptures were mostly fully dressed.

"I think we're looking for gallery numbers 13 and 16. Gallery 13 has the Hercules sculpture, and gallery 16 has the Farnese Bull sculpture."

"William, there's gallery 13."

They entered the gallery and there before them was the impressive marble statue of Hercules made sometime around 200 to 300 AD. Heavily muscled, masculine and naked, Hercules was the epitome of a magnificent warrior. Towering over 3 m tall he was leaning on a knobbed club with a lion skin draped over it.

William moved in for a closer look. Maybe he missed the sign saying "do not touch" but he carefully touched Hercules's toes and noted that they were far larger than his fingers.

Standing immediately in front of Hercules and looking directly up at this bearded face he also noted that his generous uncircumcised genitals were only a meter of so above the top of his head. That was a little bit uncomfortable for him but he tried not to show it. Let's not forget that it is not life size William thought to himself. He circled the statue so as to get a good 360 degree perspective. By now he was getting used to the majority of male Greek-Roman statues being presented fully naked.

"What do you think?"

"Excellent," replied Aoife "can it get any better? Now let's try and find the Farnese Bull sculpture."

It didn't take them long to find Gallery # 16. Aoife started reading out the information notes to William.

"Here it is Gallery #16. No way, this is fantastic. The information notes say that it was originally made in the early 3rd century out of a single block of marble and that there have been some significant restorations through the centuries, but that it basically represents the original sculpture. It was discovered in Rome in 1546 during excavations at the gymnasium of the Roman Baths of Caracalla, restored by Michelangelo and shipped to Naples in 1787. It depicts the death of the Queen of Thebes who was tied to a bull by the two sons of Antiope and torn apart over rocks. It weighs twenty two tonnes, measures 3 m wide and deep, and is just over 4 m high. I'm very impressed."

"You're impressed and I'm in awe, and we've only just started" replied William "and look over there at those sarcophagi. It looks like each one is carved out of a single block of marble and they're so ornate with hose 3-D figures and animals around the outside that it makes you wonder who was buried in them. Not your average citizen I'm thinking."

Their visit to the museum continued. Moving from room to room and gallery to gallery on the ground floor they perused household artefacts and paintings from the Farnese Collection, countless marble statues, weaponry, and jewellery. Nothing disappointed.

"Let's just work our way up to the mezzanine floor next. It's got a collection of mosaics and frescos mostly from the ruins of Pompeii and down the far end is the 'Secret Room' which houses a collection of ancient porn from Pompeii and Herculaneum. I'm game if you're game, but if you'd rather not?"

"I'm good," Aoife flashed back "and I'm open minded. I suspect things haven't changed much over the past 2000 years and ancient porn is similar to modern day porn. I'm no expert on the subject."

Neither of them could believe that they'd already been at the museum for well over an hour and had only just finished a cursory walk around the ground floor. There was so much to see and so much information to digest.

They arrived up to the mezzanine floor via a sweeping staircase and were immediately confronted by a stunning collection of wall and floor mosaics and frescos mostly recovered and excavated from Casa Del Fauno, a private home in Pompeii. It had been a large treasure filled aristocratic Roman residence until the catastrophic eruption of Vesuvius in 79 AD.

An information wall plaque stated that the highly rated "Battle of Alexander against Darius" mosaic was a standout due to its subject a matter, its detail and lighting effects, and its large 2.7 metre by 5 metre size.

"Originally it decorated the floor of a room overlooking a central courtyard garden. It depicts the Hellenistic forces of Alexander the Great doing triumphant battle with the Persian armies of King Darius III during the pivotal battle of Issus in 333 BC" explained William. He then continued.

"No way, it says it was made using 1 ½ million tiny coloured cubic tiles. It's a bit degraded and poorly preserved in parts but apparently scholars assess it as the best record of Alexander the Great's epic battle with King Darius. Seems a bit underwhelming to me Aoife but I'm no expert."

"I agree, to an ordinary person like me some of the other mosaics seem more beautiful and artistic, and are much better preserved."

They continued down to the faraway end of the mezzanine floor and the Gabinetto Segreto. The museum's previously secret room was now open to the public and housed its ancient porn collection.

"Shall we or shan't we?" asked William.

"Yep, let's have a look" replied Aoife.

William was clearly more embarrassed about going into the Gabinetto Segreto than Aoife was.

Once inside, they looked around at the large array of erotic artefacts, good luck phallic charms and sexually explicit frescoes and mosaics, taken from the villas, bars and brothels of ancient Pompeii and Herculaneum over centuries of excavations.

"Wasn't expecting that," said William shyly to Aoife as they exited.

"Just as well it was darkly lit," replied Aoife.

But in reality, both of them were excited to have seen it in the company of each other.

"One more floor to go. We might have to leave the Egyptian basement collection until another time. Just one last sculpture I'd like to see on the first floor is Farnese Atlante which is the statue of Atlas carrying a globe on his broad shoulders. Are you keen or have you had enough?"

"Yep, I'm keen to continue but I am getting hungry," replied Aoife. William laughed.

"Me too."

They wandered up to the first floor admiring the split spiralled staircase and high ceilings on the way up. They passed into the impressive Hall of the Sundial and were immediately struck by the huge painted arched ceiling and the inlaid multi-coloured stone floor. They were impressed with the inlaid brass sundial extending some twenty seven meters diagonally across the floor from opposite sides of the hall. It had the twelve signs of the zodiac embedded in it and was designed by architect Pompeo Schiantarelli in the early 1790s.

And there sitting down one end of the hall was the statue of Atlas carrying the celestial globe. The Atlas statue was dated at around 150 AD. It was impressive at just over two meters tall and the sphere Atlas was carrying some sixty-five centimetres in diameter. It was another 'no holds barred' full frontal nude sculpture with the grimacing and tormented face of Atlas tilted to the right, clearly indicating the burden of his task of holding up the celestial sky sphere.

A quick look around the rest of the 1st floor revealed a range of discoveries from the ruins of Pompeii and Herculaneum. Everyday items like glassware and ceramics, household items and armoury, wall murals and frescos.

"I don't know about you William but after four hours here I think I'm pretty much saturated for the day. So much to see and take in that my brain is starting to spin. It's been totally awesome. I'm very impressed. I feel like I've been a bit sheltered back home in Ireland to this kind of thing."

"I agree, and I'm feeling much the same. It's almost 4 pm let's go. I might have to come back sometime and do a round two. It's hard to absorb everything in just a few hours and on the first pass. Thanks for your company Aoife. It's been so much better than doing it alone."

"No, it's me who should be thanking you. It's been fantastic. Do you want to grab a pizza on the way back? We didn't have lunch so I'm getting a bit hungry. But it's only on one condition. I'm paying and it's not negotiable. And after that I want to drop by Mercato Pignasecca again to get a few fresh supplies before it closes at 6 pm."

"Sounds good. And thank you for considering and including me."

William was feeling a bit emotional. *What's that all about,* he wondered to himself. Aoife was being very kind to him and he liked it.

They walked back towards Via Toledo and Dante Metro Station taking in the local sights and sounds on the way. It was going home time for the locals so the streets were getting busy and noisy. It was only a ten minute walk from the museum to an area of bars and restaurants and cafes.

"Here's a pasta and pizza restaurant William. I had a look at the menu yesterday and a lot of locals were dining there so that's usually a good sign. OK to try this one? We can sit outside under an umbrella, have a Neapolitan pizza and wine and watch the Napoli world go by."

"It sounds perfect. After you."

They sat at a two person table, under a red umbrella, and off to the side. At 5 pm, it was still very early for dining by locals, but there were a lot of tourists milling around so most of the restaurants opened a bit earlier to cater for them. William remembered that Aoife wanted him to be her guest so he resisted the temptation to call over the waiter and start ordering.

Aoife ably did it instead. It's easy to get the almost immediate attention of waiting staff when you're as pretty as Aoife. A young female waitress came over instantly. Aoife turned to William.

"I'm going to order two pizzas. One Neapolitan pizza with tomato, mozzarella with prosciutto and peppers, and one Margherita pizza which is plain pizza topped with tomato sauce, mozzarella cheese and fresh basil. Are you OK with those choices?"

"Yes. Are you going to order in Italian?" asked William.

"No way," she replied to his cheeky challenge "I'd quite like a glass of sparkling water and a glass of chilled white wine" continued Aoife.

"That sounds good. I'll have the same thanks."

Aoife gave their order to the waitress. They sat back, relaxed and chattered while they waited for their drinks to arrive. The air temperature of 25 degrees C was still very warm and a little bit humid, but not unpleasantly so.

Ten minutes later the young waitress came back with their drink orders. She asked where Aoife came from, and also enquired where her husband came from because his accent sounded different. Aoife wasn't confident enough to respond in Italian, and didn't want to make a big deal about William not being her husband, so she just replied in English.

"I'm from Ireland and William is from New Zealand."

In broken English, the waitress responded that she had extended family in Melbourne, Australia and that she would be going there sometimes towards the end of the year. Her uncle and aunty owned an Italian restaurant in Melbourne so she would be staying with them, and working in their restaurant to start with. She then left to get their pizzas.

"*Salute* William. Thanks for inviting me to the museum. Not sure I would have gone there by myself but I'm totally glad I did. There's so much inspiring culture, history and exquisite craftsmanship to see."

The conversation flowed freely and easily as they sipped their chilled white wines and devoured their pizzas. They talked about their home towns, what a typical day back home involved for them, their rural upbringings, their love of horses and horse riding, and their general music and food interests. It was all the usual getting to know you stuff.

Although they were from opposite sides of the world it was surprising that they had so many common interests, and that their general lifestyle was similar.

He was back again. The 'ghost of Ram' was sitting there on William's right shoulder.

"Ask her mate. You're in with a chance. And she seems really nice anyway. Come on, you're balls are big enough. Be a man."

William took a sip of wine, looked Aoife directly in the eyes and then asked.

"Have you heard of the 'Veiled Christ'? It's meant to be one of the most incredible sculptures in the world. It's in a chapel museum quite nearby here. I'm going tomorrow morning. Don't suppose you'd be interested in going also? You've probably had enough of sculptures for a while."

William was expecting and prepared for a negative response.

"Actually I have read about it, and yes I would like to go, as long as you don't mind me coming along. Also there are a couple of things I'd like to do and it would be better doing them with somebody I know. In the weekend, I want to do a horse-riding trek on the slopes of Mount Vesuvius and visit either the Pompeii or Herculaneum ruins before or after the horse trek. Any interest in joining me?"

Mind, of course he didn't mind if she came to see the 'Veiled Christ' with him, and was he interested in horse riding on the slopes of Vesuvius. He was wondering how to say yes without seeming like a complete desperado. It was a long time since any female had taken this much interest in him, or been as attentive as Aoife was being right at that moment.

"I don't have anything planned for the weekend so yes to both thanks Aoife. I can give you some money now for the horse trek and the Pompeii or Herculaneum ruins trip if you like."

"Of course not. I'll book when I get back to my apartment later and then let you know tomorrow how much it is. Where would you like to meet in the morning for going to see the 'Veiled Christ'?"

Aoife trusted William implicitly. Although she had only known him for thirty six hours, she felt he was a man filled with integrity and honesty. He was different to all the men she had meet and dated previously. She wanted to go with her instincts even if they had let her down in the not too distant past.

"Are you OK to meet up at the Monteoliveto Fountain at 10 am tomorrow? We can go for a coffee first and then head to Chapel Sansevero."

"Yes, 10 am tomorrow morning is good."

With that, Aoife ask for and paid the bill and then they both got up and headed together over to Mercato Pignasecca to get some supplies for their respective apartments. After the shopping for fresh produce was completed, it was time to close the lid on what had been a great day for both of them. Aoife gave William a warm lingering hug. It was very different to the light hug they had exchanged twenty four hours earlier.

"Thanks William. It's been a great day. See you in the morning at Monteoliveto Fountain and I'll make those horse-riding and Vesuvius ruins bookings as soon as I get back to apartment."

"Yep, see you in the morning."

And with that, they departed in opposite directions to their nearby apartments. Just before he turned the corner of the side street leading to his apartment, he glanced around to see if Aoife was still in view. She was and had also glanced around. He lifted his hand, flashed his beaming smile and waved warmly to Aoife. She waved back. He was exceedingly happy at this moment in time.

Back at this apartment he put his fresh market supplies into the fridge, took out a beer and went out onto his balcony to enjoy the evening dusk. It was warm, the beer was cold, and he was content. He reflected on the day and wondered how things were going back at the farm. William was happy that everything about his trip to Naples was exceeding his expectations.

Then in the space of a few seconds, a cold chill suddenly came over him. What would happen in ten days' time when he had to return back home to

Hunterville? Would things revert back to the status quo? Was his destined to live alone on the farm? Would he ever see Aoife again? The contentment and happiness of a few minutes earlier had turned to anxiety and fear. He went back inside, showered, wandered upstairs to his loft bedroom, stripped naked and went to bed. He was usually a very quick sleeper but this night he tossed and turned before finally getting off to sleep.

Sansevero Chapel and the Veiled Christ

William woke up at 7 am on Friday 5th July after a difficult night's sleep. He went downstairs for the mandatory moka coffee and some bread, tomatoes and cheese. It was taken out to the balcony as per usual, to sit and relax and enjoy the beginning of another day. He checked his email. There was one from Ram confirming that everything was good back on the farm in Hunterville. Mr and Mrs O'Connor loved reliving the farm experience and there had been no mishaps or problems. The weather at the farm was cold and frosty but there had been some nice, clear, sunny days after the morning frost and ice had melted away.

William wanted to tell Ram about Aoife but held back just in case everything fizzled and it all turned out to be a non-event. Instead he just replied asking Ram to thank everybody sincerely for their support and help. He told Ram that the sights and sounds and 'adventures' in Naples were better than he expected. He knew Ram would wonder what 'adventures' meant, but decided to leave it there.

Over at her apartment, Aoife woke up at 6 am after a good night's sleep. The previous night, she had booked a half day trip on Saturday to the ruins at Herculaneum followed later in the day by a horse-riding trek on the slopes of Mount Vesuvius for herself and William.

She made a moka coffee, and a salad sandwich, and went outside on her small balcony to relax and contemplate the day ahead. She was thinking about William and how she enjoyed his company and how he kept surprising her with his general enthusiasm and kindness, and his friendly positive attitude to everybody. She was certain he was one of the nicest men she had ever met.

As with the previous day, William arrived to the Monteoliveto Fountain rendezvous point ten minutes before 10 am, and Aoife arrived right on 10 am. A warm embrace between the two of them seemed natural now.

"Morning Aoife. Yesterday was so good that I'm not sure today's offering can trump that. But the Sansevero Chapel Museum is meant to be really good. I'm looking forward to seeing the 'Veiled Christ'. Please, before we go any further did you manage to make the bookings for horse trekking and exploring the Pompeii or Herculaneum ruins? If yes, what do I owe you?"

"I did. Tomorrow morning pickup is 9 am for the Herculaneum ruins tour and then our personal pickup from the entrance at Herculaneum for the horse trekking on Mount Vesuvius is at 1 pm. It starts at 2 pm and finishes at 5 pm and then they will drive us back to the city centre in Naples in their minivan. The total cost for both activities is 110 euros. I hope that's OK?"

Of course it was OK. The cost could be double that and William wouldn't mind. He was just ecstatic that he was going horse-riding with Aoife to such a fantastic locality, and that he would also get to see the famous Herculaneum ruins resulting from the catastrophic Vesuvius eruption on the 24 August 79 AD. William handed Aoife the 110 euros in crisp, clean notes.

"Coffee first? I know a good café not too far from here. I've tried it a couple of times mid-morning and it's been good. Not as good as the café we went to yesterday at Piazza Bellini, but still pretty good."

"Definitely coffee first. Are you going to order in Italian again?"

"Not telling" replied William.

They smiled at each other and started walking up Calata Trinita Maggiore. It was only 100 meters to the corner café William had mentioned. They sat down outside and a waiter came over and took their order of two café lattes and two plain croissants.

Neither Aoife nor William were into the local espresso coffee ritual at cafés. Standing up at the café bar having a tiny cup of strong black coffee in less than five minutes was not the morning café experience they were used to back home in Galway or Hunterville.

"See that old classical 4-storied building opposite and that balcony on the first floor with the scattered red geranium plants and washing on the clothes line?"

"Yes."

"Well, Aoife, guess what? That's my apartment."

"Really. That's a lot closer to where I'm staying than I thought. It looks good."

William was too embarrassed to ask Aoife over to take a look around inside his apartment in case she thought he was coming on to her, or being way too forward. It wasn't his style. He checked quickly to make sure that Ram wasn't sitting there on his right shoulder telling him off. He wasn't. Not this time.

Needless to say, he was surprised at what Aoife said next.

"Can I take a quick look at your apartment before we head to Sansevero? Just to see what it's like and how it compares to mine."

"Sure, no problem."

They sat relaxing in the warm mid-morning sun enjoying the coffees and each other's company, and watching the day 'coming to life' now that the tourists were appearing in ever increasing numbers on the pavement outside the café.

"Let's go William. I want to see your apartment and then on to the 'Veiled Christ'. I emailed my parents last night and told them that I was going to see it. They texted me back almost immediately and said that they were very jealous and asked me to say a pray for them in the chapel."

"Sure, follow me."

William paid the bill and off they went across the street. It took all of fifteen seconds to get to the front door of his apartment building. He opened the door with the key pad and went inside. Aoife was surprised at how steep and narrow the access stairs were.

William explained to Aoife that there were a lot of elderly people living in the apartment building but that he never, or very rarely, saw them venturing out. He thought that it was a bit sad to be restricted to their apartments because there was no lift in the building and the steep stairs were difficult for elderly people to navigate. Not to be able to enjoy the city's piazzas and gardens and churches, especially since most of the elderly people seemed quite religious, it just didn't seem right. He wished there was something he could do but not being able to speak fluent Italian was a constraint for communicating with the elderly people.

Aoife had a quick look around William's apartment and commented that it was a bit bigger than hers, and seemed better equipped than hers. She was impressed at how neat and tidy it was. She liked the balcony area and the large balcony doors and commented that it must be a good place to sit first thing in the morning, or last thing in the evening, watching the people in the street below.

William confirmed that it was.

"You must come and see my apartment sometime," Aoife said to William as they negotiated back down the stairs. Privately he thought 'now would be good' but that wasn't the plan for today so they set off up the street towards Sansevero Chapel. It was only a ten minute walk away.

When they arrived at Sansevero Chapel it was close to 12 noon. William was expecting a long queue but there were only seven people ahead of them. From the outside, the building looked fairly ordinary, however, upon entering it was far from ordinary. Extraordinary was a more appropriate descriptive. It was confusing to know where to look first. Up at the painted frescos on the domed chapel ceiling was a good starting point.

"Wow, this is beautiful. Let's just walk around clockwise from the entrance point and see all the various sculptures and then view the 'Veiled Christ'. I can see it down towards the far end in the centre of the chapel. I don't know why I'm so nervous Aoife. It's crazy."

William's voice was quiet and he was almost whispering as he spoke to Aoife. Such was the overall reverence of the inside of the chapel. Aoife agreed with William's plan and she too was overcome with the significance of the occasion for they were about to view what has been described by art and cultural historians as the single most inspiring and incredible sculpture ever produced by a mortal man.

"I think there are around twenty five sculptures around the walls and alcoves of the chapel's interior, and also there's an underground basement vault where a surprise awaits. Let's do it."

They commenced their tour inside Sansevero Chapel. Each and every sculpture was impressive. None more so than the sculpture numbered #11 on the map guide which they had been handed with the entrance ticket. It was described as having been carved by Antonio Corradini in 1752. Called 'Chastity' it was a naked younger female form completely veiled from the top of her head, down to her ankles. The veil was so thin that it appeared silk-like and transparent, and her firm nubile breasts and youthful face could still be clearly seen under the draped veil. Her left hand rested on a large broken tablet and a garland of roses discretely covered her most intimate parts.

"How did Corradini do that? How do you create that most feminine and erotic veiled sculptural form from a slab of inert marble? Those sculptures we saw yesterday at the Naples National Museum were fantastic, but this seems even more fantastic if that's even possible."

"I agree William, it's jaw dropping."

They continued their slow walk around the chapel interior. Some sculptures were more impressive than others. All of the time William could see the 'Veiled Christ' sculpture out of the corner of his eye on the floor towards the middle of the chapel. But he wasn't yet ready to approach it. The excitement was building.

Aoife stopped at the sculpture numbered #14 on the guide map. It was the first one on the right hand side of the chapel at the faraway end to the entrance. The map notes described that it was completed by Francesco Queirolo in 1752 and called 'The Release from Deception'. She sensed that there was a lot of symbolisation in all the various components of the work which she didn't really understand. The part that stood out the most for her was a naked life sized man trying to free himself from a knotted net flung and folded over the greater part of his body. He was being helped by a winged boy-like figure standing on a celestial globe.

"William, do you think the man with the net draped over his body is carved out of a single slab of marble?"

"Must be but just let me check the map notes. Yes, it says that the support artisans who helped Queirolo were too scared to work on the delicate net part of the sculpture in case it fractured and shattered into pieces that he had to complete it himself."

"To me it's even more fantastic than the 'Chastity' sculpture."

"I agree."

They continued viewing, and assessing, and discussing the various sculptures down the right hand side of the chapel until they were back at the entrance. All the while, they had avoided stopping to look at the 'Veiled Christ' sculpture lying towards the centre part of the chapel floor. The moment had arrived. Were they really about to see what has been described as one of the most impressive, if not the most impressive sculpture, existing in the world today. They turned and walked towards exhibit # 23.

William was oblivious to the fact that he was holding hands with Aoife as they approached the 'Veiled Christ'.

They stood to the side and gazed down onto the sculpture. The veiled lifeless Christ was lying on a rectangular couch with his head and shoulders propped up by two rectangular cushions adorned with corner tassels. Lying next to the right foot of Christ was a crown of sinuous twigs with long sharp thorns. This light greyish white part of the sculpture contrasted with the larger base which comprised a dark grey marble slab with black streaks. The basal slab appeared to be a large bedspread which was finely fringed all the way around its border. Aoife quickly scanned her support notes.

"This sculpture of Christ was made from a single slab of marble by Giuseppe Sanmartino in 1753 when he was thirty three years old. What do you think?"

There was no response from William. Aoife continued.

"The veil looks so real. It looks so thin and translucent. Like you can see right through it but yet it's just made from rock. Maybe it's something you can only achieve with marble rock? It's unreal."

Still there was no response from William.

Aoife turned to William and was surprised to see his eyes welled up with tears. She couldn't tell if they were tears of sadness, or tears of joy. Or maybe they were a combination of both. She didn't want to embarrass him so was very measured about what she said next.

"Don't worry William it's all good. You just enjoy the moment and absorb it. I know you have wanted to see this ever since you arrived in Naples."

William was overcome with emotion. It was intense. He was gazing through the transparent veil covering Christ's face and the enlarged vein on his forehead directly above his eyes. He was surprised at how young he looked for he was expecting an older bearded man. This looked like a man in his early twenties. He wanted to lift the veil off Christ's face to see if there were any puncture marks from the crown of thorns having been forced on his head. Through the draped veil covering, William could see Christ's muscular arms leading down to lean long fingers and he could also clearly see his nail pierced hands. Similarly, his long lean feet and toes were nail pierced. The figure of Christ looked relaxed and at total peace.

William was not a devoted Christian or a true believer but he was strongly moved by the significance of the sculpture before him. He was spiritual but hadn't yet figured out which form of spirituality he favoured. He was still struggling with that decision. After ten minutes of staring directly at the 'Veiled Christ' he turned to move away and then suddenly realised that Aoife was with him. He was being very insensitive. He remembered that she wanted to say a pray for her parents in front of the 'Veiled Christ'. They had requested that. He held Aoife's hand and turned to her.

"I'm very sorry. Shall we do that blessing pray for your parents now?"

Aoife was joyous that he had remembered and they stood there with heads bowed towards the 'Veiled Christ' while she quietly recited an Irish blessing prayer.

May God hold you in the palm of his hand. May your days be many and your troubles be few. May all of God's blessings descend upon you and may peace be within you. May your heart be strong, May you find what you're seeking wherever you roam.

"That was nice Aoife. I'm sure your parents would be happy. You must tell them. Are you ready to go?"

"Yes, and thanks for remembering."

But William asked if he could just have a couple of more minutes with the 'Veiled Christ'. He had a quick scan of the marvel presented before him just to make sure that he hadn't missed anything. He found it difficult to leave, but it was time to go.

"We've seen a lot of marble sculptures over the past twenty four hours William but that has to be the best of all. Highlight of Naples so far for sure."

"I don't know about you Aoife but the last two days have been magic. Not just for what we've seen but also for your company. All those people that say there's nothing much to see or do in Naples must be mad. It's fantastic. I love it. *Grazie Napoli.*"

Aoife agreed with William's sentiments. It was now 2 pm.

"Do you want to stop for a drink on the way back? I thought I'd do some shopping this afternoon and not leave it all until the last minute. There's several people back home in Galway I'd like to buy presents for."

"I need to buy some presents also. A gift each for my parents and something for Ram which is going to be hard, and the ladies at the café, and Mr and Mrs O'Connor. Good idea to get it done now. I have a few ideas from the little bit of window shopping I've done since I've been here. Especially yesterday as I was looking into shop windows and displays on my way to Piazza Bellini to meet you for coffee. I might treat myself to one or two things also. But a drink first sounds good."

Aoife and William walked off back in the direction of Monteoliveto Fountain. They came across a small home-style eatery and stopped by for a salad sandwich and glass of wine.

"Sincere thanks for the past two days site seeing William. It's been great to do it with somebody who's so positive and passionate about what we've seen. It has made me feel the same."

"Thanks for your company Aoife. It's so much better than just doing it alone."

"Don't forget that we'll be meeting up in the morning at 9 am at Dante Metro Station. A minivan with 'Herculaneum Tours' on the side will collect us. They said traffic can be hellish at that time of the morning so not to worry if they're a few minutes late."

"Understood. I'll be there."

They hugged goodbye and departed off in opposite directions. William had wanted to kiss Aoife goodbye on the cheek, and better still the lips, but held back. The timing didn't seem right. Not yet. But he sensed that it wasn't too far away. He was conservative but he was not a monk.

Aoife's shopping spree was very successful. It was easy to buy for her religious parents since there were so many religious themed items on offer in all the gift shops, but a lot harder to buy for her brother who was a good reliable man but conservative and rural in his outlook. Since he was also a keen coffee drinker she bought him a branded Italian stovetop espresso coffee maker and two 500 gram cans of top quality Napoli expresso coffee. He'd love this she thought to herself. She also wanted to buy a gift for Mr O'Leary who had been a great support to her when she needed it the most. It was as difficult as buying for her brother. Eventually she saw something in an artisan leather goods shop window which seemed appropriate. It was an Italian men's wallet. It was expensive but displayed typical Italian craftsmanship qualities of luxurious soft leather and a stylish look.

Finally she wanted to buy something for Kieran. As she stood thinking about what a meaningful gift for him might be, she was suddenly wracked with terrible guilt for she hadn't thought about Kieran at all, for the past few days. That didn't seem right. Even when she was back to her Napoli apartment at night-time, Kieran was still not in her thoughts. She was very confused. But she was determined to get something useful for him despite the ongoing abusive behaviour she had been subjected to by Kieran before she left Galway a few days ago. She wandered up and down numerous side streets trying to find a suitable gift. Finally she spotted an artisan art supplies shop and walked in to take a closer look. There were so many things that she wanted to buy for Kieran but decided it should be something that she could easily fit into her bag when she left for home. The choice was difficult but she selected a gift box of Maimeri's Fine Italian Natural Earth Oil Colours. The gift set comprised eleven natural earth shades which were still made by an ancient formulation and which used Italian sourced pigments reflecting the colours of the facades of palaces and monuments and important buildings and houses in Italian city centres. They were expensive, but she was pleased because she was sure Kieran would appreciate the gift.

Having bought gifts for her family members, and Mr O'Leary and Kieran, she wondered if it was time to buy herself something. The answer was yes. Every girl loves Italian fashion she thought to herself and commenced the search. It wasn't difficult for every other shop seemed to be a ladies clothing and fashion accessory shop. She treated herself to some designer Italian sunglasses and a fine silk Italian designed scarf. When she tried them on in the shop, the assistant commented that she looked like a movie star from the 1950s. Aoife was embarrassed but thanked the lady.

Knowing that the following day would be busy and probably tiring, she decided on just going back to her apartment and chilling out on the balcony for the evening. As she walked slowly back to her apartment it was another very warm early evening in the central city and the streets were full of locals shopping for the weekend and heading home from work. She reflected on how wonderful the day had been and how she was feeling increasing affection for William.

From mid-afternoon on Friday, after he had left Aoife, William had also carried out his shopping spree in the area between his apartment and Piazza Bellini. He saw so many things he would have loved to buy but was trying to be practical about what and how much he could carry in his return baggage to Hunterville. He easily bought a gift for the ladies in the café but buying a gift for Ram was more difficult. For one hour he walked up and down all the side streets and laneways trying to find him a gift. Finally he saw something which might be Ram appropriate. It was a gift suitable for his 'chick magnet' and something which just might make it look a little bit more classy. He was sure Ram would like the set of designer natural car air fresheners and the soft black leather car seat cover with the Ferrari company logo which he had selected. If he didn't like these gifts, then he would keep them for himself. He was secretly hoping that Ram didn't like them but considered that unlikely. He still had to buy a gift for Mr and Mrs O'Connor and his parents so would keep a lookout for something appropriate.

William completed some of the gift buying he had planned and then wondered if he should treat himself to something. Clothes didn't really interest him too much. He was more interested in taking some good quality Italian cooking ingredients back home. His first purchase was a small 100 ml bottle of twenty five year old balsamic vinegar. Expensive, but the elderly man in the shop told him it was excellent quality. He tilted the bottle and the contents looked very viscous and of thick consistency. That was a good sign which convinced him to buy it. He also purchased a few 200 ml cans of infused extra virgin olive oil. From a range of ten different types, he selected cans of olive oil infused with garlic and basil, blood orange, lemon, and Italian herbs.

He walked slowly back to his apartment and once back home, he continued the same ritual as the previous few nights. A quick change from jeans and shirt into shorts and t shirts, a cold beer from the fridge, an antipasto plate and out onto the balcony to relax. It was Friday night and the street below was much busier and alive than usual. It was nearly 6 pm and as the sun was going down, mostly young people were spilling out of the bars and cafes just along the street to the outside tables.

As he sipped his cold beer sitting out on the balcony, William reflected on the 'Veiled Christ' he had seen a few hours earlier. It was sculptured by Sanmartino when he was thirty three years old. That was only four years older than him. He wished he could do magic. If he could, he would like to meet Sanmartino to see what made him tick, what sort of a man he was, ask him where he learnt to sculpture and what did he think of his own work.

It had been a great day and the next day promised to be as good, if not better. It was going to be something quite different to the first few days spent in Naples. He was excited about going on a horse-riding trek with Aoife. William was a good horseman and had ridden since he was a child. He had always had his own personal pony and then horse, and currently had a team of three working horses back on the farm which were mostly used for mustering. He assumed that Aoife was going to be a proficient rider also since she had grown up on a farm.

Come 9 pm, he had showered and was lying in bed thinking about Aoife. Things had changed significantly in the past twenty four hours for both of them, and he was wondering if things could progress further in the next twenty four hours. He fell asleep still wondering.

Herculaneum Ruins and Horse-Riding on Mount Vesuvius

William woke up on Saturday morning at 6 am. He was still thinking about the 'Veiled Christ' and he would never forget the experience of standing there and viewing that incredible sculpture. He lay in bed for another half hour and then suddenly sprung up and out of bed like a gazelle spooked by a lion. It was going to be a busy day so he thought a good breakfast was in order. But first things first, and after a good pee he put his trusty moka coffee pot on the gas burner. He then made a large antipasto plate with crusty bread, tomatoes, olives, cheese and some grilled eggplant and tuna dip. He took it out to the balcony with his freshly brewed coffee and sat down to enjoy the quietness of a 7 am Saturday morning in his Naples neighbourhood. William was going to miss his early morning balcony time when he went back to Hunterville.

Over at her apartment, Aoife was still in bed at 7 am and enjoying a mini sleep-in. She was determined to have a proper and full sleep-in the following morning. Aoife was excited about seeing the famous ruins of Herculaneum resulting from a major volcanic mud flow from the erupting Vesuvius on the 25 August 79AD. She was even more excited about going horse-riding on the slopes of Mount Vesuvius with William. Aoife suspected that William was going to be a proficient and confident rider because when they discussed going riding the previous morning, he used all the correct technical terminology and horsey jargon. Her breakfast was a little bit more constrained than Williams. A good strongly brewed coffee and a bowl of cereal and fresh fruit would keep her going for the better part of the morning and probably part of the afternoon as well. She sat out on her balcony making a quick list of the things she'd need to take in her backpack. It was going to be a hot day and they were going to be out in the full sun for a great part of it so essentials included a sunhat, sunscreen lotion, bottled water, sunglasses, a change of t shirt, her mobile phone and a little bit of cash.

Horse riding dictated that jeans and good sturdy footwear were best worn.

Being a practical and organised man, William had similarly put the same items together on his kitchen table. He knew exactly what was needed for the day ahead.

William turned up at Dante Metro Station at 8.45 am and Aoife at 8.55 am but it wasn't until 9.20 am that the mini-van from 'Herculaneum Tours' arrived to pick them up. The driver apologised profusely and was shouting and gesticulating wildly about the terrible Naples traffic but William simply said 'no problem' and *'e'una bella giornata*, it's OK' and the driver calmed down immediately.

It was only a ten kilometre drive from central Naples to the Herculaneum ruins but the busy Saturday morning traffic heading south to Herculaneum and Pompeii, and around the coastal highway to Sorrento, made it seem like a much longer distance. It took close to forty minutes to drive to the Herculaneum ruins entrance gate. When they arrived, Aoife and William were surprised at how many people were obviously about to do the same as them.

William and Aoife's tickets had been prearranged so they avoided the longish queue at the entrance gate. They were handed an audio guide, a map and a bottle of water each by the attendant. It was sunny and getting hot so hats and sunscreen were applied immediately before continuing on.

Herculaneum which had originally been a small seaside fishing town with numerous noble's residences and villa's, a theatre, gardens and bath-houses and shops, was buried underneath a sixteen meter thickness of mud flow from the 79AD Vesuvius eruption. Because the town's burial was sudden and didn't comprise superheated pyroclastics from the volcano, the Herculaneum ruins are much better preserved than those at Pompeii, only ten kilometres away.

Aoife and William walked around looking in awe at the ruins which were nearly 2000 years old.

"I wonder how many people lived in Herculaneum?"

"They say around four thousand on the audio guide but I'm not sure how they calculated that number."

"What's this William? It looks like a moat around the town. Maybe it was for protection against possible invaders?"

"No, according to the audio guide it's the former ancient shoreline. This is where the beach was at the time of the eruption but now it's several kilometres away. And also, this is where they found more than three hundred skeletons in

1980. The skeletons included men, women and children who had been trying to run down to the beach to launch their boats as the volcano erupted."

"That's terrible. Imagine how scared those poor people they must have been, especially the children."

"It's scary just thinking about it," replied William "and it blows my mind to think we're standing here now in relative safety talking about it. Apparently the last eruption of Vesuvius was in 1944 and one is overdue."

"Better not be this afternoon when we're up there riding on the slopes of Vesuvius."

They smiled at each other wryly and continued walking on around the ruins looking at impressive floor mosaics, painted wall fresco's, courtyards and gardens, shops and advertising walls, statues and earthenware containers. It was a feast of ancient Roman life on display right before their eyes.

Next it was on to the excavated ruins of the Forum bath-house for men. They were both very impressed at how organised the various sections of the bath-house were. There was a toilet area, a changing area, separate cold, tepid and hot bath areas, and even an exercise area.

"Very organised and civilised were those Romans."

"I'm just wondering if it was for everybody's use in the town or just for the nobles and aristocrats."

"Not sure about that Aoife and it doesn't say anywhere. Not sure what Roman protocol was 2000 year ago. Did the peasants mix with the nobles when naked? Probably not? "

William told Aoife he'd ask one of the group tour guides that question if they came across one as they walked around.

It was just after 12 noon and their horse-riding van pickup was timed for 1 pm so they decided to spend another half hour looking around and then head back to the main entrance gate. The Herculaneum ruins had been great and yet another fantastic learning experience, but the day's highlight for both of them was going to be the horse-riding. It was something they were both good at, and something they both enjoyed regularly back home.

They walked back around the ruins reminding themselves what they had just seen. Second time around everything seemed even more impressive if that was possible. They both agreed that it must have been quite a beautiful and picturesque seaside town before Mount Vesuvius unleashed it's fury on the morning of the 25 August 79AD.

"I think Vesuvius is the only active volcano on the European mainland Aoife. I know there's the Mount Etna active volcano on Sicily's eastern coast, and several volcanic offshore islands north of Sicily, but this the only one on mainland Europe. And we're going to be riding on it this afternoon. Guess who is excited?"

"I'm glad we came here to Herculaneum and not Pompeii. Apparently Pompeii is much busier and bustling with tourists, and on a much bigger scale, so it's hard to see everything on a half day trip."

"I agree. Good choice," replied William.

They arrived back to the main entrance gate at Herculaneum just before 1 pm. The horse-riding operator had sent Aoife a pic of the pickup minivan and the sign to look for on the van's side so that it would be easy to spot.

"There it is over there."

They opened the sliding door and hopped in the back. The driver spoke.

"*Buon pomeriggio signore and signora. Parla Italino?* Please don't worry because I speak good English also. My name is Roberto."

"Thank you Roberto. Are you the owner or riding instructor or van driver?" asked William.

"I'm everything. Yes, I'm the owner and will be accompanying you on the horse trek together with Maria. We have a stable of twelve horses but there will only be six riders this afternoon. She will lead the front and I will be at the back. Have you ridden before?"

William looked over to Aoife, and Aoife looked back to William. How do you tell somebody that you're both pretty damn good at horse riding without it seeming a bit pretentious?

"Well, I'm from Ireland and grew up on a farm so I've ridden quite a lot, and William comes from a farm in New Zealand so he has ridden a lot also. We both have our own horses."

"*Bene, bene*, I will give you the two most experienced horses. The other riders are all absolute beginners or beginners, so I hope you won't be too bored. I'll ask you to ride up front with Maria and the rest of us will follow. That will be the easiest."

Out on the main southern coastal highway around the Bay of Naples the Saturday traffic was very busy. It was almost bumper to bumper. It took them twenty five minutes to get to the mountain turnoff, and then another fifteen minutes up the slopes of Vesuvius to arrive at the horse-riding stable.

After they arrived Aoife and William were impressed at first glance. It seemed a well organised operation, the horses all looked well cared for, each had its own individual stable box for night time and there were ample outside paddocks for the daytime. The horses were all saddled and tied up waiting for the riders. They were introduced to the other four riders for the afternoon trip. None of them had ridden before so they all seemed nervous. The two girls were giggly, and the two boys were putting on a brave face.

William and Aoife understood well how they might be feeling because first time riders often found the first ride a bit daunting. Horses are big strong animals but generally respond well if ridden kindly. This ride was going to be even more tricky because it wasn't just flat ground they'd be riding on, but included a sloped surface up a mountain side.

William's horse was a pale chestnut and Aoife's a light bay. They both seemed to be around sixteen hands tall. William legged Aoife up onto her horse and William put on foot in the stirrup and ably legged himself up onto his. Aoife admired the way he mounted his horse because it looked like he had done it one thousand times before. She was impressed. Roberto could tell straight away that they were both good riders and comfortable in the saddle. He turned and spoke to them.

"Please don't worry if we lag behind on the ride. You both stay up front with Maria and I'll look after the less experienced riders at the back. We're likely to be much slower than you."

After all the riders were on their horses, the team set off along some paved roadways out of the stabling area and then on a cobbled, tree lined street past some well tendered and what looked like very productive fruit and vegetable gardens and plots on the outskirts of the mountainside village.

"Aoife, look at those tomatoes and grapes. I've never seen tomatoes so red. And those bunches of grapes are so abundant. It must be due to the rich volcanic soils here. Wish my fruit and veg garden back home was like that."

The rhythmic 'clip clop' sound of the horse hooves on the street was music to the ears for both Aoife and William. They were rearing to go up, up and further up.

Soon the group arrived at an open area where the street ended.

"We'll be heading into a low bush and tree covered area now so please go in single file and follow the instructions of myself and Roberto. I will lead the way and Roberto will stay at the back. Mr William and Miss Aoife will go second and third and the rest of you can go in whichever order you like."

"Does anybody have any questions?" asked Roberto. There was no response. Meanwhile up front, Maria was keeping a close eye on everything.

"If anybody needs help please just shout out. Don't hold the reins too tight and short missy or too long and loose. Here, hold them like this. The horses have all done this track up Vesuvius many times before so they know the way to go."

And with the group seemingly ready, they set off in single file. The first part of the horse trek was through a gently rising bushed area. William clearly loved it and kept looking behind to make sure that Aoife was alright. He was a little bit surprised at how many low hanging branches there were across the riding track so he was concentrating hard and ducking when necessary to make sure none of them flicked back onto Aoife.

"I never thought I'd be doing this on my holiday to Naples. Are you OK? Be careful of some of these low hanging branches across the track" William said to Aoife with his trademark beaming smile.

It was infectious, because Aoife responded with a smile of happiness and pure enjoyment that was as impressive as his.

"I love this William. The sky is sunny, the air is warm, the bush smells fresh, the horses are manageable and you're here with me."

He wasn't sure that he had just heard right. But did he hear her say that she was glad he was here with her? The horse trek continued up the slopes of Mount Vesuvius. Suddenly the well-defined low grade track changed to a rough track which was of a much steeper grade. Large, dark coloured volcanic basaltic and larva flow boulders suddenly appeared on either side of the track and it narrowed a lot.

From up front, Maria shouted back to the group.

"Let the horses find their own footing. They will know the best route to follow through this narrow boulder part of the track."

At the rear, Roberto was repeating the same instructions to the less experienced riders.

Aoife was directly behind William and she could see him as being almost at one with his horse. She could see light sweat patches forming on the back of his t shirt which was accentuating his broad muscled shoulders and slim waist. There was a pronounced sweat band forming at the top of his faded blue jeans. She laughed to herself thinking that if he had been born in the good old Wild West days, he would have made one hell of a fine cowboy. William's horsemanship looked very natural and he seemed super skilled. That gave her increased confidence to follow his lead although she was also a very capable rider and clearly had all the necessary riding skills to manage ably by herself. All the time William was firing encouraging calls and comments behind to Aoife.

The group continued its upwards climb through the steeper rocky part of the trekking route and then just as quickly, the track became flatter again and the tall dense bush reverted back to low scrub and flowering bushes. And then ten minutes later they rode into a flat much more open area.

"We'll stop here for twenty minutes for a drink and rest and a look at the view," instructed Maria "so please tie your horses to the railing over there. Everybody has done really well. *Grazie*."

Aoife and William dismounted, tied their horses to the railing and walked over to the edge of the flat open area. They were now discretely alone from the rest of the group. They stood there in awe for the vista that confronted them was nothing short of *bellissimo*. It was a clear, hot, sunny day and the long distance visibility was very good. Out across the seaward facing slopes of Vesuvius and the Bay of Naples they could easily see the city of Naples and it's busy harbour. Out in the bay itself they could make out the outline of the island of Ischia in the distance. Aoife spoke first.

"I can't believe I'm here. Look, it's beautiful. The horse trek up was excellent and this is our reward."

"I can't disagree Aoife. This is truly beautiful. I mean New Zealand is beautiful also, but this is as good as."

"So is Ireland but this is a different kind of beautiful. The coastline near Galway has rugged steep almost vertical volcanic sea cliffs which are eye catching, but here it's gently sloping, highly populated and intensively farmed volcanic slopes leading down to the bright blue waters of the Mediterranean. I think it's definitely got the wow factor."

Aoife then looked directly into William's eyes and spoke.

"Surely this has to be what the Italians say is *la bella vita*. Thank you for the past few days William. I've seen and experienced and learnt more with you over the last few days than I have over the past few years. You're kind and honest and smart."

"Truly? I mean thank you for including me and responding enthusiastically to everything I've said and done the past few days. I think I'm pretty ordinary. This trip is a dream come true for me. Dreams do come true."

William was getting into an emotional state which Aoife could see from the swelling of tears in his eyes so she stepped forward, gently cupped his head from behind with one hand and directed his lips slowly towards hers. William responded with a caring masculinity that was powerful. He wrapped his arms firmly around her upper body and under the hot Italian summer sun their passionate embrace and kiss seemed to last forever.

If there was a definition of happiness could this be it? Finally, the first intimate interaction between Aoife and William finished. He took out two water bottles from his backpack and handed one to her.

"It's still ice cold."

"I wrapped them in newspaper before putting them in my backpack to insulate them from the midday sun."

"How can something so simple taste so good?"

"I think the time and the place might have something to do with it Aoife."

They smiled at each other, stood up and moved back over to the others in the group.

"What did you all think of the view from here?" Maria asked the group. Everybody agreed that it was really good if not superb. Maria continued talking.

"Well, now that we're rested it's time for the journey back downhill. It will take about forty minutes. The horses will be very keen to get back to their stable but please don't let them do anything but walk. They know the way back so they'll be leading you."

There had been so many highlights from William's first six days in Naples that he would have been hard pressed to name the best one if asked. There was Nonna Russo's Cooking Class, meeting Aoife, the National Museum of Naples, the Pignasecca Street produce market, the Chapel Sansevero and the 'Veiled Christ' sculpture, the ruins at Herculaneum, the horse trek up the slopes of Vesuvius, and now, that first kiss with Aoife. When William selected Naples at the preferred travel destination back in Hunterville several weeks ago, he had no idea it was going to be this good. It had exceeded all expectations and there was still just over a week to go in Naples.

Maria asked the group to remount their horses and the trek back down from the upper slopes of Mount Vesuvius began.

"Do you want to go in front of me on the way back down?" William asked Aoife.

"No thanks William, I'm happy to follow behind you."

The trek back down the mountain was a little bit more difficult than going up the mountain. It was funny seeing all the riders leaning right back in the saddle as they were heading down some of the steeper sections. This was necessary to avoid going head over heels and forward over the horse's necks.

Now that the ice was broken, William was starting to fantasise about what the next move should be. And more importantly, when should he make the next move. It was a long time since he had intimate and lustful feelings about a member of the opposite sex. He was wondering if Aoife would really want to take it any further. She was so beautiful and he was so ordinary.

Just then, as if en queue, the 'ghost of Ram' appeared on his right shoulder.

"Good job mate. Nice to get a kiss but you can do better than that. Come on mate you know what I mean. Ask her home when you get back."

William smiled to himself. He knew that Ram's approach was very different to his own and that it was unlikely to change.

"No mate, slowly does it is the only way I know. I don't want to mess this up."

"Sorry William, I didn't hear you. What did you say?" Aoife asked as she quickly turned around.

"Nothing important, I'm just talking to myself."

The horse trek back down the mountain and through the village streets to the horse stables was completed successfully. All participants were present and accounted for. No injuries, no misgivings and everybody seemed very happy with the trip.

"Usually at the end of each horse trek we have a glass of wine and some local cheese and crackers or bread," said Roberto "please gather around that big table over there under the shade awning and we will bring it over to you."

"Wasn't expecting that but a nice gesture for sure" said Aoife to William.

The group sat around the large wooden table near the stabling area and enjoyed their glass of red or white wine with some artisan cheeses.

Roberto stood up and addressed the group.

"I hope everybody has had a great time and if you have enjoyed please let other travellers know about our service. Thank you for coming and *ci vediamo di nuovo un giorno*, or see you again one day."

William turned to Maria because he didn't want her input to be forgotten.

"*Salute Maria and grazie, grazie.*"

Maria smiled and bowed and seemed very delighted that her efforts were acknowledged.

At 5 pm the pickup minivan arrived and Roberto indicated that the driver, who was his good friend from the village, would drop everybody back to Naples city central. The traffic would still be very busy heading in to Naples so it would take up to sixty minutes to drop everybody off at their different arrival points. With thank yous and goodbyes completed, the minivan left the riding stables after what was best described as a day of total enjoyment for both Aoife and William.

During the minivan journey back to Naples, William was thinking to himself shall I or shan't I? He decided he wouldn't ask her back to his apartment to stay the night. That seemed just too forward for this man from down on the farm. Instead he'd ask her if she'd like a gelato or drink when they got back and he would suggest that they do something very relaxing, and something that the locals do on a Sunday in Naples. That's what he would do. Decision made. He remembered that Aoife had mentioned she was desperate for a proper sleep-in on Sunday morning so he would be considerate and make sure that happened for her.

It was close to 6.15 pm when they finally arrived back to Dante Metro Station. It was Saturday night and Via Toledo was bustling with people. The cafés and restaurants all looked to be doing a roaring trade on this warm summer evening.

"Aoife, how are you feeling after today's trip? Tired I'm guessing."

"Have to admit that I'm a bit tired William but it's been excellent. Basically a ten out of ten."

"Well, before you head back to your apartment can I buy you a gelato? Seems like a good night for one. I've got something to ask you."

"Sure, a gelato will be good."

The gelato shop was enticing with so many different flavours to choose from. Aoife selected strawberry and cream and William selected lemon and honey flavoured. They sat down on a bench in the nearby piazza trying not to let their gelato's melt quicker in the warm evening sunshine than they could eat them.

"I understand you've got other things to do and don't want to be always hanging around with me. But I was just wondering if you'd like to be a local tomorrow and not a tourist? Do something the locals do on a Sunday. I promise that it's something lazy and relaxing."

"Yes, that would be great. But there's one condition. I would seriously like a sleep-in tomorrow morning. Am I allowed to have a sleep-in first?"

William laughed and replied jokingly.

"Um, um, well, let me think……..of course yes."

"What have you got in mind?"

"Thought we might go sunbathing and swimming on the rocks down by the marina and breakwater on the waterfront near Castel dell'Ovo. It's about a twenty minute walk straight down Via Toledo from here. And after that, we could do aperitivo as the sun goes down."

"William, how do you come up with these ideas? It sounds excellent. Definitely count me in. But I'm having that sleep-in first so is a noon meetup at Dante Metro Station OK?"

"Yep, sounds good and thanks."

William leaned over towards Aoife and pulled her in close to him and gave her a lingering good night kiss. It had happened once, so why shouldn't it happen again. After that they stood up, embraced lovingly and then waved goodbye to each other as they walked in opposite directions towards their respective apartments.

It was 7 pm when William unlocked his apartment door. The apartment was hot and stuffy inside. His first thought was to open the balcony doors and let in some fresh night air. The noise in the street immediately below was loud but it didn't worry him at all since he was feeling happy and both mentally and physically excited. It was a long time since he'd felt like this.

I'm going to try and have a sleep-in also he thought to himself. It was something he never ever did back home on the farm. Too much work to be done. He opened his fridge and pulled out his last remaining bottle of chilled beer. He cracked it open and took it out to the balcony with a salad sandwiched he had quickly rustled together.

He hadn't seen her for a few days, but there she was across the other side of the street leaning over the balcony rails of her apartment. His number one nonna in Naples.

He raised his beer in one hand and directed a friendly wave to her with his other hand. She blew him back a kiss and he smiled at her. They had never met each other directly face-to-face, or spoken to each other, but she was one of his most favourite persons in Naples. A smile and a wave will bridge all cultures and all ages he reminded himself. That was something his mother had always taught him.

"William what's the most powerful weapon you have in your arsenal of personality traits?" she would say. When William responded that he didn't know, she fired back "Your smile William, your smile. Use it generously and the rewards will be instant."

He would never forget that piece of advice from his mother and ninety nine times out of a hundred it always worked.

Saturday the 6th July in Naples had been a day he would never forget. He was getting tired and he was hot and sweaty from the long day spent out in the intense summer sun. It was time for a shower, then an email to his parents and Ram, then a quick search on the internet and to bed. As he sat drinking his beer he was thinking of Aoife. He was having manly and lustful thoughts and it was showing. Discretely he went inside and showered dealing with the matter in hand. After that he was feeling much more relaxed. He wrote a mail to his parents and Ram telling them that he was having a fantastic time and that he was in good health and spirits. He did not mention Aoife. Not because he didn't want to, but because he knew there'd be a lot of probing questions fired back at him if he did, and he wasn't ready for that.

He retired to bed at around 10 pm after having sat out on the balcony for several hours watching 'Saturday night Naples' pass by in the street below. It had been enticing sitting out on the balcony and he was not the slightest bit bored because everybody seemed to be having such a good time. Italians know how to embrace the good life he thought to himself. He secretly wished he was a bit more like that. It didn't take him long to fall off to sleep.

Over in her apartment, Aoife was also relaxing out on her small balcony and had just completed individual emails to Kieran, her parents and brother. Unlike William, who hadn't mentioned Aoife yet to the folks back home, she mentioned to both her parents and brother that she had meet a very nice man from New Zealand called William. She wrote that they had done a few things together including horse-riding on the slopes of Mount Vesuvius earlier in the day. She was sure they'd all like him instantly and she described him as being kind and considerate, interesting and intelligent, humble and funny. She also mentioned that he had a farming background. Something that was sure to be a plus in the eyes of her conservative parents and brother. It didn't take Aoife long to receive a reply from back home in Ballinrobe. Her parents and brother all said that he sounded really nice but to please be very careful. They also mentioned that she sounded very happy and optimistic.

That was something they hadn't heard for a long time.

Aoife was also feeling the effects of being out in the blazing hot sun most of the day so decided to wash her hair. It was something that required a bit of effort due to its voluminous nature. She showered, washed her hair, went out on the balcony to let in dry in the warm night air, sipped a sparkling water, read her emails noting that no word had been received from Kieran, tidied the apartment, did some washing and retired to bed.

She was physically exhausted after the full day's exertions but sleep was not instant. She lay in bed for thirty minutes thinking about William and how kind he was to her and how manly and competent he had been on the horse trek. How sensitive he had been in not pressuring her to do something she wasn't ready for after the day's activities. She thought long and hard, but there was nothing about William that she didn't like. He didn't look like a Hollywood movie star and Kieran was a far more handsome man, but William's star shone brightly. She fell off to sleep feeling safe and secure and wondering what Sunday would bring.

Lazy Sunday Around the Waterfront

William tried to have a Sunday sleep-in but woke at 7 am. He managed to stay in bed until 8 am. That was the absolute limit for him. Considering he usually got up between 5 am and 6 am when back home on the farm, he had achieved a mini sleep-in of sorts.

Aoife's sleep-in was much more successful and she didn't wake up until 10 am. It was the best sleep she had managed since arriving in Naples. She hopped out of bed, went over and made a coffee and then went back to bed for another hour of snoozing until finally getting up at 11 am. It was just enough time to get organised for the day ahead with William. She laid out her days accessories on the kitchen table. Sunscreen, sunglasses, beach towel, and mobile phone were placed on the table. The only thing she didn't have was a swimwear specific bathing costume. It didn't really matter because whatever she wore, it was going to look great. However, that's not how it was spinning over in her mind. She wanted to look nice for William but didn't want to attract too much unwanted attention from the locals.

She thought it best to err on the side of caution so from the limited range of clothes she had brought with her, she picked out a pair of denim shorts and a pastel pink t shirt and placed them with the other items on the table. She had heard that the locals were not shy or inhibited about what they wore to the beach or seaside, but she needed to see and assess the situation for herself before deciding what was appropriate. She wondered if William would mind if they stopped for her to buy a swim costume while walking down Via Toledo to Castel dell'Ovo and the waterfront. She would ask him.

Aoife went out onto her balcony to check what the weather was doing. It was doing exactly the same as every day since she had arrived in Naples a week ago. It was clear and sunny and warm by late morning, and likely to get much, much hotter in the afternoon. They would be at the water's edge after lunch so maybe there would be a sea breeze to make things a little bit more comfortable she thought. She was both happy and excited at the prospect of seeing William again.

William had got a bit of a routine going by now and was at Dante Metro Station ten minutes before the agreed midday meeting time. Aoife turned up at 12 noon exactly. Upon meeting they hugged and kissed, and hugged and kissed again for good measure. Both seemed very comfortable about doing it even in public. Their burgeoning relationship had come a long way over the past three days.

"How was your sleep-in Aoife?"

"Best I've had in a long time. I'm feeling relaxed and rested. I feel so good. What about you?"

"I'm not really a sleep-in type of a guy but I still managed to stay in bed until 8 am. That's late for me. I'm feeling good also."

"I'm really looking forward to this afternoon. I just want to blob out and get some sun rays on the body and maybe go for a swim if it's not too cold."

"That works for me. I like swimming in the ocean but where I live the sea is a couple of hours drive away and that beach is not highly rated because of the black sand and strong rips. I do swim in the local Rangitikei River occasionally but it's really cold even in the summertime."

"Same, it's too cold to swim at the beaches in and around Galway anytime of the year."

"It should be a lot better here though. I will if you will."

"Not promising, but I'll try and be brave."

They laughed at each other's expectations of the day ahead and started walking slowly down Via Toledo towards the waterfront. They chatted and looked into the occasional shop window as they made their way down the main street. Aoife had mentioned to William that she didn't bring a swim costume with her but William suggested to just improvise since it didn't seem to matter here in Italy. He had read that most Italian men and women were not shy at the beach. They simply embraced *la bella vita* and the number one priority was the sun's rays on the body and the warm salty Mediterranean water, not how one looked.

After fifteen minutes they passed Toledo Metro Station which they recognised from a few days earlier since it had been their meeting place for Nonna Russo's Cooking Class. They continued walking past impressive 18th and 19th century buildings until they came to the Piazza del Plebiscito which was a large open square designated for foot traffic only. As they walked by William spoke to Aoife.

"Piazza del Plebiscito is home to the neo-classical Royal Palace which was built in the early to mid-1800 period and is recognised for its concave shaped facade, entrance dome, equestrian statues, and Roman support pillars. Impressive square and palace or not?" asked William.

"Impressive."

"And here's one more interesting fact. It's made of volcanic rocks from Mount Vesuvius. We've been there and done that."

They smiled warmly to each other. Where does he get all this information from Aoife wondered to herself? She was impressed with his general knowledge about all sorts of things.

They continued on a few more tens of metres and passed the Molosiglio Gardens on their left before reaching the waterfront.

"If we turn right here and walk along Via Nazario Sauro boardwalk, we should come to the marina and yacht club, and then a little bit further on, Castel dell'Ovo. I think it's in this general area that people do a lot of sunbathing on the barrier protection rocks, and swimming in the sea to cool off."

"It's such a beautiful day."

They arrived to the area they were looking for and scanned around to find a part of the boulder bank that wasn't so crowded. On first look they could see a lot of people who were young and old, male and female, fit and not so fit, alone and together, all sitting and lying on the large boulders in various stages of undress blissfully soaking up the afternoon sun.

"There's an area over there. Let's get it before somebody else does."

Aoife followed William over the rocks and they quickly staked their spot by spreading their larger sized beach towels over their preferred section of the boulder bank.

"It looks so relaxing. You're quite fair skinned Aoife so you had better use a lot of sunscreen lotion. Actually I had better also. Do you want to use this one I brought from New Zealand with me? It's eco-friendly. No harmful chemicals to the marine environment. It's a bit harder to spread on but a very effective sunblock."

"Thanks William. Mine is just the usual supermarket bought sunscreen. Happy to use yours if that's OK."

Aoife started to spread the sunscreen lotion on her arms and legs and was not concentrating on William as he stripped down to his board shorts. When she looked up and over to him she was breathless for there, standing in front of her, was one fine specimen of a man. It was obvious that all the physical work down on the farm, and his training for rugby, had kept him in peak physical condition. She tried not to stare at his slim athletic and perfectly proportioned muscled body and broad shoulders, but it was difficult to resist the temptation to take a peek. Those marble nude male statues I saw at the Naples National Museum were impressive she said to herself, but what's standing in front of me right here is the physical equal of, or surpasses, those ancient gods and warriors.

She stood up and wrapped a towel around herself while she changed from jeans to her casual shorts. And then she draped a towel around her shoulders while changing from long sleeved top to the pink t shirt she had packed in her bag.

William turned around and now it was his turn to ogle at the fair skinned Irish lady standing before him. She was simply beautiful. She could probably wear a potato sack and still look stunning he thought to himself. William was starting to feel a bit insecure. He wondered what she was doing here with him. He was losing any self-confidence he had built up over the past couple of days.

"I'm pretty fair skinned also Aoife so can you please rub some sunscreen on my back. But it's OK if you'd rather not."

She willingly completed William's request.

"I can't believe how suntanned most people are. Not just lightly tanned but deeply tanned," said William.

"Well, I did read that Italians love the sun and the beach, so it looks like that's true."

"Not only that, do you notice how uninhibited most people seem. Even some of the elderly men are wearing speedos and the elderly women are wearing bikinis. Bit and pieces squeezing out here and there and everywhere but nobody seems to care. It's a really healthy and carefree attitude to life. They're here to enjoy the sun and sea not to judge one another. That's impressive."

"I agree. It's nothing like back home in Ireland. Most people are much more self-conscious about their bodies."

Not that Aoife or William had anything to worry about for they were both fine physical specimens. Now that they were both protected with sunscreen they laid down prostrate on their towels facing each other and gently holding hands.

The air was warm and had a light salty smell to it. The background noise was mostly seagulls squawking and the quiet chatter and laughter of nearby sun worshippers.

"This is nice," said William as he smiled at Aoife.

"Just what we needed after the past few days of full-on site seeing. Time off for good behaviour."

It was William and Aoife's attempt to enjoy *la bella vita* and they were both doing a good job of it.

William glanced at his phone a few times just to make sure that their one hour maximum time limit of lying in the direct sun was not exceeded. It had been a while since their bodies were exposed to full summer sun and the last thing either of them wanted was to get sunburnt.

"Are you keen to go for a swim in the sea? It looks inviting. Quite a few are doing it."

"Definitely," replied Aoife "I wonder what temperature the water is?"

"It's 25.5 degrees C today. I checked it online before leaving the apartment this morning."

"Let's do it."

Aoife and William climbed over a few boulders to the water's edge and slowly lowered their bodies into the crystal clear Mediterranean water.

"It's so nice. If it was two or three degrees warmer would be better, but I'm not complaining" said Aoife as she went in first.

Aoife could swim enough to tread water and do breaststroke over short distances in the water, but was primarily what you'd call a weekend swimmer. William on the other hand was like a duck in the water disappearing out of sight only to come up from the depths several metres away.

"It's been awhile since I swam in the sea but this is reminding me why I like it so much. Salt water is so much better than chlorinated swimming pools. This is Sunday afternoon at its best. Thanks for saying yes to coming Aoife."

"No, I should be thanking you. Where did you learn to swim like that?"

"When I went to uni I got quite involved with swimming and was in the uni water polo team for a few years. We trained hard out a lot, so it kind of developed then. As a kid I was very poor swimmer because there are no swimming pools in Hunterville township or anywhere nearby."

Again William disappeared under the water and although it was crystal clear and underwater visibility was good, Aoife couldn't make out where he had disappeared to. She spun around in the water trying to find some tell-tale bubbles. Ten seconds later he came up from the depths such that his face was directly opposite hers. He supported her under the arms, drew her close and planted a kiss on her lips. She responded enthusiastically and wanted more, much more, but suddenly realised that people on the boulder bank nearby were staring directly at them and smiling. Not wanting to be the cause of any moral outrage from the locals, she whispered to William that might be a good idea to head back to the rocks and dry off. So that's what they did.

As William exited the water, Aoife was trying not to stare but couldn't help notice that his wet board shorts were clinging tightly back and front to his chiselled body. Beads of water were trickling down off his broad shoulders onto his chest and back. They were glistening like small diamonds in the sunlight. Aoife was feeling lustful.

Back on the rocks and having dried off, they enjoyed lounging in the warm mid-afternoon sun. Ever thoughtful, William pulled out two bottles of water from his backpack and as was the case on the horse-riding trek he had wrapped them in newspaper to insulate them so that they were still ice cold to the touch.

"An ice cold water, a day at the seaside, the warm sun's rays, a dip in the water and extra special company. We're the lucky ones Aoife. For sure we're the privileged ones. You've made my stay in Naples exponentially better than if I had just been doing everything alone. Thank you."

"It's the same for me William."

They bent towards each other and cemented their appreciation with a long lingering kiss and then Aoife spoke.

"It's still three hours before aperitivo time what shall we do now? I don't want to stay out on the full sun all afternoon in case I get burnt."

"Actually, I've prearranged something for us to do for the next couple of hours so let's get dressed and head over there to the marina. Somebody is waiting for us."

Ten minutes later they had arrived to the nearby marina. We're looking for a small yacht called "Rosa" and it's in Row E. It didn't take them long to find the boat they were looking for and they were welcomed aboard by an elderly man who was olive skinned, very charming and spoke good English.

"Welcome aboard Aoife and William. I'm Captain Marino. This is my boat. It's named after my dear departed wife. This afternoon and for the next two hours this boat is all yours. I will take you out to the centre part of the Bay of Naples so we can look back on the magnificence of Napoli to our left, and the majesty of Mount Vesuvius around to our right."

"William, you did this for me?"

"Yep, I did. I wanted to do something special so you'd never forget your time in Naples."

Aoife knew right at that moment, that this man was something very special and she wanted him to be in her life on a permanent basis. She was not sure how it had happened so quickly, but she was falling in love with this man from New Zealand.

"Before we leave can you please put these life jackets on," said Captain Marino "it's a very safe day to be out in the bay because it's very calm and sunny with only a gentle sea breeze but just in case. Better to be safe."

At the Captain's instructions, Aoife and William donned their life jackets. Aoife opened her backpack and took out the designer sunglasses and Italian head scarf she had treated herself to a few days earlier. She wrapped the scarf over her head and then around her neck and put the sunglasses on. William and Captain Marino instantly looked at each other.

When he knew Aoife was out of earshot range, Captain Marino leaned over to William and whispered to him.

"You are one lucky man Mr William to have such a beautiful wife. I hope you will both be blessed with many children."

William didn't have the heart to tell the captain that he had only meet Aoife a week ago, that they weren't husband and wife, and that they hadn't even shared a bed together. He was too embarrassed to reveal the truth. For sure it was something he now wanted, but it seemed out of his reach. He considered himself just an ordinary man. Little did he know that Aoife considered him to be an extraordinary man.

Captain Marino explained that sometimes they set the sails and sailed out into the bay, but because it was calm today it would be easier to use the yacht's backup engine. After around thirty minutes of motoring they had arrived into the central part of the Bay of Naples. The captain cut the engine and set the anchor. Aoife and William moved to the stern of "Rosa" and gazed out at the beautiful vista in front of them. It was picture perfect.

They told the captain that they had done a horse trek up the slopes of Vesuvius the previous day and looked down onto the bay admiring it's beauty. And now today, they were looking the other way around from the centre of the

Bay of Naples up to Mount Vesuvius in the distance. How many people get to do that they wondered. Few probably did and more should.

"Whoever those people are that say Naples wasn't worth visiting seriously need to contact me," said William "because I feel that everything is *bella e interessante*."

"Thank you, thank you" replied the captain "I am making you honorary Neapolitans for your very kind words."

It was now 4.30 pm and the captain said they'd be heading back inshore soon but first he wanted to take some pics of them, for them, from the bow of the boat looking towards the city. That was completed and they headed back to the marina by Castel dell'Ovo arriving there exactly at 5 pm.

They told the captain that his boat trip had helped make it one of the most memorable days for them so far in Naples. He was so appreciative of their kind words that he embraced and hugged them both enthusiastically before they departed.

"It's aperitivo time Aoife. Haven't done it yet but I'm dying to. I have read a lot about it. They say that it's a very Italian thing to do late afternoon or early evening."

"I'm looking forward to it also. Any idea where we should try?"

"Well, as we were walking down Via Toledo just before Piazza del Plebiscito, did you notice on the right hand side there were several very promising looking cafes and bars. We could choose one, sit outside under the shade of the awnings, have aperitivo and watch the Napoli world go by as the sun goes down."

"Sounds good, and William."

"Yes."

"I'm very, very happy right now."

"So am I."

They held hands and walked back up towards Via Toledo. After one hundred meters William turned to Aoife.

"Can you see those old stone buildings way up on the high hill behind that neo-classical apartment building directly in front of us? The ones surrounded by what looks like lush green gardens and bush."

"Yes."

"That's the castle and museum at Certosa di San Martino. The quickest way to get up there is by the funicular railway. I want us to go there. Tell you all about it over aperitivo."

With that, they continued walking to the area of cafés and bars a short distance past Piazza del Plebiscito on Via Toledo. They walked up past the cafés and bars, and then back past them again before they selected the one that appealed to them the most.

"How about this bar come restaurant on the corner? It's a bit smaller than some of the others but the staff look very friendly and it's got a large outdoor shaded seating area."

"Works for me Aoife."

After arriving they asked for, and were directed to, a two person table to the side but one which had a good view of Via Toledo.

"I've wanted to do aperitivo since I arrived in Naples but have been a bit shy about doing it on my own. I think it usually happens between 6 pm and 8 pm so our timing is just about right. We're a little bit early but I'm sure they won't mind."

William agreed. This seemed like it was the perfect way to finish what had been a glorious afternoon down at the waterfront.

"I'm not sure how you order it Aoife, but I think Aperol Spritz is the most common and favoured aperitivo drink and then you just ask to have it with finger food for two people."

"What is Aperol Spritz again? Is it that brightly coloured orange cocktail?" asked Aoife.

"Yes, it's a cocktail made with equal parts of Aperol Campari, Prosecco white wine and soda water with a slice of orange for good measure. I've never tried one, but they say it's a bit bitter."

"It sounds good. Let's do it."

"Shall I order in Italian?" asked William.

"I'll be very impressed if you do."

"Just joking. That might be a step too far. I'm feeling very relaxed and it's too much effort. I'm sure they have lots of tourists coming in here so they're bound to understand English."

They could see a waiter coming over towards them. It was 6 pm.

"Buona sera signore e signora. Come stai? Mi chiamo Lorenzo. Apreitivo per due persone?"

"*Stiamo bene, grazie. Si, due Campari Spritz aperitivo,*" replied William.

William couldn't help himself replying in Italian. It just seemed the right thing to do. Aoife smiled at him and admired his effort.

"*Di dove sei?*" asked the waiter.

Not wanting to be linguistically tested too much, he reverted to English. "Aoife is from Ireland and I'm from New Zealand."

"*Si*, New Zealand is the haka and kiwi right?" replied the waiter.

"Yes, you have heard of New Zealand?"

"*Si*, beautiful country. I have seen it on television."

And with that, the waiter excused himself and went off to place their order. Suddenly the outdoor seating area was filling up fast. They had timed their arrival and the placement of their order to perfection.

"Remember I mentioned the castle and museum at Certosa di San Martino on the way here, well I've heard on the grapevine that the views from up there over the city of Naples across the waterfront to Mount Vesuvius in the distance are spectacular."

"Yes, I remember" replied Aoife.

"I'd like to do that tomorrow sometime. Please come with me but only if you haven't planned something else to do."

"Of course I'll come with you."

"Let's go up and back on the funicular railway, look around the castle and museum and see if this vista they keep talking about from up at the castle is as good as they say it is."

"It probably is, so definitely worth the effort to do it. I'm keen," confirmed Aoife.

"Oh, and there's one more thing Aoife. I've got a wireless portable Bluetooth speaker with me. I want to play a special song just for you from my iPod song collection. Would you mind?"

"That's a nice and unexpected thing to want to do, but I'll only listen to your song, if you'll listen to one I select for you. Deal?"

"Deal."

What a perfect day, William thought to himself. A bit of a sleep-in, a lazy afternoon in the sun and a dip in the sea down at the waterfront with Aoife, and now aperitivo together.

The outside seating area at the bar was full now and it had just gone 6.15 pm. The waiter arrived back to their table with two Aperol Spritz cocktails and an assortment of finger food. The range of food was more than expected. It comprised bowls of salted peanuts, green olives and micro cheese pastries, and two generous plates of small, bit sized, assorted salad and meat filled bread rolls and grainy croissants.

"Aperitivo is meant to be a pre-meal drink and nibble, but crikey, I don't think I could eat anything more for dinner if we finish what's in front of us. Even if I do have a farmer's appetite."

"I'm the same William. I wasn't expecting this much finger food. No wonder it's such a huge cultural tradition in Italy."

"*Aoife, cin cin alla salute.*"

"What does that mean?"

"Cheers and good health."

Aoife took a sip of her Aperol Spritz, as did William.

"Um, it's quite bitter. I'm not sure if I like it or not."

She took another sip.

"I'm not used to that taste but it kind of grows on you. It's bitter but it seems really thirst-quenching."

William agreed that the bitter taste took a bit of getting used to, but he was soon getting stuck in to both the spritz and the food, so he was definitely enjoying it.

William and Aoife were both very relaxed and jovial in each other's company and the early part of the evening slid by quickly. Their first face-to-face meeting at Nonna Russo's Cooking Class a few days ago, now seemed like an eternity ago. They were very comfortable in each other's presence, respectful of each other, and so far, they hadn't disagreed about anything. They had a lot in common. They enjoyed doing the same things and were both kind and considerate.

What next, William pondered to himself as the evening was drawing to a close. He looked around and wondered if they were sitting on their drink and food too long but everybody else seemed to be doing the same so he didn't feel so guilty about it. It was almost 8 pm when William called for the bill. He was very pleasantly surprised when he viewed it.

"I can't believe how reasonable the cost of aperitivo is. All that for 16 euro's? I wonder if we struck lucky, or they're all equally as good. We must try the same but somewhere else next week. Just for a comparison. I'd better leave the waiter a good tip."

After dealing with the bill, Aoife and William exited the bar and started a slow stroll back up Via Toledo towards Dante Metro Station. It was Sunday evening and they were surprised how many families with young children and babies were still out and walking around. Maybe they were on their way home after family gatherings, or church services, or the movies or a show, or something similar. It had been a magical day and William didn't want it to end.

When they arrived back to Dante Metro Station he didn't want to say goodbye and head back to his apartment alone but he was self-conscious, nervous and insecure about how Aoife really thought about him. Was he just somebody nice to hang out with on holiday or was he somebody she really, really wanted to get close and personal with on all levels.

On the other hand Aoife was sure what she wanted. She was hoping he'd ask her back to his apartment to fulfil her fantasies and desires which had surfaced down at the waterfront while sunbathing and swimming together. She liked everything about him. She felt that he had physical, mental and spiritual equilibrium. All his personality traits were balanced to perfection. Not only was he smart and intelligent, but he was kind and considerate, a man who was comfortable in the country or in the city even if he did prefer the country lifestyle. He was polite and culturally aware, and that beaming smile of his was addictive. If he smiled then it was hard not to do the same.

William asked himself, should I or shouldn't I? His palms and brow were perspiring heavily and it was not because of the warm humid night air.

"Are you OK William?"

"It must be all that sun and sea and the spritz. I'm feeling a bit light headed."

Both he and she knew that it's wasn't really any of those things causing his melancholy.

He couldn't, he wouldn't and he didn't. Tonight was not the night. He felt the time was not quite right. 'Man up' he told himself but it still didn't sway him to ask Aoife back to his apartment to stay the night and take their burgeoning relationship to the next level.

Why is this sort of thing so easy for Ram but so difficult for me he wondered to himself.

"Are you sure you're OK?" asked Aoife.

With tears flowing down his cheeks William replied.

"I'm sorry. Yep, I'm good Aoife. I just want to thank you for best day ever. Thank you for making me happy. Thank you for making my stay in Naples over the past few days very special and thank you for making me feel wanted and appreciated."

At this moment, Aoife felt as close to him as she had been the whole week. She just wanted to hug him gently and hold him until she was sure that William was OK. She did and was not going to let him go until she was sure his spirits had been lifted. If tonight was not the night they'd lie together then sobeit. She was prepared to wait.

"When you're ready, I'm going to go back to my apartment and get that song ready for tomorrow and send an email to my parents. Do you mind if I send them that pic of us that Captain Mario took earlier today? Remember, the one of us standing on the stern of his yacht looking towards Naples. Can you forward it to me? They're interested to know who you are. This farmer man from New Zealand."

"No I don't mind and yes I'll send it to your email address."

With his spirits lifted by her support, William reluctantly released himself from Aoife's embrace and kissed her goodnight. He was embarrassed by his little meltdown. But he need not have worried because Aoife already knew he was a masculine man and found his manly vulnerability enduring.

"What time shall we meet up in the morning?" she asked him "Is 10 am at Dante Metro Station alright? Do you mind if I choose a café this time? I've got one in mind. We can have morning coffee and then take the funicular railway up to the museum and castle."

"Sounds good. See you then."

As had happened over the past four days they waved goodbye to each other and departed for their respective apartments.

Aoife got back to her apartment at 8.30 pm. She fired up her tablet computer, went out onto the balcony and started writing an email to her parents describing what she had done earlier in the day and how much she was enjoying exploring and experiencing Naples with William. She attached the pic of them both standing on the back of Captain Mario's yacht so they could see what he looked like. She explained that he was a 4th generation New Zealander and that his forbearers had migrated to New Zealand from northernmost Scotland in the mid-1800s. She closed her computer hoping that her email would be well received.

While she waited for a response from her parents she showered, washed her hair just in case there were any unknown nasties from her waterfront swim earlier in the day, washed a pile of clothes that had been accumulating through the week, and tidied up the apartment ready for the start of a new week.

Although she usually went to church most Sundays she hadn't this particular Sunday. Being in Italy on holiday was no excuse and Aoife wished she had asked William to accompany her to a church earlier in the day for a morning service. She started to feel remorseful about it and decided that she'd improvise and do her own personal service in the apartment. It wasn't too late. After dressing respectfully, Aoife turned off the apartment lights, lit two of the candles she had in her bag and commenced praying. She thanked God for her continuing good health and happiness, for bringing William into her life in a time of real need and confusion, and for looking after all the people she loved. She asked for guidance in everything she did, and a sign that William would be a good and honourable lifetime partner for her.

"Please send me a sign. Amen" she whispered to end her service.

Her parents responded back to her email within the hour and said they trusted her judgement even if it hadn't been fool-proof over the past twelve months. Pray for guidance they suggested.

Unbeknownst to them, she had just completed that several minutes earlier in the privacy of her apartment. They said that William looked like a decent hard working man from the pic she had sent them, and hoped that they could meet him one day in the future. They reminded her that New Zealand was a long, long way away from Galway and that long distance relationships rarely worked.

William got back to his apartment feeling positive and happy despite the moment of insecurity he had earlier suffered after leaving aperitivo. It had been a day he would never forget. He had previously wondered if days like that could ever happen to him, or if he was just destined to live alone on the family farm for the rest of his mortal life. He sat down and was ready for a good man-to-man talk with himself. He could sense the 'ghost of Ram' trying to climb back onto his right shoulder to give him and talking to, but brushed him off instinctively before he could get there. There was only one person who could deal with this current situation and that was him. He took a cold beer out onto the balcony. No need to hurry to bed tonight since I'm not meeting Aoife until 10 am tomorrow he thought to himself. He fired off emails to his parents, Ram and the O'Connors in quick succession. He desperately wanted to tell Ram about Aoife and how joyous he was feeling, and to send him the pic of them on the stern of Captain Mario's yacht, but just in case it all fizzled he decided not to. He didn't want any grubby mutterings circulating around the rugby dressing room back home in Hunterville but he was confident that Ram wouldn't say anything to other people anyway. For now he'd just sit on it.

It was late on Sunday evening and the street down below William's apartment was a lot quieter than the other six nights of the week. Although Italians have an insatiable passion for life and all its ups and downs, even they need to have a day off once a week he laughed to himself. He could see that most of the bars and restaurants in the street immediately below and along from his balcony were closed, although a Turkish takeaway place across the other side of the street was doing a steady trade in their absence. William decided to be more spontaneous going forth and not to be too clinical or hesitant. If he wanted to ask Aoife back to his apartment then he should just do it. If she wasn't keen she would simply say no thanks.

He retired to bed at peace and looking forward to tomorrow's trip up to Certosa di San Martino with Aoife. Every day he had spent with Aoife had been wonderful but he sensed that tomorrow he had the opportunity to reach for the stars. Sleep was almost instant.

Funicular Railway to San Martino Castle

Monday the 8th July was a typical summer's day in Naples. It was sunny and clear and already in the high 20s by mid-morning. Aoife arrived to Dante Metro Station at the planned meeting time of 10 am and could not see any sign of William. She thought that was very unusual given that he had arrived ten minutes before her every other day they had met there. The time had progressed to 10.15 am and still there was no sign of William. Now she was beginning to get very worried. Nervously she checked her mobile phone to see if there was any text or voice message from him. Yes there was. She opened it and read the text message.

Ram has been in car accident. In hospital. Just spoken to him. Be there 10.15–10.20 am latest. Apologies. William xx

Then she heard William calling out her name. It was 10.20 am. He arrived, hugged Aoife and apologised profusely. She told William that since Ram was his best friend back in Hunterville she would expect nothing less than what he had done. It wasn't a problem at all. That's what best friends do. She was just relieved that although Ram had been hospitalised for twenty four to forty eight hours for observation, he was probably going to be alright.

"Are you ready for that coffee now? You can tell me all about it over coffee."

"Yes. Where are we going?"

"Follow me. It's in the Mercato Pignasecca area. It's at the faraway end of the fresh market street. I came across it last Tuesday when I was wandering around getting some supplies. It's really a bakery come café and you told me that you've got a bit of a sweet tooth. So it's my treat. No ifs and buts William. It's my treat OK?"

"Ok thanks. And the Piazza Montesanto and Montesanto Railway Station should be about another 100 metres or so further on after the coffee stop. That's where we will catch the funicular railway up Vomero Hill to Morghen Station.

From Morghen Station it's a five minute walk on to the 17th century Castle and Museum of San Martino. This is perfect."

It was only a short walk to the café Aoife had selected and upon entering, William's eyes lit up like a child in a toy store as he viewed all the pastries, biscuits and cakes on display.

"Everything looks *delizioso*. I might just have one of everything," William said "joking, you just select a couple for me and a large cappuccino to go with them."

"Have I found your Achilles' heel William?"

"Guilty" he replied with a big grin on his face.

Aoife placed their order and the lady behind the counter told her to sit down at an inside shop table and she would bring their order over to them.

While they waited for their coffees, William told Aoife more about Ram's car accident. He explained that his car had slid into a deep ditch along the side of a very icy rural road. It had happened as he was going to William's farm to check with Mr and Mrs O'Connor that everything was progressing well and that they weren't having any problems. He was very badly bruised and they were not sure if there were any broken bones so he had been admitted to Palmerston North Hospital overnight for further examination and observation.

"It sounds like he will be OK but that it was a close call. It's scary when you're so far away and can't do anything to help."

Aoife agreed but was happy to hear that Ram would probably be alright. The lady arrived with their order. Together with his coffee, William was presented with a white ceramic plate upon which sat a sour cherry custard tartlet and a layered cream and pistachio flaky pastry slice. Aoife was a bit more restrained and had ordered a strawberry custard tartlet for herself.

"I've got such a sweet tooth Aoife. I could easily do this every day. I'm serious."

Aoife laughed. They sat chatting as they enjoyed their sweet treats with morning coffee. The bakery was very busy considering it wasn't even lunchtime yet.

"All finished? Shall we head off now?"

"Thanks Aoife that was a great start to the morning."

Since William seemed to know exactly where they were headed, he led the way. A couple of minutes later they were at Piazza Montesanto and the Funicular Railway Station.

"This particular funicular line has been operating since 1891. Morghen Station where we'll get off is only five minutes away but taking the funicular is much cheaper than taking a taxi and much quicker than taking a bus. Hang on a minute and I'll get a couple of return tickets."

William returned with tickets in hand.

"Let's head upstairs to the inclined boarding platform and steps."

It was all new to Aoife so she just followed William's lead. The railway car arrived and they hopped on the closest carriage to where they were standing. It was late morning and outside of the busy peak rush hour period so there were few people on board. They sat down ready for the short journey up Vomero Hill. Standing immediately in front of them was a middle aged Neapolitan man with an accordion.

The funicular railway started on its trip uphill and a few seconds later the man starting playing his accordion. For all they knew he might have been a professional such was the musical expertise he displayed. It was an unexpected bonus to have live music playing right in front of them on their short trip up the hill. William bent towards Aoife and whispered.

"Times are hard for some people in Naples so people have to be inventive. Not sure if it's allowed but who cares. It's kind of nice to hear music played so well. I'm very impressed. He's obviously trying to make a bit of money so I'll gladly give him a couple of euros for his effort."

After the music stopped Aoife responded back to William.

"Same as a few days ago when I was walking along Via Toledo. There was young woman there doing sand sculptures on a large 1.5 m by 2.5 m red canvas mat. She had just completed a life sized sculpture of a mother dog resting with two playful puppies jumping on and around her. It was really good. I'm guessing that she was just trying to make some money to pay the bills. It was definitely worth a donation and she seemed so grateful. I actually felt a bit guilty."

"Why?" asked William.

"Well, here I am on holiday pretty much paying for and doing whatever I want to do, and yet there are many people here in what is their city desperately struggling to survive from day to day. They just want dignity and to be able to care for family and loved ones."

"I know what you mean. Global inequality. It's not easy. My life on the farm is a bit solitary and sheltered so I appreciate being exposed to the real world."

A few minutes after leaving Montesanto Station they had arrived at Morghen Station and hopped off the funicular railway, walked out of the station arrival hall and onto the street footpath outside.

"Um, I'm not sure which way to go now. Hang on Aoife and I'll just check on my map app. It's showing the entrance to the San Marino Castle complex is only a ten minute walk away from here. Let's go."

They arrived to the public entrance of Castel e Museo di San Martino without any difficulty, purchased their entrance tickets, headed in and started walking around the corridors and display halls. There was a lot to see and everything was a visual feast as expected. The museum was full of wonderment including magnificent 17th century horse drawn carriages still in their original state, an ornately presented ceremonial boat, ceiling frescos in a gilded chapel, inlaid marble floors, a hall containing elaborate carved wooden and papier mâché nativity scenes some of which dated back to the 1500s. There were a lot of things to see that were very different to what they had enjoyed the week before at the Naples National Museum and the Chapel of Sansevero.

William had done a bit of online research using google maps and satellite images first thing in the morning and knew exactly where in the complex he wanted to take Aoife for the best views of Naples and hopefully a chance to play his special song for her. He couldn't play a musical instrument and his singing voice was terrible so he'd have to rely on somebody else to do it for him. But the sentiments in the song he had chosen for Aoife were how he personally felt.

William slowly made his way with Aoife over to the south easternmost corner of the complex. This was where he was expecting the best views out over the city of Naples. He was hopeful that there would be few or no people milling around since he needed to make sure the scene was set exactly how he wanted it before he played the song for Aoife.

Eventually he found what he was looking for. An area of partially covered and elevated walkways and medium sized alcoves and observation areas, adjacent to the castle walls on the south easternmost corner of the castle complex.

They stood leaning against the stone balustrades and admired the beautiful vistas of suburban Naples. They scanned the hilly suburbs of Chiaia and Posillipo to the southeast, the more industrial suburb of Santa Lucia to the east, and the busy working inner harbour just beyond that. Light coloured buildings with their ubiquitous terracotta coloured roofs, dominated the land view in nearly all directions.

"Aoife, look directly down in front of us just beyond the base of the castle walls. How beautiful is that?"

"It looks so nice. It's so green and lush. It's like an oasis in a suburban jungle" replied Aoife.

"I'm not sure if it's part of the castle complex grounds, or just privately owned. But I'm very impressed. It's probably privately owned."

As they looked down on the slopes of Vomero Hill directly in front of them, there was a hillside of green terraced gardens which comprised olive and citrus trees, a few scattered stone fruit trees, small plots of grape vines and scattered vegetable plots. Everything was well maintained and appeared very organised. It was a visually pleasing green buffer 'zone' between the densely developed area of suburban homes and the castle complex.

William held Aoife's hand and guided her to the end of walkway. Here there was a low walled, four metre high stone archway. It was at the end of a covered high ceiling area measuring five metres by ten metres. The shade of the covered area provided a welcome break from the hot glaring sun. They gazed directly out in front of them through the archway where the outline of Mount Vesuvius was presented as if it was the focal point in a picture frame. Apart from a small cluster of fluffy white clouds floating above the peak of the mountain, the sky was blue and cloudless.

Aoife was the first to speak.

"It's hard to believe that we were horse-riding on the slopes of that mountain only two days ago. Every day here in Naples seems better than the one before. Sometimes I have to pinch myself just to make sure it's not just a dream."

"I know what you mean," said William "it's like I'm living a double life. How is it all going to end?"

William looked around and they seemed to be the only ones in the area at that time. He quickly went over to the arched doorway leading inside and couldn't see anybody looking around the museum exhibits. It was 'now or never' he thought to himself.

"Did you remember to bring your song?"

"Of course, you didn't think I'd forget did you?"

"No I didn't."

Aoife put her arms around William, gave him a loving kiss.

"William, can I go first?"

"OK, just give me a minute to set the wireless speaker up. I'd better make sure the volume is not too high."

A couple of minutes later everything was ready.

"Go to 'Aoife's Playlist' and play the only song there. I downloaded it last night. Have you heard of a Belgian band called Hooverphonic?"

"No."

"Well, my song for you is sung by the lead female singer of that band which is a very well-known band in Europe. Her name is Nōemie Wolfs. This is my favourite version of the song. Listen to the words carefully. It's for you William. Do you understand? It's only for you."

William was nervous and expectant. He held his breath and selected the play button. He sat on one side of the arched window and Aoife on the other side. They looked intensely into each other's eyes as the music began.

A hypnotic orchestral introduction was followed by a slow tempo song with a reoccurring line which William heard loud and clear. 'Mad About You'. He was concentrating and trying to get his head around the significance of what he was hearing. Yes, he heard it right. 'Mad About You'. One minute into the song he couldn't stand it any longer and he was overcome with intense joy and passion. He understood clearly what she was attempting to convey to him. She was mad about him. He stood up, asked Aoife to stand up, held her in a loving embrace and started a gentle swaying to the music. He was shy but determined. He kissed her so erotically that it was borderline indecent. The song finished as William and Aoife were left standing in front of the arched stone window silhouetted against Mount Vesuvius in the far distant background.

Their moment of passion was suddenly interrupted by a female voice speaking out with joy.

"*E bellissimo, e bellissimo. La bellezza del giovane amore.*"

It was accompanied by polite group clapping.

William and Aoife turned around and they were mortified and shocked to see a group of five elderly ladies and two elderly men standing over in the corner looking directly at them with expressions of pure joy and happiness on their faces.

"I'm so sorry, I'm so sorry," said an embarrassed William "I thought we were alone. Please accept our sincere apologies. We were not meaning to be offensive or disrespectful."

One of the nonnas spoke back in English to William and Aoife.

"No, no, no, no. It's the highlight of our day. It makes us feel glad to be alive. Better than all the pills we have to take. Where there's young love, there's hope. Be good to each other and may you be blessed with many children. God bless you both."

"Are you sure you're not offended?" William asked the lady.

"No, we're all delighted and happy. It makes us feel young. We're not offended. We will leave you alone now."

As they shuffled and moved away from the area and back into the museum proper, they were all chattering and smiling to each other and waving cheeky and appreciative goodbyes to the young couple.

Now that the group had all left and the coast seemed clear, Aoife turned to William and spoke.

"Oh my goodness, I wasn't expecting that. But they seemed to be OK with it. Did you understand my song to you?"

"I did and you have answered my doubts and addressed my anxiety. Thank you for making the message loud and clear."

"You must hear my song now Aoife. It's just for you. I've never ever done this for anybody before."

They sat back down over by the arched window and William explained his song choice to Aoife.

"Have you heard of an Australian group called Nick Cave and the Bad Seeds?"

"Vaguely."

"This song is 'Into My Arms' and Nick Cave is the singer. People interpret it differently. Some consider the lyrics melancholic but I have my own personal take of it. I interpret them as being kind and hopeful lyrics. I don't have as much pure faith as you Aoife, I know that, but I do believe in something. I just haven't figured it out yet. And I believe in love and I know you do also. I think you'll understand when you hear it. Shall I play it?"

"Yes."

William dashed over and attached his iPod to the Bluetooth speaker, pressed play and quickly went back to sit with Aoife. As the song started he could see that Aoife was listening intently and it wasn't long before he observed her eyes filling with tears as she heard the words 'Into My Arms'. She held his hands tightly and he felt that the song was conveying what he wanted to say to her. There was only one place he wanted her to be right there and then and that was

'Into My Arms'. And she didn't disappoint. She stood, placed both her hands around his head and gently lowered it to rest on her bosom. He carefully grasped her and put his long arms gently around her upper body. She was now into his arms. They stood silently for several minutes until the song finished. This time there was no appreciative audience and William and Aoife were able to enjoy the moment in total and unbridled privacy.

"Nobody has ever done anything as beautiful and personal as that for me before. I know that you're not as religious as I am, but that doesn't and shouldn't matter. Not to me anyway. You're a good and kind man who loves and appreciates the world about him. You see good in everything and the good in everybody. William."

"Yes."

"I love you."

"I love you to Aoife."

Monday was a special turning point in their relationship. It had taken only a few days to go from that first face-to-face meeting at Nonna Russo's Cooking Class, to them now expressing their sincere love for each other as they stood together on a castle on Vomero Hill looking eastwards out over the city of Naples towards Mount Vesuvius. Naples had been generous it providing William and Aoife with magical moments and sensory delights and a setting for their love to develop, blossom and grow. It had been perfect and they moved slowly inside.

It was heading towards mid-afternoon as William and Aoife sat on a stone bench down in the castle's inner courtyard garden.

"What would you like to do for the remainder of the day William?"

"I have an idea so please say yes."

"Are you going to give me any clues?"

"Oh sorry. Acting bit a goofy is this man from New Zealand."

They laughed together knowing that today was a huge step forward and there was no going back. They both sensed that. They just had to work out the immediate and longer term plans for their journey ahead. That was not going to be easy given they lived on opposite sides of the world.

"How about coming back to my apartment and I'll make dinner for you. Back home most people think I'm just a bachelor who can't look after himself. Good on the farm but useless around the home. I'm actually pretty handy in the kitchen and I'd like to make something special for you tonight."

"Yes I'd love that, but can I do one thing first. I'd like to go home and shower and change. And buy a bottle of good sparkling wine to celebrate the occasion. To celebrate that I'm 'Mad About You' and can't wait to fall 'Into Your Arms'."

"Very good" replied William as they bounded off hand in hand, and for once, Aoife's smile was almost but not quite as beaming as William's. That was one thing he couldn't be beaten at.

They arrived back at Montesanto Station as the time was closing in on 4 pm.

"I'll just get a few supplies from Pignasecca Market and then head back to my apartment. I know what I'm going to make," confirmed William.

"OK, I'll head home to shower and change and get a bottle of sparkling wine on the way over to yours."

"I'll wait downstairs on the footpath outside the front of the apartment for you just before 6 pm. I'll wait for you to arrive. Will that be OK?"

"Perfect William, I'll see you later."

With that, they hugged and parted.

William hurried to the nearby market to make sure he purchased all the fresh produce supplies he needed. He bought some firm white fish, Arborio rice, cherry tomatoes, a packet of vegetable stock, a few spices, some fresh herbs, four fresh peaches, a small bag of shelled walnuts and a packet of mascarpone. Everything else he required was already available back in the apartment kitchen cupboards. As he started walking back to his apartment he suddenly remembered that he had forgotten to buy something special for Aoife so he dashed back and got it. He wanted to go all out and make the evening one that Aoife would never forget. By the time he got home it was close to 5 pm, and although time was tight before Aoife would be downstairs, he told himself to make a plan and not to panic.

As soon as he arrived back to the apartment William sent a 'how are you doing?' text to Ram. He was surprised to get an almost immediate reply back saying that he was fine apart from some bad bruising to his legs and some strained back muscles. There were no broken bones indicated from x-rays. He had a lucky escape this time. William responded back to Ram that some magic had just happened in Naples and that he would explain all soon. He knew that would make Ram perk up to the point of being desperate to know what had happened.

After checking the health status of Ram, he quickly shaved, showered and changed into something a little bit more formal than the faded blue jeans and loose fitting t shirts he usually wore. He put on a crisply ironed white shirt, dark grey dress pants with black belt and some shiny black leather shoes. It was the only half decent outfit he had brought with him. Not too bad considering what I have to work with he said to himself as he quickly looked in the mirror.

He flung open the balcony door to let fresh air circulate around the apartment and then went to the kitchen to start what he hoped would be some 'kiwi chef' magic. All the while he was keeping a very close eye on the time so as not to be late downstairs to let Aoife into the apartment building.

Over at Aoife's apartment she had showered and was deciding what to wear. Not that she had a huge choice, but just in case, she had brought one half decent outfit with her. She put on her floral summer dress, a pair of yellow high heels and tied her hair up in a loose bun.

She placed her sunglasses in her hair ready to use if it was too glary outside. Simple but stunning was the result.

On the way over to William's apartment she stopped by a wine store and purchased a bottle of Prosecco DOC Rosé and two bottles of sparkling water. It was still sunny and glary when she left her apartment building so she did lower her shades. As she walked the short distance from her apartment to William's apartment she felt that many eyes were looking at her and she was starting to feel self-conscious about it. She didn't like being the centre of attention and even more so when she sensed it was one dimensional and just based on looks.

It seemed like an eternity, but finally she arrived at the front door of William's apartment building a couple of minutes before 6 pm and he was there waiting to let her in. After a quick hug they went inside, up the very steep stairs and into William's apartment. William immediately turned to Aoife and stated the obvious.

"Oh my goodness, you look simply stunning Aoife. Beautiful on the inside and the outside. How did I get to be so blessed?"

"Thank you but hang on a minute William. The man standing in front of me from down on the farm doesn't present to badly either. I'm blessed also, so don't ever forget that."

They smiled, laughed and kissed lovingly.

"Before we go any further, there's something I want to give you."

He handed Aoife a bunch of yellow and purple wild flowers, which he had managed to find with some difficulty at the market.

"Do you know what these flowers are? Have you seen them before?"

"Yes I do. They're all those beautiful wildflowers which were in full bloom when we stopped up the slopes of Vesuvius on the horse trek on Saturday afternoon to see the views over the Bay of Naples."

William thought to himself that he had probably scored a few brownie points with his bouquet of wild flowers and was delighted with Aoife's reaction.

"Thank you William. It's kind and thoughtful. But hang on a minute you're not getting off so lightly. I've got something for you."

From her bag she pulled out what seemed to be a gift wrapped book. She handed it to William. He unwrapped the gift, scanned the title and immediately hugged Aoife tightly. He didn't want to let her go. Not ever. It was titled 'Chapel of Sansevero Museum' and was a written and pictorial history of the chapel and each individual monument and statue within, including his beloved 'Veiled Christ'.

"I'll treasure this always. I'll use it frequently. I love it. Thank you."

The evening was off to a good start and was about to get much better.

"I've half prepared dinner already. When we're ready to eat it will take me just ten minutes to finish off each dish. Fingers crossed that it will be edible."

William was being just a little bit pretentious because he loved Italian cooking, had made numerous Italian meals back home on the farm, and had bought good quality fresh ingredients from the market. He didn't need to follow a recipe because some of it was already catalogued in his head and the balance was impromptu. He knew that the chances of the meal being anything but delicious, or close to delicious, were slim. Tonight of all nights he was out to impress.

"Shall we go out on the balcony and sit for a while, have a drink and watch the sun set down at the end of the street?" asked William.

"Sounds good. Let me pour you a drink. *Prosecco Rosé o acqua frizzante?*"

William laughed as he admired Aoife's attempt to use Italian.

"Are we on the same wavelength or what? *Acqua frizzante por favore. Con una fetta di limone.*"

Aoife obliged and they went out on the balcony and sat down with their drinks. It was getting close to 7 pm and the sun was about to set at the end of the street. Slowly over the course of thirty minutes the evening went from full light to full darkness. The air was still warm and there was a light breeze. Aoife and William chatted about the week which has just been, their visit earlier in the day to San Martino, how wonderful Naples had been to them both and life back home. Aoife avoided mentioning anything about the deleterious relationship she had been in over the past six months. She felt that she needed to explain it to William at some stage, but that tonight was not the right moment.

As they sipped their drinks and chatted, Aoife observed an elderly lady on the balcony across the street who seemed to be beckoning and gesticulating over their way. Yes, she was definitely smiling and waving over towards them.

"William, look at that lady over there. She seems to be trying to get our attention. She seems very excited. Wonder what that's all about?"

William explained that the waving nonna was his 'Napoli friend' and how she had observed him sitting out on the balcony on his first morning in Naples in his jocks and nothing but his jocks. How she seemed to be very friendly and waved to him frequently. William and Aoife stood up and waved back across to the elderly lady. She simply waved back, put her hands on her heart, and went back inside her apartment.

"So cute, if you can make people smile and happy it must be good," Aoife said to William.

"I'm hungry William. No pressure but I haven't really had anything to eat since out morning tea at the bakery cafe this morning."

William laughed. He was confident that he would perform both now and later. No problem.

"What are you making? It smells really good."

"Well, I'm making fresh fish and cherry tomato risotto for main, and stuffed roasted peaches with mascarpone for dessert."

"Sounds delicious. I know you can cook but that sounds really professional."

"Fingers crossed I can pull it off."

Before William went over to the small kitchen area to do his magic, he attached his iPod to his portable speaker and selected 'William's Playlist'. He pressed play.

"Hope this music is OK for you Aoife. It's just a selection of the type of music I like."

Aoife sat down on the sofa, threw off her heels, sipped her remaining drink and listened to the music as she watched William navigate the small kitchen area. He explained that he had already pre-prepared the risotto but he added more stock to it and stirred constantly for another five minutes. He then added a large handful of the reddest of red cherry tomatoes and a cup of finely chopped fresh herbs, a teaspoon each of dill seeds, cracked pepper and lemon salt, put the lid on and turned to Aoife.

"Four or five minutes on a low simmer and then we'll be ready to eat."

William had set the table as best he could with what was in the apartment. He had put Aoife's wildflowers in a vase on the table and lit two candles. He invited Aoife to sit at the table and opened the bottle of Prosecco Rosé and poured them each a glass. In the background Caro Emerald was singing 'A Nite Like This'. The scene was set and everything was perfect as William brought the hot pan of simmering risotto over to the table. He served them both a generous plate of his risotto.

William spoke first.

"Aoife, I was a lost soul when I came to Naples. I was struggling with the direction of my life journey. I love my life on the farm, my parents, Hunterville township and the few close friends I have in Hunterville, but I don't want to live a life that's unfulfilled. I'm curious to know about anything and everything. The first day I met you things seemed better. We have shared sights and sounds and personal experiences over the past week thanks to the magic of Naples. You're non-judgemental and you accept me for what I am. I feel complete. I want more. Please let there be more. I love you."

Aoife replied.

"Thank you William for being the kindest man I have ever met. You're a gentle man. An interesting man. A masculine man who is in touch with his emotions. You know how to cry and how to be vulnerable. You know how to be comforting and caring. You have included me in everything the past week without any pressure or expectations or demands. I treasure that. It's the beginning not the end. I love you also."

They raised their glasses and toasted the future. It was still unclear to both of them how they would navigate that.

"*Bon appetito*. I hope you enjoy."

After a few minutes, the verdict was in.

"William, this is delicious. The fish is moist, firm and flaky. The tomatoes are so sweet and red, and the risotto is so creamy. How did you do that? That's the best meal I've had in a long time. Perfect."

Not wanting to be too pretentious, William said he was pleasantly surprised at how tasty it was. Aoife asked him if he had any update about Ram's accident and he reported that it was a close shave but everything seemed to be alright with x-rays indicating no broken bones or worse. All the while, music was playing in the background and they were both enjoying it.

"Time for dessert. It shouldn't be too long. I've already halved and stoned the peaches. I've just got to make the filling for the top of each half of peach, and then oven bake for ten to fifteen minutes."

"How did you make the filling?"

"Two tablespoons of flour, half cup of chopped walnuts, generous knob of butter, teaspoon of vanilla essence, the zested rind of a lemon, a pinch of cinnamon and nutmeg, and two tablespoons of this this secret ingredient."

"What is it?"

"I'll give you a teaspoon of it and you try and guess what it is."

Aoife tasted the thick liquid on the teaspoon William handed her. She said it was sweet, had a slight grainy texture and a strong buttery taste. She also noted that it left a strong lingering floral aftertaste on the tongue.

"Is it some kind of fruit syrup or honey maybe?" Aoife guessed.

"Yes, it's 10+ Mānuka bush honey sourced from beehives around the district I live in New Zealand. I buy it from Mr Bates at the Mānuka Honey Shop in Hunterville. It's really strong floral and bush-like taste is very addictive to me. I love it because it reminds me of home and the bush. That's why I always travel with a one kilogram jar of it in my luggage."

"What does 10+ mean?" asked Aoife.

"10+ is it's UMF. Short for Unique Mānuka Factor. It's a grading system. Higher the grading then the better the honey supposedly is for medicinal and antibacterial purposes. UMF 25+ Mānuka honey can sell for hundreds of dollars for a small 250 gm jar. A bit out of my league, but 10+ is affordable. But only just."

"When I see my brother I'll mention it to him. He'll be impressed I know so much."

William deftly mixed all the ingredients together, then spooned it on top of each peach half, placed them into a greased baking dish and slid the dish into the oven. As they waited for dessert to cook, Aoife poured them another glass of the remaining wine and they continued talking about the week that had just passed.

"If I was to ask you what was the number one highlight for your first week in Naples, other than meeting each other of course, what would you say?"

"That's really hard," replied William "because there's been so many. Either horse-riding on the slopes of Vesuvius, or seeing the 'Veiled Christ' at the Chapel of Sansevero. Are you allowed first equal? What about you?"

"It's impossible to select just one thing. Probably the best way to respond is to say that I haven't done anything in Naples that has disappointed. Everything has been fantastic."

"Nice reply," smiled William, "dessert smells ready so let me go and check."

William went over to the oven, prodded the peaches with a fork and announced that they were ready. He served two peach halves into each dessert bowl together with a quenelle of mascarpone. Dessert definitely smelt and looked good.

"Be careful Aoife the peaches are still very hot."

There was silence as Aoife took her first mouthful of the desert.

"This dessert is totally delicious. Seriously William, it's possibly the best dessert I've ever had."

"Blame it on the Mānuka honey from the honey shop in Hunterville," responded William "I call it my liquid gold. Thanks to the magic of bees."

They finished their dessert, and the wine, and there was no doubt that the meal had been a huge success.

"Let's have a quick coffee out on the balcony to say goodnight to, and thank Naples for bringing us together."

William put the moka coffee pot on the stove, made a quick coffee for both of them and they went and sat out on the balcony. It was close to 10 pm and the streets below were becoming quiet. The air temperature was still warm but it was starting to cool down. It had been a spectacular day. Coffee finished and with that, William led Aoife inside from the balcony. Neither of them wanted the night to finish and it wasn't finished.

William drew the curtains, turned to Aoife and kissed her gently and lovingly all over her neck and shoulders. He slowly undressed her as he gazed at her beautiful naked body emerging from her floral dress. Her dress and then undergarments fell gently to the floor. Those marble Greek goddesses at the National Naples Museum, if they were not so inert, would surely be envious of the erotic beauty that stood before William. She slowly and excitedly undressed him and let his clean crisp clothes fall gently to the lounge floor. From top to bottom and back to front, he looked every inch a lean, fit man who worked the land and was blessed with the physical rewards of having done so. Standing there naked before her, William was nothing less than she had visualised and expected. Neither of them were disappointed with what they saw standing in front of them. A vision of youthful physical perfection.

William led Aoife up the stairs to the loft. Not a word was spoken as they lay onto the bed and commenced their night of unbridled passion and lust. William was the gentle and consummate lover Aoife had expected. He may have been a little bit out of practice over the past year or two, but like the simple act of breathing, it was intuitive and instinctively it all came flooding back to him. Aoife was very responsive to William's manliness and natural physicality and trusted him implicitly. She was happy to be with such a considerate lover who took her to places she'd never been before. The night ended with the two lovers from opposite sides of the world falling asleep together in each other's arms under the cover of a thin crisp white cotton sheet. A stand fan to the side of the bed blew a gentle cooling breeze over their drained bodies.

All in the space of just under a week, they had progressed from being friends to lovers and were now both totally committed to making and building a life together no matter what obstacles were presented. It was a day neither of them would ever forget. How could it be any better? It could be and it would be.

Subterranean Naples and the Palaeontology Museum

The following morning Tuesday 9th July, William and Aoife woke up still in each other's arms. They smiled sensing that something very special had happened between them the night before.

"Is it OK if I shower before breakfast?"

"Of course it's OK. There are clean towels over there on the dresser," replied William.

His eyes were focussed on Aoife's nakedness as she rolled out of bed, grabbed a towel and wrapped it around her like a sarong. Until he drew open the curtains of his balcony doors each morning William was comfortable walking around his apartment naked. However, now that Aoife was there in his apartment he was unsure if he'd be able to hide his manly intentions if he was naked, so he elected to pull on some denim shorts and wear a white t shirt.

He also rubbed a splash of his favourite sandalwood oil around his face because he loved the fresh, spicy and woody smell of it. For one brief moment he had thought about joining Aoife in the shower and satisfying his rekindled morning lustfulness, however, being the ever considerate man he was, he didn't want to appear too demanding or too overbearing towards to Aoife. He decided to err on the side of caution and respect. The day was young.

When Aoife exited from having showered, William had already made their coffee and arranged some pastries and freshly sliced fruits on a plate.

"Sorry William, but I don't suppose you've got a spare t shirt and pair of shorts I could wear. Putting my dress back on seems a bit overkill?"

"Yep, of course I do. Here's some gym shorts and blue t shirt. Will that do?"

"Great, thanks."

Now that they were both were suitably attired, they went and sat out on the balcony with their simple breakfast. It had just turned 7 am and the street below was still quiet. The air temperature was a perfect 23 degrees C.

"Thanks for making me dinner last night William. Seriously, it was one of the best meals I can ever remember having. Totally delicious. And thanks for be gentle and loving with me afterwards. I knew you were special the moment I met you. I'm very happy."

"It's the same for me. Thanks for making me feel wanted. I don't feel alone anymore."

They continued chatting and eating their breakfast until Aoife discretely leaned forward and spoke to William.

"That same lady over across the street on that apartment balcony seems to be trying to get your attention again. She's pointing to you."

William looked across and sure enough his favourite nonna was trying to get his attention as she lowered a plastic bucket on a rope down to street level. She was beckoning to William to come and get whatever was inside the bucket. William waved and shouted out good morning and indicated that he'd go downstairs, cross the street and collect whatever she had lowered down for him. But first he wanted to write a note to her.

"*Momento, momento,*" he shouted across to her.

"I don't think she speaks English so I'm going to have to try and write it in Italian," he said to Aoife. He composed a note as best he could.

Buongiorno signora. Mi chiamo William. Io sono dagli Nuova Zelanda. Grazie per tatto qullo che c'e cestino. Grazie for essere un vicino felice e amichevole. Buona giornata, William.

"What did you write?"

"Good morning madam. My name is William and I come from New Zealand. Thank you for whatever is in the basket. Thank you for being a happy and friendly neighbour. Have a nice day, William."

William rushed carefully down the steep internal stairs of the apartment building, crossed the street and took a plastic container from the bucket. He put his note inside the bucket and rushed back to his apartment balcony just as the elderly lady was pulling the bucket back up to her balcony.

They looked across and could see her reading the note. She waved to both of them, and shouted across, "*Bellissimo, grazie. Che ti benedica.*"

They opened the plastic container as she watched from across the street. It was full of an assortment of homemade Italian style cookies.

William shouted back, "*Grazie, grazie. Sembrano deliziosi.*"

The nonna waved to them with both arms, blew them kisses and then disappeared back inside.

"What a sweet old lady. I think she's probably a widow. Do you think that maybe she's lonely? That was a truly beautiful moment William, but at the same time, I feel a bit sad. Sad because she probably doesn't know that you're leaving at the end of the week."

Right at that moment, Aoife was feeling as emotionally close to another person as it was possible to be.

For a few minutes it put a damper on their breakfast but their spirits soon lifted and it was time to plan what to do for the rest of the day.

"Honestly Aoife, I've done a lot, you've done a lot, we've done a lot of sightseeing over the past week that I'd just be happy to hang out with you and do some low key stuff around the immediate area. Just walk around the nearby streets, explore and see what's on offer. Maybe we can plan to do something more significant on Wednesday, Thursday or Friday if you're keen?"

"That sounds great. I'm ready for a day off being a revved up tourist."

Neither of them were wanting to mention the end of the week, and especially Sunday, for that was the day they'd both depart Naples and fly off and return to their homes on opposite sides of the world.

"I know that you like visiting churches and chapels and monasteries. I'm keen and there are lots in this general area all within five to fifteen minutes' walk from here. Apparently they're all inspiringly beautiful inside. Why don't we go do that tomorrow after we've had morning coffee?"

"It sounds perfect William and it is something I really want to do so thanks. What shall we do today?"

William had already given it some thought. They had five days left together in Naples before they flew home. He wanted to try and make the remaining days count, and at some stage, to discuss the forward plan with Aoife.

"Well, we could start off at a cafe, just look around all the artisan shops in the general area especially up near Piazza Bellini, and then perhaps do the Subterranean Naples tour which is only ten minutes' walk away from here. It's highly rated. And there's one more thing I'd like to do today if possible but I'm bit shy to ask. We don't have to do it. Please don't think I'm a complete nerd."

"I wouldn't and I don't, so what is it?"

"Well, about ten minutes' walk from here is the University of Naples Federico 11 campus. Not only is it the oldest public university in the world, but it's a very large campus and includes several very historical buildings. One of them is the Cloister of Saints Marcelino and Festo and within that convent complex is the......are you ready? The Museum of Palaeontology. I want to go there but I'll understand if you don't."

Aoife was starting to realise that William was a multifaceted man. He was happy just enjoying a simple natural life on the farm and being in the bush exploring how everything worked and interacted and depended on each other. At the same time, he embraced the arts and culture, history and science and was interested in all of those topics also. He was very adaptable and keen to experience everything life had to offer.

"Yes, of course I want to go with you. I've never been to a palaeontological museum so it's all going to be new for me."

Aoife's affirmation was sweet music to William's ears. He was very happy.

Aoife reconfirmed to herself that she had done and seen more, and developed more as a person in the past week, than she had done over the previous twelve months. William and the magnificence of Naples had been responsible for that.

"Before we get going do you mind if I dash home and change into some more casual clothes. Your gym shorts and t shirt is a bit underkill, and my floral dress I wore last night a bit overkill."

"No problem. Do you want me to accompany you?"

"It's OK. I'll be less than half an hour for sure. Straight back, I promise."

William accompanied Aoife downstairs and kissed her lovingly before letting her out onto the street. He went back upstairs, showered and shaved, tidied the apartment, made the bed up in the loft area and waited patiently for her return. There was one further thing that William hadn't yet shared with Aoife. There was somewhere special he wanted to go, and something he wanted to do before he departed Naples, and he was desperate for Aoife to be a part of it. It was out of character and not something he had done before, but Naples was the perfect place to do it.

It was approaching 9 am and William sat out on the balcony checking to the street below to see if Aoife was in view. She was, so he dashed downstairs and let her in to the apartment building.

"Aoife, before we head out for coffee, just one more thing I want to ask you."

"Yes."

"Several weeks ago when I knew I was coming to Naples, I went online to see if there was any chance I could go to the opera. I might only do it once in my life but I want to go to an Italian Opera. Usually it's booked for months ahead."

"You're not going to tell me you managed to get a ticket?"

"No, better than that. I managed to get two tickets for Friday night. It's a long story. The lady online at the booking site helped me after I explained where I was emailing from. Call it fate. Call it a premonition. Something told me that I'd go to the opera with somebody I meet in Naples."

"Wow!"

"That somebody is you Aoife. Will you go with me on Friday night?"

Aoife sprung to her feet, wrapped her arms around William and hugged him intensely.

"I've always wanted to go to an opera. I don't know what's going on, or who our guardian angel is, but yes, yes, yes. Of course yes."

William was beside himself with excitement.

"I can't believe we're going to the opera on Friday night."

"Hang on William. Problem. I've got nothing with me to wear to an evening at the opera. I know you've got to be dressed appropriately."

"Neither have I, but there is a plan. I'll tell you about it over coffee."

"Where shall we go for coffee this morning? Back to same place at Piazza Bellini, or somewhere different?"

"Let's try along Via Dei Tribunali which is where the entrance to Subterranean Naples is. It's only a ten-minute walk from here. I know there are several cafés fifty meters either side of it on Via Dei Tribunali and we can look at artisan shops on the way there."

"Sounds good."

It was 10 am when they set off from William's apartment to enjoy the rest of the day in each other's company. William used his foldout street map of the Old City central area to find Via Dei Tribunali and they spent almost an hour walking in and out of various shops along the street. Not being able to resist the artisan foodie shops, William stocked up on some handmade pasta, dried porcini mushrooms and several packets of dried herb mixes. Aoife bought several cans of Naples roasted coffee powder, a pair of leather gloves and some hand crafted blank writing paper and envelopes.

Aoife was thirsty and hungry.

"Time for coffee and cake. This one looks good. Let's try here."

They sat down and a pleasant middle aged lady came across and took their order. They were surprised to see that they were the only customers inside the café at 11 am.

"I think it's empty because of the time of the day. Most of the coffee drinking by locals is done first thing in the morning, usually on the way to work."

"Ok William tell me more about Friday night and the opera. What are we going to wear? I imagine that's it's quite a formal event."

"It is, but I went online when you went home to change and I found that there's a vintage fashion and accessory shop in the street behind the Basilica of Santa Chiara which is open every night until 8 pm. Santa Chiara is just three minutes' walk away from my apartment.

"Remember, we passed it on the way here. That impressive religious building I pointed out to you on the right. Too easy. I'm sure we can find something appropriate in that vintage clothing shop."

"When shall we go and look?"

"How about tomorrow later in the day after we've explored a few churches and monasteries. Will that work?"

"Definitely. Exciting."

The lady returned with their order comprising two cannoli filled with ricotta, orange zest and nutmeg, two almond and orange biscotti, a vegetarian salad roll to share and two cappuccinos. William and Aoife sat and enjoyed their late morning coffee and food while they watched the world go by on the street outside. They were now very relaxed in each other's company. Most people would have assumed they were a married couple, not a young couple from opposite sides of the world who had only just met one week ago.

"I'm really going to miss Italian coffee time when I go back home to Hunterville. Love everything about it. The coffee's good, the sweet treats are even better, it's affordable and the service is always great."

"Me too. I mean I do have a favourite café in Galway called the 'Secret Garden Café' but it's different to here. Coffee time here seems more cultural. It's more passionate."

By the time they finished their morning drinks and food it was 12 noon and the street outside the café was becoming a lot busier. Office workers were having their lunch break and an ever increasing number of tourists were appearing on the streets.

William and Aoife spent the rest of the early afternoon at the Subterranean Naples tourist site. They explored a network of aqueducts and tunnels, cavities and burial chambers, ancient streets and theatres buried beneath the Old City area. They were awed by its long and often tumultuous history going as far back as 2400 years.

As part of a small tour group, they descended down one hundred and thirty six steps to a well-lit underground world forty metres below the current street level. They marvelled at large water cisterns and aqueducts which had been hewn out of the relatively soft and porous yellow tuffaceous sandstone rock by the Greeks and then the Romans going back to 470BC. The tour guide mentioned that 470BC was the period they commenced building the city of Neopolis. They were surprised at how clean and crystal-clear the water flowing in the still operating aqueducts appeared to be. They were told by the tour guide that early Christians had dug secret caves to worship and to bury their dead and that Neapolitans of various centuries had used the cavities as dumping grounds. The cholera epidemic of the mid-1880s had shut down the underground city, but during World War II it was in use again as an effective underground shelter from the heavy aerial bombing that decimated Naples city between 1940 and 1944. They learnt that as recently as the 1990s, criminal mafia gangs had used the underground caverns and tunnels for their drug cultivation and distribution endeavours.

Once they exited the underground site and were back out onto the main street level, they looked around for a moment and then towards each other in surprise. William spoke first.

"How would you know all that infrastructure and all that amazing archaeological history was directly there underneath your feet just forty meters below the surface. It's unreal."

"I'm so glad we did that. Talk about an eye-opener."

"It's 3 pm, so we've still got enough time to go to the Museum of Palaeontology in the Saints Marcelino and Festo Convent Complex. But if you'd rather leave it until another time that's OK also."

Aoife knew that William was super keen to go there and have a look, and she was still keen also. She responded accordingly.

"No William, I want to go."

"It's less than a five minute walk away. Let's do it. It should only take one hour maximum to look around."

They left hand in hand like they were now a serious couple and walked the short distance to the palaeontological museum. At first glance it was hard to find the museum's entrance but after walking around the beautiful church complex and an internal courtyard garden, and then asking a student for directions, they finally found the museum entrance. They paid the reasonable entrance fee of three euros each.

Once inside the museum William lead the way and he seemed knowledgeable about the different exhibits which was just as well because nearly all of the information cards and explanation notes were in Italian. They walked around the exhibits. William pointed out different fossils of the main geological age periods, the skeletons of a sabre tooth tiger and a large cave bear, full articulated dinosaur skeletons of a raptor and pterodactyl, a baby woolly mammoth corpse lying on its side, and various other objects of interest.

"When I fossick around the rock outcrops back home in the Rangitikei District I dream that one day I'll find a fossil that's something very special. Maybe I'm just a dreamer? Definitely would be exciting to find something like a dinosaur skeleton or even a dinosaur bone. Shame the rocks are far too young geologically for that to happen where I live."

William was pleased they'd made the effort to visit the museum but was apologetic to Aoife for having done so much when it was meant to be a day of chilling out.

"It's been another great day William. Shall we head back now? I noticed a takeaway homestyle food type place on the way here. It looked like good authentic nonna type food. Shall we get some for dinner and a bottle wine and go home and chill out?"

"Let's do that."

They walked back to the apartment stopping on the way to get several medium sized takeaway containers of food, and a bottle of wine. It was close to 5 pm when they entered William's apartment.

"That food smells good. When do you want to eat?"

"I know it pretty early still but we haven't eaten since that late morning coffee. Is now too early?" asked William.

"Now's good. I'm hungry to."

"If you serve the meal, I'll pour the wine."

"Nothing like a bit of teamwork" smiled Aoife to William as she patted him on the buttock on her way to the kitchen.

William poured them each a generous glass of Salento rosé, put his iPod music on and they sat at the table to enjoy what looked like a delicious home style cooked meal.

"It looks like something my nonna friend across street might make. Aubergine lasagne, ricotta filled pasta, grilled capsicum and sautéed vegetables. No meat for the boy from the farm but still looks delicious."

"Not having meat occasionally is good for you, William. Cleans out the system."

They smiled at each other. They were acting like a well-oiled married couple already, however they were far from that. William realised that time was running out since they were both taking international flights in five days' time. That made him nervous. They were taking flights going in opposite directions. How could that be? He had to come up with some sort of workable plan before that and he didn't want to leave it until the last minute. He decided that he'd discuss the matter with Aoife on Thursday when they hadn't planned to do much. He thought it would be good if they had time to concentrate and discuss possible scenarios that would reunite them as soon as practical after their separation on Sunday.

"Cheers Aoife. Do you like this song playing? Simple but appropriate."

"I think I know who it is. Is it 'What a Wonderful World' sung by Katie Melua?"

"Yes."

"I remember her being all the rage about ten years ago. She was and probably still is, very popular."

William stood up and walked around the table to Aoife and asked her to hold his hand and dance with him. Far too many times he had danced all alone. Many times he had wondered if any significant other would ever be there, or would want to dance with him. He held her gently and closely, very closely, as they slow danced to the music. Usually it was William who was prone to tears in emotionally situations, however, he seemed composed this time and it was Aoife who slowly released a stream of glistening tears down both cheeks. It was obvious to William that these were not tears of sadness but rather tears of joy. Total joy.

She was madly in love with this man from Hunterville, New Zealand. "William I don't want us to part on Sunday. It's going to be too hard."

"I know it's going to be hard but we can do it. We'll make a plan to be reunited as soon as possible. Do you trust me?"

"Yes."

"I will make it happen. We will make it happen. Shall we talk about it on Thursday?"

"Ok."

William escorted Aoife the few metres back to the dining table and they continued their dinner.

"Don't tell anybody I said this but this meal is so delicious and seems so healthy even though there's not a molecule of meat anywhere on the plate. And the wine is perfect with it."

"William, before we leave Naples I want to cook dinner for you. How about Thursday night? It's just a small way to say thank you for coming into my life when I needed it the most."

"Do you want to cook here?"

"No, I want you to come to my apartment. I'll get some produce from the market on Thursday afternoon."

"I'll be there. And one more thing. You know the nonna across the street, well I want to give her a little something before I leave. She has been an unexpected and special friend to me during my stay here in Naples even though we've never actually spoken directly standing in front of each other."

"What are you going to do?"

"Several things, but firstly I want to give her a signed picture of me and you. Maybe the one that Captain Mario took for us when we were out on his boat in the Bay of Naples. I've still got it on my phone. I just need to get it printed somewhere. I'll look around for a print or stationary type shop tomorrow. I'm also going to look for a few gifts to give her. I want to give it all to her on Friday morning if possible along with a personal note."

Aoife was not the slightest bit surprised that William was planning on doing something like this. That's the kind of man he was. She did wonder to herself how he was going to make this all happen but knew William would have a credible plan and half the joy of it all would be how it unfolded.

Dinner ended, the music ended and the bottle of rosé was finished so William got up and put the moka coffee pot on the stove. He went over to his backpack and pulled out a small box of artisan chocolates.

"To have with our coffee."

"I didn't see you get those."

"No I got them a couple of days ago at the market. I wanted to keep them for a special occasion which is now."

"Shall we go out onto the balcony or would you rather just sit inside on the sofa?"

"We could go on the balcony for a while. Let dinner settle. Will you please stay tonight?"

Aoife smiled and replied to William "I was hoping you'd ask me and of course the answer is yes."

They went out to the balcony, sat down and reflected while they drank their coffee and tried the artisan chocolates. It was now just over a week since they'd first met at Nonna Russo's Cooking Class.

"Coffee and chocolate. It might be caffeine overload but it works big time for me."

Aoife agreed. Was there anything William and Aoife didn't agree about? If there was it hadn't yet surfaced. They both relaxed and gazed out to the street below. The tourists were all heading back to their accommodation and there were scattered mainly younger people sitting outside of the bars and restaurants up the street.

William glanced at his mobile phone and it was showing 9 pm. The previous night the magic had started at 10 pm and William was keen for a repeat. In his mind he was already undressing Aoife. The warm night air, the vision of beauty sitting opposite him and the promise of things to come was making him lustful. He couldn't wait any longer. He held Aoife's hand and led her inside and closed the curtains behind them.

He stood there in front of the closed curtains which shielded the world from seeing what Aoife was seeing. His manhood was fully aroused and he could wait no longer. He undressed her as considerately as he could, ripped his own clothes off like a man possessed and carried Aoife over to the sofa where he gently started to explore every part of her beautiful body. She responded enthusiastically and performed things which showed William that he was now the most important person in her life. They continued to enjoy an emotional and physical connection until they became one and then ultimately reached the point of no return. A point which was to have a significant outcome in the journey ahead.

They lay and smiled and kissed and were at the point of almost falling asleep.

"Let's shower and go to bed. Do you mind if I shower with you?"

Aoife didn't say anything, she just smiled and led William to the shower where they gently bathed each other, dried off and walked upstairs to the loft. William laid in bed thinking to himself that if he died right here and right now, he wouldn't mind. It was the happiest he'd ever been. It was a different kind of happiness to being on the farm or in the bush or with his family and friends. This was a kind of happiness that only Aoife could have gifted him.

The night was a bit humid and even more so in the upstairs loft so he hopped out of bed and put the stand fan on low speed, then slid back into bed, cuddled up to Aoife and drifted off to sleep in a state of total bliss.

Churches in the Old City Area and the Vintage Clothing Shop

It was very unusual for William to have a proper sleep-in but on Wednesday morning the 10th July he did. It had been a busy past few days for both himself and Aoife and they were playing sleep catch up. Neither of them stirred until well past 9 am. When they did wake up they were surprised to find out what the time was.

"I had such a good sleep. We're a bit late rising today but no problem because everything we've planned is in the immediate area and a maximum of fifteen minutes' walk away."

Aoife agreed.

"I'm really looking forward to today William. Not only for all the amazing Baroque, Renaissance and Gothic churches and other religious buildings we'll likely see, but also going to the vintage clothing shop and finding something for the opera. Exciting."

"Whatever you want to do today Aoife you just say. This is your day."

"There are a dozen churches at least from the 12th to 17th centuries worthy of visiting in the Old City area but let's stick to four or five of them otherwise it will be a bit overload. Honestly, I think it would take two to three full days to do all of them."

They placed William's foldout map of the Naples Old City area on the kitchen table and William asked Aoife to put a circle around the ones she wanted to visit. Aoife circled and explained a little about each of the ones she wanted to visit.

"Let's do the Church of Gesu Nuovo first and then head across the street to the religious complex and cloisters of Santa Chiara because they're opposite each other and they're just two minutes away around the corner. We can then head straight up Via Benedetto Croce to the Church of San Domenico Maggiore which has amazing wall and ceiling frescos and tombs, and continue up the same street to the Church of Saints Filippo and Giacomo, and finally branch off down Via San Gregorio Armeno to the Basilica of San Lorenzo Maggiore. Underneath this church there is a partly excavated roman streetway which they say is worth seeing."

"It sounds good. I'm sure it's going to be incredibly spiritual and historical, and the craftsmanship and artwork will be mind-blowing."

"Thanks William. Not only do I want to do it for myself but I also want to do it for Mum and Dad. They will enjoy hearing about it when I go home. It will mean a lot to them. Apart from The Netherlands and France, they haven't travelled much around Europe. Our generation is much luckier and more mobile than theirs thanks to cheap air travel."

"No problem. I'm excited as you."

William was impressed that Aoife had it all planned out as to exactly what she wanted to do and he was determined to make it a special day for her. He was happy to take a back seat and let Aoife decide how long they stayed at each religious stop. The vintage clothing shop didn't close until 8 pm so there was no pressure to get there before 6 pm.

"Shall we have breakfast before we go, or just do our usual café visit?" asked William.

"Let's just have a quick coffee now, then go to the two churches around the corner, then have a late morning coffee and eats somewhere, and then do the rest of the stops. I think we'll be finished by 3 pm or 4 pm and then we can go to the vintage clothing shop."

"Did you say late morning coffee and sweet treats?"

Aoife laughed.

"No mister sweet tooth, I said late morning coffee and eats."

They were starting to act like real Neapolitans in that the café scene was now an integral part of their daily ritual. They both enjoyed it immensely. If it hadn't already, it was becoming a real passion for both of them.

Aoife and William set off from the apartment at 10 am and headed around the corner to Piazza del Gesu Nuovo and their first stop, The Church of Gesu Nuovo which was a 16th century Renaissance-Baroque church.

"That's a very strange façade for a church. Very unchurch like. I've never seen anything like that before. Look all those dark grey protruding low pyramid shaped blocks of stone."

"Wonder what that was all about?"

Aoife had done a bit of research and knew a little bit about each of the religious stops they'd make during the day. She turned to William and explained.

"That façade is the original one from the Palace of Sanseverino built in 1470. The palace was confiscated due to political rumblings, bought by the Jesuits in the 1580s, and then a church was built in the late 1500s by altering and renovating the palace. But the façade of the palace was kept intact. I'm not sure why it was kept, but maybe because it's so unusual? The church was badly destroyed during the Second World War and restored in the 1970s."

"It's definitely volcanic rock. Wonder if it's from Vesuvius?"

"Let's go inside. I know it's going to be spectacular."

William and Aoife stepped from the outside into a dark foyer area and then through another door to the church proper itself. It did not disappoint. Spectacular was an understatement. They both stood there in silence gazing around and trying to take it all in. It was magnificent. From the elaborate fresco ceilings and walls, to the inlaid marble flooring, and from the ornate side chapels with their altars and statues to the gold gilded church treasures. It was sensory overload of the best kind. William turned and whispered to Aoife.

"It's incredible. For people with faith I'm sure it's a very spiritual place and very special experience just being here. Think of all the people that have prayed here and confessed here in the last four hundred years."

Aoife didn't respond and William knew that she was having a private spiritual moment. He discretely moved to the back and waited for Aoife to finish. She walked back and William could see that she was very moved by the whole experience. He waited until they were back outside before hugging her and telling her that even he was affected in some mysterious way.

They walked across the other side of the street and a very short distance along Piazza del Gesu Nuovo and entered the grounds of the Santa Chiara religious complex.

"This complex was built in the 14th century but the basilica was completed destroyed during the Second World War. It was reconstructed to give the church we see now, however, the monastery cloisters and courtyard garden were largely unaffected by the Allied bombing.

"The cloister courtyard garden is decorated with brightly coloured 17th century majolica tiles and frescos and was largely designed and landscaped in the 18th century."

"It looks good."

"Let's do the church first William, and then the cloisters."

They walked through the church and were impressed. They were greatly impressed. They then paid a small entrance fee of a few euros each and walked into the larger monastery part of the complex. It didn't disappoint. They walked past bright colourful hand painted tiles on octagonal columns and benches at the edges of the pathways crossing the central garden area. The painted tiles depicted hunting and fishing scenes, rural farming scenes, climbing flowers, grape vines and lemons trees. Both agreed that everything was beautifully presented.

"It's so peaceful and largely free of people in here William. It's hard to believe that there's a very busy urban city on the other side of the monastery walls. You can hardly even hear the street noise."

William continued exploring and was equally impressed by the frescos on the walls of the covered walkways surrounding the central garden area.

"I'm not sure what those 14th century frescos depict as they're a bit faded but on the wall plaque over there, it says they illustrate Franciscan tales. They might be faded and dull but are still very impressive given they're so old."

"Psst, William, I feel like going over and picking one of those oranges from that orange tree over in the central garden area. Suppose I'd better not. Might get arrested or at the very least told off."

"Please don't. Awesome first two stops Aoife. It's been really good. Is it time for coffee and food maybe?" William asked.

"Yes. It's that time. Where shall we go?"

"Well, our next stop is the Church of San Domenico Maggiore just a few minutes' walk up the street. There's bound to be several cafés around the Piazza San Domenico. Let's just go and take a look first and then decide."

They ambled slowly up the street and a few minutes later they had reached Piazza San Domenico. As expected there were four cafés to choose from. They looked around to determine which one looked the more inviting. They had timed it well because it was just before 12 noon and there were still plenty of empty seats at all of the cafés. That would change quickly straight after 12 noon.

"I'm not sure where I read it but this one is highly rated for coffee and aperitivo so shall we try it. It's open until very late at night. Maybe we could try aperitivo here later today?"

William just wanted to eat as soon as possible so immediately said yes.

"Do you want to sit inside or outside William?"

"Outside is good. We can people watch and it's such a nice day."

They checked with the young waiter standing at the entrance to the café and he directed them to an outside table with umbrella shade right at the edge of Piazza San Domenico.

"Please sir, sit here at this table. A special one for you and your wife. My name is Leonardo? Where do you come from?"

William knew and had observed that all of the younger people working in the hospitality industry in Naples were keen to practice their English as a precursor to trying to work internationally, so he didn't mind having a conversation with the waiter to help him out a bit.

"It's nice to meet you Leonardo. My name is William and I am from New Zealand. This is Aoife and she is from Ireland. We are tourists in Naples for two weeks. We love everything in Naples. Everybody has been very kind."

"*Grazie signore.* Thank you for coming to Naples. We love our city. Thank you for loving it also."

"Coffee or wine Aoife? Share a pizza OK or you prefer something else?"

"Chilled white wine and pizza sounds good."

"Leonardo, two glasses of chilled white wine, a bottle of sparkling water and two slices of pizza please. Surprise us with the pizza type. *Ho fame e ho sete.*"

Leonardo laughed.

"Yes Mister William sir, I will arrange for you now."

After the waiter had departed to get their order, Aoife spoke to William.

"Are you OK with all these church visits William? If it's getting boring please just tell me. We don't have to do all five of them."

"Are you kidding? I'm loving it. I'm blown away by the craftsmanship and spirituality of both churches we've visited so far. And I'm enjoying seeing you so happy."

Ten minutes later Leonardo returned with their drinks. And then another five minutes after that, he delivered their pizza lunch comprising two large slices of pizza. Each slice of pizza came on its own white ceramic plate.

"Looks good Leonardo. What are the pizza toppings?"

"One is grilled summer vegetable and the other is Napoli salami with porcini mushrooms. OK for you both?"

"*Perfecto, grazie Leonardo.*"

"*Prego.*"

William and Aoife sat and talked and enjoyed their lunch. The adjacent street was very busy by the time they were ready to leave one hour later. William grabbed Leonardo's attention and indicated that he wanted to pay the bill. Leonardo arrived with the bill five minutes later and William paid, adding on ten percent gratuity for the friendly service they had received.

As they left to continue exploring all the historical churches in the area, Aoife spoke to Leonardo.

"*La pizza era deliziosa Leonardo*. Is the aperitivo good here also?"

"*Si signora*. It's very good and not expensive. I'm working until 9 pm tonight. Please come back later for aperitivo. I will look after you. *Arrivederci.*"

"We will try. *Ciao*."

And with that, William and Aoife waved goodbye to Leonardo and walked over to the opposite side of the piazza where the entrance to the Church of San Domenico Maggiore was. They walked up the flight of stairs to the entrance. Before they stepped inside the church, Aoife gave William a brief rundown on the church's history and what they might see inside.

"This church is mostly of Gothic design was completed and consecrated in 1324 by friars of the Dominican Order. For a long time, it was a church for royalty and nobles. Wait for it. Forty-five Aragons of royal descent and nobility are entombed inside. The church is full of magnificent artworks and frescos by 14th century artists. It has a separate gallery where they keep historical clothes and accessories taken off the mummified bodies of entombed 15th and 16th century Aragonese royalty and nobles for safe keeping. There is also a separate gallery housing the churches huge range of religious treasures. Ready?"

"It sounds amazing. Yes, I'm ready."

They stepped inside. The sight before them in the main part of the church was nothing less than visually incredible. They both stood there in silence looking around and craning their necks to look up at the ornately painted and gilded arched columns and ceiling. It was as magnificent as, if not more so, than the Church of Gesu Nuovo which they had seen a few hours earlier. They explored the side chapels and the separate galleries of tombs and treasures. Not a word was spoken between Aoife and William as they looked around.

They both wanted to be respectful of the sanctity of the church.

It wasn't until their tour of the church was over one hour later and they stepped back outside onto Piazza San Domenico that they spoke to each other.

"Oh my goodness Aoife. That was too beautiful. Talk about the wow factor. You don't have to be a strong believer or a Christian to appreciate what we just saw. Very reverent. I'm seriously impressed. And I'm thinking that you are even more so?"

"Yes. Can't wait to tell my parents about it and I'm just happy that you're doing it with me. These memories will last me a lifetime."

"Let's just get a gelato from over there and sit down on the monument steps and reflect for ten minutes so we can come back down to earth. What flavour would you like?"

"Pistachio or strawberry will be good."

William walked across and purchased two gelatos. They sat down on a bench and talked and enjoyed their gelatos before getting up and moving on to the next stop. It was only two or three minutes' walk away up the same street.

They arrived to the Church of the Saints Filippo and Giacomo. It's entrance was right beside the main street.

"William take a look up. Can you see those two sculptures on either side of the main entrance door? Any idea who they might be?"

"Yes I can see. Maybe they're Saint Filippo and Saint Giacomo?"

"Correct and they were sculptured by Giuseppe Sanmartino. Remember who he is? That's the same man that sculptured your favourite work, the 'Veiled Christ'."

William was impressed.

"I know all the churches in the Naples Old City area have their own uniqueness and special features. What's this one known for?"

"This was originally the site of a church going back to 1593 when it was known as the Church of Silk Art because it was commissioned and paid for by traders and merchants dealing in the silk industry. From between 1580 to around 1630 Naples was an important centre for silk production. The church we see now was built in 1758 in the Renaissance style by the Roman Catholic Church. As well as the beautiful inside of the present day church, there is also a burial crypt for members of the 16th century Silk Corporation, 16th century frescos and a wooden Neapolitan vestry going back to 18th century."

"That is a bit different to the others we have seen earlier today. Let's do it."

William and Aoife wandered around inside the church and as was the case for the earlier churches they had visited, the ceiling and wall frescos, side chapels, marble sculptures, main altar and inlaid stone floor were all visual treats.

They managed to find the old burial crypt of the original church, and the 16th century frescos.

Totally amazing as expected was William's summation of the Church of the Saints Filippo and Giacomo. Aoife was in complete agreement. They finished their tour and stepped outside into the glaring mid-afternoon sun. It was hot and a little bit humid.

"One to go," said William "and you're absolutely right. If you want to visit all the historic churches in the Old City area you definitely need to allow two or three days. I guess there must be modern-day pilgrims who come to Naples just for that."

They arrived to the Basilica of San Lorenzo Maggiore which was directly opposite the small Piazza San Gaetano. They stood on Piazza San Gaetano looking towards the basilica. William encouraged Aoife to give him a rundown of what this church was noted for before they went inside.

"I will but I feel like I'm starting to act and sound like a school teacher." Aoife laughed composed herself and then continued.

"This church was opened in 1235 and is mostly of the Gothic style except the two side chapels which were added later in the Baroque style. It has high arched internal ceilings supported by marble columns and very high windows, a terracotta coloured marble floor, all of which gives an overall sombre feeling to it. This contrasts with the later added two chapels which are magnificently art and sculpture filled, made of highly ornate polychromatic marble and much more colourful overall. There's the church, a side entrance to the ruins of the 5th century underground covered Greco-Roman market and a side museum covering 3 floors."

"We can probably give the underground market ruins a miss because they're just a lateral extension of Subterranean Naples which we visited yesterday, but it might be good to have a quick look at the museum because that gives an archaeological history of the site going right back to the 5th century."

William and Aoife walked around admiring everything inside the church, and then perused all the artefacts, holy treasures and maps on display in the three chronologically arranged floors of the adjoining museum.

William had reached the point of total information overload and once they were back outside on the street again, he gave Aoife his verdict of their just completed churches tour of the Old City.

"Crickey. How good was that? Totally loved it Aoife. It's not something I would probably have done by myself but it's definitely been a learning experience for lots of reasons. Just the craftsmanship of the stonemasons and sculptors, the beauty the artists and metalworkers have created, the overall history and archaeology of the Old City as told by its churches, well it's all inspiring to me. Something I need to get my head around and process over a few days."

He sensed that Aoife was getting a bit tired also for the same reason.

"Did you enjoy it? That's probably a silly question."

"I loved it William. And I loved it even more because you were sharing it with me. My parents are going to enjoy hearing about it. They'll be very impressed that you spent the whole day doing it with me."

"We've got to go to the vintage clothing shop yet but before we do that I'm just going to try and find a print shop to get that photo of us together on Captain Mario's yacht printed off for nonna across from my apartment."

They walked back along the street they had come from but couldn't see any likely looking shops. William went into a souvenir shop and asked the man behind the counter if he knew anywhere he could get a print made from his mobile phone. He did and he pointed out the directions to go on William's foldout map. They found the shop and made two A4-sized colour prints of the photo of them standing on the back of Captain Mario's yacht in the Bay of Naples.

"If we both sign it and I write a brief message I'm sure she'll enjoy. I'll shop for a gift tomorrow. Not in the mood now. Shall we head back and checkout the vintage clothing shop on the way?"

Their concentration was now firmly fixed on being prepared and suitably attired for going to the opera on Friday night. William had one final look of his map to check its location.

"It's on the small side street which branches off to the left just one hundred meters up this main street. Let's go."

Aoife was very excited. She had no idea if she'd find something suitable to wear or if she'd even be able to afford it.

They arrived to the shop, walked in and starting looking around. They were initially surprised at how many racks of clothing there were for sale. Neither of them would be considered fashionistas but they had a good idea of what they were looking for. A lady shop assistant approached them and starting speaking in English.

"Good afternoon. Can I help you? Are you looking for anything special?"

"Hello madam. My name is Aoife and this is William. We are going to the opera at the San Carlo Theatre on Friday night before we leave Naples on Sunday. It was last minute decision and we don't have anything suitable to wear in our belongings. William is looking for a black jacket, waistcoat and bow tie and I'm looking for some kind of formal evening dress or gown. Do you have anything suitable?"

"Yes, I think I can help you. Please follow me to the men's section. How lucky you are to be going to the opera. It's very hard to get tickets. I have never been but maybe one day and everybody says the theatre is beautiful inside."

"William and Aoife followed the lady over to the racks of men's clothes and she pulled out a black jacket with matching waistcoat. This is from the 1960s period when men dressed more formally even when doing ordinary everyday things. Please try it on to check the sizing."

William tried on the black jacket and waistcoat pairing and it was a perfect fit. The pricing labels on the clothing indicated thirty euros and twenty euros respectively, which William thought was reasonable.

"We'll take these items, thank you. Do you have a black bow tie to go with it?" said William flashing one of his trademark beaming smiles.

It must have worked because the shop assistant went over to the tie rack, picked out a black bow tie and told him it was complimentary to go with the outfit he had chosen.

"Thank you kindly madam, can you please try and find something very special for Aoife to wear."

The shop assistant turned to Aoife and asked her if she had any idea what she might like to wear. Aoife explained what she wanted to the lady.

"I definitely want something long and formal. Maybe a gown or dress from the 1950s or 1960s. Not patterned. I'd like it to be just one solid colour. I don't wear a lot of dresses so please help advise me."

"Of course, it's my pleasure. Please follow me. Over there is a rack of formal gowns and dresses we can look through."

They went over to the rack of formal gowns and dresses and started looking through them. The lady could tell immediately from both Aoife and William's facial expressions, that none of them were 'the dress' that Aoife had to have for their night at the opera on Friday.

"Please wait a moment, there is a dress which came in a few days ago and it just came back from the drycleaners this morning. It hasn't been put out on the formal dress rack yet because we need to do a little bit of repair work. It was owned by Madam Ricci who was a very well-known Napoli socialite during the 1950s to 1970s period. I'll get it and show you."

The lady went to the office area at the rare of the shop and then came back with a flared and fully accordion pleated, black glossy satin gown. The bodice of the gown which was also black satin was accentuated with vertical rows of small silver sequins. The lady asked Aoife if she liked it.

"I love it. Shall I try it on? I hope it fits."

Both William and the shop assistant indicated that she must try it on. She disappeared into the dressing room with the black satin gown and a pair of black high heels and a few minutes later emerged and stood there before William and the shop assistant.

William couldn't speak and the excited shop assistant's eyes lit up as she did the talking for him.

"*Bella, bella. Tua moglie è bellissima.*"

William finally composed himself and then spoke to Aoife.

"You look beautiful, Aoife. That dress was made for you. Oops, and of course the lady who it belonged to originally. It's perfect for the opera. That's the one. Do you like it?"

"I do but how much is it?"

The shop assistant apologised for it being rather expensive at one hundred and fifty euros but that was because it had a colourful history. If Aoife bought it, they'd do the small repair to the sequins on the bodice immediately, and not charge for the black high heel shoes, and she would also gift Aoife a black satin shawl to wear with the gown.

Aoife discretely took William to the side and whispered anxiously to him.

"It's too expensive William. I can't afford that much."

"No, it's OK Aoife. I want you to have it for the opera. My gift to you. Keep it always to remember this shop and our going to the opera for the first time in Naples. What price can you put on special memories like that? Please accept it as a gift from me."

Aoife didn't feel totally comfortable accepting William's offer to pay for the black satin dress but didn't want to disappoint William, or the shop assistant, so she said yes. It was the dress she'd wear to the opera on Friday night.

William settled the bill with the shop assistant lady and thanked her for being so helpful. She then confessed to them that she was actually the owner of the vintage clothing shop and wished that she could be at the opera on Friday night to see them in the vintage clothes they'd bought from her. She told them if they came back tomorrow at the same time all the repairs would be done and she would have an extra special surprise for Aoife.

"I didn't think it was going to be that much fun but we both got what we needed, so opera here we come."

"Thanks again William. You're kindness is overwhelming and greatly appreciated."

They exited the shop and William immediately put his arms around Aoife and gave her a long passionate kiss. The time had moved on to almost 6 pm. William wanted to confirm the forward plan with Aoife.

"Shall we do aperitivo again before heading back to the apartment? It's been a busy day and I'm not in the mood for making dinner back at the apartment. Let's just end what has been yet another special day in Naples with a relaxing evening."

"Ok William it sounds good. But……"

"There's a but?"

"Yes, only if you promise that I can pay for aperitivo tonight."

William flashed his signature smile at Aoife and indicated the affirmative.

"Where shall we go?" he asked.

"Let's go back up the main street to where we had lunch at that café in Piazza San Domenico Maggiore. Leonardo the waiter who served us at lunchtime said he'd be there and look after us. Is that OK?"

Again William indicated the affirmative by nodding and smiling. They strolled up the street hand in hand, canoodling as they went. They were in a world of their own and mostly oblivious to the passing by crowds in the street.

When they arrived to the café they couldn't see Leonardo so asked one of the other waiters. He went inside the café and Leonardo immediately came out. When he saw Aoife and William he was excited and embraced them both warmly.

"*Buona sera, buona sera. Benvenuto, benvenuto.* Thank you for returning. The evening crowds haven't arrived yet so there are still a few empty tables. Inside or outside? Can I recommend outside on a warm evening like this."

"Outside will be good thanks Leonardo."

He showed them to their table. Leonardo was impressed that they had remembered his name. To him it indicated that they were a kind and thoughtful couple.

"I'm feeling pretty hungry tonight Aoife. Let's have aperitivo but ramp it up a bit. I'll ask Leonardo if we can have the best aperitivo they've got and a small antipasto meat platter with ciabatta and some dips."

"That sounds good."

"Oops, apologies. Crickey, that seems very rude me planning to order all of the higher end stuff when you're paying."

Aoife smiled lovingly towards William and clasped his hand.

"Not at all. I want you to enjoy dinner after our special day visiting all the churches. I'm dreading Sunday but let's not talk about that now. We can discuss it tomorrow. Let's just celebrate the magical day we've just had."

Leonardo returned and they explained to him as best they could, what they wanted for their aperitivo even if it wasn't exactly on the menu.

"I will arrange for you. *Non problemo.*"

Fifteen minutes later they were presented with aperitivo drinks and nibbles plus an additional antipasto plate comprising cold meats, olives and cheeses.

"Thanks Leonardo. It looks really good. Probably enough for four people but we'll do our best to finish it all up."

"William, I'm quite enjoying the Aperol Spritz. It seems a lot more enjoyable this time than when we had it a few days ago. Maybe I'm becoming used to its unique taste. Despite the bitterness it is really refreshing."

They spent a relaxing couple of hours sitting outside the café in the Piazza San Domenico Maggiore sipping on their drinks, eating the aperitivo nibbles and plate of antipasto, and just watching the Neapolitans and tourists pass by.

Leonardo the waiter came by every twenty minutes or so to check that everything was alright at their table, and to have a quick chat with William and Aoife. Although he was very excited for them when he found out they were going to the opera on Friday night, he was not so happy when he found out that they were leaving Naples on Sunday because their two week holiday would have come to an end.

"How was your food? Did you like it?"

"Leonardo, it's the best antipasto and aperitivo we have had in Naples. Please tell the chef we loved it."

"*Grazie signora.*"

"Have you both had a good time in Naples Mister William?"

"Leonardo, we have had the best time. A fantastic time. We are sad to be leaving but we will return one day."

Leonardo was very happy to hear those words. His smile indicated that. But William hadn't finished.

"*Napoli e bellissima. Napoli e amichevole. Napoli e interessante. Ma soprattutto, Napoli e stata gentile con noi.*"

"*Grazie Mister William. Grazie.*"

"Can we please have the bill now Leonardo. It has been a very long day of sightseeing for us. It's time to say goodnight."

Leonardo left to get the bill for them, while Aoife checked with William what he had just said to Leonardo in Italian.

"I got some of what you said, but lost it a little bit at the end."

"I told him that Naples is beautiful. Naples is friendly. Naples is interesting. But best of all, Naples has been kind to us. Hopefully he understood. I think he did."

"Nice. And don't forget I'm paying the bill when it comes."

Leonardo returned with the bill which Aoife paid, they all hugged and said goodnight. Leonardo stood there waving goodbye as William and Aoife disappeared down the street into the crowd and the darkness.

When they got back to William's apartment it was 8.30 pm. They were tired but full of happiness. They both agreed that it had been a day to remember. As had all of the previous days they had spent together. Aoife was glad that they had visited the five different religious sites together, and grateful that William had been enthusiastic about going with her even though he wasn't religious himself.

"You know what tomorrow is don't you? It's Thursday the 11th. We've got three more full days in Naples together. We need to have a serious talk tomorrow Aoife. We need to talk about our future. Are you OK with that?"

Aoife agreed while holding William's hands as she responded.

"Let's have an early night and discuss tomorrow when we're not so tired. We don't have anything much planned for tomorrow other than collecting my dress from the vintage clothing shop in the afternoon, and you getting a gift for nonna across the street. And don't forget I'm making you dinner at mine tomorrow night."

"Sounds like a plan."

They showered, stripped and slipped into bed. It didn't take long before they both dozed off to sleep.

Dinner at Aoife's Apartment

Aoife and William stirred and woke simultaneously at 7 am on Thursday. They stared into each other's eyes while lying in bed both sensing that the day ahead was going to be monumental in determining if they had a future together. William had a plan but was nervous how Aoife might react to it. Aoife knew what she wanted but was shy about making her feelings known to William. The past nine days in Naples had been joyous for both of them. William was the first to speak after he had cheekily touched and cuddled her.

"Quiet day ahead Aoife but I'm glad because we need to talk seriously. I need to know if you feel the same about me as I feel about you? And if the answer is yes, what are we going to do about it because on Sunday we're both taking international flights in opposite directions."

"I know. Sunday can't be the end. Let's get up, make coffee and breakfast, and sit down to discuss."

They sprung out of bed, showered together, dressed and went downstairs to make breakfast. William's supplies were getting very low but there was still enough left for a decent breakfast. Since it was such an important day, William made an effort in setting the table as nicely as he could with a clean tablecloth, a few red geranium flowers he picked from the flowering pot plants on the balcony, and clean white crockery. They sat down to have the discussion. William knew what he wanted to say to Aoife and didn't hesitate to speak first.

"Just under two weeks ago I came to Naples for a break to try and sort out my life. Why did I do that? I had become totally lost. I was lonely. I was scared for the future. I just want the normal things that ordinary people want. A happy home and a secure future. A lifetime partner and children. A few adventures along the way and somebody significant and special to support and encourage me. I meet you nine days ago at Nonna Russo's Cooking Class. Over the past week we've explored and enjoyed the magic of Naples together. Every second, every minute, every hour with you has been beyond my wildest dreams. The simple truth is that I'm madly in love with you. I embrace the similarities and respect the differences. And I don't want it to end but I need to know how you feel. Please be brutally honest with me Aoife. If you don't feel the same way it's best to say now. I'll understand. Please be honest."

William could see the tears forming in Aoife's eyes. He held her hand across the table as she tried to compose herself and respond to William's heartfelt words. He didn't rush her. When she was ready she replied to William.

"I've never mentioned to you why I came to Naples. I was in a bad, bad headspace. I was in a physically and mentally abusive relationship. Then I met you at the cooking class. I wasn't looking for a substitute for what I had just lost, but over the space of just a few days I became aware of your kind and caring nature. Not just to towards me, but towards everybody you met. You have this ability to simply smile and make everybody feel good. I love your gentle but masculine demeanour. I have been happy beyond belief for the past week. Naples has been wonderful to me but you have been more so. I want to be with you William. I want us to take the journey of discovery together. A journey which will be full of kindness, honesty, love and support. A journey which will be full of surprises and unexpected twists and turns. The love I feel for you is pure and unwavering. I don't want Sunday to come."

Upon hearing Aoife's response William knew exactly what he wanted to say next. There would be a short pause in the journey as they departed their separate ways on Sunday, but as soon as possible after that, they must be, and would be reunited. He revealed his plan to Aoife.

"I know this might seem overwhelming Aoife but I want you to come to New Zealand. I know it's the other side of the world and very far away from your family, but I'll be waiting for you. I promise I'll look after you. Come to my farm in Hunterville when you're ready and I'll let you see and experience the life I live. And if you feel inspired and contented and want to stay, then I'd be happy beyond belief. We can sort all the details out once we both get home."

By now Aoife was crying uncontrollably. They were tears of joy. William stood, took her in his long lean arms and held her tightly and protectively. This was a time for both of their full emotions to be fully displayed. Finally Aoife was able to respond back to William.

"I want to William but I was too afraid to mention it. Yes, yes of course yes."

With the difficult matter of 'what happens next' sorted and out of the way, they were free to enjoy the rest of the day.

"I was dreading that talk Aoife but it seemed easier than I was expecting. What a relief. I'm so happy that we've got a plan. You've made me one very happy man. Thank you. I've got to answer a few emails sometime this morning. Especially the one from Ram who's now back in Hunterville. He sent me a text last night saying that he's making good recovery and that he would definitely be at Palmerston North Airport on Tuesday to pick me up. He wants to know about you so I'd better tell him something. I've got to get a small gift for nonna across the street and we've got to pick up your opera gown sometime this afternoon."

"I've also got to do a few emails, especially one to my parents. They want to know what's been happening. I won't tell them the forward plan just yet. I'd rather be face-to-face when I do that. Later I've got to go to the food market and get a few produce supplies for tonight's dinner."

"Why don't we do our emails now, and then go out for the ritual morning coffee and 'you know what' at around 10 am, and from there I can go shopping for that gift, and later this afternoon collect your dress from the vintage clothing shop."

"Sounds good William. I'll head to the market after our café visit, and then back to my apartment and tidy up, do some washing, and get sorted for dinner."

"Would you like me to buy a bottle of wine on the way over to yours?"

"That would be great."

"When I collect your opera gown later this afternoon shall I just take it back to my apartment? We can get ready for the opera and leave from there. It's too far to walk in formal attire so I'll organise a taxi to take us there."

"Perfect and thanks."

William poured another coffee for the both of them and they sat down in the lounge to deal with their emails. Coffee in the apartment was good but nowhere near as good as having one at a café.

William let Ram know that Naples was a ten out of ten holiday destination and that he had met a beautiful woman from Galway in Ireland named Aoife. He told Ram that they had been inseparable for the past nine days while they had explored and enjoyed the magic of Naples. Out of respect for Aoife, he didn't tell Ram any of the intimate details of their turbo charged relationship. He also mentioned to Ram that he had asked Aoife to come and visit him on the farm in Hunterville and was awaiting her reply to that. As he was about to press the 'send' key, he wondered if he should send a pic of Aoife to Ram since he was his best friend and one of the few people he could trust with his life secrets and dreams. He wanted to share his happiness with somebody so decided he would send Ram the pic of them together taken on the stern of Captain Mario's yacht out in the Bay Of Naples. He hoped that everything was OK on the farm and mentioned that he would be forever grateful to Mr and Mrs O'Connor for looking after the farm for him for the past few weeks. He finished the email off with......... 'it's a nice 25 degrees C here and been enjoying swimming in the Med. Not looking forward to returning to colder temperatures. Catch up soon.'

Aoife sat at the other end of the sofa and sent her parents an email on her mobile phone. She told them that Naples had been fantastic and that she had done many new and wonderful things including an almost full day of church visits with William. She sowed a seed by saying to them that she was very saddened to be leaving William on Sunday since he was flying back to New Zealand the same day she was flying back to Ireland. And she ended the email by saying that she hoped to see him again one day soon, knowing full well they'd wonder what that meant. She would be happy to tell them about it when she was back home in Ballinrobe. Aoife confirmed to her parents that she would love to be picked up at Galway Airport by her brother and taken back to the family farm in Ballinrobe for a few days.

Both William and Aoife felt relieved that they had discussed the forward plan and come to a decision that left them both in a state of euphoria. It was a lot easier than they thought it might be.

"I've finished my emails William, how are yours going?"

"I've finished mine also. Coffee and sweet treat time? Race you there."

"I would if I knew where we were going."

"Oops, bit too keen."

They both laughed and then embraced and kissed passionately before exiting the apartment building onto the street.

"Where shall we try this morning? We haven't visited a dud café yet so they are probably all good. Let's walk down Via Toledo in the direction of the waterfront and just stop at the first one which has lots of Neapolitans inside enjoying *café italiano*."

Aoife thought that William's suggestion was as good a way as any to select their next café experience. They strolled slowly down Via Toledo for five minutes until William stopped and indicated that the café in front of them might be a good choice. Aoife laughed under her breathe because she knew immediately that it had nothing to do with the coffee on offer, but more to do with the large display cabinets full of small cakes, pastries and biscuit delights that were seductively beckoning William to step inside.

"OK, let's try this one. I'll order if you select a table."

William stepped over to the counter and asked the young lady serving for two cappuccinos and a selection of small cakes and biscuits. He paid the bill at the counter and the young lady smiled and said that she would bring the order over to their table.

Aoife and William sat and chatted while they enjoyed their morning coffee and sweet treats at the café. They both felt relaxed and happy despite there being only three days remaining until their holiday was over.

"That was great as usual. Not sure what I'm going to get for my nonna friend across the street. Have you got any ideas?"

Aoife thought for a minute, using her own grandmother as an analogy, before replying.

"It's hard to buy for older people sometimes. They often already have everything they need. How about something practical and foodie she can enjoy and use daily rather than a keepsake. Perhaps a bottle of red wine, a bottle of white wine and a bottle of premium extra virgin olive oil. All presented together in a nice gift box or carton."

"Good idea, I know where there's an Italian food speciality and wine shop quite close to my apartment. I'll try there. Good team work, thanks. What time shall I come to yours for dinner?"

"Come at 5 pm and we'll have a drink first on my balcony and then eat after 6 pm. You know the address don't you. Text me when you're at the apartment building and I'll come down and let you in."

Aoife and William hugged outside the café and then waved goodbye as they headed off separately to do their errands.

William went straight back to the speciality food and wine shop near his apartment and got exactly as Aoife had suggested. The shopkeeper also had a cardboard presentation box which was suitable for holding three one litre bottles so that was perfect. William was pleased with his gift for nonna across the street. He considered it to be a practical gift which she could enjoy either alone, or with family and friends. He thought to himself that if only he had been more organised, he would have bought some extra jars of his beloved honey from the Hunterville Mānuka Honey Shop with him. 'Next time' he said to himself.

He decided to drop nonna's gift back to his apartment before heading out again. It was now noon and the streets were filling up with the lunchtime crowds. It was also a very hot day and had already reached 32 degrees C. William thought it best to just hang around his apartment until 2 pm before heading back out to get a bottle of wine for dinner at Aoife's and before collecting her opera gown at the vintage clothing shop.

As soon as he entered his apartment door he got a beep on his mobile phone indicating a text had been received. It was a reply from Ram to the email with attached pic that he had sent him earlier in the morning. He sat down and read the text.

William, what the f mate? How did you score such a beauty? She looks gorgeous and she's a really nice chick from what you say. Mister studly finally wakes up. You lucky man. Hope she comes to Hunterville. See you Tuesday. Ram.

William smiled. He wasn't overly impressed with Ram's choice of words and knew his reply would be a bit crass, but at least he was genuine and honest. William knew that his best friend would be very excited for him. He was very, very excited about introducing Aoife to his parents, and Ram, and everybody else he knew in Hunterville sometime in the near future.

Aoife had dropped by Mercato Pignasecca on the way back to her apartment. She knew how to cook Italian food well and wanted to impress William. She was going to make an antipasto plate of prosciutto with honey roasted figs and pesto stuffed cherry tomatoes, and then for main, a dish of pennoni rigati pasta with cauliflower florets and summer peas and broad beans in a rich cheesy sauce. The cream, yellow and vivid green colours of the main course would be a visual feast for the eyes. Well, that was the plan she was hoping to execute. She had seen all the necessary fresh vegetable ingredients at the market a couple of days ago and was hoping they'd all still be available.

On arriving to the food market and walking up and down the various food stalls, she found everything she required. That brought a smile to her face. Aoife wished she had access to William's jar of Mānuka honey from New Zealand for the roasted figs, but since she didn't, she substituted with a small jar of wildflower honey collected from beehives on the slopes of Mount Vesuvius. She was sure that William would be impressed with the significance of that.

After she had left the market and gone a short distance towards home, she suddenly felt a little bit guilty. She knew William had an untamed sweet tooth and loved to finish off any meal with something sweet. Wanting the evening meal to be as special as she could make it, Aoife headed back to the market and looked around but was unable to find anything suitable. Then she recalled that the café they had enjoyed before heading up the funicular railway was only one hundred metres up past the market. She headed up there and the lady behind the counter remembered her.

"Do you have any of those small custard cream filled profiterole pastries left?"

"*Si signora*, what flavour would you like? We have chocolate, vanilla, amaretto or lemon."

"Two chocolate and two vanilla please."

Mission accomplished. She had all the provisions she required and headed back to her apartment. None of it was difficult, but there was quite a lot to do for the dinner preparation. After she arrived back home she immediately showered, tidied the apartment and sat down with a glass of cold water to go over her food preparation and cooking plan.

William looked at his phone and it was showing 3 pm. It was time to go and collect Aoife's opera gown. The vintage clothing shop was only a few minutes away from his apartment so before collecting her gown he'd still have time on the way there to stop and get a bottle of wine from a small boutique wine store just fifty metres along from his apartment. He entered the wine shop and was confronted with wall-to-wall bottles of wine.

"*Buona pomeriggio signore*. I'm going to a very special dinner tonight so I need a very special wine but I only want an Italian wine. Do you have any suggestions?"

"Have you tried Franciacorta?"

"No. What is Franciacorta?"

"It's Italian champagne made by the traditional method. This comes from the Lombardia region. It's usually forty euro's but last few bottles and I want to clear stock so it's on special for twenty euros."

"Sounds perfect sir. Can I have a bottle please?"

William walked out of the wine shop happy with his purchase. A few minutes later he arrived to the vintage clothing shop.

"Good afternoon William."

"*Buona pomeriggio signora.*"

"I was expecting you. We repaired the satin gown for your wife this morning. It's in the bag together with the black shoes and black shawl."

"Thank you. Thank you."

"Before you go I have one more thing for you. Remember I said this gown belonged to Madam Ricci. Well, I have something to tell you. She was my aunt. I am a widow and I will never be able to go to the opera. I wish I could."

William was sorry to hear that because he could see the pain and disappointment on the shop owner's face. He felt sad that the shop owner's dream would not be fulfilled. She continued.

"I know your wife will look beautiful in the gown. I want to loan you this jewellery for your wife to wear with the gown if you promise to return it to me on Saturday morning. It was Madam Ricci's jewellery and is a family treasure. I know you are an honest man and will make sure it's returned to me. But there's one request I have of you."

William listened intently noting that the word 'wife' was mentioned. If only he thought to himself.

"I will loan your wife the jewellery unconditionally of course, but could you please take some photos of her wearing my auntie's gown, and especially anything to do with your night at the opera? That would make me the happiest *signora* in Naples."

William was moved and as long as Aoife didn't mind wearing the jewellery and having some photos taken, he would make sure the shop keeper lady got her treasured jewellery back on Saturday morning together with a few photos of their night at the opera.

"Are you sure you want to have this jewellery going out of the shop? It looks very expensive. It seems too kind. It seems very trusting."

"Yes, I'm sure. The jewellery needs to be worn and not left just sitting in the safe."

William could see the anticipation and excitement on the lady's face. He was nervous but accepted the loan of the jewellery. He exited the shop, waved goodbye and made his way back to his apartment grasping the bag tightly. Very tightly. It was quite a responsibility to look after somebody's family jewels especially when you had no idea of their true worth. The fact that they were kept in a safe suggested they were valuable. Not knowing their actual worth was probably a good thing he thought to himself. William couldn't wait to tell Aoife what had transpired and was hopeful that she'd be on board with the plan. However, if she gave any indication that she wasn't, he would not pressure her under any circumstance.

William arrived back to his apartment, put Aoife's gown and accessories in a drawer of the dresser in the loft bedroom, sat down at the dining table and pulled a cold beer out of the fridge.

It was almost 4 pm and he was expected at Aoife's at around 5 pm. The only remaining thing to do was to get Aoife some flowers on the way to hers. He wished he had asked her what her favourite flower was, but in the absence of that information, he decided to try and get a small bouquet of green, white and red coloured flowers in memory of their fantastic time together in Naples. He wasn't sure if Aoife would recognise the bouquet as the tricolours of Italy but he sensed she probably would.

Aoife had spent the afternoon back at her apartment getting everything prepared for dinner. It was a lot more work than she had anticipated, but for William, the effort was worth it. Stuffing the cherry tomatoes with pesto and roasting them off had been a fiddly job but everything else was pre-prepared and just needed cooking which she'd do once William was there and they were ready to eat.

At 5 pm precisely, Aoife's phone beeped and there was a text from William informing her that he was at the front of her apartment building. She immediately went downstairs to let him in.

"These are for you Aoife."

She hugged and kissed him and looked at the flowers for a few seconds before she clicked.

"I can see the tricolours of Italy. Nice gesture. Thank you William."

William was impressed that she had figured the significance of the bouquet of flowers so quickly.

She led William upstairs and they entered her apartment. It was the first time he had been inside her apartment since they had first met. It was noticeably smaller than his apartment and everything was on the one level but it was neat and tidy. The balcony was more private than his in that it looked out onto a quiet laneway. Directly opposite was a warehouse type of building without any windows. Privacy walls separated Aoife's balcony from those to the left and right.

"Something smells good. Here's a bottle of wine to celebrate our time in Naples and the journey ahead. It's Franciacorta which according to the wine shop owner is Italian champagne. No idea if it's any good but definitely worth trying. Not that I'm an expert in champagne tasting."

"Thanks William. It should be good. It feels nice and cold. Shall I open now and we can have a glass with the antipasto plate I've made? Just let me roast the figs off for five or ten minutes and then it will be ready. We can take it out and sit on the balcony."

"How about I'll pour the champagne when you tell me it's time, and you can deal with the antipasto."

"That will work. Thanks."

Ten minutes later Aoife's antipasto plate was ready, William had poured them a glass each of the Franciacorta, and they went out and sat at the small table on the balcony.

"*Salute* Aoife, this is turning out to be the best day ever. After our talk this morning I'm feeling so happy and so excited. Plus I've got some news to tell you about the opera gown."

"Good news I hope? Please tell me it's ready and you collected it."

"Yes, I've got it and the shoes and shawl, but there are a couple of other developments."

Aoife had no idea what William was talking about when he said 'other developments' but she was definitely intrigued.

"Let's have some antipasto first and then you can tell me."

Aoife served William a plate of her antipasto which looked stunningly delicious. William was impressed with everything on the antipasto plate but especially the pesto stuffed cherry tomatoes. He had never come across those before.

"I wished I had access to some of your Mānuka honey to drizzle over the figs but I managed to find an artisan honey from the market that was collected from beehives on the slopes of Mount Vesuvius. I thought that would be a meaningful alternative."

"Wow, that's awesome Aoife. It's such a nice thought and such a powerful memory." He leaned forward over the table and kissed her.

"I haven't had a lot of champagne William but this is really nice and matches the figs and cherry tomatoes really well. It tastes crisp and clean and dry and it's not too sweet."

Curiosity was starting to get the better of Aoife.

"So what happened when you went and collected the opera gown? Don't ask me to guess because I've got no idea."

"Oh yes, the vintage clothing shop. Hold on to your chair tightly. Are you ready? Well, it turns out that the lady who owns the vintage clothing shop is actually the niece of Madam Ricci. Remember that's the lady that originally owned your gown."

"That is a surprise. I wasn't expecting that."

"No wait, there's more. The shop owner was left some valuable jewellery by her aunt. She has loaned it to you for tomorrow night and asks if you'd wear it with the gown when you go to the opera. She said you will look like a movie star. Although it is her dream to go to the opera herself, she thinks she'll never have the chance and just wants you to have a very special night instead. And finally she asked if we could take some pics of our night and the opera in memory of her aunty. I did tell her that only if you wanted to and that it was solely your decision. She was good with that. I was very hesitant to take the jewellery because they look very expensive and valuable. But I can't think of anybody that could do them justice other than you. I promised her I'd return the jewellery back to her at the shop on Saturday morning."

"That sounds like something you'd read in a Bronte sister's novel. It's a bit sad really. She wants to have a night at the opera but thinks she'll never have the chance so wants to live it through somebody else. Do you think I should?"

"I don't want to say Aoife. It has to be your decision."

"I'll do it. Definitely. If it's going to make her happy I'll do it."

"Nice and wait until you see the jewellery. I think you'll be very surprised."

William continued to enjoy the antipasto plate. He was very impressed. It's going to be hard going back to more simple everyday type of meals when I get back to the farm he thought to himself.

"That's a ten out of ten Aoife. Take a bow. It was totally delicious."

"I've got everything prepared for the main, but let's wait twenty minutes before I do the finally cooking and bring it all together. Can your stomach wait another twenty minutes?"

William smiled at Aoife.

"I think it can survive but only just."

This time they both laughed. Aoife excused herself to go and prepare the main course while William went over to his backpack and took out his iPod and portable speaker.

"Do you mind if I put some music on? It's nice to have a bit of mood music for dinner. And there's a special song I want to play for you later. It expresses how I'm feeling today."

"Sounds good. Five more minutes and main will be ready. You go sit on the balcony and I'll bring it out."

William put on his playlist of mood music and then went back to sit out on the balcony. Aoife arrived soon after with her rustic pasta dish.

"Smells so good and looks so appetising and healthy. Yum."

"Thanks William. *Salute*."

Their refilled glasses of Franciacorta gently kissed and made a faint clinking noise, and then William tried the first mouthful of the main course.

"You said I can cook, but this is way up there also. It's so delicious. Could easily be the best meal I've had in Naples."

"Best equal, William. Yours was delicious also."

How could the night get any better? It would.

Dinner was over and William was feeling as contented as any man could feel given how the day had unfolded. It was a day full of positives and he was convinced that he had finally found what was missing in his life.

They sat out on the balcony listening to William's mood music as the sun finally set and darkness descended on the laneway. There was a gentle breeze which made the warm evening seem pleasant even at 8 pm.

"I wonder if it ever rains in Naples in the summertime? We've been here nearly two weeks and there hasn't been a drop of rain."

"I think it's like this for a couple of months at least. Dinner's not quite over yet William. I didn't make them, but I got us some custard filled pastries to go with coffee. I got them from that bakery up by the funicular railway station. Have you got room?"

"Think I could squeeze a couple down, but seriously, when I get back home and the body clock has adjusted back to kiwi time I'm going to have to get back into training and get active on the farm. I think I might have gained a bit of weight."

Aoife just smiled for she couldn't see an ounce of weight gain on her fine physical specimen of a man from Hunterville when they showered together twelve hours previously.

She excused herself and went to the kitchen to get dessert and to put the coffee pot on the stove. Less than five minutes later she was back. Aoife and William sat out on the balcony enjoying their dessert and coffee while recalling all the wonderful things they had done together since that first face-to-face meeting at Nonna Russo's Cooking Class.

"What would you like to do tomorrow morning Aoife? You decide. We've got the opera in the evening. That starts at 8 pm and they recommend being seated by 7.30 pm so we don't have to leave the apartment for the opera house until 6.30 pm latest."

"One thing I'd like to do and since it's a weekday, it might be less crowded."

"A morning café visit?"

"Yes that as well, but mainly I'd like to go to the waterfront for another swim. I loved it when we went on Sunday. And it will probably be a long time before I'll swim in the sea again. What do you think?"

"Loving it. Let's do that. We'll do a café visit on the way to waterfront. Sunbath again on the rocks and then swim in the sea, and I can also show you the opera house on the way to the waterfront. There's little chance of me swimming in the sea when I get back home because it's still the tail end of winter."

William was pleased that they had a plan of activities organised for Friday since it would probably be their last full day as tourists in Naples. He then looked Aoife directly in the eyes and the tone of his voice became more serious. Aoife could sense that.

"Do you remember that first coffee we had together as friends at Piazza Bellini?"

"Yes I do."

"I think I've already mentioned that I came to Naples because I knew I was lost. I was a happy man, but a man with a lost soul if that makes any sense at all. Then after being in Naples for just two days I met you. You instantly left me breathless with you physical beauty and quickly made me feel wanted with your appreciation and support. There were no conditions attached for your affection. You help me overcome my personal insecurities. I call them my demons. And over the past week it's been nothing but 24/7 sincerity, honesty and love directed from you to me. I wish I could find the right words to say and tell you how I feel more eloquently than what I've just said. Please listen to this song carefully. Every word has meaning and significance to me."

William went over to his iPod and searched the menu for his special song for Aoife. He pressed play and the music came through loud and clear on his portable speaker. Aoife listened intently to William's song choice. It was Bryan Adams singing 'I Finally Found Someone'. They held hands and not another word was spoken between them as the song was played from start to finish. William could see that Aoife was concentrating and listening intently to the words of the song as she smiled at William. By the end of the song both Aoife and William were in tears. William composed himself as best he could and wiped the tears trickling down his cheeks on the sleeves of his shirt.

"Aoife, please tell me that me that my search is over. Please tell me that you feel the same about me as I feel about you. Please don't make me wait too long after we separate on Sunday because that would destroy me mentally and emotionally. The separation will be unbearable until I see you again. Don't let me get lost again. I need you and I love you. I'm sorry about all the tears. Does that make me seem weak?"

"Don't you understand William, tears don't make you bad or weak, they make you appear strong. They make you a real man who's in touch with his real emotions."

Aoife knew that William was very venerable right there and then and summed up all her inner strength to reply to William and reassure him that she was totally addicted to him. She loved him dearly.

"William you've done so many nice things for me over the past week. I thought I was damaged goods but you restored my faith in everything. You picked up the pieces and put them back together so they are better than they were before. I've had more happiness in the past few days than I've had in the past few years. Your respect, kindness and love towards me leave me speechless. Your kindness is a beautiful thing."

William acknowledged her reassuring reply to him with his trademark smile. He went over and touched replay, and his song which was now their song, played again as they walked hand in hand to the bedroom to show their true love for each other.

Friday Night at the Opera

It was Friday the 12th July and only two more days before they'd head to Naples Airport for their flights back home.

Aoife woke first, sneaked out of bed and into the kitchen to put a pot of coffee on the stove. When she returned to the bedroom William was still asleep. She smiled and went around to his side of the bed, sat down gently and stared at this man from New Zealand who had captured her heart in his steely grip. She bent forward and pecked him on the cheek. That was enough to stir him.

"Morning, what time is it?"

"It's 8 am. I've just put some coffee on."

"Seriously? I never sleep until 8 am. I hope I'm not getting too used to it. What time do you want to go for a café visit?"

"The usual. 10 am is good."

"I'd like to swing back by my apartment first to get a few things before we head down to the waterfront. Is that OK?"

"Of course and maybe I can take a peek at the jewellery I'll be wearing to the opera tonight. Can't deny that I'm excited to see what the lady has loaned us."

"Let's leave here around 9 am, go over to my apartment, check out the jewellery, get my board shorts and sunscreen, towels and shades, and then we can head out to a café."

With the morning's plan sorted, William and Aoife took their coffee and some pastries out to the balcony. Initially they didn't say anything and just sat enjoying the stillness of the warm morning air as they sipped their coffee.

"Forty eight hours from now we'll be heading to the airport. I'm starting to get nervous Aoife but I'll try not to think about it today. Instead I'll just make today a day to remember for both of us."

"It will be special. Just like every other day for the past week. I'm basically ready so if you want to go now."

"Yep, let's go."

William and Aoife walked hand in hand the short distance from her apartment to his apartment. They entered William's apartment and he quickly pulled together his sunbathing and swimming requirements and put them on the kitchen table.

"Hang on a minute and I'll get the jewellery for the opera from upstairs."

He came back down from the loft in less than a minute and unwrapped the black velvet pouch the vintage shop owner had given him. Aoife looked at the contents and seemed amazed.

"They look like diamonds but surely they can't be diamonds? It must be some sort of high end costume jewellery. Nobody would loan out a diamond necklace and earrings to basically what are a couple of strangers. Who would do that and why would a person do that?"

"Hang on a minute I know a way to test if they're diamond."

William got a drinking glass from the kitchen and brought it over to the table. He gently scratched one of the gems in the necklace against the glass and it cut deeply into the glass. He looked at Aoife and gave her the surprising verdict.

"I'm 100 percent sure that they are definitely diamonds. Diamonds are harder than silica which glass is made from. And the diamonds in the necklace have a made a deep mark into the glass. Crikey. Now I'm even more nervous about the security of them than I was carrying them home."

"I can't believe it William. This is crazy. They must be worth tens of thousands of dollars. I wonder if our going to the opera for a night is a substitute for her thinking that she'll never have the chance. That's really quite sad. It doesn't seem fair."

"If the timing was different and it was easy to get tickets, I'd gladly give up an evening and take her to the opera. If it resulted in extreme happiness for somebody, especially an elderly person, why wouldn't you do it?"

That was exactly the type of response Aoife would expect from William and was the reason why she wanted to spend the rest of her life with this man from Hunterville. Her only hope was that in the journey ahead, she would be able to give as much to him, as he would undoubtedly give to her.

"Let's go and embrace the night. I'll wear the jewellery and we'll take lots of photos to make it a night to remember for us, and a night to remember for her."

"Let's do it. We're going to the opera. One thing though. There's no way we're walking there for obvious reasons, and now I'm also nervous about using a taxi. The owner of this apartment said to call her if I wanted to be driven anywhere special since her son is trying to earn a bit of extra money for his university costs. It's a bit short notice but I'll call her now and ask if he might be free tonight."

William went over and sat on the lounge chair and called the apartment owner. She answered immediately. He explained the situation to her and apologised for the short notice. He mentioned pickup from the apartment at 6.30 pm going to the San Carlo Opera House and pickup from the opera house going back home at 10.30 pm, and he also enquired if her son could take them to the airport at 9 am on Sunday morning.

"She said yes to all those requests. It's sorted. There is a plan. Her son's name is Carlo, he would be driving a silver Toyota and she gave me the car licence plate number. The god's are smiling on us Aoife."

With the plan for transportation to and from the opera all sorted, and a decision made regarding the jewellery, William and Aoife left the apartment, checking twice to make sure that it was securely locked. They headed down Via Toledo towards the waterfront.

"I'm ready for a café visit William."

"Me too. You know this is our penultimate Naples café visit. I'm just saying. We'll have to make tomorrow's café visit something special."

"What do you mean by something special? You're not having a plate of sweet treats to yourself Mister William from New Zealand."

They both laughed as they continued walking down Via Toledo. The time was just after 10 am and it was already 25 degrees C and brilliantly sunny. It was a perfect day for sunbathing and a swim. Walking down to the waterfront was a route they'd taken a few days earlier so everything was familiar. Just before they reached the large Piazza del Plebiscito area and the Royal Palace of Naples across the street from it, there was a major traffic roundabout with a central fountain.

"Look over there to the left Aoife. See that dark grey stone building with the white stone columns and arched windows above? Well, that's the San Carlo Opera House."

"It looks grand. Something tells me that it's going to be spectacular inside."

"I won't give any clues away other than it was opened in 1737 and it is the oldest continuously running opera house in the world. How impressive is that?"

"I'm so excited about going to the opera. Look, over there just along from the opera house I can see a café. Shall we try there?"

"Yep, let's go there."

William and Aoife spent forty minutes at the café enjoying a cappuccino and their usual plate of assorted sweet treats. Aoife gave her assessment of the café to William as they got up and left.

"Not the best one we've been to but still pretty good. I'm ready for a bit of sun and a swim."

Ten minutes after exiting the café they were down at the yacht club marina and boulder bank area near Castle dell'Ovo. It wasn't as busy as the previous Sunday but it was still busy.

They guessed that in a city of over three million people there were still many with the day off, and as the air was warm and the sun was shining brilliantly, it was a recipe for many citizens to go to the boulder bank area to enjoy *'la bella vita'*.

Although it was only five days since their last visit to the waterfront area, their relationship had progressed in leaps and bounds. They were now a seriously committed couple.

"That same boulder bank spot we went to last Sunday is vacant. Shall we go there again? It was good last time."

Aoife didn't wait for William's reply because she was very keen to grab a spot that wasn't too busy and to claim their territory. William was happy to follow Aoife to the exact same spot they had been to on Sunday. As per their Sunday visit, there were many scantily clad Neapolitans of every conceivable shape and size soaking up the full rays of the sun. Most were moderately to deeply sun tanned.

William discretely changed from his jeans to his board shorts with towel wrapped around his waist. Aoife laughed to herself thinking that the masses probably wouldn't even bat an eyelid if his towel happened to slip down or fall off since everybody was too busy worshipping the sun god.

"I don't want to get too carried away in the sunshine. I don't mind a little bit of vitamin D for good health, but I'm not going to get fried. Can you rub some of my sunscreen on my back please?"

"Of course William and it's same for me. One hour lying in the full sun is my absolute limit after you have helped me do a slip, slop, slap."

Once they were both suitably protected against the sun's most harmful rays, they laid their towels down on the rocks and stretched out for an hour of sunshine therapy. Both agreed that the sun's rays were warming and relaxing, the setting was beautiful and the waterfront atmosphere addictive.

"Please let me know when one hour is up William. I don't mind a light tan but I don't want any more than that."

"Will do. I'm the same. I don't want to get burnt and I'm not looking to be a bronzed god."

The hour passed without incident as they both half snoozed and half chatted as they lay on the rocks.

"Hour's up, Aoife. I don't want to do any more lizarding. It's swim time."

William was first in the water but Aoife was close behind him. With her confidence flying high from Sunday's swim, she was more adventurous this time and swam further out from the rocks. She noted that William remained close by and was guarding and protecting her just in case. As was the case for their Sunday sea swim, he disappeared under the surface of the water for a good ten seconds and resurfaced right in front of her. He took a deep breath and then while supporting her as he tread water, he planted a long lingering kiss on her lips. Both were in happy land and they were oblivious of all the 'lizards' sunning on the rocks.

They continued playing in the sea for another twenty minutes and then made their way back to their spot on the rocks.

Aoife did a quick, sly check of William from the rare as he dried off. She convinced herself that he had not gained a single ounce of weight from all the eating and drinking they had done over the past ten days. In her eyes he remained a fine physical specimen of a man.

"It's 2 pm. That was magic. Sun and sea, all that's missing is the sand. I feel great. I feel so alive. Shall we go back and have an afternoon siesta in preparation for tonight?" asked William.

Aoife agreed that their repeat visit to the waterfront had been perfect. She was also feeling alive and well. They dried off, dressed, packed their belongings and left the boulder bank and waterfront area. Half an hour later they were back in William's apartment.

"Let's have a rest upstairs for a couple of hours and then start getting ready for the opera. You'd better set the alarm on your phone for 4 pm William and I'll do the same. I'm feeling very sleepy and I don't trust myself to be awake at 4 pm."

"Will do."

It was just as well that William had set his phone alarm clock because both of them were still fast asleep at 4 pm as a result of all the salty sea air and abundant sunshine they had been exposed to a few hours earlier.

"Pickup car will be here at 6.30 pm so we've still got a couple of hours to get ready. That's plenty of time for me to shave, shower and smarten up. Will it be enough time for you?"

"Not really. I'm joking. It's plenty of time for me William."

"You first or me first to shower?"

"You go first and I'll lay out my satin gown and the jewellery on the bed and sort out what makeup I'm going to wear. Girl stuff. "

William stripped and went downstairs butt naked. First thing he did was to put the aircon in the lounge area on since it was starting to get very stuffy in the apartment. He shaved, showered, wrapped a towel around his waist and then got himself a cold beer from the fridge. He laid out his opera clothes on a chair next to the sofa. He sat on a chair and sipped his cold beer.

"Everything OK up there Aoife? Need anything? Bathroom's free now."

"All good William. I've got it all sorted now. I won't get dressed for the opera yet. I'll leave that until 6 pm."

"I'll do the same. We can check over the balcony to see if and when the pickup car arrives. It's a silver Toyota."

Aoife came down from the loft and joined William on the sofa.

"I don't get dressed up very often but kind of enjoy it when I do."

"I'm the same," replied Aoife "but I'm very excited about tonight for lots of reasons. First time going to an opera, I'm wearing some fabulous jewellery and a nice gown, we're going to take photos to make somebody's life better, but most of all, because I'm going with you."

"Thank you. Appreciate that."

Aoife went to the bathroom and showered. She came back to the lounge with towel wrapped around her sarong style.

"How long is the opera performance? I've got no idea."

"The one we're going to tonight is *Cavalleria Rusticana*, or in English, Rustic Chivalry. As far as operas go it's actually a very short one. It's only seventy five minutes and one act. Most operas are two or three acts long. The write up says it's an extremely emotional and passionate story and the music is outstanding. I'm sure it will all be in Italian so not sure how we'll handle that."

"Can't wait. Have we got good seats?"

"When I booked them, the ticketing lady said they were side centre box seats three levels up so I'm guessing they'll be pretty good. Not the best in the house and definitely not the worst in the house."

"It is 6 pm yet?"

"Just gone 6 pm Aoife. Is it time to put our glad rags on?"

"Yep, now's good. I'll get dressed upstairs and you get dressed down here."

Ten minutes later William was all ready and went to check in the bathroom mirror. Not too bad he thought to himself, definitely presentable enough for a night at the opera. He especially admired the combination of his vintage black jacket and waistcoat with his white shirt and black bow tie. While he was in the bathroom he rubbed some of his favourite sandalwood oil on his neck.

"I'm ready Aoife. Do you need any help?"

"No I'm good thanks, just give me another five minutes or so and I'll come down."

William remained downstairs and checked that he had the opera tickets, some cash for the driver, his credit card and that his mobile phone was fully charged. He would need a fully charged phone to take photos for the lady at the vintage clothing shop.

William was busy at the kitchen table when he heard Aoife coming down the stairs from the loft. He went over towards the stairs and was greeted by a vision of beauty that was nothing short of sensational. He choked up to the point of being unable to talk for a few seconds.

After he regained his composure, he flashed a beaming smile towards her and spoke.

"Aoife, wow you look spectacular. The lady in the vintage shop was right. The diamond jewellery makes you look like a movie star. And I'm the lucky man taking you to the opera very soon. Something tells me that I could be the luckiest and happiest man in Naples tonight."

"Thanks William. You look pretty smart yourself. I wouldn't want anybody else but you taking me."

Aoife was wearing more makeup than usual but still not a lot, and it accentuated her natural beauty. The black satin gown was a perfect fit and the high heel shoes elevated her to the same height as William. She wore her hair up such that the magnificent diamond necklace and earrings sparkled seductively against her fair skin. William also noted that she was wearing perfume and it smelt really nice. That heightened his level of emotional arousal. He felt very proud of the beautiful woman standing in front of him and walked over to her and planted a very gentle kiss on her lips.

"Opera here we come. I'll check from the balcony and see if the pickup car has arrived yet."

William opened the balcony door and peered over and down to the street below. Yes, there was a car waiting and it appeared to be a silver Toyota.

"Let's go down and I'll just check it's the right guy before you come out the apartment building door. I'm pretty sure it is though. Is that OK?"

"Yes, let's go."

William went over to the passenger door and spoke to the driver while Aoife waited just inside the door.

"Hello, what's your name?"

"Hello sir, I'm Carlo. Are you Mister William going to the San Carlo Opera House?"

"Yes I am."

William quickly double checked the car's registration and it was correct. "Please wait just a minute. I have a friend coming to the opera with me."

Aoife exited the apartment building and William shut the entrance door behind. They hopped into the back seat of the car.

"Thanks for taking us Carlo. Will you be able to pick us up at the pizzeria across the street from the opera house at 10.30 pm? We are going to have something to eat after the opera finishes. I'm sorry it's a bit late."

Carlo turned around to address to William and Aoife.

"*Che bella. Che bello.* Mister William you both look very nice. I'm very happy to be your driver. I hope the opera will be good for you. I have never been to that famous opera house but one day I will. Yes, I will pick you up at 10.30 pm at the pizzeria. Here is my mobile number in case any problems."

Aoife spoke next.

"Thank you Carlo for your kind words. We are both very excited to be going to the opera."

Carlo started driving but due to the very busy Friday night traffic in the central city area, they didn't reach the opera house until close on 7 pm even though they could walk the distance on foot in around fifteen minutes. Before they got out of the car William asked Carlos if he wanted to be paid there and then, or later when they had arrived back to the apartment.

Carlo confirmed that later would be best. William exited the car first and helped Aoife out. As she exited she said a goodbye to Carlo.

"We will see you later. *Ciao Carlo.*"

Carlo drove off waving enthusiastically to them both while William looked around to try and figure out the protocol for a night at the opera. He sensed that there were many eyes looking at them and felt both shy and proud. He realised that being with Aoife tonight was bound to attract glances and stares, but he was looking for somewhere less in the open for the next half hour.

"It's still thirty minutes before the doors open for audience seating. There's a wine bar right next door shall we try and have a drink there first? I'm not sure if we'll be able to get a seat though. It looks really busy."

Aoife was happy to just go along with whatever William thought was best since it was his determination that had secured the tickets.

"Sounds good. Let's have a glass of Franciacorta to celebrate."

They walked the short distance to the wine bar adjacent to the opera house and were greeted by an impeccably dressed waiter who initially stared at Aoife, but then finally addressed William.

"*Buona sera signore. Buona sera signora. Prego entra. Vai all'opera?*"

"Good evening sir. Yes, we are going to the opera. It's our first time. We only want a celebration drink before we go in and sit down. Is that possible? You look very busy."

Possibly as a result of William's trademark beaming smile as he spoke, but more likely as a result of Aoife's simply stunning beauty, the waiter confirmed that he would find them seating for two.

There was no doubt that everybody in the wine bar at that moment, was bedazzled with the vision of loveliness that had walked in and over to a table in the faraway corner.

"Where do you come from?" asked the waiter.

"I am from New Zealand and Aoife is from Ireland. We have been in Naples for almost two weeks. Naples is beautiful and has given us a gift that you cannot buy. Love and happiness."

The waiter smiled and went over to the bar area. William could see him talking to several people at and behind the bar including a handsome middle aged man who appeared to be watching over the wine bar with an eagle eye. William thought he might be the manager or even the owner. The waiter returned with two glasses of Franciacorta.

"Sir these drinks are compliments from the owner over there. He thanks you for your kind words about Napoli and wishes you a good night at the opera."

William stood up and bowed in gratitude and mouthed 'thank you' towards the owner, while Aoife made a love heart with her hands and directed it towards the owner. The owner smiled and waved back at them both.

Aoife and William sat and sipped their drinks both agreeing that Italian champagne was the perfect drink as a precursor to the opera. After they had finished their drinks, and just before they were about to get up and leave, William suddenly remembered that they were meant to be capturing some photographs of the evening for the vintage clothing shop owner. He beckoned the waiter back over and asked if he could take a few photos of them for their family and friends. He obliged with pleasure.

Upon leaving, William confirmed with the waiter once more that no payment was required. The waiter was adamant that it wasn't and wished them a great night at the opera. It was 7.30 pm and time for Aoife and William to take their seats in the opera house. Many eyes in the wine bar tracked their exit for obvious reasons.

William and Aoife walked the very short distance to the opera house entrance. Although the outside of the opera house was described as ordinary in the travel guides there was nothing ordinary about the inside. It had the wow factor and then some more as it exceeded all their expectations. They gazed at towering internal ceilings, marble floors, sweeping staircases leading to the upper floors, dazzling chandeliers, and exquisite wall murals.

With the help of the ushers, they made their way to their allocated box seats on the centre left hand side at the third level. On the way there, William asked a lady usher if they were allowed to take photos. The usher replied yes as long as it was done discretely, but definitely not once the performance began, or at any time during the performance. William got to work and took numerous photos of the internal surroundings and décor of the opera house, and of Aoife wearing Madam Ricci's black satin gown with the beautiful diamond necklace and earrings her niece had loaned them. He agreed to have a few photos taken of himself, but it was with some reluctance, since he didn't consider himself photogenic or photo-worthy. As they entered their seating box on the third level, a visual feast confronted them as they looked out into the auditorium.

"William look how beautiful it is."

William smiled back as they gazed out at the horseshoe shaped auditorium with its ground floor seating area surrounded by levels of seating boxes around the outside. They admired the plush red velvet seats, the elaborate gilded royal boxes, the exquisite central ceiling fresco which depicted Apollo showing Minerva the greatest poets of the world, and the ornate banisters at each seating level.

"From the outside you'd never know how breath-taking and beautiful it was on the inside. I'd be happy going to the opera just to see this, never mind an actual operatic performance."

Aoife agreed. They took their seats and readied themselves for the performance to begin. Having taken a good look around at the seated audience, William was sure in his mind that Aoife was 'the belle of the ball'. He was both humbled and proud that he was the man of choice accompanying Aoife to the opera that night.

It was a long, long way from the farm in Hunterville, and a long way from the pub in Galway, but William and Aoife embraced the formality of the evening and were excited as the red velvet curtain lifted exactly at 8 pm and the performance began.

For the next seventy five minutes they watched and listened. Since it was all in Italian, they understood very little of the dialogue and arias but this didn't detract from their enjoyment of the overall experience. When it ended there was an encore followed by another encore. It was clear the audience wanted more.

"I remember reading that because this opera is considered a short one, it is usually performed together with another short opera. I guess that's why the audience wants more. But I'm satisfied, happy and ecstatic I made the effort to get tickets."

Aoife agreed and said for her first opera experience it had been something she would always remember for lots of reasons. They exited the opera house which took a good twenty minutes.

"I don't usually eat so late at night, in fact I never do, but when in Naples do as the Neapolitans do? Are you still OK with having a bite to eat at the pizzeria across the street before we head back? I asked Carlo to pick us up at 10.30 pm which still gives us an hour yet."

Aoife thought it was a great idea. Something they hadn't done, but something they should do. They made their way across the street with William staying very close to Aoife's side in consideration of her precious jewellery. They made it to the pizzeria just in time to avoid the post opera rush. The waiter, who seemed to be fixated on Aoife, led them to a two person table inside and near the front.

"It seems strange eating out so late at night. Can't remember when I've ever ordered a meal at 9.30 pm. But it shouldn't be a problem since we don't have a lot to do tomorrow so maybe a sleep-in is on the cards."

"We can do that," replied Aoife "what shall we order? Will a large Neapolitan pizza and a shared side salad do?"

"Sounds good. I'm not super hungry but would like something."

Aoife and William seemed very over dressed for the pizzeria but since other formally dressed people arrived soon after them, they assumed the staff would all understand that they had just been to a performance in the opera house across the street. Aoife continued to get side glances and stares while they dined at the pizzeria.

They enjoyed the pizza, the Mediterranean side salad and their quartino of white wine. It was 10.30 pm and since William didn't want Aoife to be waiting out on the street with all the expensive jewellery at that time of night, he went outside and had a quick look to see if Carlo had arrived. He saw Carlo so went back inside, paid the bill and escorted Aoife out to Carlo's vehicle.

"*Buona sera signore e signora.* How was the opera?"

"*Molto bene Carlo. Molto bene.* The opera house is beautiful inside. I hope you get the chance to go one day."

"Thank you. I will try. Shall I take you back to the apartment now?"

"*Si, grazie*" replied William.

The traffic was lighter at 10.30 pm so it was only a ten minute drive back to the apartment. William paid Carlo in cash and thanked him for his very reliable and friendly service. He confirmed with Carlo that they'd see him again on Sunday morning at 9 am to take them to the airport. They bid Carlo goodnight and William and Aoife disappeared into the apartment building.

Once they were inside William's apartment they kissed and cuddled. Both agreed that going to the opera had been the perfect end to a perfect day. It was an evening neither of them would forget for a long, long time. It must have been the salty sea air and sunshine from earlier in the day, combined with the champagne and wine, but sleep was the only thing on their mind. They walked upstairs hand in hand, stripped and slipped into bed before falling asleep very quickly in each other's arms.

William and Aoife's last full day in Naples had arrived.

It was 8 am on Saturday 13th July and William and Aoife hadn't yet stirred after their big day out the previous day. They were both still sleeping soundly.

It was only ten days ago that they had met at Nonna Russo's cooking class as total strangers. Now they were a totally committed couple who had expressed their love and admiration for each other and wished to embark on a unified life journey as soon as possible.

William stirred first, rolled over and looked at his phone. It was showing 8.20 am. He rolled back towards Aoife and nibbled on her ear to which he got an immediate response. She rolled over and pecked him on the forehead.

"Aoife, it's nearly 8.30 am. How are you feeling this morning?"

"Morning William. I'm happy, sad, nervous, anxious, thankful, excited, blessed. You name it and I'm feeling it. This is going to be a big day for us."

"I know, but don't worry we'll work thorough it as the day progresses and discuss the forward plan until we're both happy with it. Are you OK with that?"

"Yes. Let's get up, have a coffee and just check again what we have to do today and how we're going to organise tomorrow morning."

Aoife picked up a long t shirt of William's from the dresser and flung it over her nakedness while William simply went downstairs letting it all hang out and put the moka coffee pot on the stove. While the coffee pot was boiling he went into the bathroom to gargle and brush his teeth and came back out with a towel wrapped around his waist. Now that he was more modestly dressed, he went over and flung open the balcony doors to let some fresh morning air into the apartment. It was another typical mid-July summer's day in Naples. Not a cloud in the sky and the temperature was rising. They sat down at the kitchen table with hot coffee and went over the day's activities.

"We definitely have to do a last Italian café visit this morning. Maybe we could do that after we have returned the jewellery to the owner of the vintage clothing shop. Seriously, I'll be relieved once we hand it back. I'll get the owner's email address and forward those opera photos to her. Something tells me she's going to love them. Plus I need to give my nonna friend across the street her gift, the signed pic of us on the yacht and I want to write a brief note for her.

That's all I can think of. Anything you'd like to do or anywhere you'd like to go?"

"No that sounds good William. That's already a lot to do. Remember that homestyle takeaway restaurant we went to last week? Let's pass by there again and if they're open on a Saturday morning, get some food for this evening. It will be our final proper meal together before we depart."

"What about tomorrow morning? Are you happy to leave from here together at 9 am which means we'd need to go over to your apartment sometime later this afternoon, tidy up and get your belongings and bring them back here? Is that how you want to do it? Honestly, whatever you want is fine. You say."

"No that's perfect. I just want to hang out this afternoon and evening with you and spend some quiet time together. And of course I'd prefer to go to the airport together in the morning since we've both got departure flights around noon."

"I'm just going to write a note first to nonna across the street."

William got pen, paper and then composed his note on the kitchen table. After ten minutes he told Aoife that it was completed.

"What did you write?"

"I'll read it to you in English. I tried to write it in Italian because I'm sure she doesn't speak English. Hopefully she'll understand my pigeon Italian, but translated, I wrote something this."

Hello nonna, this is William and Aoife in the apartment opposite. Thank you for your friendly waves and smiles from across the street. The home baking was delicious. We enjoyed it. Tomorrow morning at 9 am we leave for airport to return home. Naples is beautiful. I will miss you. I will not forget you. God bless you. Health and happiness always…William.

"That's really nice William. She will love it. I love it."

"I'll put the note together with the yacht photograph we both signed and the boxed gift of wine and olive oil. Now I've got to try and get it to her."

"How are you going to do that?"

"I'm going to get dressed and go out onto the balcony and pray and hope that if we sit there long enough she might come out and wave hello. Then I'll indicate to her with sign speak, to lower her bucket and I'll rush across and put our gifts in her bucket and she can pull it up to her apartment balcony."

"Awesome. I'll get dressed also and sit out there with you."

Aoife and William got dressed and went and sat out on the balcony with another coffee. Five minutes passed, ten minutes passed, fifteen minutes passed and then finally after twenty minutes, nonna appeared. William waved enthusiastically across to her and she waved enthusiastically back. He then indicated to her what he'd like her to do. She seemed to understand really well. Nonna went inside her apartment and came out again a couple of minutes later with her bucket and rope and started lowering the bucket down to street level. William gathered all the items he wanted to give her off the kitchen table, dashed across the street and put the items in her bucket. As she started pulling it back up to her apartment balcony he dashed back and joined Aoife on his apartment balcony.

They waited as nonna read the note, looked at the signed photo and opened the gift box.

"I'm not sure but I think she might be crying William. It looks like she's wiping her eyes. I hope she'll be OK."

Nonna from the apartment balcony across the street then put the bucket down and blew kisses towards them both.

"*Grazie William, grazie, grazie. Sei un uomo gentile,*" she shouted out.

William tried to indicate back to nonna that they had to go up the street to do some errands. She seemed to understand. They went back inside and prepared themselves for their next 'must do' which was to return the jewellery to the owner of the vintage clothing shop.

"Let's return the jewellery first and then go to a café somewhere over that way. How about Piazza Bellini where we had our first coffee together as friends?"

"That sounds really good. You must show the lady some of the opera photos on your phone before you send them to her digitally. I've got a good feeling about this. And then we'll head to Piazza Bellini for our final Italian café visit. That takeaway food shop is up that way so we can stop there on the way back and get something for dinner if it's open."

William and Aoife's morning was progressing well as they headed out of the apartment building onto the street below. It was 10 am and the tourists were just starting to appear in the street. Most of them appeared to be heading towards the Old City area. William checked once more that the precious cargo was safe in his backpack and that all the bag's zips were done up. He wore the backpack on the front of his body as a precaution. The finishing line was in sight and he didn't want any dramas before the jewellery was handed back to its owner.

"The vintage clothing shop opens at 9 am so hopefully she'll be there now since it's nearly 10 am. She told me she'd be there all morning on Saturday."

It was a short walk to the shop and they entered the front door. The shop was empty of customers. Immediately the shop owner came over to them. She was very excited.

William opened the back pack and put the black velvet bag containing the jewellery on the counter. He opened the velvet bag so the owner could see that everything was there and all returned in good condition. He breathed a sigh of relief. He had taken the responsibility of looking after the valuable jewellery very seriously. Aoife spoke first.

"Thank you very much for loaning me the diamond jewellery. I've never worn anything like that before. It was an honour to wear it to the opera. It was also an honour to wear you auntie's formal satin gown. I will never forget our night at the opera. William has some photos to show you before he sends them to you digitally."

William opened the pictures gallery folder on his phone and started showing the photos to the lady. He had only shown her four of the photos when she started dabbing her eyes with a handkerchief. He sensed that she was about to cry. She scanned through the rest of the photos on William's phone. There were thirty in total.

"Thank you very much for doing that. *Signora* you look absolutely beautiful. You look like a movie star. Just as I guessed you would. You look handsome also *signore*. I will treasure these photos. The memory of my auntie will live on thanks to you both. It's like going to the opera with you. I am very happy. *Grazie, grazie.*"

William asked the shop owner if she used any sort of a photo app to which she replied that she did. He got the details from her and confirmed that he'd send to her the complete suite of opera photos when they got back to the apartment. William and Aoife left the shop and the owner came out onto the street to say goodbye to them. She hugged them both very warmly, and stood there waving goodbye until they disappeared around the corner.

"Let's head to Piazza Bellini now. I'm ready for coffee and you know what."

"Yes William I know what." replied Aoife as they laughed, held hands and slowly made their way to the café they had last visited as friends just over a week earlier.

"My check in luggage is getting a bit full and heavy now and although I'd like to buy anything and everything, I supposed I had better try and constrain myself. I've got presents for everybody back in Hunterville. If I see anything 'must have' at the airport duty free I might try and squeeze it into my hand luggage. What about you?"

"I'm the same. I've got presents for everybody that I needed to get something for."

They arrived to the café just after 10.30 am and decided to sit at the same outside table they had last time. Just as they were about to call for a waiter, they were greeted enthusiastically from behind.

"*Buongiorno signore e signora. Che bello rivederti.* How has Naples treated you?"

"*Ciao, grazie.* You remember us? We have had a fantastic time. Everything in Naples is beautiful. Today is our last day. We fly home tomorrow at noon. I'm very sorry but I don't know your name."

"No problem. My name is Giovanni Bianchi."

"I am William and this is Aoife."

"If this is your last café visit in Naples I will try and make it special. What would you like to order?"

"Aoife is going to order for us," said a smiling William knowing full well that she'd make sure his sweet tooth was catered for.

"Giovanni can we please have two large hot cappuccinos and a plate of small Sicilian biscuits and also two of those delicious cannoli. Ricotta with pistachio if you have them, otherwise whatever you recommend is fine."

"*Si signora*. We have all of those things. I will get the order now."

Out of the corner of her eye, Aoife could see that William's eyes had lit up indicating that he was obviously happy with the order she had made.

Giovanni went inside while William and Aoife lovingly held hands and reminisced about the past ten days and all the wonderful things they had done together. They were both very happy. Ten minutes later Giovanni reappeared with a full tray of drinks and eats which he placed on the centre of the table.

"It looks great Giovanni. The prefect way to say goodbye to café culture in Italy. We have loved it. It's a ten out of ten for us."

"*Grazie signore*. When you get home will you be playing rugby again?"

"You remembered. Well, New Zealand is a long way to travel and my body is sure to be tired from the long journey and the change in time zones, so maybe not next Saturday. But yes for sure, the weekend after that. Giovanni, I have been eating and drinking so much in Naples that I'll need to do some serious night-time training first."

Giovanni laughed and said he thought that Mister William would soon get back into peak condition for playing rugby. Aoife didn't say anything, but privately, she totally agreed. She hadn't noted any physical change over the past week.

"Would you like me to take a photo of you and your wife to remember your last café visit in Naples?"

William did note that Giovanni had referred to Aoife as his wife again but he just let it slip. For sure it was what he wanted, but he would deal with that possibility at a later date.

"Good idea to take some photos of us Giovanni, thanks. Can somebody also take a photo of us all with you in the middle? We'd like that."

Giovanni took a few photos of William and Aoife enjoying morning coffee and then called a fellow waiter over to take a photo of the three of them. Once that was finished, he went about dealing with the other customers.

"This is so good Aoife. I'm going to miss it big time. There is a café in Hunterville and it is really good but it's different to the café experience here in Naples. It might take me a week or two to readjust back."

"It's the same in Galway. Good cafés but they are very different to here."

William and Aoife hung out at the café until it was almost 12 noon and until they noticed the lunchtime crowd were starting to arrive. Reluctantly they decided it was time to leave and draw the curtain on their enjoyment of the café culture in Naples. They asked Giovanni for the bill and he returned ten minutes later. They paid the bill and William left a generous tip.

"It's been good meeting you Giovanni. If I can score a try when I start playing rugby in a couple of weeks' time then it's dedicated to you. To remind me of the man in Naples who loved rugby!"

Giovanni was very moved by this expression of friendship from William and embraced him firmly. Just like a brother would. He then hugged Aoife and kissed her respectfully on both cheeks.

"Thank you Mister William. I won't forget you both. I will remember you as the *coppia amichevole* from New Zealand. *Grazie and arrivederci*."

Giovanni stood waving to them both as they disappeared around the corner and back onto the main street.

"How nice was that?" said Aoife to William.

They decided to head back to William's apartment to spend the rest of the afternoon and evening. As they passed by the homestyle takeaway food shop on their way back, Aoife went in and got a selection of dishes for their dinner. Just before they got back to the apartment William went in to the nearby wine shop and got a bottle of dry rosé wine. It would be their last dinner in Naples together and they both wanted it to be a good one.

It was close to 1 pm when they arrived back to the apartment. The morning had gone well and they had ticked off most items on their 'must do' list. They discussed and agreed that they'd head over to Aoife's apartment at 3 pm to do the final clean-up, checkout and bring her belongings back to his apartment. After that they'd have a farewell dinner together and go over the forward plan.

William sent a quick text to Carlo just to confirm that he'd be there at 9 am in the morning to drive them to the airport, and then he went on to his laptop computer and sent the suite of opera photos to the owner of the vintage clothing shop. It wasn't long before they both replied back. Carlo confirmed that he would be there at 9 am, and the vintage shop owner replied back thanking William and Aoife one more time.

The temperature outside was in the mid-'30s and inside the apartment it was getting hot and stuffy. William put the aircon on and told Aoife that he was going up to the loft to have a siesta. Aoife said she'd join him. They spent the next two hours dozing on the bed. By the time they woke up properly it was 4 pm.

"We'd better head across to yours now."

"I agree. Let's go."

Once they had arrived to Aoife's apartment it took them a good hour to do the cleaning and tidy-up, and for Aoife to pack her bags and do a final check to make sure that nothing was left behind. She left the apartment key in the drop box on the way out and they headed back to William's apartment.

"What time shall we eat William? Is 6 pm OK?"

"6 pm is good. Let's just sit down and go over the plan again."

They sat down at the kitchen table to talk and suddenly the atmosphere got a lot more serious.

"You're going to get home a lot quicker than I am Aoife. With the time difference and much longer travel time, it's going to be almost two full days after departure time before I'll finally arrive back to Hunterville. I'm going to be stuffed. Let's make a commitment to video call each other on Wednesday at 8 am Ireland time which will be 8 pm New Zealand time. Promise?"

"I promise William."

"I can't wait until you get to New Zealand. I'll try and be patient Aoife but it's going to be really hard. I'll be waiting for you. This is going to sound really dumb but you do still want to join me. Right?"

"Totally, madly, deeply, so the answer is yes, of course yes."

Aoife's reply made him feel a lot more relaxed. What happened from now on was in the lap of the gods although he would not be happy with them if they kept Aoife away from him in New Zealand.

They went up to the loft and spread all their clothing and presents out on either side of the bed. They packed their bags and separately laid out what they'd be wearing in the morning for the trip home.

"Shall we eat soon?"

"I've finished packing so I'll head downstairs and set the table. Put some music on. Pour a glass of wine. I want it to be nice tonight. I want to try and make it something special for us."

It was 6.30 pm by the time they started eating. Everything was delicious especially the rolled chicken breast with prosciutto and pecorino cheese stuffing. All the pasta dishes accompanying it hit the spot for William.

"Nice choices Aoife and the rosé wine goes well with it. *Perfecto*."

The atmosphere over dinner was relaxing and happy for them both. Aoife was listening intently to the music and some of the songs now had special significance to her.

As the meal ended, she gazed across the table to William and wondered how this modest farmer who lived near a very small rural town in New Zealand could have captured her love and devotion so easily. It had all happened over the short space of eleven days. He had all the attributes she was looking for in a life partner but thought impossible to find. Now she couldn't imagine a life without him. She was not going to let that happen. There was only one way forward and that would be by William's side. There were complications which she'd have to deal with when she got back home to Galway but they could wait for now. Right here, and right now, there was only one man on her mind and she wanted William to know that.

Aoife stood up and went around the table to William. She took him by the hand and led him up to the loft. They undressed each other slowly and carefully. What followed was a moment of pure physical lust and emotional ecstasy. William liked to be in charge and gave Aoife everything she craved. His manliness was satisfied. It was a highly intimate exchange between two persons deeply committed to each other. The journey was just beginning.

They fell asleep in each other's arms knowing that they had now reached a point of total trust and dependency.

Farewell to Naples

The day they were both dreading had arrived. William and Aoife woke around 7 am and lay in bed looking directly at each other in the eyes.

"Penny for your thoughts," said William.

"I'm going to make this happen William. You already know there are several personal matters I have to deal with back in Galway. I'll sort them as soon as possible, let my family know what's happening and then sort all my belongings. Can you wait three months for me to make it back into your arms?"

"However long it takes Aoife. I'll be waiting. It will be hard, but I'm mentally prepared. Two weeks in Naples has changed my life for the better."

"It's the same for me William. Thanks to you."

William kissed Aoife on the lips, sprung out of bed and started walking downstairs while he spoke back over his right shoulder to Aoife.

"I might have a quick shower and shave, have a coffee and then get dressed. Carlo the driver won't be here until 9 am so we've still got a bit of time yet."

"Ok you go first, let me know when you've finished in the bathroom and then I'll do my stuff."

William was trying not to think too much about the long journey ahead. He was thankful he only had to do flight changes with relatively short transit waiting times in Dubai and Auckland.

William had supplied all the flight details and times to Ram who had confirmed back that he would personally be at Palmerston North Airport to drive him back to his farm near Hunterville.

William was experiencing mixed emotions as his last morning in Naples unfolded. Not only was he sad to be leaving Naples and Aoife, but he was also happy to be returning home to Hunterville, the family farm, catching up with his best friend Ram and his own parents. It's a wonderful world he thought to himself. The past two weeks had been extraordinarily generous to the man from Hunterville. He didn't want to be greedy knowing that many people all over the world were struggling daily with the basics of life, but if he was worthy, he couldn't wait for the next adventure to anywhere, except this time, he wouldn't be doing it alone.

"I'm finished Aoife. Bathroom's all yours."

William dressed casually in jeans and a semi-formal dress shirt in preparation for the long journey home. He left out a jacket and jersey to hand carry because it would still be cold when he arrived back home to New Zealand and he'd definitely be in need of those items of clothing on arrival.

Aoife soon finished in the bathroom and went back upstairs to dress. She was flying to Galway where it would be the height of summer when she landed, so she just wore blue jeans and a smart white blouse. She was expecting to be picked up by her brother at Galway Airport and driven home to the family farm in Ballinrobe. Her priority was to explain the rapidly evolving situation to her parents including her impending departure to start a new life on the other side of the world. She was unsure how they would accept that news, but was hopefully they'd be supportive.

Aoife also wanted to contact Mr O'Leary as soon as possible after getting back to Ireland to share her good news with him. He had been instrumental in suggesting and then supporting her holiday to Naples.

She was much less enthused about seeing Kieran and explaining to him that their destructive journey could not continue and that it had reached its inevitable conclusion.

At 8 am they sat down at the kitchen table with a cup each of freshly brewed coffee. Both knew that their temporary physical separation would start in around three hours' time when Aoife boarded her aircraft in preparation for a 12 noon departure time. William's flight was scheduled to depart soon after at 1 pm.

"I'm getting nervous, Aoife."

"So am I."

"Take a deep breath, be brave and I know three months separation will pass by quickly."

"I think it will, and anyway, we'll be able to contact daily via the internet so it won't be too bad."

William checked his phone and it was ten minutes to 9 am.

"I'll just check over the balcony and see if there's any sign of Carlo yet."

William returned almost immediately.

"He's already down there waiting. I can see the car. Wonder how long he's been there for? OK let's go. I'll take all the bags down and then come back to do a final check before I put the apartment key back into the drop box."

Five minutes later, everything was in the car and Aoife and William did a final check of the apartment to make sure that nothing was left behind. They walked down the stairs together for the final time and stepped out into the street. Just as they were about to hop into the car for the ride to the airport, Aoife spoke urgently, "William, wait. William."

"Yes Aoife. What's the matter?"

"Look up there."

William looked up to where Aoife was pointing. There standing on the balcony dressed in her best black dress and waving goodbye with a white handkerchief was his nonna friend on the balcony opposite his apartment.

"She waving us goodbye," said William as he waved goodbye back to her and blew her multiple kisses. "I told you she was a special lady. I'll never ever forget this moment."

Aoife knew there and then that this man she was with had a special gift to make people feel happy and appreciated with his kindness and compassion. See was proud of her smiling man from Hunterville.

They hopped into the car, rolled the windows down and both waved a final goodbye to nonna as the car pulled away and drove out of the street. Both William and Aoife's eyes were welled up with tears. This time they were solely tears of sadness. Even Carlo the driver had tears in his eyes.

They made the forty five minute journey to the airport in busy traffic and not a word was spoken between the three of them the whole way. It was a time for reflection and private thoughts. They arrived to the airport close to 10 am as planned. William got out the last forty euros of cash he had in his wallet and handed it to Carlo.

"Thank you for driving us to and from the opera on Friday night and for driving us to the airport this morning. All the best with your university studies Carlo. Work hard."

"Thank you Mister William. Thank you *signora*. I will try and work hard. My mother said you are welcome back to the apartment any time. I hope you both liked Naples. Safe travels."

"No Carlo, we didn't like Naples, we loved it. It was perfect. *Arrivederci*."

Carlo smiled and waved them goodbye as they walked over and into the departure building.

They were flying different airlines so went to their respective check-in counters separately to complete check-in formalities. The plan was to head back to a designated meeting point after check-in so that they could pass through the immigration channels and the hand luggage x-ray areas together. After a seamless check-in they met up again and went through immigration and x-ray scanning together. There were no problems.

"We've still got one hour before you have to board Aoife. Shall we have a coffee? It's not going to be like our usual café visit in Naples but at least it's a chance to sit down. Let's find the nearest one to your boarding lounge."

With coffee in hand and boarding passes to the ready they sat down with the masses. Sunday was clearly a very busy travel day in Naples.

"It's only twenty minutes to your boarding time. Don't forget I won't get back to Hunterville until later on Tuesday and I'll be pretty tired and will crash for don't know how long, so we're going to talk on Wednesday at 8 am Ireland time which will be 8 pm New Zealand time."

"Absolutely no way I'll forget. I can't believe we're going to be on opposite sides of the world when we next talk face-to-face. It seems weird. Please tell me this is not just a crazy dream."

William held Aoife's hands, sent her one of his trademark beaming smiles and spoke.

"It's not a crazy dream Aoife. Be brave and come back to me soon. We can continue the life journey destiny has planned for us."

When William flashed one of his smiles, it was virtually impossible not to smile back. Aoife felt reassured by William's supportive words.

"That's the call for your flight."

William stood up and escorted Aoife over to the boarding gate. It was time for goodbye. With eyes full of tears and unable to speak any more, William hugged and kissed Aoife passionately. He didn't want to let go but was clearly holding up the boarding queue. Not that anybody seemed to mind.

Aoife walked through the boarding gate and waved goodbye to William. For a few seconds, he was completely lost and felt abandoned but quickly regained his composure. This is going to happen, he thought to himself. I'm going to make sure it happens. He picked up his bag and walked towards his departure gate.

By the time he boarded his Emirates flight to Dubai, Aoife had already been airborne for an hour. Aoife had a direct return flight to Galway which would take three and a half hours flight time.

William's direct flight to Dubai was a six hour flight. William would still be in the air by the time Aoife had arrived back to Galway.

He sat down in his allocated seat, buckled up and the long journey back to his farm near Hunterville began. He would have plenty of time over the next thirty six hours to reflect on what had happen over the past two weeks in Naples, and to dream about his future and their future together.

Return to Galway and the Surprising Development

Aoife's direct return flight to Galway touched down mid-afternoon. As he had promised, her brother Finn was there to meet her and drive her home to Ballinrobe.

"Welcome home, Aoife. I hear from Mum and Dad that you've had a fantastic time in Naples and met a man from New Zealand while you were there. They said he's a farmer. Is it serious?"

"It's more than serious Finn but can I tell you and Mum and Dad all about it tomorrow?"

"Of course you can."

It was just under an hour's drive from Galway Airport to the family farm in Ballinrobe. As they drove home Aoife scanned the local countryside. It was beautiful and she had missed it. She wound down the car's window and breathed in the fresh air. She wondered if William had a made his flight OK. She would send him a text as soon as she got home. As her brother had started up an artisan honey business on the family farm he was interested in all things honey related.

"Finn, do you know what Mānuka honey is?"

"I do, how do you know about Mānuka honey? It's a special type of honey from a native New Zealand bushy tree. It's meant to have antiseptic and medicinal qualities. Very expensive though. Have you tried some?"

"I did. William made me a dessert one night and it had Mānuka honey in it. It was delicious. William never leaves home without a jar of it in his luggage. He asked me to taste test it before telling me what it was."

Aoife was saying all the right things to her brother. Finn thought that any man that liked honey and knew something about honey had to have some good qualities. Privately he wished he could meet this man named William because he sounded like somebody he would get on well with. Finn noticed, even whilst he was driving, that whenever Aoife talked about William her eyes lit up and there was a beautiful smile on her face. Obviously this man from 'down under' had captured his sister's heart.

"Aoife don't answer if you don't want to, but have you fallen in love with William?"

"Yes. I wish I was with him now."

Aoife was starting to get very emotional so Finn decided to try and change the subject and they could revisit the 'William effect' tomorrow after she had rested.

Aoife arrived home just on 5 pm and her parents were waiting at the front door to greet her. They were a close family so there were hugs and kisses aplenty.

"I'm not sure how hungry you are Aoife but I've made your favourite for dinner anyway. A traditional Irish stew with sweet cabbage and mashed spuds on the side."

"Sounds good mum. I'll definitely have some but not a huge plate like Finn always has. Just a small to medium serve is plenty."

Aoife took her bags to her bedroom and immediately got her mobile phone out. She was desperate to send William a text even though she knew he wouldn't get it until after he arrived to Dubai which was still an hours flying time away for him. She sent him a text.

Hello William. Home in Ballinrobe now. Missing you. Love you. Want to be with you. Safe travels. Aoife xxx

She was a lot happier now that her text had been sent and went back to join her parents and brother for dinner. Most of the table talk was about what had been happening on the farm, not what Aoife had done in Naples. They thought it best to leave that until the following morning.

After dinner Aoife couldn't wait to hand her family the presents from Naples. Her mother and father loved the two framed photos she had bought for them. One was of 'Jesus on the Cross' which she told them she had blessed by the priest at the magnificent Gesu Nuovo Church in Naples, and the second was of William's beloved 'Veiled Christ'. She told them that she had recited a blessing for them standing right in front of the 'Veiled Christ' in the Chapel of Sansevero. They loved the gifts and promised Aoife that they'd be up hanging on the lounge wall the following day. Aoife handed Finn his present.

"Nice one Aoife. I'm loving it. I'll make us a brew in the morning. Can't wait. It will be welcome home to Café Finn."

"I'm in a full café mood at the present Finn because I've been going to a different one every morning in Naples with William so I've got high expectations for Café Finn. No pressure."

Finn laughed and hugged his sister.

"Dinner was nice thanks mum. Love you all. I'm pretty tired so I think I'll go shower, unpack and then head to bed even though it's only 8 pm. See you all in the morning. I've got a lot to tell you. Nite."

Aoife couldn't wait to get to her mobile phone sitting on her bedside table and true to form there was a text reply from William who was now waiting in transit at Dubai Airport. She read it several times.

Arrived Dubai Airport. Boarding not for 3 hours yet. Flight time to Auckland is around 16 hours. Help. Miss you heaps. Be brave. Love William xxx

That was exactly what she wanted to hear. Aoife didn't know there were direct flights that long, but since she would be doing it in the near future, she was interested to find out more about the flight options when she went back to Galway.

Aoife showered and then went to bed. She read through William's text several more times and it didn't take long before she went off to sleep.

Aoife woke up early on Monday morning and had one of those moments where you ask yourself 'where am I?' She was confused for a few seconds but soon realised she was back home in Ballinrobe. She lay in bed and went over the past two weeks in Naples in her mind and how she would tell her family about William and their plan for the future. She hoped they would be understanding and supportive. She could hear somebody in the kitchen and guessed it might be Finn. She put on a robe and went to the kitchen. It was Finn experimenting with his new coffee pot.

"I've got it all figured out Aoife. Take a seat and coffee will be ready very soon. Plus I've put some scrambled eggs on. Couple more minutes and it's ready to serve."

Finn's coffee and eggs were good but not quite as good as the Naples version.

"I can hear Mum and Dad getting up. Do you want to tell us about Naples now before we head out to do farm chores, or leave it until later?"

"Now is good."

Her parents entered the kitchen and sat down at the table. Finn poured them all a coffee. Aoife's father spoke first.

"We sense that you had a great time in Naples and did some great activities and sight-seeing with your friend from New Zealand but we also sense you've got something bigger to tell us. We want you to be happy and we want you to find somebody worthy of our daughter but we also want you to be safe Aoife."

"Mum, Dad, Finn you're right. I wasn't looking for anybody but I found William. He came into my life via a cooking class. We did lots of things together. Horse-riding, visited cafés and castles, swimming, dinners, church visits, museum visits, went to the opera, walked the ruins at Herculaneum, visited Mount Vesuvius, shopping, lots of crying and lots of sharing. I love him dearly. He wants me to go to New Zealand. I want to be with him. Not tomorrow or next week but soon. How do you feel about that?"

Aoife's father replied first.

"Janey Mack Aoife, I wasn't expecting that. He seems like a nice fella from what you've told us and from the photo you sent us of you both on the yacht, but it's so far away. I'd be worried that you were alright."

"I know dad, but honestly he's very special. He's kind and considerate, he's caring and compassionate, and he's hard working and smart. You'd like him I know that you would. You'd all like him. You'd all grow to love him."

Aoife's brother gave his verdict.

"Any man that works the land and tends animals, plays rugby, prays at church with my sister, loves the 'Veiled Christ' sculpture and carries honey with him when he goes away on holiday has got to be someone very different and someone very special. Despite a few brotherly reservations, he's got my vote."

Aoife's mother gave her opinion.

"We've not seen you this happy for a long time Aoife. The past six months has been difficult for all of us. William sounds like a nice man who is genuine and sensitive. I'm scared but we want to support you in anything you decide. We love you and want to see you happy but it's hard thinking you'll be so far away."

"I know being on the other side of the world is difficult, Mum, but with the internet we can communicate visually and talk as much as you want. I promise I'll let you know if things are not working out or if there are any difficulties. I promise."

They held hands around the table and Aoife's parents prayed for protection, guidance and love especially for their daughter Aoife and for William also.

"I'm so happy I've got your support. Thank you. William is on a long direct flight from Dubai to Auckland still but I'll let him know. He will be so happy and thankful. I'm so happy."

The family conference ended well. Aoife told her family that she'd spend the rest of the day around the family farm and help her mother do some baking, but wanted to go to Galway the following morning to deal with some important personal business. She didn't say exactly what that was to her family, but she wanted to thank Mr O'Leary for his support and she wanted to talk with Kieran. Her job at the pub was still open and the apartment was still available. There would be a lot to sort out over the next days, weeks and months.

The following morning Aoife took the bus to Galway and arrived there mid-morning. She had called Mr O'Leary the night before and they had arranged to meet at a café near the King Brian Pub. When she walked into the café Mr O'Leary was already there waiting for her. They hugged warmly.

"Welcome back Aoife. Come and sit down and I'll order a coffee for us both."

"Thanks Mr O'Leary. I've got a small gift for you from Naples. Hope you like it."

"Very stylish, thank you Aoife. I need a new wallet and this one looks really smart. It's very kind and thoughtful. Judging from that smile on your face and sparkle in your eyes, everything went well. I've got some news for you but you go first."

"Naples was excellent. Everything about it was beautiful. I meet somebody there. A man named William from New Zealand. I didn't know men like that existed. He has changed my life and I'm madly in love with him. He wants me to go to New Zealand. Of course I want to but I need to talk with Kieran first and tell him that we cannot continue. I'm very worried about how he will take the news. I did send him a few texts and an email while I was in Naples but I haven't heard anything back."

"I can see you're happy, Aoife. It's like you're a different person. Well, the news I have for you might be tending towards good news, rather than bad news."

"Good news? I don't understand."

"Well, four days after you left for Naples, Kieran packed up and left Galway suddenly. The grapevine tells me that he has gone to London to join some of his artist friends. He craves a bohemian lifestyle. It seems like he has a history of abusive behaviour, drugs and is fighting personal demons."

"That's terrible. I wonder if I should try and help?"

"No Aoife, I don't think you should. Apparently, his close friends and family are dealing with it. You are free to get on with your life and to embrace it and start afresh. I've heard that New Zealand is a beautiful country. A little bit like Ireland with lots of green grass and grazing horses, but of course, there are a lot more sheep there. Go and see if it works for you."

"But I feel guilty."

"Don't feel guilty. Feel blessed. I'll miss your friendship, of course, but William sounds like a good man. You decide what's right."

"My family is very supportive and you're supportive and Kieran has moved on. I think it's a sign. I prayed for a sign. I've got my answer."

Going forward, there were no obstacles in Aoife's way and she was very excited. She'd be able to tell William when they spoke face to face the following day that she was free to join him in New Zealand. Aoife and Mr O'Leary said goodbye and she thanked him for all the updated news. On the way back to her Galway apartment, she passed by the pub and confirmed with the duty manager when she'd start working again after her holiday to Naples. They asked if she could work the late afternoon and evening shift the following day.

Aoife arrived to her flat and was shocked to see it empty of all of Kieran's belongings. She'd have to arrange a new flatmate but that wasn't going to be difficult. A single female was her preferred choice.

Return to Hunterville and the Mānuka Honey Shop

William's flight to Auckland arrived very early morning on Tuesday 16th July. He had managed to grab some short catnaps on the very long flight from Dubai to Auckland but was still shattered and very tired on arrival. He sent a quick text to Aoife to let her know that he had arrived safely and only had one more short domestic flight to go.

After going through all the arrival formalities and walking from the international terminal to the domestic terminal, he still had three hours of waiting before his flight to Palmerston North was due to depart. All this mindless waiting he thought to himself. He just wanted to be horizontal in his own bed and fast asleep.

Finally, he boarded his flight from Auckland to Palmerston North. During the flight he started going over in his mind what he had to do after he arrived back home to the farm. It was almost the start of the spring lambing and calving season so that would be the main priority on the farm for the next few weeks.

He was looking forward to catching up with Ram and hearing all the local gossip. He wondered if his rugby team had been managing OK and secretly hoped that the team hadn't been posting large winning scores in his absence. He was looking forward to telling them all about the waiter at the café in Piazza Bellini who had wondered if he was an important kiwi rugby player. They'd laugh when he told them that story. Most of all he was looking forward to telling his parents and Ram and anybody else that was interested, about the wonderful Irish girl he had met in Naples.

His domestic flight landed in Palmerston North mid-morning, and as planned, Ram was there to meet him. It was hard to tell who was the more excited. William couldn't wait to tell Ram about Aoife, and Ram couldn't wait to grill William about her. William thrust out his hand expecting Ram to grasp it and shake it vigorously. Instead, Ram gave him a warm bear hug which didn't seem to end. William sensed that Ram was glad, very glad, to see him back home. Finally, Ram released him from the bear hug.

"Hell William I knew you'd have a good time but I wasn't expecting you to have such a bonza time mate. Sounds like you've been busy. Aoife sounds really nice. And she's a real looker. How'd the hell did you manage that?"

"Ram she's very special to me. We're in love so please be kind when you talk about her."

Ram immediately sensed that William was telling him something important and he wanted to be respectful to his best friend so he continued the conversation with caution.

"Well, on the drive to Hunterville you tell me whatever you want about her. Do you think she'll come to New Zealand? You look really happy mate. I'm happy for you. Everybody around town has been asking about you."

William had elected not to go and visit his parents in Palmerston North immediately on his arrival back home. He wanted to be well rested and alert when he visited to tell them the good news. He'd call them as soon as he got home, but would leave visiting them until sometime over the weekend.

It was almost a one hour drive from Palmerston North airport to the farm. On the trip home William told Ram about his adventures in Naples and how he came to meet Aoife, and Ram told William about progress on the farm, how the rugby team had been going and general Hunterville happenings.

As they passed through Hunterville, William asked Ram to stop briefly at the Mānuka Honey Shop while he dashed inside and bought a jar of their best quality 10+ Mānuka honey. As he exited the shop he stopped and turned back to speak to the proprietor.

"Tell you all about it later in the week Mr Bates, but this 10+ Mānuka honey helped me find the love of my life in Naples. There's something magical about this honey. I think it might be a love potion?"

They both laughed and Mr Bates shouted out that he was looking forward to William filling him in further. He knew that the local Mānuka honey was good if not very good, but it was the first time he'd heard it be described as a love potion.

William arrived back to the farm right on 11 am. He was happy to be home. No sign of any lambs or calves in the holding paddocks yet but he knew their arrival was only days away. Mr and Mrs O'Connor were there to meet him.

"Welcome back William. You look very tired. We'll stay until the morning if you like so you can get some sleep after the long journey home."

"Do you mind? I'm totally shattered. If I don't go to sleep soon I'll collapse on the floor. But before I go to bed I just want to give you all a small gift to show my appreciation and to thank you for helping me out. It has changed my life for the better."

William handed Mr and Mrs O'Connor two bottles of wine he had bought from a vineyard on the slopes of Mount Vesuvius at the end of the horse- riding trip, together with a bottle of limoncello liqueur from the Amalfi Coast. He had carefully packed the bottles in bubble wrap before putting them in his luggage. Thankful there was no sign of breakage when he unpacked the gift. They were delighted and said they couldn't wait to try them.

"Here's a gift for you Ram. Thank you for the pickup and ride home from the airport. And thank you for being my best friend and helping me when I was down. Seriously down. I won't ever forget that. I think you'll like the gift. Please don't open it until you get home."

Ram was overcome with emotion at William's kind words and sincere smile. A lot of people didn't understand how he and William could have formed such a close friendship. Ram didn't care what most other people thought, but he did care what William thought.

William's affirmation of their special friendship was music to Rams ears. It meant a lot to him. Not wanting to have a meltdown in front of Mr and Mrs O'Connor and William, he took the gift and left telling William that he'd open it at home and catch up with him in the morning.

William then excused himself from Mr and Mrs O'Connor's presence and retired to his bedroom where he immediately sent a text to Aoife.

Have arrived home to Hunterville. I'm totally shattered from long trip. Everything is good on farm. Wish u were here. Talk tomorrow. William xx

Given the time difference between Hunterville and Galway, William was pleasantly surprised to get an almost immediate reply.

Great to hear u safely home. Good news this end. Tell you about it tomorrow. I'm so happy. Love you. Aoife xx

He then called his parents and had a brief conversation with them telling them he'd visit over the weekend. It was time to hit his bed. William showered quickly, hopped into bed and didn't need to count sheep because sleep was almost instant.

William woke up on Wednesday morning somewhat, but not entirely, refreshed. He dressed and went out into the kitchen where Mrs O'Connor had already prepared a welcome home breakfast for him.

"Sit down William and I'll bring your breakfast over. Tea or coffee?"

"Coffee thanks Mrs O'Connor. It's a habit I've developed while away in Naples."

William smiled to himself at the 'real mans' farmhouse breakfast placed down before him. Naples had been great, Hunterville was great and life in general was great. He was definitely in the happy zone. He thanked Mr and Mrs O'Connor for their fantastic help while he was away. Mr O'Connor updated William on the status of the farm.

"Everything has gone well William. No problems at all. It's been pretty quiet over the past couple of weeks. No lambs or calves yet but they're not too far away. There are a few hints of spring in the air. We've both enjoyed it. A lot of memories for us William but it's time to revert back to living the life of retirees."

William stood up and went over and hugged Mrs O'Connor and then shook Mr O'Connor's hand.

"Come back here William, you're not getting off that easy lad."

And with that Mr O'Connor gave William a warm hug and told him that it was their pleasure to be able to help out.

"And by the way William, we hear on the grapevine that you've met somebody significant while you were away in Italy and that she might be coming to Hunterville. If and when she does, please introduce her to us also."

"Of course I will. I've already told her about you both. She is excited about coming to Hunterville. I'm hoping that will be soon."

After breakfast and the departure of Mr and Mrs O'Connor, William saddled up one of his horses and set off on a ride around the farm. The air temperature was still cool but the air itself was clean and fresh and filled his hungry lungs. There was spring blossom on some of the trees around the farm house, the very first spring daffodil flowers had appeared, and the pregnant ewes and cows in the holding paddocks looked rotund and healthy. The worse of winter was over now and all the paddocks and hill slopes were greener than green thanks to the start of the lush grass growth typical of springtime in the Rangitikei District.

William rode up to the highest point on the farm and gazed around. He felt on top of the world both figuratively and literally. He felt good to be alive. He was thankful. It was a beautiful vista. He loved his farm and the people in the district, and life was a lot sweeter now that he had somebody special to share it with. That person was still on the other side of the world but if the 'gods were smiling' it wouldn't be too long before she would be right by his side. He sat on his horse on the hilltop for more than ten minutes thinking about and reliving all the wonderful things he had done in Naples over the past two weeks with Aoife and wondering how his face to face call with her later in the day would go.

He knew that he'd only a have a few quiet days left before work activities on the farm increased significantly so he'd enjoy them as much as possible. When he got back to the farm shed and unsaddled his horse, he checked what supplies he had, and what supplies he might need for the weeks ahead. He then went inside his home knowing that it was hard to concentrate on farm requirements until after he had spoken with Aoife. In order not to overthink it, he called Ram.

"Morning Ram. How's it going? Have you opened the Naples gift yet?"

"I did William. It's awesome mate. Thank you. My car is going to be upmarket now. There's something I've got to tell you."

William went quiet not knowing if it was going to be good news or bad news.

"It's about me and Suzie. We're a serious item. Not something I've ever done before. No more rabbiting every weekend and all weekend for me mate. It's time for me to get serious and show commitment. It might be time for me to settle down."

William was very surprised at Ram's news but he was delighted.

"Nice one Ram. Congratulations. How much better can my day get? I'm not going to be fit enough to play this weekend's game but I'll be at rugby practice next week and available to play that weekend. That's if I haven't been replaced?"

"We wouldn't do that to you William. You're our star winger mate. I wouldn't allow it."

William and Ram ended their call and William went about getting back into the swing of things on the farm. As the day ended and the scheduled 8 pm call time with Aoife approached, William's anxiety level started to increase. What if she had changed her mind, or there were complications with her previous boyfriend, or her parents didn't want her to go to New Zealand? All of these possibilities swirled around in his head.

Finally 8 pm arrived and he made the call to Aoife. She answered immediately. It was good to hear her voice and see her face again after their three days apart.

"Morning Aoife. Miss you, love you, how are you?"

"Everything is good William. I miss and love you also. And I miss that smile. I'm back in Galway now and started back at the pub yesterday. It's 8 am so I'm just relaxing this morning and enjoying a Napoli coffee now. I'm not going to work until late morning. I'm back in my old apartment and sharing it with a girl work colleague."

"I saddled up and took a ride this morning up to the hilltops and looked down on the farm. It's truly beautiful. Spring has just sprung and the countryside is so green. There was only one thing missing. You of course. "

Although William was desperate to ask her about the Kieran situation and what her parents and brother said when she mentioned the possibility of going to New Zealand, he thought it best to let her bring up the subject.

"Thanks William, I needed that. Everything is good on the family farm and back here in Galway. Town is busy because it's the summertime tourist season. Do you miss Naples?"

"I do. I've got so many fantastic memories etched in my mind it's unreal. And I miss our morning café visits. They were very special. And I miss my nonna friend, and all the characters we meet and the food and history and architecture. I basically miss everything. It's different here but really good also. It's much quieter of course."

"Same here. I've adjusted back to Irish life much easier than I thought."

That statement set off alarms bells in William's mind. Was Aoife trying to tell him that it was a great summer fling but she was contented just to stay back in Galway. Was she about to say 'adios amigo'.

"And I've got some good news William."

"What is it?"

"Kieran left Galway while I was away in Naples and is now completely out of my life. I spoke to Mum and Dad about going to New Zealand and although they're nervous, they want me to be happy so I have their blessing. Even have my older brother's blessing. There's nothing stopping me. I want to as soon as possible. That is if you still want me to?"

"Want you to. I need you to. Get on the next plane. I'm so excited Aoife."

Aoife could see from William's beaming smile that he was a very happy man at the news she had just delivered.

"I think it will be weeks rather than months. Few things to sort out here in Galway and at home but that shouldn't take too long. I'll let you know a possible date in the next few days. I'll look at flights and all that stuff also."

"Have to admit Aoife that I was a bit nervous about what you might say but this news is the best news. I can't wait. When you look at possible flights just book to Auckland. I'll be there to meet you."

"Ok I'll do that. It might be half way around the world, but at least it's not a different planet."

They both laughed heartily, and the conversation slowly drew to an end. Neither of them wanted to be the one to press the 'end call' tab on their video call. Finally the call ended. Both were happy and excited.

William showered and retired to bed having had a great first full day back on the farm in Hunterville. He lay naked in bed thinking about Aoife. He wished she was there lying by his side. He was lustful and it was showing. He did what men do in situations like this and after dealing with the matter William drifted off into a deep blissful sleep.

Back in Galway and after the call had ended, Aoife sat drinking her coffee knowing that she would be busy getting things sorted over the next few weeks prior to her departure for 'down under'. Seeing William and discussing the forward plan with him cemented the special bond and love she had with this man from Hunterville. Going forward, there was no other and there would be no other. Her fate had been determined during the eleven days they had spent together in Naples. Since she had arrived back to Ireland she did wonder if there had been some sort of divine intervention in bringing them together. Was something or someone was lending a helping hand? Something seemed strange but she couldn't put her finger on it. Rather than get too intense thinking about it, she elected to just concentrate on making plans to get to William as soon as practical.

After the call to Aoife, William was 'floating on clouds' and woke up on Thursday morning a very happy man. In his head he planned out the things he needed to do over the next four days before speaking with Aoife again on Sunday evening. He would concentrate on farm work Thursday and Friday, go into Hunterville briefly on Saturday morning to see the ladies in the café, and after that visit his parents in Palmerston North. On the way home on Saturday he would go watch his rugby team play their scheduled afternoon game at Marton. If all went well, he'd be back playing in the Hunterville team the weekend after. He smiled to himself when he recalled the friendly waiter at the café in Piazza Bellini who though the he might be an important rugby player from New Zealand.

After very productive days on the farm on Thursday and Friday, William set out early on Saturday morning to visit his parents in Palmerston North. However, his first stop was at the café in Hunterville to have a coffee and say hello to the ladies there and to give them each a small gift.

"Welcome back William. We have missed you. Having the usual?"

"Yes please Connie and whatever sweet treat has just come out of the oven. Smells good whatever it is."

"We hear that you had a fantastic time in Naples and met somebody really nice."

William smiled to himself knowing that good news travelled fast on the grapevine in small towns. Not that he minded at all. In fact he was pleased because he wanted to share his happiness with all the regulars he knew in town. He considered them his extended family. They would all be a part of Aoife's life in the future so he wanted them to get to know her.

"I did. Can I tell you all about it during the coming week whenever I'm next in town? I'm off to see Mum and Dad in Palmerston North very soon. They are super curious about what happened to their son in Naples."

"Of course" said Connie "but we'll be expecting you back again soon so don't you dare try and hide."

"No chance of that."

William finished his coffee and cake and departed. It was only a short drive from Hunterville to his parents place in Palmerston North. He was excited about seeing his parents and giving them his presents from Naples. It hadn't been easy selecting presents for his parents but he knew they would like what he had brought for them. He knocked on the door of their townhouse at 9 am and the door flung open. Both parents were there to welcome their son home from his trip to Italy. They were overjoyed to see him and neither his mother nor father was shy about showing William how much they loved him. He was their only child and only son. They had never told William why they had him later in life, and why he was their only child. They had been told by several doctors and specialists that they'd never be able to conceive a child. That was the reason. His arrival into their lives had been their own personal miracle and they were eternally grateful for it.

"Come in and sit down William. I've made some morning tea for us. It sounds like you had a fantastic time in Naples. And it sounds like you found something very special while you were over there."

For the next hour, William described to his parents all the wonderful things he had seen and done while in Naples while showing them pics on his phone of many of the things he had experienced and places he had explored. They were very impressed.

"Are you going to tell us about Aoife?"

"Yep, I will dad."

William spent another hour telling his parents about Aoife, how they had met and what they had done together. His parents listened very intently and both seemed impressed with what he was telling them. Knowing his parents were conservative, he skirted all the personal happenings. They could easily tell from his energised body language while talking, and his beaming smile, that he was deeply in love. They were overjoyed because the biggest worry they had, was that William might be alone on the farm after they were gone. He told them that he wanted Aoife to come to see him in Hunterville and that she had agreed to that. It wasn't going to be immediately, but he hoped it would be soon. They were working on plans to make that happen.

"Oops, I nearly forgot to give you some presents from Naples. This one is from me, this one is from Aoife and this one is from the beautiful city of Naples."

William's parents opened the presents. They loved the framed photo of William and Aoife standing at the stern of Captain Marino's yacht in the Bay Of Naples. Both William and Aoife had personally signed it. They loved the box of Irish shortbread biscuits Aoife had made for them in her apartment kitchen. And they loved the hand-made nativity scene William had bought for them from the Old City Centre 'Christmas Street'. That was a very special gift to both of his parents and would take pride of place in their house over the upcoming Christmas period.

"William the gifts are perfect" said his mother "we will value them all. Thank you and Aoife kindly."

William discussed with his father what had been happening on the farm and confirmed that everything was ready for the approaching lambing and calving season.

"Well, Mum and Dad that was my trip to Naples. I don't want to sound dramatic but it's been my salvation. I didn't know I could be this happy."

"You're happy and that makes us happy. We can't wait to meet Aoife. Keep us updated. When are you talking to her next?"

"On Sunday night mum. She might have a better idea of dates then. I'll let you know."

It was only a small family unit but it was a close family unit. Their love for each other was clearly evident throughout the morning's get together.

"I might head away now if that's OK. I told Ram that I'd try and drop by and watch their game in Marton this afternoon on my way home. Is there anything you want or need?"

"No son we're good. Hear from you again soon. Drive safely."

William departed his parents' home and headed off on the forty minute drive to Marton to watch the Hunterville rugby team play their Saturday fixture. The team were pleased and excited to see William back.

"Hope you'll be playing next weekend William. We're doing OK, but you have been missed. Will we see you at training mid-week?" shouted the captain of the team.

"Ok rubbish, were not doing OK William. We've lost the last three games mate," shouted another player.

"For sure. I'll be there. Looking forward to it."

William smiled to himself. It was nice to be missed and he hoped he could turn his team's fortunes around. His rugby team lost their game in Marton but not by much. It was less than ten points between the teams at the final whistle.

William arrived back home late afternoon and did a few jobs outside in the farm shed. He was determined to use the Italian cooking ingredients he had bought himself in Naples and try to make something authentic Napoli for dinner. The resulting dinner he made was average, and in his mind, nothing spectacular. To do his best cooking he needed an incentive, and dining alone was not one of them.

William and Aoife Make Plans to Reunite

William was determined to get the farm back and running as he wanted it and was resolved to using the days ahead wisely. Other than rugby practice on Tuesday and Thursday nights, he would concentrate fully on the farm during the week ahead. His body clock seemed to be adjusting nicely back to New Zealand time so he woke up on Sunday morning close to his usual wake up time of 6 am.

His body clock might have adjusted well, but some of the habits he had picked up whilst in Naples were not so easy to forget or change. He jumped out of bed butt naked thinking to himself that he'd make a moka coffee, slip some shorts and a t shirt on and go and sit out on the balcony in the warm early morning air. Very quickly he realised that he wasn't in Naples anymore such that the early morning routine he had enjoyed while on holiday would have to change a little bit. He chuckled to himself at the confusion. Instead, he'd get fully dressed and go into the kitchen and make himself an instant coffee and sit at the kitchen table before planning out the day.

He was looking forward to talking to Aoife again at 8 pm that evening, but until then, he'd get outside on the farm and busy himself with farm activities. His two farm workers would be turning up early on Monday morning and when they arrived, he wanted them to know that he was fully back into the swing of things.

William completed a good day out on the farm and returned back to the farmhouse just as it was turning dark. After he had shaved and showered, he made dinner and had a glass of wine. He prepared himself for the 8 pm call with Aoife.

Neither William nor Aoife had a pet or amorous name for each other. Throughout his life various people had tried to call him Will, Willy, Willie, Bill and Billy but he always insisted on being addressed as William. It was a generational name that had been in his family for several hundred years and he was very proud of it, and being a bit conservative, he liked to maintain the formality of his Christian name. Similarly, Aoife who was even more conservative than William, liked her traditional Irish name and didn't much respond to nicknames like Fifi, Eef, Aoif and effa-beefa. Maybe it would change sometime in the future but for now they were both happy addressing each other with their exact given Christian names. In many ways they were like peas in a pod.

William video called Aoife exactly at 8 pm and she responded almost instantly.

"Evening Aoife. Hunterville in New Zealand calling Galway in Ireland. Miss you. Love you. How is everything?"

"Good thanks William. Ditto. So much has happened and it's all good. Do you want to go first or shall I?"

William was very excited to hear Aoife's update. "You go first."

"I discussed it again with my family and work and have been looking at flights. I can get a flight from Galway to Dublin, and then all the way with Emirates Airlines from Dublin to Dubai and on to Auckland. It takes so long though. If I leave on the 28th August I would be there on the early morning of Saturday the 31st August. Not sure if I'll sleep on the plane so I'll probably be a wreck when I get there. Is this OK or is it too early a date? I can amend if it is."

William was beside himself with excitement. He had hoped it would be sooner rather than later, and the end of August would be perfect because the busy lambing and calving season would have finished by then and he could easily make his way to Auckland so as to be there to meet and collect Aoife.

"Don't amend those dates because they're perfect. That's almost seven weeks total we would have been apart but I can live with that. I'll be there to collect you Aoife. I know you'll be exhausted from the flights but don't worry, I'll look after you."

"I know you will William. I just want to be there with you. The travel part is freaking me out a little bit. I've never flown any more than a few hours. I hope I can sleep a bit on the plane. Especially on that really long flight between Dubai and Auckland."

"I know, I did it last week. Do you need any help with flight costs and all that?"

"Definitely not. I'll sort it all. I've got it covered. I've been saving for something special."

"I'm just going to pinch myself to make sure that I'm not dreaming. Ouch. I'm not."

"I'll sort it all out next week and confirm the exact travel details when it's all arranged. I'm going home to Ballinrobe in the weekends to spend time with the family before I head away."

"That's a good idea. Everybody at this end is very excited about meeting you. No pressure."

They laughed nervously at that prospect and then spent the next hour discussing what they had been doing over the past four days since their last face to face call.

"What are you going to do today?"

"Finn is picking me up soon and I'm heading home for the day to spend some time with Mum and Dad and address any concerns they might have. Of course they're nervous for me but happy it's you I'm heading to and not anybody else. Finn will drop me back to Galway same time tomorrow morning."

"Sounds good. When shall we call and talk again? I've got rugby practice Tuesday and Thursday nights. Is Wednesday OK?"

"Yes Wednesday is good and I should be able to confirm about flights then. Time to sign off William. I can't wait to join you."

"Neither can I. Love you. Talk Wednesday. *Ciao*."

William reluctantly pressed the 'end call' tab on his computer and was thankful they had a good forward plan. In six weeks' time Aoife would be in Hunterville. How did that happen he thought to himself? Six weeks was just enough time to get his act together, smarten up the farm and homestead grounds and make sure his home was clean and comfortable for Aoife's arrival. Sleep didn't come so easily to William on Sunday night. He was too excited.

After the video phone call with William on Sunday morning and the visit home to her family that same day, Aoife was feeling a little bit apprehensive but mostly super excited. Finn dropped her back to Ballinrobe on Monday morning and she started making plans to travel to New Zealand to be reunited with William. It was a lot easier than she thought. She didn't need any special immigration visa before arriving and since she was in the right age bracket, she could apply for a twelve month visitor's visa as long as she had sufficient funds on arrival.

She would make sure she did. Aoife finalised the travel route she wanted to take, got the best airfare available and went online and booked it. It was exactly as she had told William on their Sunday call. Unable to hold on to the exciting news any longer, she flicked a text off to William.

Just booked flights. Arriving to Auckland Saturday morning 31st August on direct Emirates flight from Dubai. Can't wait to see u. Love Aoife xx.

The reply was quick.

Made my day. B there to meet u. Love William xx.

Life reverted back to near normality for William over the next few days. He thought about what he would do once Aoife arrived in Auckland on the morning of the 31st August. She would be exhausted from the long journey so he decided it was best that they just stay in Auckland and relax that first day and night, and then the next day he'd start the leisurely drive back home to the farm at Hunterville. It would be a five to six hour drive home but he decided he'd break it up by stopping at the scenic jewel of Lake Taupō. They'd have lunch there and maybe even go for a dip in the famous Wairakei geothermal hot pools if Aoife was feeling up to it. He was sure she'd find that novel and different since as far as he knew, there were no active geothermal and hot pool areas in Ireland.

On Tuesday night he went to rugby practice at the Hunterville rugby club grounds right in the centre of town. He wondered if word had got out about his misplaced 'celebratory status' at the café on Piazza Bellini. If it had, William knew the lads in the team would tease him about it. That was a certainty.

William walked into the changing rooms and it didn't take long for the team to start teasing him.

"Welcome back to practice William. Excuse me mate but is there any chance I could have your autograph and is there any chance you'd sign this rugger ball for us?"

To raucous laughter and good-humoured banter from all of the team, William replied back.

"Don't blame me, the waiter added one and one together and got five. So is there still a spot for me in the team game this weekend?"

"We'll see how you perform on the field tonight at practice before deciding" replied the team captain to continuing laughter and teasing.

It was obvious from all the good humoured exchange between the team that they were pleased to see him back. Given that William had indulged in a lot of food and drink while he was on holiday in Naples, he still did well at practice and didn't appear to have lost any of his speed and agility.

"What do you reckon guys? Shall we let him play on Saturday? Is he up to it?"

The reply from the team was a unanimous yes for not only did they all without exception like him a lot, they thought that he might just be the man to change their fortunes around. Three losing games on the run was not a good record. Williams' speed on the wing could make a big difference.

"Practice again Thursday night lads and this weekend's game is in up the road in Taihape. They'll be hard to beat but I think we can turn things around," said the team captain as they filed out the clubroom door.

William was pleased with his first rugby practice after getting back home from his holiday. He felt physically fit despite the excesses of the holiday in Naples. It wasn't all eating and drinking he thought to himself, I did do some exercise. There was the horse-riding and swimming and a huge amount of walking.

William went to bed happy and contented after Tuesday night's rugby practice. He lay in bed reflecting on the past three weeks and how his life had changed for the better. How it had not just changed a little bit, but how there had been major changes. He also had a feeling that somebody or something was helping him but he couldn't put a finger on it. He suspected that there were going to be some momentous events happening in his life in the near future but that they were completely out of his control. He became confused and started sweating. He wished Aoife was by his side to help him unravel it all. William decided that he'd go on one of his bush and river treks sometime during the weekend ahead to clear his mind and make time to think about it all in a more spiritual setting.

Finally he drifted off to sleep.

The next few days were busy ones for William. No lambs of calves had been born as yet but they were only a few days away. The farm was well prepared for their arrival. He had his usual face to face call with Aoife mid-week and she confirmed that all the travel arrangements were going well. Rugby practice on Thursday night was intense but at least his mates at practice had stopped teasing him about his "celebratory" rugby playing status. The practice went well and the team was hoping for a better result on Saturday.

On Friday morning William took himself and his two farm workers into Hunterville for a café treat. He valued what they had done on the farm while he was away in Naples and wanted to show his appreciation. His kindness was well received.

Saturday afternoon arrived and William made the short drive from his farm to the Taihape rugby grounds twenty minutes away. He was in a very determined frame of mind. His rugby mates all seemed energised. The weather was fine and sunny but a little bit cool. However, the playing field was dry and firm and that would suit his speedy style of play much better than it being waterlogged and slow under foot. He hoped they could win even if the prospect of that happening was a bit of a longshot. If they did, then on his next call to Aoife he'd be able to have bragging rights and jokingly tell her that maybe the waiter at the Piazza Bellini café knew something they didn't know.

It was a good game of provincial club rugby and the final score was a respectable 16 all draw. Not a win but not a loss. William had even scored a try out on the left wing.

Considering Taihape were the second placed team in the competition, all of William's team mates were well pleased and thankful to have him back playing in the team.

William went to bed on Saturday night a little bit muscle sore from being on the receiving end of a few hard tackles at the rugby game, but it was par for the course and he knew he'd recover quickly so no need to worry. He lay in bed thinking about where he'd go exploring the following afternoon. There was a stand of dense native bush on the banks of the Mangaweka River just a few kilometres inland from the old single lane Mangaweka Bridge. He'd been to the general area previously but not that particular stand of native bush. Plus there were several very good rock exposures in the area along road cuttings and bluffs so he would fossick around those also.

Sunday arrived and although it was the day of rest for most people in the district, William couldn't afford the luxury of taking the whole day off especially since he was to go exploring by himself in the afternoon. The very first thing he did after waking up and dressing was to go outside and see if there had been any birthing activity overnight. He scanned all the holding paddocks near the homestead for calves or lambs but couldn't see any new-borns.

Once back inside and for one brief moment, he wished he was back in Naples taking a moka stovetop coffee out to his apartment balcony and relaxing in the warm morning air. But he soon snapped out of that indulgence and considered himself lucky to be where he was when there was so much turmoil in the world. He had safety and security with good health and happiness so was very thankful for that.

After breakfast William headed out on the farm on his all-terrain quad bike just to check that everything was alright with his scattered livestock. It wasn't a small farm so that task took him most of the morning. Everything was in order. He was free to spend the afternoon out on one of his beloved wilderness exploratory trips. The weather was fine and sunny but cool so he knew he'd need to dress appropriately and make sure his mobile phone was fully charged just in case he got into trouble.

William set off from the farm at 1 pm and twenty minutes later arrived at a parking spot just past the old Mangaweka Bridge. He looked across the deeply incised river valley to the native bush area he had selected to visit. It was an area that he had not been to previously. The stand of native bush across the river looked densely wooded and primeval from a distance. Around the area where he parked his car, and along the roadside verge in both directions, the sprawling Bright Bead Cotoneaster bushes were still covered in their pea sized bright red berries. Although he knew it was an introduced and invasive species he still marvelled at their beauty when they were growing en masse. He gazed across the river valley at the steep native bush covered slopes he was going to visit. His first task would be accessing the area because there was no way he'd be able to directly cross the river alone and on foot. It was too deep and too fast flowing. He scanned upstream and noticed a narrow foot bridge going across the river approximately one kilometre in the distance. It was likely to have been a farm-to-farm access bridge built decades ago. If he did decide to use it he would have to proceed with extreme caution.

William was adventurous but he was not stupid. He scanned the rickety foot bridge very carefully and assessed that it would hold his body weight. He was a little bit nervous during the crossing and was glad to get across to the other side safely. After reorganising the gear in his back pack, William started walking back downstream close to the banks of the river until he approached the area of native bush.

The ground leading into the bush was steep and there didn't appear to be any existing man-made or farm animal tracks going into it. He entered the tall tree canopy slowly and cautiously and then almost immediately it became darker and damp. Despite those constraints the air was intoxicating and luscious. William inhaled to full lung capacity. He felt extraordinarily alive and was sure that he had never smelt air that was so refreshing. Apart from a few melodic bird calls, the bush was eerily silent. He could just make out the muffled sound of the river flowing by downslope.

He continued walking through the bush on a parallel upslope bearing to the river. William was mesmerised by the various bird species. He wasn't an expert but he could easily identify at least five different species. They all seemed so fearless and inquisitive. They all acted so trustingly. William was encroaching into their world and he was mindful of that. A small group of pīwakawaka fantails fluttered around him and one landed on his left shoulder. Then another landed on his right shoulder. Several others landed on branches only a few tens of centimetres away from him. He froze completely still and breathed as quietly and slowly as he could not wanting to startle or frighten them. For several minutes the group of pīwakawaka fantails scoped William and he scoped them. William was feeling emotional at the overpowering spiritually of the event and the place. Tears of happiness started to fill his eyes. Life is full of beautiful experiences and this is one of them he told himself.

William. William.

William was startled and glanced around quickly in all directions thinking he had heard a quiet voice call out his name. The pīwakawaka fantails sensed that he was anxious and fluttered away quickly out of sight. William was sure he had heard that same female voice before.

"Hello, hello is anybody there? Is somebody calling me?"

Nobody answered. William reluctantly assumed it must have been a bird calling and chirping that sounded like somebody speaking. Maybe it's the spirituality of the place getting into my mind he thought.

Although a little bit scared by his close encounter of the unknown kind he continued wandering through the stand of native bush. As he went he was touching, listening, looking, smelling, moving around trees and changing his body position. It was sensory overload such that apart from his sense of taste, all the other six of his seven senses were being fully utilised. He couldn't wait to bring Aoife into the bush with him and see what she thought of it. In his mind he was sure that she would be just as impressed as him. A quick glance on his mobile phone told him that it was time to head back.

William returned home to the farm without incident. That night he was going to try and make a decent Italian meal for himself with some of the cooking ingredients he had brought back from Naples. He wanted to spend a bit of time with Ram also so would invite him and Suzie over for dinner one night during the week ahead. As it was Sunday night he would and did make his usual 8 pm call to Aoife.

"Aoife it's William, can you hear and see me OK?"

"Yes I can."

"How have the past few days been at your end?"

"I've booked my flight tickets and have received them online. All confirmed now. Hunterville here I come."

"That's great news. Send me a copy of your Dubai to Auckland ticket just so I know flight number and ETA to Auckland. I'll be at the airport."

"Just over a month to go but that's OK. It will speed by, and anyway, I want to spend some decent time with the family before I head away. I'm surprised, but they seem OK with me heading to the other side of the world. If it was anybody other than you, I'm not sure they'd be so happy."

"That's cool. I played rugby yesterday and we drew 16 all. The team was very happy to break a three game losing streak."

William wanted to tell Aoife about his walk into the stand of native bush earlier that afternoon and the female voice he thought he had heard, but he didn't want Aoife to think he was acting weird so he just let it drop.

They spent the next hour reminiscing about their time in Naples, about the trip ahead and what each of them had been doing over the past few days since they last talked.

"When you pack your bags, don't forget to bring your black opera dress with you. I've got a surprise planned when you get here but that's all I'm saying."

"Are we going to the opera again?"

"Stop fishing Aoife," replied William laughing "no not the opera but somewhere special to do something special."

"Can't wait William. I know it will be memorable. Love you."

"I love you to. I'm expecting the first of the spring lambs and calves to be born in the next day or two so it's going to be busy few weeks for me. That's good because it will make the time pass by more quickly."

"Will we be able to talk again Wednesday?"

"Of course that's set in concrete. Talk then, and text me whenever you feel like it."

Aoife and William said their goodbyes and as usual, the actual ending of the call was drawn out as neither of them wanted to be the one to tap 'end call'.

William was an excellent stockman and as he had predicted, when he woke up the following morning and went outside there were six new born lambs in the holding paddock. He couldn't see any calves but he was certain they'd start arriving within the next forty eight hours.

Over the next few days William was very busy on the farm. It was an unusually mild spring and this greatly aided the ease of the lambing and calving season. There was not a single new-born lamb or calf lost, the grass feed was green and lush, and the evenings were cool but not cold.

Over the next few weeks, Aoife and William kept in regular contact via calls and texts. During this period, William's life was very busy with his farm work, rugby practice, Saturday rugby games and regular visits to his parents. There was however, one thing he was not very happy about and felt he had neglected somewhat. He was determined to address that.

"Evening Ram it's William here. Sorry I haven't been in contact mate but the lambing and calving season has been full on. It's almost over now, in fact I think it's finished, so I just wanted to ask you if you'd like to come over for dinner on Friday night and bring Suzie with you."

"Are you sure?"

"I'm definitely sure. And I'll make dinner. Something Italian of course. Will Suzie be OK with Italian?"

"She loves food from different countries and has been trying to get me to branch out and be a more adventurous foodie. She'll love it. Can we bring something?"

"Bottle of wine maybe, ask Suzie what she likes, but honestly nothing else. Is Friday night 6 pm OK?"

"That will work. Thanks William, you're a good mate."

"It works both ways Ram. You're a good mate also. Friday night 6 pm. See you guys then. *Ciao*."

"Goodnight William. Thanks again."

William already had most of the ingredients he wanted to use to make dinner from the Italian foodie supply he had brought back with him. The few other items he'd need, he could easily get in Hunterville at the local general store. He knew exactly what he was going to make for Ram and Suzie and it was only Wednesday so everything was well under control.

Friday night arrived and William could see the headlights of Ram's car coming up the long driveway to the farmhouse while he was in the kitchen. He immediately stopped what he was doing and went to greet his guests at the front door. After giving them both a warm welcoming hug William spoke.

"Evening Ram. Evening Suzie. Thanks for coming. Please come in and make yourselves at home."

"Evening William" they both replied in unison.

"Dinner is pretty much ready so let's have a drink it the lounge first. I've put the fire on. Makes it seem cosier. Do you like Italian food Suzie? Please say yes."

"I love it William. Joseph tells me you're a pretty good chef so I'm looking forward to it."

"I don't know about the chef bit, but I do like global cuisine and I do like cooking. Fingers crossed."

Dinner was ready and the three of them sat down and enjoyed a main course of beef osso bucco casserole with mushroom polenta. When they were all finished, Suzie gave her verdict.

"Totally fantastic William. The meat is so tender and so tasty. Joseph said you were an excellent cook, and seriously, that was of restaurant quality."

"Thank you kindly. I've got some ice cream and brandied apples for dessert but it's not store bought ice cream. I made it. First attempt so I'm not sure what it will be like. There's no back-up plan so fingers crossed. It's got 10+ Mānuka honey from 'you know where' swirled through it."

All three of them tasted the ice cream simultaneously. The verdict was unanimous.

"I know this is going to sound a bit pretentious especially since I made it, but it tastes pretty good to me."

Ram agreed.

"Pretty good. William it's damn delicious. You should enter it in one of those ice cream competitions they have mate."

William was getting a little bit embarrassed with all the compliments so he tried to change the subject.

"You're the first people I've told other than my parents, but Aoife is arriving in Auckland on the morning of Saturday 31st August and I'm going to drive up there to meet her and bring her back to the farm. She'll be very tired from the long journey so we'll overnight in Auckland and we'll drive down home the following day. So on Sunday 1st September Aoife will be here with me in Hunterville."

Suzie and Ram could see from the sparkle in William's eyes and the smile on his face as he told them about Aoife's arrival, that he was very, very excited.

"William, that's awesome mate. We can't wait to meet her."

"I promise that you guys will be the first."

Ram already knew that William was a special friend to him and the fact that they would be the first ones to be introduced to Aoife after her arrival in Hunterville merely confirmed this. William was more like his close brother than a mate. Ram's parents lived in the South Island and it was a long time since he'd been in any sort of contact with them. His two older sisters lived in the North Island but they wanted nothing to do with him. He knew that for many years his behaviour had been aggressive and hurtful towards his family and since meeting and getting serious with Suzie, he wanted to try and change that.

"William, I've got a big favour to ask you. Suzie means a lot to me and I want to try and make some changes for the better. She doesn't like people calling me Ram. Those days are over. Since you're my best friend, is there any chance that you could start calling me by my real name Joseph? I'd like that."

"Going forward and right from this moment, I will call you Joseph. It's a good name. It has biblical significance. Ram is no more. The only Ram I now know is the one I have out in the paddock. Joseph it is. I like calling you that name. It suits you."

Joseph knew that he could rely on William's support. Suzie approved. Joseph and Suzie said their good nights to William and thanked him for a great evening and a perfect meal. Suzie who had sat on the one glass of wine all evening said that she'd be driving.

"Please drive very carefully Suzie and we'll catch up again soon."

"Thanks mate and fingers crossed that you have a good game tomorrow. I'm not playing tomorrow. I've got some important things to do with Suzie."

"Ok. We're playing the Mangaweka team just up the road. They're good but I think we can beat them."

"Hope you do. Text me if you win. Good night mate."

"Good night William and thank you for a nice evening and for being such a kind friend to Joseph" added Suzie.

Joseph's car disappeared down the long driveway. As they were driving down the driveway Joseph turned and spoke to Suzie.

"Do you think we should tell anybody else about Aoife's arrival to New Zealand on the 31st August. William didn't say keep it a secret or anything like that. If he had wanted it to be kept secret I'm sure he would have said. I'm so happy for William I have to let other people know. I'm sure they'd all be happy also."

"I think you're right Joseph. He didn't say not to tell anybody else so it should be alright to mention it."

After Joseph and Suzie had left, William showered and went straight to bed. It wasn't very late but he had his rugby game the next day and wanted to be physically alert and mentally primed for it. An early night seemed appropriate. William woke up the next morning in a positive frame of mind. He was determined to try and put his Hunterville team in a winning position when the final whistle blew.

It was an even game and the leading score changed several times throughout the game, but at the final whistle, the score was twenty four to eighteen in favour of the Hunterville team. William had scored two tries out on the wing and was well satisfied with his performance. At the end of the game in the dressing room, he flicked a quick text off to Joseph.

Gidday Joseph, we won 24–18. Guess who scored 2 tries? Life is good.

Joseph's text reply was immediate.

Good job William. Catch up soon.

The day was fast approaching for Aoife's departure from Ireland. William had been working hard out on the farm and inside the house to make both presentable for Aoife's arrival. He was ready.

Thanks to Joseph's excitement and desire to share the news immediately after the memorable Italian dinner over at William's house, word had got out around Hunterville that William's 'special female friend' from Ireland was arriving into Auckland on the 31st August. Most knew a little about how they had met in Naples as strangers, explored the city together and quickly developed a close and loving relationship. Without exception, everybody was very happy for William and hoping for a fairy-tale happy ending.

Aoife's date of departure from Galway was the late afternoon of Wednesday the 28th August and William called her at his usual scheduled time of 8 pm. It was 8 am in the morning in Galway.

"Morning Aoife. William here. How are you feeling?"

"Morning William. I'm very excited but nervous as well. I'm dreading the length of the journey to reach you. But I'll be OK once I get going. It was hard saying goodbye to the family. Finn drove me to Galway last night. I slept reasonably well."

"I know it's a long way and a long journey. Text me from Dubai if you can. I'll be at Auckland Airport to meet you. The whole town knows you're coming and everybody wants to meet you. But I know you'll want to rest for a few days so don't worry. No pressure. Just want you to be here."

"Can't wait. I'm heading to the airport around 2 pm. Mr O'Leary is picking me up and dropping me there. Everything is sorted. Any tips?"

"I'm no expert at long distance flights but just try and rest. Any catnaps are good. Drink lots of water and not too much alcohol."

"Ok. See you on Saturday morning. Love you. Not long now."

"Safe travels and you're in my mind 24/7. Love you. Don't forget to text me from Dubai."

"I will. See you soon. Bye."

The long distance calling was completed. In two days' time Aoife would be physically reunited with William in New Zealand. She would be back in his arms. She would see that beaming smile again.

William had arranged for the farmhands to look after the farm while he was away up to Auckland to collect Aoife. He had asked them if he should get extra help in for two days but they insisted they'd look after things for him especially since the lambing and calving operation was now over. They'd both stay overnight in the self-contained workers units to ensure farm security. Not that a breach of farm security was a likely possibility. Things like that very rarely happened in the district. Local people cared and looked after each other's wellbeing and property.

Reunited

Aoife's flight in to Auckland Airport was due to arrive at 6 am on Saturday morning the 31st August. William knew he wouldn't be able to drive up north that morning so he elected to go up the afternoon before, and book a motel close to the airport for two nights. That would give Aoife a chance to rest and recover from the long journey before heading down to Hunterville on Sunday. He explained to the rugby team why he wouldn't be at the Saturday afternoon game and they all understood that he had a far greater calling. Every man in the team was supportive of their friend.

The day when they would be reunited had finally arrived. William's wait was almost over and his excitement was palpable. In retrospect, the six weeks since he had last held Aoife in his arms at Naples Airport had passed by quickly thanks to busy times on the farm and his other interests. William's drive up to Auckland all passed without incident. At 5.30 am on Sunday morning, William left on foot from his airport motel having checked the arrival time of the flight. He'd rather be early and have to wait, than be late and not there when Aoife came out into the arrival hall.

Aoife's flight arrived a little bit behind schedule at 6.20 am. William stood in the arrivals area patiently waiting. His heart was beating much faster than normal. He was lightly sweating and his breathing had accelerated. The waiting was unbearable until exiting through the custom area doors into the arrival hall was Aoife. She had arrived safely to Auckland. He was overcome with emotion and ran forward with tears streaming down his cheeks to greet her. They were tears of unbridled joy and happiness. He flung his arms around her and kissed her lovingly. She reciprocated with equal joy and happiness. Even after a journey time well in excess of forty eight hours she was still a vision of beauty.

"I missed you so much Aoife. Welcome to New Zealand. I'm not even going to ask if you're tired. Give me your bags and let's go to the airport motel I've booked for you to rest."

"Thanks William. I missed you more than……well, more than you could ever imagine. I miss that smile of yours. And that never ending kindness you dish out. I am feeling really tired even though I slept a bit on the flight to Auckland. And I feel a little bit nauseous.

Probably shouldn't have eaten that spicy meal last night on the flight. My stomach not used to it. I just want to sleep."

"Of course you do. Let's go it's less than ten minutes' walk away. Are you OK walking or shall I get a taxi?"

"Walking is good. The fresh air might perk me up a bit."

After arriving at the motel Aoife had a very quick shower, went straight to bed and slept deeply and continuously for the next eleven hours. It wasn't until 6 pm that she woke up again. William was sitting on the side of the bed when she woke up.

"Hello William. What time is it? Please don't ask me to guess?"

"It's 6 pm. You slept for eleven hours straight. How do you feel?"

"Eleven hours! Really? I'm feeling a bit better. A bit washed out. That's not a journey I'd like to do again in a hurry. It might be OK in business class where you can lie horizontal and sleep, but economy class is so tiring."

"It's not good I know. Just rest. We are not going to drive back until the morning so there's plenty of time yet to try and recover. Like anything to eat or drink?"

"Something light, and a cuppa tea rather than coffee."

He had brought a few very basic provisions with him from home.

"No problem. How about scrambled egg on toast and nice cup of English breakfast?"

"Sounds perfect. Thanks."

William set about looking after Aoife. She had come a long way to be with him and that was something he didn't ever want to forget. Aoife got out of bed and joined William at the small kitchen table. They sat gazing into each other's eyes, held hands and chatted about the past few weeks apart, and the next few weeks ahead. Aoife listened intently to William's plans.

"It's a six hour leisurely drive from Auckland to Hunterville so I thought we might leave around 9 am tomorrow morning. We can stop at Lake Taupō for some lunch which is just over half way and then continue home. How does that sound? I'll point everything out to you on the way because the landscape changes frequently. Promise me one thing."

"OK, what is it?"

"If I rabbit on in the car too much about all the sights and geography and farming and all that stuff on the drive south, and you just want some peace and quiet, please just tell me. I promise I won't be offended."

"OK, I'll try but I want to hear what you say. I love it when you're so enthusiastic and positive about everything. That's one of the many reasons why I'm attracted to you."

William stood up and went around and leaned over and kissed Aoife passionately on the lips. He wanted more but thought it would be far too disrespectful to be wanting of Aoife when she had only been in the country for twelve hours and was obviously tired from the long journey. That would be unacceptable and wasn't going to happen.

Aoife and William spent the rest of the evening in simple conversation, happy to be back in each other's company again. They retired to bed at 10 pm. Despite having woken up from a long sleep just four hours prior, Aoife fell asleep again in William's arms. She knew she was with a man that would love and respect her. This night, just lying next to Aoife and comforting her was all he wanted. It felt good and was something he had missed for the past six weeks.

William was surprised to wake up in the morning and find that Aoife was already up and had started making breakfast for them with the few provisions she could find.

"I'm feeling a lot better this morning William. Those two big sleeps must have done the trick. Moka coffee on the balcony? Sorry, just joking."

William laughed joyously and sprung out of bed butt naked and rushed over to scantily clad Aoife. Testosterone was flowing freely through his body and he couldn't contain himself any longer. He acted like most men would in such a situation. He made sweet morning love with Aoife until both were satisfied.

Finally back to the kitchen after both of them having showered and dressed, William spoke first.

"Sorry, no balcony here or on the farm Aoife, but we'll have to come up with something that has equal significance. Let me work on that."

"You did say there was a café in Hunterville right? I'm looking forward to our first café visit together."

"It's not going to be anything like Naples, but it's still going to be enjoyable. Don't be surprised if the ladies in the café fuss over you when we visit. Joseph aka Ram has already spread the word about our arrival time back to Hunterville so most people already know that we'll be arriving to the farm later this afternoon."

"Nice. What does Joseph aka Ram mean?"

"Ram doesn't want to be called that anymore. Joseph is his real name. He seems to be in a committed relationship with Suzie so thinks it's a more appropriate to use his real name. I hope it works out."

"OK, I'll try my very best to remember to call him Joseph."

Aoife and William spent the rest of the morning enjoying each other's company and checked out of the motel just after 9 am to start the drive south.

"Are you ready? Hunterville here we come. Excited?"

"Definitely. Can't wait to get there William."

And off they went. Aoife was interested in everything she observed and asked William many questions as they drove south. She was amazed at how green the countryside was. Ireland was very green but from what she had observed on the first part of the drive south, New Zealand was its equal and possibly even greener. She mentioned to William that back home in Ireland the farm fences were mostly built of stone, whereas here they were all wire strand fences.

"There are so many sheep and dairy cows and the grass is so green. No wonder New Zealand meat and dairy products are so popular all over the world. Do animals graze outside all year round?"

"Yep. No indoor livestock in kiwiland even over the cold winter months. I can't imagine that type of farming. Even in the winter I like to get out on the hills and valleys and tend my animals."

"The countryside in Ireland is beautiful William but this is easily its equal. It's stunning."

"Well, get ready, because as we drive south, it's going to be even more scenic."

Three and a half hours later they had arrived to the outskirts of Lake Taupō and the central North Island town of Taupō. Aoife had observed steam rising from the hills and countryside in many places as they approached Lake Taupō and asked William what it was.

"The area surrounding Lake Taupō is a famous active geothermal area in New Zealand. They use geothermal steam to generate electricity, there are hot pools for bathing and health spas in several places, and there are famous active volcanic and geothermal areas that you can carefully walk around all over the place. We'll definitely come back here sometime in the future for a few days. I love coming here. I think you will also. We can even go horse-riding or mountain biking or both. How cool would that be?"

"I can't wait until we go horse-riding together again William. New Zealand is so different to Ireland. But it's a good and an exciting kind of different."

William was happy that Aoife was impressed with everything she was seeing. It would make the process of settling into life in New Zealand a lot easier. There was no doubt in William's mind that he wanted to formalise his relationship with Aoife. He hadn't yet finalised where and when that would happen, but he had been thinking about it a lot and had a good idea of how he wanted to do it. It would happen back on the farm. He was a man on a mission.

"Let's stop here for lunch. There's a café near the town that I go to when I'm here. Not like the cafés in Naples of course but still good, and there's an excellent view over the lake whether you sit inside or outside. Let's sit inside. I don't want you to get a chill."

"Sounds good. Thanks."

After lunch and before they continued their journey south, they took a moment to walk over to and stand at the edge of the boardwalk around the lake margin. They gazed out across the lake towards two very well defined and snow-covered mountain peaks in the far distance. Aoife was impressed.

"William that café lunch and coffee was good. I can't believe how friendly and cheerful everybody is. And this lake is so clean and the air is so fresh. I hope we come back here sometime."

"I promise we will Aoife. See those snow covered volcanic peaks in the distance. We're going to drive right by those via a road called the Desert Road. It's not really a desert by international standards but it has a lot of barren and poorly vegetated slopes due to a history of ongoing volcanic activity in the area. If we're lucky we might see a volcanic eruption as we go by. Not. I'm just joking. They close all the roads in the immediate area if there are any significant volcanic rumblings or actual volcanic explosions."

Aoife smiled and lent over and kissed William. She loved it when he joked about things and teased her. She felt safe in his presence. This was a man that knew the countryside and was interested in all things earth science related so there's no way he'd jeopardise their safety. As least that's what she hoped.

"It's about another two and a half hour drive to the farm. Ready to go?"

"I'm ready."

William and Aoife continued their journey to the farm by driving around the margin of the lake and then heading inland and southwards across the Central Plateau. Aoife was amazed by the constantly changing landscape. To say she was impressed was putting it mildly.

"There's nothing like this in Ireland. What's that large mountain called? It's beautiful."

"It's the largest active volcano in New Zealand. It's called Ruapehu and means 'pit of noise' in the Māori language. The last major eruption was twelve years ago during September 2007. There are a couple of ski fields up there which are very popular. Do you like skiing? Not really my thing but I've done it a few times."

"No, I've never been skiing."

William slowed down, pulled over and stopped the car at a clearing adjacent to a stand of low scrubby bushes and densely growing trees.

"What's wrong?"

"Nothing is wrong. I just want to show you something very quickly."

They got out of the car and walked the very short distance over to a stand of bushes.

"See these bushy trees here with their small spikey leaves and blackened branches and scattered small white flowers. Guess what they are?"

"No idea William. Sorry."

"It's the Mānuka tree. Botanical name *Leptospermum scoparium*. Those little white flowers with the pink centres are where the bees gather Mānuka honey from. Luckily it grows in many parts of New Zealand. I know it's cold but I just wanted to show you quickly. Sorry about that. It's easier to see it here than on the farm."

"Thanks William. Glad you stopped. Don't be sorry. I know Mānuka honey is special to you so happy to learn about it."

"Let's go it's getting cold. I don't want you to get sick."

They hopped back into the car and continued their journey.

"At the next town coming up called Waiouru, which is an army town, we're going to branch off to the south and after about twenty or thirty minutes we'll enter the Rangitikei District which is a farming area in New Zealand very well known for its sheep grazing and beef cattle fattening farms."

As they drove south of Waiouru, Aoife continued to gaze with delight at the rugged landscape, the lush green paddocks, valleys and hillslopes. Out her side of the car window she could see the Rangitikei River Valley in places and freshly exposed rock cliff slopes at the bends in the river. She was very impressed and turned to William.

"This is beautiful William. It's so, so scenic. I had a picture in my mind but this is much better. Lots of animals in the paddocks but there doesn't seem to be many people. Not that I mind."

"No there isn't a huge number of people in this part of the country, just small friendly farming service towns scattered along and a short distance in from the main state highway."

"We're almost there. We are going to branch off to the right in about five minutes and head up Murimotu Road. Murimotu Road is just a few kilometres north of Hunterville township. We can go into Hunterville tomorrow or the next day to have a look around if you want to or just spend time together around the farm. Depends on how you feel. No rush and no pressure."

"Don't ask me why William but I'm both excited and nervous. A few days ago I was home with family in Ballinrobe and a few minutes from now I'll be at your home in Hunterville on the other side of the world. Crazy."

"As soon as we get home send your family a text and tell them you've arrived safely. And we can video call them whenever you feel like it."

"I will and thanks for being so considerate. They'll be wondering what's happening."

"This is Murimotu Road and home is less than ten minutes up the road."

Aoife went silent as they turned into Murimotu Road and drove the final few kilometres towards William's farm. And there it was. Aoife's jaw dropped as they drove up a long driveway lined both side with trees with arched branches. On both sides of the driveway she could see the paddocks filled with ewes and their newly born lambs frolicking and playing in the late afternoon spring sun. At the end of the driveway there was an open parking area for vehicles, and adjacent to it, William's home. She noted how neat and tidy everything was outside including the driveway, the paddocks, and the garden around the home.

William jumped out of the car and took a quick look at his phone. It was showing 4 pm. He rushed around to Aoife's side, opened her car door and helped her out. He held her from behind as she gazed around the homestead.

"Welcome to the farm but most of all welcome to my world Aoife. I have been dreaming of this moment. It proves that dreams do come true."

"Thank you for being so kind and making me feel so welcome William. I know I've done the right thing."

"Let's get your things and head inside."

William took Aoife inside and she felt at home straight away. The inside of William's house was neat and tidy and had some of the indications that it was the home of a bachelor. It had been his parent's house since the 1960s and possibly needed a little modernising inside.

"How are you feeling? I reckon it takes five or six days for the body clock to completely readjust when the time difference between locations is twelve hours. This is only day two for you. Do you feel like any dinner? I've got stuff already made in the fridge. But first I'll put the heating on because it's a bit cold."

"Maybe some dinner would be good but no alcohol I'm still feeling a bit queasy. It comes and goes. I haven't travelled extreme long distance before so I wasn't sure how my body would react."

William sat Aoife down in the lounge and made her a warm tea while he went to the kitchen and dished them out and then heated up some lamb casserole and vegetable rice in the microwave.

"It's not Italian but I hope you'll like it."

"Looks good William but before we eat, I'll just flick off a text to the family."

Aoife composed a short text and sent it back home separately to her parents and her brother.

Mum, Dad, Finn...long tiring journey but with William on the farm now. It's so beautiful. New Zealand is beautiful. Everybody is so friendly. Safe and sound in Hunterville. Can't wait to explore everything with William when over this jetlag. Love u all. Aoife xx.

Knowing that it wasn't yet 6 am back in Ballinrobe she wasn't expecting a quick reply so Aoife was surprised to get instant text replies back from both her brother and her parents.

I knew I could rely on William. I'm happy u safely with the man you love. Any problems let me know. Rest and when recovered keep us updated...Finn xxx.

Morning Aoife. Thank goodness u safe and sound. Rest and then face call us soon. We will pray for you and William at church this morning. Take care. Mum and Dad xxxxxx.

William and Aoife chatted over dinner and discussed what they might do over the next few days depending on how Aoife felt after the long trip. He told her that she was welcome to use and access anything in the house.

William asked Aoife if it was OK for him to get out and do some farm work in the morning. She answered that he must. If she was feeling up to it he suggested they might head into Hunterville on Tuesday morning to check out the café and he wanted to show her his beloved Mānuka Honey Shop. He also mentioned that he would not be going to rugby practice on Tuesday and Thursday evening of the coming week. He felt that he was in such good physical condition that he didn't really need to. He didn't want to leave Aoife alone more than absolutely necessary during her first week in Hunterville.

There were so many things William wanted to do with Aoife over the next days, weeks, months but rather than overwhelm her when she was obviously still tired from the trip to New Zealand, he suggested they shower and head to bed for an early night. Aoife was in total agreement.

Having showered, they slipped into bed. It was warm and cosy. Aoife feel asleep almost instantly in William's arms while he lay awake for several minutes reflecting on how lucky he was to be lying naked with this beautiful soul brought into his life at Nonna Russo's Cooking Class. Had it been predetermined or was it by chance? He didn't have an answer but right at that moment he didn't care. He was the happiest he'd ever been in his life. William drifted off to sleep.

William and Aoife Settle into Life on the Farm

William woke up at 6 am the following morning. He didn't want to get out of bed but reality beckoned. There was work to do on the farm and his farm workers would be arriving at 7 am and be looking for instructions for the day's activities. He looked over at Aoife and she was stirring but not fully awake. He got out of bed, dressed and made them coffee using a packet of Napoli coffee he had brought back from Naples with him. He delivered a coffee to Aoife while she was still in bed. She was very appreciative.

"Thanks William."

"How are you feeling this morning?"

"Not too bad but I'll just rest and acclimatise today. You go out on the farm and do whatever you have to and I'll potter around. In a day or two when I feel better I'd like to come out on the farm with you."

"If you don't mind me getting back to work that would be good. And midweek we'll go into Hunterville and visit the café and the honey shop if you're up to it. How does that sound?"

"Sounds perfect. Do you mind if I rummage through the kitchen for supplies and ingredients? I want to make us dinner tonight. Maybe I'll make something Italian."

"Treat it as your own home. Rummage through anything you want. All the Italian cooking supplies I brought back are in the pantry, the fridge is full, and there's a freezer full of various meats and frozen veggies in the washroom."

William sat on a chair in the bedroom and chatted with Aoife while they sipped their coffee.

"I've got one final thing to ask you and please say no if you're not keen about it. Joseph is my best friend and I promised him that he and Suzie would be the first to meet you after you arrived to the farm. I don't want to break that promise. Can they come around later on Tuesday to say hello and meet you?"

"Of course they can. Tell them I'm looking forward to it."

"Thanks Aoife."

William kissed and hugged Aoife and reluctantly left her so he could carry out a good day's work on the farm. There was stock to move, fertilising of the paddocks to be completed before the full spring rains arrived, and a few fences needed mending. The lambs and calves were thriving and it wouldn't be long before they'd need docking, crutching and tagging.

William was also very keen to starting planting some native bush areas on the farm. He was keen to reduce his carbon footprint. It was something he had promised himself to do while away on holiday in Naples. He wanted to work out the best areas on the farm for doing that with the help of his farm workers.

William was tired when he returned to the farmhouse at 5 pm. He had been working hard all day and was physically spent. He was totally buggered but when he walked into the house he perked up considerably. Aoife had the heating on, dinner was almost prepared and she was ready to pour them a pre-dinner drink. He hadn't been spoilt like this since his mother and father were last living in the house.

"Evening Aoife. How's your day been?"

"Good, I think the body clock is adjusting because I've been feeling a lot better today. I found everything I needed. I made us something Italian for dinner. Memories?"

"Thanks Aoife. Appreciated. It's been busy day out on the farm. We got a lot done today."

"Remember that I come from a farming family so I know there's always work to be done. You do what you have to. And hopefully in a few days' time I'll feel a bit better and be able accompany you. I seriously want to. In fact, I can't wait. I know Dad and Finn will be very interested to know what the farming life is like in New Zealand."

"Thanks Aoife. You're always so kind to me. Sometimes I really wonder what I did to deserve it."

"It works both ways William. Your kindness to me is never ending so you deserve the same in return. It's as simple as that. But enough of that, it's time to eat."

William and Aoife sat down and enjoyed a delicious dinner of Italian roasted lamb cooked in white wine and garlic served with polenta chips and a salad slaw. William enjoyed a cold beer with his dinner but Aoife just wanted a warm lemon tea. Her choice of drink with dinner went unnoticed by William. They laughed and joked and reminisced about their holiday in Naples and discussed what they might do for the rest of the week.

"Excuse me mister sweet tooth I made you something special for dessert. I made a small apple crumble and some…wait for it…some Mānuka honey and vanilla custard."

William smiled and then laughed and held Aoife's hand across the table. "*Delizioso*, it sounds good. I love crumble."

"Well, now that I'm a bit more educated about the Mānuka tree and its prized honey, and since you like it so much, I thought I'd better start getting inventive. When are we going to the Mānuka Honey Shop in Hunterville?"

"I thought Wednesday would be good when we stop by the café in town."

"Sounds like a plan and tomorrow night I'm meeting Joseph and Suzie right?"

"Yes. I'll call him now and check that they can come over."

"How about I make a couple large pizzas and we can share those for dinner and get to know each other."

"Are you sure?"

"I've got all day William so no problem."

William called Joseph and invited him and Suzie over the following evening for a pizza night.

"He's so excited that he's going to meet you. It sounds like he desperately wants us to form a good friendship with him and Suzie. I've never known him to act like this before."

"Just shows how important your friendship is to him William. That's kind of special. Really special."

William thanked Aoife for the enjoyable dinner, a fantastic evening and told her that it was the perfect end to a busy day. Aoife told William that her first full day on the farm had been enjoyable from start to finish. They retired to bed early and before you could count to twenty, William was fast asleep. Aoife smiled lovingly at the sleeping William knowing she had made the right decision joining this man in Hunterville.

Tuesday was another busy day on the farm. Aoife did a repeat of what she had done the day before. Although William craved and enjoyed the attention and support he was receiving from Aoife he was starting to feel a little bit guilty. He didn't want Aoife to feel like she was being used, but in reality that was the furthest thing from her mind. He promised her that after their café and Mānuka Honey Shop visits on Wednesday, he would make dinner for her.

At 5 pm there was a knock on the front door. Joseph and Suzie had arrived. William went to meet them. He led them into the kitchen where Aoife was putting the finishing touches to dinner. She turned around, flashed a big smile at them and immediately went over, introduced herself and then warmly hugged them both. Joseph and Suzie were extraordinarily quiet. William had never known Joseph to be so quiet. He wondered to himself what that was all about?

"Evening Suzie. Evening Joseph. I'm Aoife. William has told me all about you. I'm so pleased to meet you both. I hope we'll be good friends."

Finally Joseph seemed to muster the courage to talk.

"Thanks Aoife. Welcome to Hunterville. We're so happy to meet you. I'm William's best friend. Have you met anybody else in Hunterville yet?"

William and Aoife glanced at each other knowing full well that Joseph was checking if William's promise to him had been kept. William was a man of integrity so of course it had been.

"No, you're the first people I've seen since I arrived here on Sunday afternoon. I've been really tired from jetlag so I've just been taking it easy around the house."

Once he had heard the reply he was hoping for, he opened up and the conversation flowed more freely. The back and forth conversation between the four of them continued. William listened and was in shock. He had never heard Joseph articulate without cussing and using suggestive vulgarities. He was polite and charming towards both Suzie and Aoife. This is indeed a changed man he thought to himself. The evening passed and was a huge success as were Aoife's pizzas and the ice cold beers.

"When are you guys going in to Hunterville? You know the whole town is keen to meet you Aoife. William is special in this town. He helps everybody, doesn't judge anybody and makes everybody feel happy. Men, women, children, cats and dogs, we all respect and admire him."

Aoife could see tears welling in Joseph's eyes as he spoke. He discretely tried to wipe them away. This was a man telling Aoife that the town was proud of William, and that he was even prouder to be his best friend. William was surprised. In all the years he had known Joseph he had never seen him this emotional, let alone shed any tears.

The evening was a great success and had paved the way for the four of them to be good friends. William and Aoife accompanied Joseph and Suzie outside into the cold night air to wish them good night and wave them goodbye as they departed down the long driveway.

As they drove down the driveway Suzie put her hand on Joseph's thigh and told him how she had enjoyed the evening.

"Aoife is so nice. Just like William. They make a perfect match. I'm so happy we'll be best friends with them."

"I agree. I hope we can copy them. I'm trying to be a better man Suzie and I think William is showing me how to do that. Something tells me we in for more big surprises. I'm sure he'll propose to her soon."

Visit to the Café and Mānuka Honey Shop

William woke up first again on Wednesday morning and got out of bed to make himself and Aoife a coffee. He was missing having a proper cappuccino coffee so was looking forward to visiting the Hunterville Café later in the morning with Aoife. Aoife was still fast asleep when he came back to the bedroom so he put her coffee on the side table and scribbled a note for her.

Just going out to the shed for an hour to let the guys know what the day's work plan is. I've got a couple of other things to do out there. Be back in 9 am latest to shower and change and then we can head in to Hunterville around 10 am. xxxxxx

William came back inside exactly at 9 am. Aoife was up and dressed. She was sending some emails to her family and friends in Ireland. William shaved, showered, and got dressed. He was ready to go when she was ready. They left the house at 10 am. It was less than a ten minute drive to the café in Hunterville so he expected they'd be seated and sipping a decent coffee before the quarter hour.

"I do know why I'm so nervous William. I feel a bit like I'm on show or going to be judged."

"Oh, please don't feel like that. We don't have to go if you don't feel comfortable. It's just that everybody knows me in town and I've been alone for so long they're curious as to whom this lady is that has totally captured my heart. Word has got out that you're on the farm now and they just want to welcome you to Hunterville. Maybe even thank you for saving me from what was looking like a life of loneliness. Do you still want to go or shall we turn back?"

"Sorry William. Now that you say it like that I understand how people might be feeling. People in small towns are generally much closer than the people in big towns and cities. It's the same in Ballinrobe. Let's do it. I'm proud to been seen out with my man William anywhere around Hunterville."

They had arrived. William easily found a parking spot on the main street. They entered the café.

Instantly, Connie and Kathy dropped what they were doing behind the counter and rushed over to William. Luckily there were only two other customers in the café at that time and they had already been served. William proudly introduced Aoife to the ladies. Connie and Kathy fussed and gushed over William and Aoife as they led them to a table. Everybody was smiling. If any strangers had walked in, they might have thought there was a smile-fest going on. Even the two elderly customers already sitting in the café enjoying their morning tea were smiling from ear to ear. The happiness atmosphere in the café was infectious.

"Aoife this is the regionally famous Hunterville Café. It's been my salvation on many a morning. This is Connie and Kathy. They own the café. Kathy does all the baking herself."

"I'm pleased to meet you ladies. William has told me a lot about this café and your delicious baking and cooking. I can't wait to try some of it."

"It's nice to meet you also Aoife. Welcome to Hunterville. William is our favourite customer. We call him mister sweet tooth."

Aoife laughed out loud and told the ladies that this was also the name she often referred to him as.

"Connie can we please have two large cappuccinos and a plate of sweet treats. Just whatever you think it good for Aoife to try on her first café experience in Hunterville."

"No problem. Be back with your order soon."

It was a small cosy café. Aoife felt immediately at home and the ladies' welcome had been very warm and sincere. Connie returned five minutes later.

"Here are your cappuccinos. They're nice and hot. And I have put two blueberry and lemon muffins with a pottle of butter, and a peanut butter and chocolate slice on a plate. Enjoy."

"Thanks Connie. Everything looks great. Yum." replied William.

William and Aoife didn't hesitate to get started. The coffee didn't disappoint and the muffin was delicious. Aoife was impressed.

"It's hard to beat home baking straight from the oven. The ladies are so nice and I'm impressed that everybody is pronouncing my name correctly. Usually strangers get it completely wrong."

"I think word went out via Joseph and everybody has been telling each other how to say your name correctly. Nobody wants to make a mistake. Everybody wants to create a good impression."

"Great café stop William. No problem coming back here as much as we can. Couple times a week maybe?"

"Yep, we can aim for that as a minimum but more if possible."

Aoife and William finished their café visit and as they stopped to pay on the way out, Aoife thanked the ladies again for their kind welcome to Hunterville. Connie and Kathy asked them to please revisit again sooner rather than later.

"Did you enjoy that? I love visiting there."

"Yes, it was really good. I loved it also. Where to now?"

"Down the street a little bit is the Mānuka Honey Shop. That's our next stop. Don't let me buy too much because I have a tendency to get carried away. I want to introduce you to Mr Bates. He knows me well. He's got bee hives set all over the district and produces artisan honey products. Where we're going is his retail shop."

"Do you think he'd mind if I took a few pics? Finn is developing an artisan honey business back in Ballinrobe and he'd be really interested to know about it."

"I'll ask him. It shouldn't be a problem."

As William and Aoife entered the honey shop William's eyes immediately lit up.

"Morning Mr Bates. I'd like you to meet somebody."

"Morning William. Morning, you must be Aoife. Welcome to Hunterville and I'm very pleased to meet you. I hope you'll like it enough to stay here. William is my most loyal and enthusiastic customer."

"Thank you Mr Bates. Everything is great. You probably don't know but the very first meal William made for me in Naples used your 10+ Mānuka honey in the dessert. It was delicious. I think I'm also addicted to it now."

Mr Bates turned discretely to William and gave him a smile and a wink. Now he understood what William meant several weeks previous when he had mentioned that his honey was a love potion as he exited the shop. Mr Bates was very impressed with Aoife. Not only was she a natural beauty but she was totally charming and her affection for William was obvious. They were both very touchy-feely. In a world that was often filled with cynicism, Mr Bates found it very endearing and refreshing. Although he had only known Aoife for ten minutes, he considered that William had made a good choice in a potential lifetime partner.

William asked Mr Bates if Aoife could take a few pics of all the different products on display to send to her brother back in Ireland. He explained that her brother Finn had just started an artisan honey business on the family farm in Ballinrobe.

"Yes of course. Please take as many pics as you'd like. I'm flattered."

Aoife started taking a few pics. She asked if she could get one of William and Mr Bates standing in front of the honey display. They were both a bit shy initially, but it was virtually impossible to resist Aoife's Irish charm so they obliged willingly.

"Finn will be so excited to see these pics. Thanks so much. I can't believe how many different types and grades of honey there are."

"Before you go William I want to give you something to try. I haven't packaged it yet so it'll just pour some into a small container. I'm not sure if it will go commercial because I only have a very small quantity of it. It's got the highest UMF of any Mānuka honey I've ever collected over the past twenty years."

Mr Bates explained that the analytical company he used to rate the UMF quality of his different batches of Mānuka honey were shocked at the initial result for the 'MB' batch of honey. They repeated it two more times just to make sure their equipment wasn't malfunctioning. They told him that its super high quality made it something very special and they were certain it was 100% monofloral Mānuka honey. That was the only explanation they had for its exceptional quality.

"Where's it from, and what does 'MB' mean?"

"You know the old single lane Mangaweka Bridge, well just past there on the left hand side as you're driving inland there are some stands of dense native trees and Mānuka bush in the river valley and on the hill slopes. I set a few hives there close by a patch of densely flowering Mānuka bush and trees on the other side of the river."

William knew exactly the area Mr Bates was talking about. That seemed a bit strange. It was where he had explored that first Sunday he arrived back from his Naples holiday. It was the stand of native trees and Mānuka bush across the river where he thought he had heard somebody calling his name.

"It's a gift to welcome Aoife to Hunterville. Plus I want you to try it and give me your opinion."

"Thanks so much Mr Bates. Fantastic. I'm cooking dinner for Aoife tonight so I'll use it in something and let you know what I think next time I'm in."

"Yes, thank you Mr Bates for being so generous. I love your shop. And when we get back home I'm going to send those photos I took straight off to my brother in Ireland. He'll be so interested. And probably amazed at all the different types of honey you sell."

William and Aoife left the Mānuka Honey Shop. William hadn't purchased any of his favourite 10+ but had come out of the shop with something far more special. He couldn't wait to use it later that evening.

"Well, Aoife that's the café and the Mānuka Honey Shop in Hunterville. What do you think?"

"Love them both William. Everybody has been so kind and welcoming to me. Now I can see why you love living here."

"Shall we head back to the farm and have a bite of lunch? Then after that I'll do a bit of farm work before coming in around 5 pm to make dinner. Will that work?"

"That will work. Sounds good. I'll send off a few emails back home. Finn's going to love the photos."

As they drove the short distance back to the farm William discussed with Aoife his plans for the rest of the week. He thought that if he did a full day of farm work on Thursday and then again on Friday, he'd be free on Saturday morning to take Aoife to meet his parents in Palmerston North. Then in the afternoon, depending on what Aoife thought, he could either drop her back to the farm and go to his weekly rugby game alone, or she could come with him and cheer him and the Hunterville team on. Her preference was to go to the rugby game with him.

After arriving back to the farm, William changed, had a quick bite of lunch and then went outside to do farm work while Aoife got her tablet out and started writing emails. As promised William came back inside at 5 pm.

"Right, it's time for William to make dinner. Um. Um. What can I make? Joking. Give me an hour and a cold beer and everything will be ready at 6 pm. How does that sound?"

"Sounds good William. Are you going to use that special Mānuka honey Mr Bates gave you this morning. I don't remember him saying what it's UMF was?"

"On the way out he did whisper something to me but he asked me not to spread it around because he wants to try and keep the area he sourced it from a secret. The world record UMF grading for Mānuka honey is in the low 30s. That container he gave us to try was rated 36. There's something very, very special about that area it was collected from but he said he couldn't figure out what."

"I won't mention it to anybody. Not even Finn. I'll let you guys figure it out."

William set to work making dinner as promised. He didn't use a recipe book. It was just an off the cuff recipe. He was good at impromptu cooking. Right on 6 pm dinner was ready.

William came into the lounge with the small container of Mānuka honey Mr Bates had gifted them earlier in the day.

"Before we start dinner and while our palates are fresh, let's taste the honey in its raw state. Not too much, just a level teaspoon each. Here, you go first Aoife."

Aoife put the teaspoon in her mouth and let the honey melt on her warm tongue. The flavour was intense and sweet but not too sweet. She let it trickle down her throat. The sensation in her mouth and down her throat was pleasurable. She perked up. It left her in a euphoric state.

"Wow, it's so intense William and it leaves a lasting pleasurable feeling in the mouth and throat initially, and then over the whole body. Might be the nectar of the gods? You try."

William had tried a lot of Mānuka honey in his time and considered himself a bit of an expert taste tester. He put a teaspoon of the honey into his mouth. Aoife observed William as he stood there swirling the melting honey around his mouth and letting it eventually trickle down his throat. He tilted his head back and closed his eyes. An image appeared in his mind. It was a strangely dressed woman standing in dense native bush holding her hand out and beckoning him to follow her. He tilted his head forward and opened his eyes. The image had disappeared. He was silent.

"Are you OK? What did you think? Powerful stuff isn't it."

He dare not tell Aoife what had just happened in case she thought he was losing the plot. The last thing he wanted to do was scare her and send her heading back to Ireland.

"Haven't taste anything like that before. Wow, that's powerful stuff. Could well be the nectar of the gods. That was a happening of sorts. Are you ready to eat?"

"Yes please. It smells good."

William placed the first course on the table together with a glass of wine each.

"It's Italian beef meatballs on a bed of tomato and capsicum infused spaghetti and some crumbed eggplant slices on the side. *Buon appetito.*"

"*Grazie*. It looks good William."

William lifted up his glass and toasted Aoife. He thanked her for making the effort to embrace everything on the farm and everything and everybody in Hunterville. Aoife lifted her glass and took a sip. William didn't notice that it was a miniscule sip.

Aoife enjoyed the main course and was looking forward to dessert. If it had the 'special' Mānuka honey in it then it was bound to be delicious.

"It's not exactly an Italian dessert. I made stuffed baked granny smith apples to be served with whipped cream. I hollowed out the centre of the apples and filled with sultanas, butter crumble and a generous amount of the UMF 36 Mānuka honey from Mr Bates's shop. It smells good."

It wasn't good. It was exceptional. Aoife wouldn't and couldn't stop complimenting William on yet another great meal. Her wine sat on the table undrunk.

"Awesome dinner William. Thanks for looking after me so well."

Aoife and William spent the rest of the evening chatting about what they might do over the next few days. Aoife told William that she hoped she'd be able to get out and about with him on the farm, and help in any way she could, sometime over the next few days. If that wasn't possible, then she'd definitely do it the following week. She wanted to see all the things William had described to her when they were in Naples.

It had been a great day with the highlight being their visit to the Mānuka Honey Shop. Prior to meeting William, Aoife didn't know what Mānuka honey was even though it had an international reputation. Now she considered herself reasonably well informed on the subject. She was probably one of the very few people in the world that had tried a UMF 36 Mānuka honey. That was very special. Before they went to bed Aoife checked her tablet computer to see if there was any reply from Finn. There was. She opened the email from him and read it out to William.

Hello Aoife and William. Thanks for pics. Loved them all. Envious of the Hunterville Mānuka Honey Shop. Hope I can develop something like that. I know about Mānuka honey. It's rated very highly. Look forward to meeting William one day. Thank him for looking after you. Love to you both, Mum and Dad send their love also. All good here. FINNxxx

"That was a nice reply. Hope I can meet him one day also. It sounds like we would get on well."

Aoife shut her tablet, took William by the hand and led him in to the bedroom. She asked him not to say anything. Aoife stood in front of William and undressed. William ogled the fair skinned nubile beauty standing in front of him. She then undressed William slowly. It was intense. She could see that he was ready for a night of erotic love making. She knew William was mostly conservative tending in public, but behind closed doors and in private she had only known him to be an inventive, hungry and lustful lover. He always delivered what she wanted. This night was no exception.

William and Aoife got into a good routine on Thursday and Friday. He had a lot of work to do on the farm and was determined to make every hour count so that he could take time off on Saturday. Aoife was feeling a bit up and down and blamed it on jetlag. She was sure her body clock would right itself soon, but in the interim she was contented to just stay around the farmhouse. She was not lacking in domestic skills and her being there in the farmhouse did make a difference. She added a feminine touch to the home. This was something which was lacking when William was living there alone.

William Scores a Try

Saturday arrived and William had a busy day planned. He had checked with Aoife the previous evening to determine if she wanted to attend his club rugby game at Bulls on Saturday. Bulls was a small town half way between Hunterville and Palmerston North. Aoife confirmed that she was keen to see William play and cheer him on. She asked if he could 'please score a try for me'. He laughed when she said that, telling her tries were not that easy to come by, but he'd try his best.

They left the house at 8 am and drove down to Palmerston North to see his parents. It took less than an hour. Aoife commented that all the lambs in the paddocks looked adorable and wondered how anybody could eat them. William quickly changed the subject not wanting to admit that his freezer was half full with various cuts of spring lamb.

William knocked on the door of his parent's townhouse in Palmerston North and the door opened immediately. Initially, it was if William wasn't even there for both his parents rushed forward to greet Aoife and welcome her into their home. They already knew from photos William had shown them of his Naples holiday that Aoife was a very attractive female. In the flesh she was even more beautiful. When she spoke it was a delightful Irish accent they heard. She was softly spoken, polite and articulate. They were both very impressed. Neither of them would dare say it out loud, but they were privately ecstatic that their son had managed to capture the heart of such a beautiful girl.

Deep down, they knew that although William didn't have rugged good looks or Hollywood movie star looks, he had an arsenal of other very desirable and attractive qualities. And then there was that beaming smile which few could emulate. They knew their son was a good and decent man, but rarely did good and decent average looking men capture the hearts of beautiful girls. This made their admiration of Aoife grow even stronger. William had courted and dated the odd girl through his late teens and twenties but had never brought any of them home to meet his parents.

William bringing Aoife to meet them was like a dream come true.

Finally, his parents remembered that they had a son and fussed over him also. They all went into the lounge and William's mum had prepared an expansive morning tea knowing that William was playing his Saturday rugby game later in the afternoon and wouldn't eat any lunch. Instantly Aoife felt at home because William's parents reminded her very much of her own parents. Both his parents, and her parents, were old school and conservative.

"Welcome Aoife. William has told us so much about you. How is everything going in the farmhouse? Is William looking after you? Have you been into Hunterville yet? Has William showed you around the farm?"

"Whoa Mum, you're asking Aoife so many questions."

"I'm so sorry Aoife. I'm just so excited. We just want you to be happy on the farm knowing you're so far away from home."

"No problem at all Mrs Thomson. Everything is great and I appreciate you asking. William has been outstanding. We went to the Hunterville Café and Mānuka Honey Shop yesterday morning. I loved them both. And everybody in Hunterville is so kind and friendly and they're smiling all the time. Is there something special or magical in the water?"

They all laughed.

"Hunterville has always been like that Aoife. Sometimes I think to myself, why don't they change the name of the town to Happytown. It was like that when I first arrived there back in the late sixty's" replied William's mother.

William's parents backed off and let the conversation between the four of them flow more naturally. William and Aoife enjoyed the morning tea spread Mrs Thomson had prepared. William was in his element choosing from plates of various cakes and slices, club sandwiches, and small savoury meat pies. Everything Mrs Thomson had made was deliciously old school.

Aoife observed that William's father was much quieter than his mother. When he did talk it was just a little bit formal. As the morning wore on she noted that William had a very close bond with his father. She admired how respectful, patient and inclusive he was towards his father. She listened as William gave his dad an update on what was happening on the farm and addressed all his father's questions carefully. He asked his father several times during the morning if he wanted anything, or if he could do anything for him.

"Mum, dad, I think we had better be making tracks now. Why don't you both think about coming up to the farm for a few days?"

"We'd like to William but I'm just a little bit scared because there are no medical facilities available in Hunterville if Dad gets into trouble or has a relapse."

"Ok but just think about it anyway and if you'd like to visit I'll come and pick you up and return you back home."

William's father spoke just as they were about to leave.

"Thank you for visiting us this morning Aoife. It's been our pleasure to finally meet you. William is a good man. Please be kind to him always."

Aoife wasn't offended by these words. She simply considered them to be the words of a father that loved his son dearly. She was moved by this request of her.

Similarly, William wasn't offended or embarrassed by these words. He simply considered them to be words of fatherly concern and love.

"Of course I will" replied Aoife.

Aoife and William said their goodbyes and went on their way to the Saturday afternoon rugby game in Bulls. Kick-off was at 2 pm. Rugby had a reasonable following back in Ireland and her brother Finn had played it at school so Aoife knew the basics.

William and Aoife arrived to the rugby ground just after 1 pm. William introduced Aoife to a few of his team mates and was surprised at their behaviour in front of her. Without exception they were all polite and respectful in her presence. No mouthing off, no swearing and no tom-foolery. That was a bit different to usual. It was a reflection of their respect for William. They didn't want to do anything which might present them or him in a bad light.

Before going into the changing rooms, William escorted Aoife to the stands and suggested a good place to sit. He was delighted when Joseph and Suzie unexpectedly appeared to watch the game. Suzie immediately came over to Aoife and insisted she sit with them. William excused himself and went down to the changing rooms located under the stand.

Aoife, Suzie and Joseph chatted about what they had been doing over the past few days. At ten minutes to the hour the Hunterville team came running out onto the field and did a few warm ups. Aoife stood up in the stands and waved to William. He very quickly acknowledged her.

"There's William. I've never seen him in white rugby shorts before. Sexy legs and cute firm butt. Oops, sorry about that. 'Twas a slip of the tongue."

Joseph and Suzie looked at each other and just smiled. It was affirmation to Joseph that Aoife was deeply in love with his best friend William. He wanted what William had and was trying very hard to achieve that with Suzie.

At 2 pm exactly, the referee blew his whistle to commence the game. The Bulls team was favoured to win. The score seesawed back and forth. Ten minutes to go and it was level at 12 all. Aoife wasn't being shy in her support of William. Five minutes to go and he was passed the ball out on the wing. Whether it was the presence of Aoife in the stands which spurred him on, or him wanting to impress his friend Joseph, he boldly ran forth like a man possessed and scored in the corner. His team mates rushed over and enthusiastically congratulated him. Aoife was very proud of her man. William's try was not converted and the final score was an unexpected win to the Hunterville team 17 to 12.

Knowing that William would want to have a celebratory beer in the changing rooms with his team mates, Aoife, Suzie and Joseph waited around until William reappeared.

"Here's my hero" said Aoife as she ran forward to greet him.

"You said you wanted me to score for you. Your wish is my command," replied William. Everybody was in a buoyant mood.

"Do you want to stop off in Hunterville at the pub on the way home and have a couple beers and pizza?" asked Joseph.

"Joseph I'm driving so that might be a bit tricky."

In a flash, Aoife had a solution.

"It's OK William. I'll be the designated driver. I won't drink any alcohol. Let's celebrate with Joseph and Suzie. You deserve it."

They drove separately back to Hunterville and meet up again at the pub at 5 pm. The four of them had a great early evening dinner. The pizzas were tasty, the beer was cold and they had a good reason to celebrate. The boy's drunk heavily, Suzie drunk modestly and Aoife wouldn't drink any beer or wine at all.

Suzie noted Aoife's steadfastness when it came to refusing any alcoholic drink during the evening. It had been the same a few nights earlier at farmhouse when Aoife and William invited them over for pizza and beer. Call it female intuition, call it curiosity, but Suzie wondered if Aoife could have something more than a case of lingering jetlag. She was nervous for Aoife, but for now, her lips were sealed.

"Ok Joseph, Suzie, it's time for us to head home. It's been a great evening thanks and it's been good to catch up again. We're doing something very special tomorrow so we need a good night's sleep."

Aoife couldn't remember what special thing they were doing on Sunday. She escorted a jovial William out to the car, said farewell to Joseph and Suzie and drove William home. It was still early, but her rugby hero looked tired. As she undressed and helped him into bed she reflected on what had been another great day. She showered quickly, checked her emails and also went to bed.

Celebration at the Mānuka Honey Shop

William woke up on Sunday morning with a minor headache. It was the type of headache that soon disappears after a good strong coffee. Aoife was still snoozing when he hopped out of bed to go and make them a coffee. He was about to take it back to her to bed when she appeared in the kitchen.

"Morning William. How's my rugby hero this morning?"

"I'm feeling surprisingly good after last night. Poked my head out the door and it's a beautiful early spring day. It's meant to get to 20 degrees C after lunch. The daffodils are out, the spring lambs are jumping in the paddocks and the grass is green. I love spring time."

"Me too it's really nice. What are we doing today? You said you had something special planned. I can't remember you mentioning it to me."

"Well, since it's going to be such a nice afternoon I thought we might go on a horse ride up to the highest point on the farm. I want to take you there because there's fantastic views of the whole farm. Are you feeling up for a ride?"

"Definitely. I feel good today. Things are settling down."

William assumed she meant the jetlag had all but disappeared now. Aoife continued.

"I haven't been on a horse since the Mount Vesuvius trek. Have you got a horse that's not too keen or headstrong?"

"Yes, I've got one for you that's perfect. An ex thoroughbred but he's quiet and very reliable. I call him Plod."

"Can't wait. It's going to be so good the both of us just getting out on the hilltops for some peaceful alone time. How about I make a picnic lunch, a flask of tea and some lemon cordial using those few lemons left on the tree and we can take that with us?"

"It's getting better by the minute. That sounds good. I can't even remember when I last went on a picnic. I'll head out and do a few small jobs over in the farm shed now and then get the horses ready. How about we aim to leave just after noon? It will take around half an hour to get to where I want to take you. Is it a plan?"

"It's a plan."

"OK, I'll just grab some toast, go out and do those jobs and see you later. I'll be back in just before noon to change and we can go."

William had an ulterior motive for wanting some alone time out in the farm shed. He had to confirm some confidential arrangements for later in the day and evening. Those arrangements would go ahead if everything went according to plan during the afternoon horse trek with Aoife. If things didn't go according to plan, he just wanted to make sure one final time, that his friends would abort and not feel offended.

William came back inside just before noon, changed into his riding gear, packed and fussed around with his backpack several times, and then asked Aoife if she was ready. He loved seeing her in faded jeans and tight fitting t shirt with her hair tied up. He thought it was casual and sexy. William was rearing to go. He packed a woollen picnic blanket and their picnic lunch into the side pack on his horse. Was this Sunday about to become the happiest day of his life?

"Here's Plod. Look how cheeky he is. He's eyeing you up and down. Watch it mate. She's taken."

Aoife laughed and just spent a couple of minutes getting familiar with Plod. She gave him a carrot from her pocket to nibble so they would become 'friends'. When that was consumed she then felt confident enough to hop on. Willian legged her up and then sprung up onto his horse. As she remembered from their horse trek back on Mount Vesuvius, William looked good on his horse. Really good. He was a confident rider and knew what he was doing.

"Ready?"

"Yes."

"Let's go. We'll follow some of the sheep tracks and gradually make our way up to that hilltop over in the distance."

"Which one, there's several?"

"See that one over there with the small patch of native bush. That's one of the few remaining areas of native bush left on the farm. I've seriously got to do something about that. There needs to be a lot more pockets and stands of native bush on the farm."

William and Aoife set off on their horse trek. It was the first time that Aoife had been out on the working part of the farm and she loved every minute of it.

William was a careful, caring and very attentive leader on his horse. He looked after Aoife the whole way. Where the tracks narrowed, she rode behind William. She had no complaints slotting in behind and watching her lean, physical man with the killer smile ride ahead of her in full control of his horse. She observed William in his element and realised that this was where he belonged.

Gradually the elevation increased and Aoife was getting a much better perspective on the spread of the farm. The air was clean and clear so she could easily see across to the horizon. It was nothing like the family farm back in Ballinrobe. William's farm was much more rugged in places, significantly larger and much more intensively stocked.

"See that patch of native bush in front of us right at the top. It's about ten minutes ride away. That's where we're going."

"The scenery is so beautiful William. I can't believe how green it is. Even right on the hilltops."

They arrived to the hilltop where they'd have their picnic. It was the highest point on the farm. William dismounted his horse and let Aoife slide off Plod and into his arms. He kissed her lovingly several times. On a windy or wet day they would be very exposed to the elements and it wouldn't be a pleasant experience but this day was exceptional. There was virtually no wind and the air temperature was 18 degrees C. It wasn't warm and it wasn't cold, it was somewhere in between. Most people would call it pleasant.

"Are you cold, I've got a couple of jackets in my backpack if you need?"

"No I'm good William, I brought a jumper with me if I need it."

"Let me just tie the horses up to that tree over there and we'll spread the picnic rug in this open area to the side, and then I want to show you something."

Having tied up the horses, William took Aoife by the hand and led her to an open area about twenty metres away from the stand of native bush.

"Look over to your right. That's the farm. Can you see the farmhouse and farm buildings way down in the distance?"

Aoife scanned around taking in the vista presented before her. She was impressed.

"It's impressive William. It's a credit to you and your parents and your ancestors."

"Can you believe this whole area was densely bush covered in the early 1800s before the settlers arrived and started clearing it all away? How impressive that must have been.

"Imagine a dense bush full of tall towering native trees with countless native birds including the flightless kiwi and no predators in sight."

"It's sad to see that most of it has now gone. I know farming is progress but how much is too much?" replied Aoife.

William and Aoife cuddled together and spent a few minutes looking down on the farm. For a fleeting moment it felt like they were the only two people alive in the world.

"Don't know about you but I'm hungry. Picnic time?"

William went over to where the horses were tied up and got the picnic gear and food. He returned a couple of minutes later to where Aoife was waiting and spread the woollen rug on the grass. Aoife arranged the picnic lunch out on the rug and they sat down.

"Wow Aoife it looks fantastic. Did you do prepare this entire picnic this morning?"

"I did. While you were in the farm shed."

"Well, it's superb. Hate to ask but is that chocolate brownie in the plastic container?"

"Yes mister sweet tooth but that's for later. I brought a flask of tea to go with it."

It was a perfect picnic in a perfect setting on a perfect day. Aoife didn't think it could be any more perfect but William was about to make it an exceptional day.

"Aoife quick stand up. There's one of those very poisonous spiders on the picnic rug." Aoife stood up quickly and started brushing her clothes frantically.

"Where, I can't see it? Where is it?"

William seized the moment. He knelt before the standing Aoife and pulled a small box out of his left jean pocket. Aoife calmed down. He looked up directly into her eyes.

"Aoife will you make me a happier man than I ever thought possible? Will you marry me? Will you join me on a journey into the unknown? It's a journey that will be based on mutual respect, love and kindness, adventure and security. Will you say what I'm longing to hear?"

Aoife was silent. The silence continued and William became visibly anxious. Aoife could see that he was confused, totally confused, because she had said neither yes nor no.

"William I've got something to tell you. Let's sit back down on the picnic rug."

William was sure she was about to tell him no but he wasn't sure why. In his mind everything had been going perfectly. Had he done something wrong but didn't realise it. They sat down and Aoife spoke to William as she held both his hands.

"Aoife have I done something wrong?"

"William, I'm pregnant."

Now it was William's turn to be silent. Stoney silent. It was a statement that he needed a little time to process. But he wasn't silent for long. He leaned over and hugged Aoife to show her that she wasn't alone.

"Are you sure? But when?"

"I'm sure. You know I hadn't been feeling that great just a few days before I left Galway, and for that first week after I arrived in New Zealand. I thought it was jetlag causing the ongoing tiredness and nausea but deep down I knew. I did have some morning sickness after I arrived to Hunterville but discretely kept it to myself. I didn't mention it to you because I didn't want to scare you or make you feel like you owe me anything. As to when, well the most likely date is the evening we spent together after taking the funicular railway up to the Castle of San Martino. That night you first made me dinner in Naples. Or it could have been the next night when I stayed over at your apartment again. Nobody knows I'm pregnant apart from the two of us."

"But Aoife don't you understand, this is not bad news, this is great news. It just means I love you even more if that's possible, and I want to be with you even more. I'm ecstatic. I'm so excited. I'm so happy. It's what I've always wanted but never though it would come to me. I'm going to be a dad? Crikey."

William started crying. Aoife could tell from the sparkle in his eyes and the smile on his face that they were tears of absolute joy. It was just the type of reaction Aoife expected and confirmed to her that this was definitely the man she wanted to spend the rest of her life with.

"When is the baby due?"

"Sometime between the 7th to 15th May next year plus or minus a few days."

"Wow, this is turning out to be some picnic."

William and Aoife laughed and hugged each other.

"I didn't want to say yes or no until you knew that news. It wouldn't be fair. If I didn't tell you it would seem like entrapment."

"Well, now that I do know can I ask you again?"

"Yes."

Aoife stood up on the grass hill top overlooking the Thomson Farm. The sun was shining and the air was still. William knelt down a second time and pulled out the box containing his choice of engagement ring.

"Aoife will you marry me."

"Yes William I will."

William slipped the ring on her finger, kissed her passionately and put his hand gently on her stomach. The picnic hadn't gone exactly as he was expecting, but the end result far exceeded his expectations.

William and Aoife made their way back down to the farmhouse and buildings. William had a beaming smile on his face which remained all the way back down from the hilltop. When they got back home William unsaddled the horses, gave them some feed and a drink, and asked Aoife to come inside because there was one more thing he wanted to ask her.

"By the way William that music you had playing when you proposed to me was beautiful. I'll never ever forget that. It's something to tell our kids. How did you do that? Your wireless speakers and a remote? It really made it sound like it was coming out from the native bush. I saw you rummaging over by the horse when you tied them up at the edge of the bush."

"What music?" William was confused.

"That flute like music. Sounded like a wooden flute or something similar. That very pure and natural sound. It seemed spiritual. That was very special. Thank you."

William found it hard to reply to Aoife. He didn't want to say anything that would spoil the day. He was completely perplexed. He hadn't heard anything while he was proposing to Aoife and definitely hadn't arranged anything. He wondered if she had perhaps got caught up in the romanticism of the moment. He just smiled, and held her hand as they went inside.

"Have to admit that I was expecting you to say yes when I proposed. Honestly I would have been gutted if you said no. On the basis that you would say yes, I've arranged an intimate celebration dinner in Hunterville for us tonight. It's at a surprise venue. No crowds or anything like that. The only diners will be you and me. I thought we might get dressed up like when we went to the opera and make it the perfect end to a perfect day. What do you think? But if you're too tired or don't feel like it well that's OK also."

"No William I want to go out. I'm feeling good today so might as well make the most of it. It's not every day I get proposed to."

"You did bring your opera dress and accessories with you to Hunterville?"

"I did, you asked me to remember."

"It's going to be so good Aoife. We should aim to leave here at 6.45 pm. I won't be driving. There'll be a pickup. I'm just going to dash out to farm shed to make sure those horses are OK and put them out in the paddock."

"OK, I'll start getting things ready for tonight. Who's picking us up?"

"It's a surprise."

Knowing that William was big on surprises and a bit of a romantic she decided to just wait and see who arrived to pick them up and how the evening panned out.

William rushed out to the farm shed and sent a text to those key persons involved in making sure the evening was a success. They needed to know by 3 pm and it was exactly 3 pm as he sent off his text.

"Green Light. See you later, appreciate, William."

He had told them all that it was Aoife's 25th birthday and she was feeling a bit homesick so he wanted to try and cheer her up. He had hated telling them that 'little white lie' but was sure they'd all understand when the truth was revealed. It wouldn't have been fair if they all knew he was going to propose to Aoife before he actually did, hence the 'little white lie'.

By 6.45 pm William and Aoife were ready in the lounge in their 'opera evening' outfits from Naples. Aoife looked stunning in her black satin dress and William looked very smart in his vintage black suit and white shirt.

"Wow Aoife this brings back some special memories. You look even more stunning than you did on opera night in Naples. You're glowing."

"Thank you William. You look very smart."

William kept staring at Aoife's stomach. It was a look of both pride and curiosity. He was just a little bit naïve when it came to human pregnancy even if he knew all there was to know about sheep and cow pregnancy.

"William the first signs of a bump don't appear until three to four months. It's only gone a little over two months since conception so it's a bit early yet."

"I'm sorry Aoife. I'm just so excited."

"I know you are."

William could hear that their transportation had arrived and he escorted Aoife outside to the waiting car. It was Joseph and Suzie who would be their chauffeurs and chaperones for the evening. The male chauffer and his assistant opened the passenger doors on either side of the car simultaneously.

"Good evening William. Good evening Aoife. Wow you guys both look awesome. Your carriage awaits. Where to sir?" said Joseph obviously relishing the role play.

"Hunterville please. The Mānuka Honey Shop."

William and Aoife hopped into the car and settled down in the back. Suzie immediately turned around to Aoife and stated the obvious.

"Aoife you look so beautiful. Like a movie star. That dress is fantastic. And happy birthday."

Aoife glanced sideways to William and looked confused. He discretely held his finger up to his lip and then raised his right hand as if to indicate 'don't say anything now, all will be revealed soon'. It was only a short drive into town and they arrived right at the door of the Mānuka Honey Shop spot on 7 pm.

William and Aoife got out of the car and before entering the shop, William stopped to speak.

"Joseph, Suzie please forgive me. I sincerely apologise. I've told you a 'little white lie' about this evening. It's not Aoife's birthday and she's not homesick, it's something else."

"Is everything OK? What going on?" asked Joseph.

"Well, it's something even better. This afternoon we did a horse trek up to the highest point on the farm and I proposed to Aoife. She said yes and we are now engaged. But wait. There's one more thing. Aoife is pregnant. We've having a baby."

Joseph and Suzie were silent for about ten seconds, looked at each other and then all hell broke loose. There were overjoyed that they had been the first ones to hear William and Aoife's exciting double news. It was a joyous and happy moment for the four of them. After hugs and handshakes and kisses on the cheeks, the happy couple finally entered the Mānuka Honey Shop. The stoic Mr Bates was there to meet and greet them.

"Evening Aoife and William. What a beautiful couple. You look like you're going to an evening at the opera."

William smiled to Aoife. It was funny that Mr Bates should say that. We've been there and done William chuckled to himself. Mr Bates continued.

"That's been very noisy outside. What's going on? Is there a problem in town?"

Suzie couldn't contain her ongoing excitement. She was dying to ask the happy couple when and where but managed to contain her enthusiasm for the time being. Even Joseph was standing there with a smile on his face that was almost, but not quite, as good as William's.

"This afternoon William and Aoife got engaged and they're having a baby."

Mr Bates might have had a reputation in town for being a stoic man but his reaction to the news was far from that. It was totally unexpected. He rushed forward, put his arms around Aoife and William and hugged them tightly and kissed them both on the forehead to show that he cared for them both deeply.

"I think it was my Mānuka honey that did the trick" said Mr Bates winking at William.

William smiled back acknowledging that it was indeed Mr Bates's 'love potion' that had help make him the happiest man in the world that night.

Aoife turned around and was in awe of the formal setting presented in front of her. The honey shop had been converted into an intimate restaurant for two. It was exactly the kind of surprise that she knew William was capable of pulling off.

The newly engaged couple sat down at the table which was dressed with white tablecloth, silver cutlery, crystal glasses and a big pottery vase of William's favourite red bead cotoneaster branches. Then William revealed to Aoife who was in on the act.

"Suzie and Joseph are our chauffeurs and chaperones for the night, Mr Bates is the maître de and host, and Connie and Kathy over at the café are making our celebration dinner as we speak."

"William your friends in Hunterville are exceptional. If your good friends become my good friends then I'm blessed."

Aoife was amazed and impressed that William had prearranged the evening but suspected that her life ahead with William was going to be full of moments like this.

The evening of intimate celebration commenced. While Connie and Kathy cooked in the café, Suzie and Joseph ferried each course the short distance down to the honey shop and Mr Bates fussed around making sure everything was nicely presented and flowing. William enjoyed some red wine and Aoife stuck to sparking water. William hadn't specified with the girls at the café what they'd like for dinner. He just knew that whatever they presented, it would be tasty and healthy. Their celebration dinner comprised a starter of spiced carrot soup, a main of wild pork, fennel and kumara pie and a dessert of pear and ginger tart with lemon cream. True to form, William had two servings of the pear and ginger tart.

"Was that good or what Aoife. Totally delicious."

"Thank you William. Today has been a day I'll never forget. It has been truly outstanding."

Finding it impossible to keep the secret of the day to herself, Suzie had already shared the good news with Connie and Kathy over at the café. They were very excited and decided they must stop by the honey shop on their way home to congratulate William and Aoife.

They arrived just as William stood up and made an announcement in a quivering voice.

"Aoife this is for you. You're my salvation. I'd truly be lost without you. I thought I was destined for a life of loneliness but we meet in Naples and I soon knew that I'd finally found someone to love and cherish. Until today I didn't know that happiness had no limit. This will forever be our song. I'm a bit rusty but will you dance with me?"

William turned and nodded over to Mr Bates who pressed play to start the music.

Before the music even started Aoife knew what song it was going to be. It was their special song from the night she first made dinner for him at her apartment in Naples. Aoife stood up and tears flooded down her cheeks. Again the roles were reversed because it was usually William that had a propensity for emotional tears. She silently went around the table to William and kissed him gently and lovingly. She was deeply in love with the man she was dining with.

As Bryan Adams sung what was now their song, they danced slowly while gazing silently and deeply into each other's eyes and souls. By the time it ended there wasn't a dry eye in the Mānuka Honey Shop. William was thankful that he could share the moment with his special friends in Hunterville. The ones who were right there with them as they slow danced to end what had been a day to remember for the rest of their lives.

"Ok William and Aoife. We'd better get you home and bolt the front door behind you both. Holy f—friar, what a day."

Although he was trying very hard, some habits were harder for Joseph to change than others.

"Ok Joseph but before we go, Aoife and myself want to thank you all for making this a night to remember. You're all truly outstanding people and it's a privilege to count you as our friends. I will never forget your collective kindness. Before we go can I please ask just one special favour from all of you."

"Of course William, what is it?" asked Joseph on behalf of the group.

"I don't want Mum and Dad to find out what happened this afternoon until we tell them personally. I'm planning on going to see them first thing in the morning to share the good news with them. We know people around town will want to know, and we're good with that, but can you leave saying anything to anybody until after lunchtime tomorrow."

Joseph, Suzie, Connie and Kathy and Mr Bates all promised that they'd say nothing to anybody until after lunchtime the following day.

The newly engaged couple said their finally goodnights to everybody and then Suzie and Joseph drove them home. It was 10 pm when they stepped in the front door of the farmhouse.

"Thanks Joseph. Thanks Suzie. Goodnight and god bless you both" said Aoife as her parting gesture.

And with that, Joseph and Suzie drove back down the long driveway while William and Aoife readied themselves for bed. When Aoife woke up on that Sunday morning she had no idea that it would evolve as it had. She was excited to discuss with William in the days ahead, where and when their marriage might take place. She didn't want it to be anywhere else but in the Hunterville area. Although it was her new home she would never forget her Irish roots and was hopefully that one day in the not too distant future she could take William and their new baby to visit Ireland.

The following morning William woke up very early. He had experienced difficulty sleeping during the night. He was worried that his parents might find out about their engagement and Aoife's pregnancy before they had a chance to tell them. If they found out from somebody else other than him and Aoife, that would devastate them and he was determined it wasn't going to happen.

He went to the kitchen and made a coffee and waited impatiently for Aoife to wake up. That seemed to take an eternity, but finally she woke up.

"Aoife, I didn't have a good night. I had a terrible sleep."

"It's OK William I know why. Let's get dressed and have a quick breakfast and then go immediately and visit your parents and tell them the news."

"Thanks Aoife. If we leave just after 7 am we should be there around 8 am. I can let the farm helpers know what has to be done this morning on the way out. We should be back at lunchtime latest. Possibly earlier. I don't want Dad to receive any shock news even if it's fantastic news. His condition is a bit fragile."

"Understand. Do you think they'll be OK with the news? I'm getting a bit nervous now."

"They probably won't be expecting it but I think they'll be delighted. They've always been very supportive. They've never ever scolded me for any choices or decisions I've made in life even when they've been a bit dubious."

William and Aoife had a quick breakfast with their coffee and then met the farm workers on the way out. William explained that there had been an emergency and they had to drive to Palmerston North and should be back before lunch time. Both farm workers knew that William's father had poor health so they assumed it was something to do with that.

William's parents were having their breakfast and hadn't yet dressed when they arrived and knocked on the front door. William's mother was very surprised to see them immediately thinking there must be something wrong. She didn't understand why they were making an unannounced visit so early in the day.

"Good morning. Come in, sorry we're still in our jammies. Is there something wrong at the farm? What's happened? Has somebody been in an accident? You and Aoife are here very early."

William breathed a sigh of relief for it was obvious that they hadn't heard Sunday afternoon's news yet. William went over in his head how he might reveal the news. He didn't want to hurt them in any way so he asked for a cup of coffee first. Mrs Thomson made them coffee and brought it in to the sitting room. They all sat down and William held Aoife's hand so as to discretely hide her engagement ring. He took a deep breath before he spoke.

"Mum, Dad, we've got something to tell you. Well, you know that small stand of remnant native bush up by the highest hilltop on the farm, yesterday we went up there on a horse trek for a picnic…the picnic was great…and I proposed. Aoife said yes. We're going to be married. But that's not all. You're going to be grandparents."

There was silence. William's parents didn't immediately grasp the meaning of what he had just said so he said it again but phrased it a different way.

"We're engaged to be married and you're going to be grandparents because we're having a baby."

This time it registered and just to make sure, Aoife flashed her engagement ring towards Mr and Mrs Thomson.

William was unsure of what reaction they'd get from his parents but he need not have worried because it was one of sheer delight. Although they were conservative they were not judgemental. They couldn't believe they were going to be grandparents.

"Congratulations to you both. How very exciting. That means a wedding and a baby to look forward to. When is it all going to happen?"

"Mum, we only got engaged yesterday afternoon so we haven't discussed any wedding plans yet, but the baby is due early to mid-May."

"Of course sorry, I can't wait to tell everybody. Is it OK if we tell our friends?"

"Yes, of course it is. We just wanted to make sure you heard it directly from us before the bush telegraph gets going. Aoife hasn't told her parents and brother yet so that's next."

"Mum, Dad, we'd better get going back to the farm. The weather's going to be really good for the next few days and there are a lot of things I need to do."

William and Aoife stood up and made their way to the front door. William's parents followed them to say goodbye. His parents hugged Aoife warmly knowing that she was away from her family during these momentous events and would need their love and support. William's father hadn't said a lot up to this point but as he hugged William goodbye, he whispered into his son's ear.

"William, thank you. I love you dearly you know that. I'm so happy and very proud. I wouldn't want any other son but you. Take care of Aoife. Let us know what you decide as to where and when."

William and Aoife made their way home to the farm and arrived there around 11 am.

William headed straight out to the farm shed and joined his farm workers in the daily tasks. He told them the good news and they were both very excited. He needed to make preparations for docking the lambs, separating out the bobby calves and worming and irrigating all livestock on the farm. On his way out, he promised Aoife that when he came back in later in the afternoon they would discuss how they'd tell her parents, and also where and when their wedding would take place.

By the time he came back into the house at 5 pm, his phone was running hot with text and recorded phone messages. It was a sign that the Hunterville bush telegraph had gone into overdrive after lunchtime with William and Aoife's double news from the previous day.

Everybody in Hunterville, maybe with one or two exceptions, liked William a lot and wanted to wish him and Aoife all the best. It was a while since the town had celebrated a local wedding and everybody was hoping that another one might be on the horizon. William was also well known in the wider district and beyond so the good news travelled further afield also.

Rather than just read through all the messages himself, he wanted to sit down with Aoife and go through them together. This way he could explain to her who each message was from. William and Aoife sat down and enjoyed a quiet dinner together mainly reminiscing about the day before and discussing how well William's parents had taken the news earlier in the day.

"Leave the dishes Aoife, I'll do them later before I go to bed. Let's go through all the messages on my phone. There's a lot."

William went through each text and phone message with Aoife. They were from a wide range of people and organisations. There were messages of congratulations from townsfolk who had known William and his parents for a long time, from his close farming neighbours and other local farmers, from various business owners around town, from his old school teachers, from the local federated farmers organisation, from his rugby team mates, and from his university mates.

"Gosh William, is there anybody that hasn't sent a message of congratulations? And they're all so kind to include me also. Most of them haven't even met me."

"I know and that's why I don't want to live anywhere else. Here is just perfect. Have you thought about how you'd like to tell your parents?"

"I am nervous about it especially telling them the pregnant part. Shall we face call them on Wednesday night? I'll tell them the news but you must be there with me because I don't think I could do it alone."

"Of course I'll be there Aoife. We'll call on Wednesday night at 8 pm our time. Will you mind if I say something to them during the call?"

"Mind? No, I'd love that."

William then asked Aoife if she had given any though as to where and when she would like to get married. Aoife had thought about it and happily shared her thoughts with William.

"I definitely want to get married here in Hunterville since I feel that this is my new home now. I want us to share the occasion with all your friends and family. It will be hard for my family because they're so far away but I'll discuss it with them. In case my parents can't make it, I'd like to get married in church out of respect for them. Do you have any ideas for a reception venue? As to when, I just want to be married to you as soon as possible."

"Well, in terms of a when, Saturday the 2nd November is the annual Hunterville Huntaway Festival and just about everybody in town is involved with that. It's a big deal. The town numbers swell by 4000 to 5000 on the day. We definitely want to avoid that weekend, so I'd say the weekend before, or the weekend after. What do you think?"

"The weekend before is good. That's only six weeks away William. Do you think we'd have enough time to make all the arrangements?"

"Yep, I know lots of people in town will want to help and if you don't mind them being involved then six weeks from now is definitely possible."

"What about a reception venue?"

"I have somewhere in mind between the farm and Hunterville township but it's a surprise. I'll take you there sometime in the next few days. If you don't like it just say and we'll find an alternative in Hunterville itself."

William and Aoife had set the ball rolling. They now had a pretty good idea of when they'd get married and William at least, had an idea of where the reception might be. The next big step was to call Aoife's parents. They wouldn't make any final decisions about the wedding until after that call.

Wedding Plans

Wednesday evening arrived. William and Aoife sat in front of the computer together at 8 pm. Aoife was extremely nervous. She felt sick in the stomach and it had nothing to do with her pregnancy.

"Hello mum, dad, Finn. How is everybody? William is here with me."

"Hello Aoife. Hello William. How are you both? How is everything on the farm?"

"We're good thanks. Everything on the farm is really good. It's springtime here and the days are getting warmer and longer and the paddocks are full of lambs and calves."

"Hi everybody, it's William here. We have some news for you." Aoife took a deep breath, held William hand's and spoke next.

"Mum, dad, Finn, William took me on a horse trek in the weekend up to the highest point on the farm. He wanted to have a picnic overlooking the whole farm. Of course I wasn't expecting it but he proposed to me and I said yes of course."

"That's fantastic news, congratulations to you both," said Aoife's delighted father "I can't say we're surprised. I assume you'll be getting married locally?"

"Congratulations sis," added an equally delighted Finn.

"Yes, we've been discussing it the past few days. In Hunterville, in church, and at this stage we've pencilled in the last weekend of October. Of course we know the logistics and distance will make it difficult for you to travel here but we understand that."

"Hello again, it's William. Thank you for being so kind and generous and supportive with your congratulations. I promise you all that I'll look after Aoife always. She will always be my priority. She has given me something I thought I'd never find. And I'm thankful to her and you all for that. I'll never forget so thanks again."

"Thanks William, we're relying on your to look after her. Give us a couple of days and we'll get back to you and let you know how we'll celebrate the day with you" replied Finn.

Aoife quickly whispered into William's ear. William discretely whispered back that his parents had taken the additional news well so her parents and brother might also. Aoife held William's hand tightly to the point of it almost being painful.

"Mum, Dad, Finn we have one more piece of news. We are having a baby. It's due in early May."

The line went dead silent and the image of Aoife's family went offline temporarily. William and Aoife could hear loud chaotic whisperings at the other end. The picture returned after a minute or so. Finn spoke.

"Sincere congratulations Aoife and William. That's fantastic news. I'm going to be an uncle. Uncle Finn. It sounds good. Nice one. Mum and Dad are a bit shocked as expected but they are so happy for you both and love you both. They can't believe they're going to be grandparents. They're a bit gaga at the moment. They asked if we can call you again same time on Friday after we have formulated a plan to your news. Wow what a call. I wasn't expecting that."

"Hope it's good news and not bad news we've just given you. Love you all and talk Friday night."

"Of course it's good news. It's the absolute best news. We'll talk again Friday. Bye now and take care of each other." Finn signed off.

Aoife was upset. She was sure her parents had reacted well to the first piece of news but badly to the second piece of news. William did his very best to comfort and reassure her.

"It will be fine Aoife. Trust me. They just need a bit of alone time to get used to the idea of a wedding and a baby in quick succession. Let's wait until we talk to them on Friday before we make any forward plans, OK?"

"Ok. Well, at least it's all out in the open now," replied a dejected Aoife.

William and Aoife busied themselves around the farm on Thursday and Friday. Joseph texted William, and Suzie texted Aoife, asking if a decision had be made about a wedding date and venue. William responded that they hadn't but would have it sorted by the weekend. They'd get back to them then.

Friday night arrived and William and Aoife were ready for the follow up face to face call with Aoife's family over in Ireland.

"Hello Aoife, hello William, it's Dad, Mum and Finn here in Ballinrobe."

"Hi, how are you all?"

"We're good. We want to apologise for our laboured and muted response to your baby news on Wednesday. Can't deny that Mum and I were a bit shell shocked but now that we've thought about it, we're over the moon and very excited. We know that you will both make excellent parents. Finn has already been planning what he's going to do with his niece or nephew. Once again please accept our sincere apologies."

"Thanks Mum and Dad that means a lot to us. I'm so happy now. We knew you'd be shocked but we just want you to be happy for us, and for yourselves. Being a grandparent is special because it's a gift from god. How cool is that?"

"Mum wants to say something now."

"Aoife, William, congratulations on both the wedding and the baby news. It's going to be hard for us to make it over for your wedding day but Finn insists he comes and will be there to represent us all. We'd like it if he can be the one to give you away in marriage in place of dad. Remember how you always admired grandma's crème coloured vintage lace and satin wedding dress. Well, Finn will bring it with him and if you want to wear it on the big day, please do but only if you feel like it. Honestly, if you'd rather do something else that's alright. We'll save hard and arrange things here on the farm so that we can visit you when you have the baby. I want to be with you when you have the baby in May."

In the background William flashed his beaming smile and gave both thumbs up to indicate to Aoife his delight with, and approval of the plan. Aoife's mood was completely reversed to one of happiness and relief.

"Thanks so much mum, dad, Finn. I'm so happy now. We're delighted that Finn will be here and of course we'll send you lots of videos of the day."

"William wants to say something."

"Finn I'm looking forward to meeting you mate, and for sure I'll be taking you to the Mānuka Honey Shop in Hunterville. Mr and Mrs O'Brien thank you for your blessing and I'm looking forward to seeing you both here in Hunterville when the baby arrives."

Everybody said their goodbyes. Once the call was over, William and Aoife hugged knowing that they could proceed full steam ahead with planning the wedding.

The weekend was a busy one for William and Aoife. As well as completing routine farm work, they invited Joseph and Suzie around for a barbeque burger evening on Saturday night. They indicated that there were matters they wanted to talk to them about and had firmed up a where and when for the wedding. Joseph and Suzie arrived with an assortment of salad bowls for the barbeque. They were full of expectations and were not disappointed as the conversation unfolded.

"Joseph and Suzie, it's full steam ahead with the wedding now that we have spoken to all our parents. Aoife's parents were a bit shocked initially, but once they had processed it all they gave us their full blessing. That was important to us."

"I can imagine that it was a bit of a shock to them, especially the baby part. Will they be able to come to the wedding?" asked Suzie.

"They won't be coming to the wedding but my brother Finn will come to represent the family. Mum and Dad are going to make the trip here for the baby's arrival" replied Aoife.

"Nice."

"Suzie I haven't known you for very long, but in the short time I have, it's been a supportive and caring friendship. Will you please be my bridesmaid at the wedding?"

"Oh my gosh thank you so much Aoife. I've never been a bridesmaid before. Nobody has ever asked me. I'd love to."

Seeing that Suzie was becoming teary, Joseph moved over to comfort and hug her. This was a side of Joseph that William hadn't seen before and he fully approved of his friend's maturing personality. William noted that Joseph had the look of 'and what about me' on his face.

"Joseph, you have been my best friend for a long time now. You were there to help me a few months back when I had my meltdown and was struggling. There's no other person I'd want to be my best man other than you. If you can't be my best man then I won't have one. Will you please do that for me?"

"Thanks William, of course I will. Thank you for having faith in me. I promise that I'll do you both proud."

The rolls were suddenly reversed and it was now Joseph becoming extremely emotional with his partner Suzie having to comfort him.

"Have you decided on a date?" asked Suzie.

"We have," replied William "it's the Huntaway Festival in town the first Saturday in November and a lot of townsfolk are involved with that, so we've decided on the weekend before that, Saturday 26th October. We're going to have a formal church ceremony in Hunterville and then a reception at a venue yet to be decided."

"Reception in town or have you got somewhere else in mind?" asked Joseph.

"There's one potential venue in Hunterville and one just out of Hunterville. I want to show Aoife both tomorrow afternoon and I'll let her decide."

"Any clues?" asked Joseph again, sifting for information.

"Sorry Joseph. I'll let you know on Monday."

They all laughed and then enjoyed the evening's BBQ meal. After Joseph and Suzie had departed William discussed further wedding plans with Aoife.

"Aoife are you OK with the plans so far?"

"More than OK William, I'm so happy. Everything is falling into place nicely."

"I know I'm not exactly the same as most other guys Aoife and there are a few things I want to do differently for our wedding. These are things that mean a lot to me. I just want to make sure none of them will be offensive to you so here goes."

"William, I love you so much because you are different. I already know that none of what you're about to say will not offend me, but go ahead anyway."

Aoife listened very intently as William started telling her his personal thoughts and plans for the wedding.

"I'm happy just to have Joseph as my best man and no other groomsmen. Of course I want my other mates to be there as my friends, but not as groomsmen. If you decide to wear your grandmother's vintage lace wedding dress then I'll wear my opera suit from Naples. It has special significance to me. However, if you want to wear something more modern then I'll dress accordingly. I want to write my own wedding vows. They will be promises and commitments from my soul not from a random online website. I want to wear a spring of Mānuka flowers on my left lapel and a sprig of red cotoneaster berries on my right lapel. I'm going to ask Connie and Kathy if they would like to do the reception food and I'd like to ask Mr Bates if he will be the church ceremony and reception usher because I know he'd enjoy that role. I'll show you possible reception venues tomorrow and let you pick one. If neither appeals then we'll keep looking. And finally, when it comes to deciding who to invite to the wedding my plan is a bit unconventional."

"Wow William everything sounds perfect so far. I love it all. We need somebody to video parts of the wedding and reception to send to Mum and Dad.

I know it's a bit of a longshot and a strange request but do you think there's any possibility that we could grow some 4-leaf clover for the wedding day? If I could have a simple bouquet of late spring freesias mixed with sprigs of 4-leaf clover to signify my Irish heritage, well that would be all I need."

"It's definitely possible Aoife. I'll ask the guy that supplies all the seed for grassland planting on the farm. I know him well and he's super knowledgeable. He'll know where to get 4-leaf clover seed from and the best time to plant it so it's ready at the end of October. There'll be somebody in town that would be happy to be our video technician for the day. We've got time, no problem."

William continued telling Aoife about the reception plan.

"Since you are newly arrived to town and the district you don't know a lot people yet. You will and they'll all embrace you. That's a given. Basically I know everybody in town, and there are lots of other people I know through the farm activities and my rugby mates and old university friends and all of Mum and Dad's friends. They don't have many weddings in Hunterville so I thought that I'd put out an open invitation to anybody and everybody that might like to come and share the day with us. Put the word out via the grapevine and then word will spread very quickly on the bush telegraph. The only proviso I'll make is that people should let us know prior to Friday 18th October so we can organise and cater for the numbers. It could be forty, one hundred or it could be four hundred. No idea."

"Wow, that's pretty radical William to invite the whole town and sundry, but the more I think about it the kinder a gesture it seems. I know you're well liked around town so I didn't think we'd be celebrating the day alone."

"Is it a plan then?"

"It is. I'm so glad Finn will be here with us."

"Me too. Between now and the 26th October we'll concentrate on the wedding planning and I'd better get serious on the farm. There's a lot of farm work needs to be done over the next six weeks."

William and Aoife retired to bed knowing that wedding arrangements were well and truly underway and that their relationship would be formalised to husband and wife status in around six weeks' time. The minor bumps which had presented over the past few days had all been navigated successfully.

The following morning William and Aoife woke up hungry for each other, and hungry for a good breakfast. Ever inventive, William got up first on the pretext of making them a coffee in the kitchen. He did that, but also went to the bathroom. It was a long time since the oversized bath tub had been used. In fact, he couldn't even remember when he last had a bath in it. He started filling it up and poured some of his favourite sandalwood oil in the bath. He readied some thick crisp white towels on the towel rack. And as a last touch he rummaged around in the kitchen drawers and managed to find a couple of long stemmed old school type candles left over from when he parents were living in the house. He anchored them into a couple of very small vases, lit them and placed them on the basin benchtop in the bathroom. Finally William carried the coffee to the bathroom and put one at each end of the bathtub. He tested the water temperature to make sure that it wasn't too hot or too cold for his pregnant wife to be.

William had hatched his plan and returned to the bedroom door from which he addressed Aoife.

"Coffee's ready Aoife. Come and get it while it's hot."

"OK, want me to make breakfast or will you?"

"I will. It's almost ready."

He returned to the kitchen and Aoife followed soon after. When she entered there was no sign of breakfast being ready. There was just William leaning against the kitchen table clad in a pair of loose fitting boxers with that alluring smile of his. He took Aoife by the hand and silently guided her from the kitchen to the bathroom. Aoife flashed a smile of surprise and then approval upon entering the bathroom. No words were spoken. Aoife turned to a naked William as he deftly undressed her. William shut the bathroom door. He had always been a gentle and respectful lover and was even more so now that Aoife was pregnant. What followed was an hour of private intimacy and passion. Since they were both conservative leaning, what went on behind the bathroom door was destined to stay behind the bathroom door.

Later in the day when William had completed some farm work and Aoife had completed a bit of gardening outside and a bit of housework inside, William reappeared and asked if she would like to go and visit the potential wedding receptions sites. Aoife didn't need to be asked twice and ten minutes later they were heading down the long farm driveway.

"The first one is an indoor venue in Hunterville, the second is an outdoor venue just a few minutes from the farm which we'll visit on the way back."

William smiled at Aoife as they drove past Simpsons Reserve on their way into town. He smiled because this is where they'd be stopping on the way home and she was oblivious to its existence. William drove into Hunterville and turned to the right in the centre of town. One hundred metres down the street he stopped and they got out.

"This is the first possible venue. It's the fully restored town hall. It's really large and roomy inside and can accommodate three hundred and fifty people or thereabouts. It's close to the café which would be a real advantage if Connie and Kathy confirm they'll do the catering."

"It's nice but I'm curious about the second possibility."

"OK, let's get in the car and go there. It's only five minutes away. We drove past it on the way here."

William drove back towards home and a few minutes later stopped at a pair of white concrete and stone commemorative gates each about ten metres in length. The entrance gates were erected either side of a secondary vehicle road leading into a forested area. The white gate on the left hand side was emblazoned with the words 'A. G. Simpson' in black lettering, while the one on the right just had the word 'Domain' also in black lettering.

"This area is known by the locals as Simpsons Reserve. I'll drive in off the main road and park on the grassed area on the left. Then we can walk across the small bridge by foot and I'll show you the area I was thinking of."

After parking the car and getting out, Aoife's initial facial expressions indicated to William that she was confused. A wedding reception in a forest was not what she had in mind.

"OK, come with me. Here hold my hand. The bridge needs a bit of repair."

Aoife and William held hands as they carefully walked across the small bridge and then immediately entered a densely forested area. Aoife was impressed because they didn't have such densely forested areas like this back in Ireland.

"This is a remnant of native podocarp forest. The trees are all evergreen. They've calculated that some of the trees in this forest are 800 years old. See how there are different layers of trees. There's the tall canopy trees reaching for the light, and beneath those, there are several lower levels of many different species of shade loving trees and tree ferns, and then a huge variety of ferns thriving on the forest floor. Can you believe that before the first European settlers came in the mid-1800s and starting felling and clearing the native forests for lumber and farming, the whole of the Rangitikei District was covered in this type of forest. What a site that would have been. It must have been magnificent."

Aoife listened intently to William and noted how articulate and enthusiastic he was when he talked of something he was passionate about. She was very proud of him. As they walked through the forest she took in some deep breaths of air. It was sweet and had a wholesome vegetative smell. She could hear birds singing and moving within the forest but it was hard to see them due to the subdued light at ground level. Everything felt so natural and in balance.

William stopped several times to gaze upwards at individual kahikatea and rimu native trees. He didn't say anything. He just scanned the tree trunks slowly with his eyes, touched with his fingers and rubbed his palm along the bark, and then looked up at the magnificent canopy of branches towards the top of the trees. Aoife could tell that he was awed by their significant age and majesty.

It was only a short walk through the forest and then they suddenly emerged out to a large grassed clearing. She scanned around and the grassed clearing was completed surrounded on all sides by dense forest.

"Going way back, there used to be a large sawmill nearby here, and this block of forest was part of a large farm before being gifted to the community by the owner. In 1933 it was officially opened as a domain for the public. They used to hold a lot of social events here like picnics, brass bands parades, local anniversary day celebrations, but they rarely do these days."

"Are you suggesting we have our reception here? But what if it rained? It's too much of a risk William."

"I know it's a risk and don't ask me how I know, but it will be a fine weekend when we get married. I had a dream. Something or somebody has promised me it will be sunny and warm. I'd love this reserve to come alive with happy people and fun and laughter even if it was just for one day" replied William flashing his trademark smile towards Aoife.

"It's hard to reply to that William. Your reasoning is a bit abstract. It would make everything logistically more difficult but if you seriously want to have our wedding reception here I'm good with that. I'll trust your instincts. And even if it did rain guess what? I don't care. It's what we want to do that counts. So decision is made. Our reception will be here. I can't believe I just said that to you."

William and Aoife laughed and then hugged and kissed as they stood in the middle of the expansive grassed clearing at Simpsons Reserve. They were as happy as they had ever been.

Over the next five weeks, William and Aoife with the help of their dearest friends and the Hunterville community at large, made preparations for their wedding day. There was an excited buzz around town. People were genuinely happy for William and his bride to be, and wanted to show that they too could put on an event that had a feel good factor. They wanted William and Aoife's wedding day to be one that people would remember fondly for a very long time. Being a town and district full of practical and artisan people, nothing in the planning phase was overlooked. The bridge to Simpsons Reserve was repaired, a large marque tent was ordered from Palmerston North to erect in the domain as a contingency in case of bad weather, flowers were tended, transportation from town to Simpsons Reserve and back was pre-booked and William's farm advisory friend took on the responsibility of having masses of 4-leaf clover ready for Aoife a day or two before the wedding.

Joseph, Suzie and Mr Bates were outstanding in preparing for the event. There wasn't anything they hadn't considered. Connie and Kathy had confirmed that they would love to be involved with catering for the event and were just waiting on the confirmed numbers attending.

The local woman's farmers club who all knew William's mother very well, insisted that they make some food for the reception also. Being mostly but not exclusively of the older generation, they remembered back to the days when Simpsons Reserve had been used regularly for community events. They were all very excited that it would come back to life even if just for the day.

William's rugby team mates asked if they could be ushers and waiters at the reception. They wanted to wear their rugby uniforms at the reception. William chuckled when he asked Aoife if that would be alright. They both agreed that whatever made people happy was the way they wanted to go on the day.

William had been feeling guilty for several weeks about not having given his father proper recognition on Father's Day back on the 1st September. That had been the weekend Aoife arrived to Auckland Airport after her long trip from Ireland. He mentioned his misgivings to Aoife and knowing that William was very close to his father, she responded exactly how he hoped she would.

"You must do something. I know you're really busy but how about this coming Sunday? You go to Palmerston North and collect your dad. I'll make a nice lunch. You can spend the day showing your dad around the farm and take him to Simpsons Reserve and see if he can tell you anything about its past history. Then you can drive him back home later in the day."

"That sounds perfect. And I'll also take him to Hunterville Cemetery down the road. His parents, my grandparents are buried there. I know he'd like to pay his respects."

William's belated Father's Day celebration was completed as planned. William drove his father up to the highest point on the farm on his quad bike and showed him exactly where he had proposed to Aoife. From that vantage point, he showed his father all the improvements he had made on the farm. His father was impressed. Later during the visit, William could tell from his father's reactions that it was very nostalgic visiting Simpsons Reserve and the Hunterville Cemetery. The day had been a resounding success and William felt happy that he had given his dad the recognition he deserved, even if it had been a few weeks late.

The days passed and the wedding plans were now in full swing. As far as they could tell, everything was going smoothly. So far, there had been no hiccups.

The evening of Friday the 18th October had arrived and after dinner, William and Aoife tallied up the number of people that indicated they would be attending their wedding day the following weekend. Some people asked if they could bring children. Others asked if they could bring girlfriends and boyfriends and children. William and Aoife decided they get back to those people and confirm yes, yes, yes. The final tally including adults and children and cats and dogs was three hundred and sixteen.

"Crickey. That's a lot of people Aoife. Do you think it's too many?"

"It's too late now. We've committed but don't worry. With everybody's help, we'll make it happen."

"You're right. I'll let Connie and Kathy and the farmer's club ladies know. I don't care how much it costs I just want it to be a day to remember."

William and Aoife decided to proceed on that basis. But they had more pressing matters at hand because the following day Finn was arriving in to Auckland. William and Aoife were on overload, so Joseph had offered to drive up to Auckland very early on Saturday morning, collect Finn, and drive him straight back to Hunterville. Finn would be tired after the long journey from Ireland to Auckland but it was a full week until the wedding which they hoped would be sufficient time for his body clock to readjust.

On Saturday evening at around 5 pm, William and Aoife heard a car with its horn tooting coming up the farm driveway. They immediately knew that Finn had arrived and went out to meet him. Aoife was very excited and threw her arms around her brother. He embraced her warmly. William hadn't met Finn before in person but Finn greeted him with just the same enthusiasm he had shown towards Aoife. Aoife sensed that her brother and William would be instant good friends since they were both around the same age, had both lived most of their life on a farm, and both loved all things honey related.

"I know you'll be tired Finn but just one question before you go and rest. Did you bring grandma's vintage wedding dress?"

"I did. Do you want it now?"

"Is that asking too much?"

"Let me show you to your room Finn and where the bathroom is, and then after that you can unpack. How about that?" suggested William.

Aoife immediately sent a text to her parents letting them know that Finn had arrived safely to the farm. Finn disappeared for half an hour and came back showered and changed. He was carrying the wedding dress in a box for Aoife. Aoife was excited to show it to William who was just as excited to see it.

Aoife opened the large box and let the wedding dress unfurl. William knew that whatever Aoife wore on their wedding day she would look beautiful, but wearing the crème coloured satin and lace vintage wedding dress held up before him, he knew she would look stunning.

"It's going to be a bit like beauty and the beast walking up the aisle."

William had never seen Aoife displeased before but he sensed that he might have said something wrong. All the while Finn was observing and listening.

"William. Please don't say that. It hurts me when you say that about yourself. You'll never be my beast. You the kindest, smartest most caring man I've ever known. Looks will never impress me. I see nothing but a handsome quality man when I look at you."

"I'm sorry Aoife, I just have these self-doubts that people will wonder why you're with me."

"I'm with you because I adore you. Looks don't last William but I know that smile of yours will endure forever."

William apologised and promised that he'd never think those thoughts again. Finn could tell that his sister was deeply and madly in love with this man living in a small rural town in New Zealand. He retired to bed knowing that she had made the right choice for a lifetime partner.

The day of the wedding was fast approaching. There was a lot to do but the townsfolk in Hunterville had taken it upon themselves to make sure that Aoife and William's wedding day was one to remember. Those that could help did so in many different ways. Mr Bates from the Mānuka Honey Shop made it his personal responsibility to ensure that everything was ready for the big day. He was particularly diligent about arrangements for the reception at Simpsons Reserve. He had considered everything. Music, a dance floor, scattered sunshade areas, hay bales for seating, a sound system, lighting, shuttle busses, the catering, the drinks, and close family seating arrangements. People around town were amazed at his organisational skills and wondered if he had done this before in a past life. Nobody actually knew what he had done before he came to Hunterville and set up his successful honey shop business.

Joseph and Suzie had been stellar. They both took their responsibilities very seriously.

It was only three days before the wedding and William and Aoife decided that they'd go in to Hunterville and have a final café visit before the wedding, and at the same time, introduce Finn to Mr Bates.

The café visit went well as did Finn's visit with Mr Bates. Connie and Kathy confirmed that they were shocked when first told how many people would be attending the wedding reception, but once they got used to the idea, it was full steam ahead with the help of the ladies from the women's branch of the farmers club. There was a plan.

Mr Bates was very interested to hear about Finn's fledgling honey business back in Ballinrobe, and Finn was interested to tap in to Mr Bates' expertise. He was amazed at how many different types of floral and bush honey Mr Bates sold in his shop. On the way out of the honey shop Mr Bates handed Finn a gift.

"Has William told you yet about the 10+ Mānuka honey?"

"No, not yet. Is it special?"

"I think it might be. Ask William to explain. It worked for him."

Finn didn't really understand what Mr Bates meant but promised himself that he'd ask William at the first opportunity. When they got back to the farm and Finn was alone with William he asked the question that was on his mind.

"William, Mr Bates said to ask you about this 10+ Mānuka honey. He gave it to me as a gift as I was leaving the shop. He kind of suggested that it was special. What did he mean by that?"

William laughed and proceeded to explain to Finn. "Do you have a serious or significant partner?"

"No, but I'm looking."

"Take a teaspoon of this honey daily."

"Is it an aphrodisiac or something like that?"

"Can't say. Not telling. But let me know what happens."

Finn was none the wiser for William's vague explanation but was determined to do as William had suggested.

Wedding Day and Celebration at Simpsons Reserve

It was Saturday, 26th October 2019. The day of William and Aoife's wedding in Hunterville had arrived. Upon waking up, William leaped out of bed, went outside to check the weather, quickly checked the weather forecast online and then rushed back inside to give the good news to Aoife.

"Aoife, it's going to be a fine sunny day. The god's are smiling on us." Aoife who was still half asleep gave a simple reply.

"Nice. We're lucky."

Meticulous planning had been completed over the previous six weeks to make sure it would be a day that William and Aoife and the whole of the Hunterville community and district wouldn't forget in a hurry.

William's parents had arrived up the night before from Palmerston North and were staying at the farmhouse. Finn was staying there also. He had recovered from the long journey from Ireland the week before and was ready for the big day.

The formal church service in Hunterville was timed to begin at 12 noon exactly and the reception was due to commence at 2.30 pm at Simpsons Reserve.

William had made sure that word got out on the grapevine that the formal church service was very important to Aoife and her family, and as such, he requested that it was undertaken in a dignified and respectful way.

William got dressed in his black vintage opera suit from Naples resplendent with colourful sprigs of flowers and berries from his favourite Mānuka and red bead cotoneaster trees. He was visibly nervous as Finn drove him to the church in town. He arrived at 11.30 am and by that time, the church was already full of people. There were also many gathered on the grass areas outside of the church. William's parents had been collected from the farm by family friends and were already seated in the front row inside the church. A local person was also waiting to record the event on video and another to take photographs.

Immediately after William left, Suzie helped Aoife get dressed in her grandmother's cream coloured satin and lace vintage wedding dress. Her wedding dress was snug fitting but not so tight as to be inappropriate for getting married in church. Her bouquet of spring freesias and 4-leaf clovers was unique and meaningful. She wore no veil. Her hair was tied up in a bun and a small sprig of freesias and 4-leaf clovers pinned to her hair. Suzie was a doting bridesmaid and double checked that everything was in order before Aoife walked out into the lounge.

Joseph paced around nervously in the lounge. His biggest fear was of being late and keeping William waiting. At 11.45 am Aoife was ready and emerged into the lounge.

"Holy s—shipwreck Aoife. William's going to melt in front of us like butter on a hot frying pan. My goodness, I guarantee his tears will flow like a river in flood when he sees you."

Aoife smiled at Joseph. She was impressed with his down to earth eloquence. Joseph and Suzie escorted Aoife out to the car.

Suzie sat in the back with Aoife and they drove the short distance to the church in Hunterville arriving there exactly at 12 noon. Joseph jumped out of the driver's seat and bounded around to Aoife's side and opened the door for her. Aoife got out of the car.

Initially, there was silence from the wedding crowd gathered in the grassed area just outside the church, and then there was polite chatter and whispers. Finally when William's mates couldn't stand holding back their admiration of the bride any longer, there were loud whistles, cheering and spontaneous clapping. It was a sign of unanimous approval from the crowd waiting outside. William could hear the noise from inside the church and wondered what all the commotion was about. He had told everybody to be respectful inside the church, but he didn't say anything about outside the church, and the wedding guests were taking full advantage of that.

Aoife stopped just outside the church doors and waited for Finn to come to her side and escort her down the aisle. Finn came to his sister, kissed her on the cheek, and told her that he was very proud.

"Mum and Dad will be overwhelmed when they see you in grandma's wedding dress. I've never been so proud in my whole life Aoife. You're amazing. William is going to flip. Nothing is more certain."

"Thanks Finn. This is for William. I love him more than people will ever understand. Can I go to him now?"

Prior to wedding day, Aoife and William had met with the minister to discuss various aspects of the wedding service they wanted. The youthful minister told them that what they were planning was a bit unconventional and in one or two places a little bit controversial.

However, he wanted to be seen in the community as progressive and inclusive so he agreed to most of what they had requested. It was to be a service that combined traditional with modern, old world with new world, and sacred with bold. A video feed has been set up by some of William's mates so that those people outside the church could see the service on a large screen.

"Are you ready Aoife?"

"Yes, I am."

Finn asked if they could start the music. Aoife had personally and carefully selected the song she wanted to be played as she walked down the aisle towards William. It was her personal gift to William. She hadn't told him what her unconventional song choice was. It had been approved by the minister, but only just and with some reservation.

'Lovin You' sung by Minnie Riperton began playing and there was instant silence from all the people gathered to formalise William and Aoife's marriage. You could have heard the proverbial pin drop. The song could be heard both inside and outside the church.

Aoife held onto Finn's arm and commenced a slow walk down the aisle towards William. William was listening carefully to the words of Aoife's song choice, and as she got closer Aoife could see that as expected, tears were rolling freely down his cheeks, and Joseph's cheeks and those of half the congregation. Life can be full of beautiful moments that leave a lasting impression, and this must surely have rated as one of them.

Many of the older people inside the church thought the song choice a little bit liberal and raised their eyebrows in surprise, however despite their reservations, they all clearly decided it was appropriate for William and Aoife since they were deeply in love and had brought a lot of happiness to the town.

William's parents sitting in the front pew were very proud of their only son. He was a very respectful man who always listened to what they had to say, but in the end, usually did it his way. They were conservative and controlled but admired their son's much freer spirit.

Aoife arrived to William's side. She could see the joy and happiness in his tear filled eyes. Aoife was a picture of composed ethereal beauty and dignity as she glanced towards William and sent him a reassuring smile. The moment they both wanted had finally arrived.

The minister stepped forward and the serious part of the wedding ceremony began. After exchanging their personal vows, exchanging rings, and reciting prays and readings which both sets of parents had selected at Aoife and William's request, the minister pronounced them husband and wife.

Not wanting to make an embarrassing mistake William waited and waited and waited for the minister to give his final blessing. Just when his patience was starting to be sorely tested, the minister realised his slip up.

"Oh sorry William, you may kiss the bride."

And that's exactly what he did to raucous laughter and clapping in the church. The cheering and clapping continued once they were outside the church. Aoife whispered into William's ear.

"Thank you William. The church service was perfect. I can't wait for Mum and Dad to see the videos."

Mr Bates was fully in control of proceedings outside of the church and announced that the wedding reception would start at 2.30 pm at Simpsons Reserve. Transportation was available for those who needed it and he reminded everybody that if they were drinking to make sure they had a designated driver for the return home after the reception. It was a long time since most of the people going to the wedding reception had been anywhere near Simpsons Reserve so there was a lot of curiosity and expectation about the venue.

William and Aoife had gone home to change into something more comfortable. They wanted it to be a casual affair and dressed accordingly. Everything was ready for their arrival. The townsfolk had made sure it was going to be an afternoon and evening that the town wouldn't forget in a hurry. Connie and Kathy together with the ladies from the farmers club were in a designated tent making sure that all the finishing touches to the buffet meal were underway. William's friends from the rugby club and others from the music club in town had an afternoon and evening of entertainment planned. They were confident it would cater to the wide age and gender demographic that was expected to be at the reception.

Lights, cameras, action, it was 2.30 pm and the newly married couple arrived. William was dressed in snug fitting faded blue jeans, a checked shirt and his outback hat. Aoife thought it would be cute if she dressed the same. The crowd waiting for them at Simpsons Reserve approved of the informality and clapped and whistled enthusiastically when they arrived.

William went up on the small stage with Aoife and spoke into the microphone.

"Ladies and gentlemen, boys and girls, and my mates from the rugby club, thank you for a very special wedding day. You're all incredibly kind and generous. So many people have worked hard to make sure that this wedding reception here at Simpsons Reserve does justice to the setting. Aoife and I feel blessed. Please have a good time, kick back and we'll talk to as many of you as we can later. Buffet food will be served at 5 pm and we'll crank up the scatted barbeques around the perimeter at around 4 pm. The music should be good.

They promised me it would be. Let's do it. Let's relive the good ol' days."

The music started, the beer and wine was flowing and the dancing commenced. A few clouds had arrived after lunchtime so it wasn't as hot and sunny as they expected. It was just a beautiful 20 degree C spring afternoon. It was perfect for outdoor partying.

The reception had commenced and Simpsons Reserve was buzzing. At 5 pm, William went back onstage to announce that dinner would be served. After he had everybody's attention, he thanked the team involved in presenting the mouth-watering buffet they were about to enjoy.

"I'd like to thank Connie and Kathy from the café, and the ladies from the farmers club and various other people around town for preparing this fantastic spread. And I'd also…"

William's speech was cut short by the sound of haunting music emanating from the surrounding dense bush. The sound was breathtakingly pure and spiritual. It sounded like somebody was playing a flute. It didn't come from the same spot. Short bursts seemed to come from different places in the bush. There was complete silence from everybody as they listened to the haunting pure sound surrounding them. Then as suddenly as it had started, the flute sound stopped and it was replaced by the sound of hundreds of birds simultaneously singing in the tall trees surrounding the grassed clearing. Their joyful melodic chirping completely filled the air and then it also stopped suddenly.

Everybody just assumed that William had organised it for Aoife in recognition of them now being husband and wife, and they showed their appreciation by enthusiastically clapping before getting back to the party.

Aoife glanced over to William knowing that she had heard this exact sound before. It had occurred at a previous momentous point in their lives. She rushed over to William.

"William did you arrange that? It was so beautiful and so romantic."

"Aoife it wasn't me."

"But it's that same sound I heard coming from the bush up on the hilltop when you proposed to me."

"Very strange. I'll ask the guys later. I'm sure one of them has organised it or set it up."

Aoife didn't say anything more to William about it. Something was responsible for the flute music they heard but she had no idea what or whom that could be.

The wedding reception continued into the evening. The buffet meal was a resounding success and the ladies who had prepared it were congratulated over and over again.

The music was eclectic and appropriate for both the older generation and the younger generation. There were no complaints. The seating was plentiful for those who were running out of energy. Several of William's university mates had formed a band and they played some live music. The alcohol and non-alcoholic drinks didn't run out and everybody had as much as they wanted, even if there were a few who should have stopped drinking at an earlier stage of the evening.

Holding the wedding reception as Simpsons Reserve had been a resounding success. There wasn't a single person that hadn't enjoyed William and Aoife's wedding reception. A lot of townsfolk commented that they didn't realise such a fantastic event venue existed in their own backyard very close to town. They hoped it wouldn't be the last gathering at Simpsons Reserve.

William and Aoife left the wedding reception with William's parents at 8 pm. It had been a long day but one which they wouldn't forget for a long, long time to come.

William Loses His Father

Married life was bliss for William and Aoife. They had been married one month. Christmas was only four weeks away and the arrival of the baby was just under six months away. Farm commodity prices were attracting a premium. Everything was perfect until the morning Aoife received the phone call from William's mother in Palmerston North.

"Morning Aoife, this is Mrs Thomson, is William about?"

"Morning, he's out on the farm but said he'd come in for lunch. What's wrong?"

From the tone of her mother-in-law's voice she instantly knew that something was terribly wrong. She assumed that William's father wasn't well or had a relapse and that William needed to know as soon as possible.

"Mr Thomson had a massive stroke earlier this morning and passed away an hour ago. I'm at home alone."

Aoife could hear her uncontrollable crying on the phone. She became frantic and desperate wondering what to do.

"I'm so sorry. OK, please just wait at home and I'll get William and we'll be there as soon as possible. I promise we'll be there soon."

"Please come soon."

"We will. Bye."

Aoife put down the phone and sat in stunned silence for a couple of minutes. She realised that sitting in silence wasn't helping the matter so immediately called Suzie and told her what had happened. Suzie called Joseph and within thirty minutes they had both arrived to the farm. They had to act quickly knowing that word of William's fathers passing would spread like wildfire in the community since he was well respected by everybody, but especially the older generation.

"This is going to be difficult. If I go up and get him he'll know something is wrong and I'll need to tell him. I think it's better coming from you Aoife. Are either of the farm workers around?"

"I think George is out in the farm shed."

"I'll tell him to let William know that there's a problem at home and ask if he can come back down to the house as soon as possible. He'll be worried but at least he'll get here quickly and we can try and get prepared to break the news to him."

"Suzie, Joseph thanks for coming so quickly. I can't do this alone. William will be devastated. You know how much he loves his father."

Joseph ran out to the farm shed, explained to George what had to be done but didn't explain exactly why. George left immediately on a quad bike saying he knew where William was working.

Ten minutes later William rushed in to the house. He had seen Joseph's car in the driveway but didn't understand what was he was doing there at that time of day. He ran to the lounge and was even more surprised to see Aoife, Suzie and Joseph all standing and waiting for him. He could see that Aoife was alright so knew it had to be something else.

"What's wrong?" he asked frantically.

Aoife ran over to him and hugged him tightly. She didn't want to let him go, knowing that the next few minutes would be a difficult time. She was dreading having to tell him.

"Please tell me what's wrong."

"William, it's your dad. He suffered a massive stroke earlier this morning. He passed away a couple of hours ago."

William burst into uncontrollable crying.

"No, please no. Please no. Please don't tell me that. No. Not my dad."

William was inconsolable. His grief was palpable. Aoife, Suzie and Joseph all felt helpless at that moment. Aoife knew she had to do or say something.

"William, your mum is alone at home. Imagine how she's feeling. You need to go to her immediately. Joseph said he'll drive you there. Do you want me to come?"

"Of course. My mum. I need to get to Mum and Dad immediately. No Aoife, best you stay here for now and I'll call you when I find out all the details. Joseph, Suzie I'm sorry about this inconvenience."

"Don't be crazy mate. We're here to help you. Everybody would want to help you and everybody will help you. Come on let's go right now. Your mum needs you."

Joseph helped William out to his car and they set off to Palmerston North.

Suzie said she would stay with Aoife. No ifs, buts or maybes. She phoned her work, explained to them what had happened and they all agreed that the priority should be for her to stay and help William and Aoife.

The following few days were difficult. William was taking it hard. Aoife and William's best friend Joseph had made a bad situation just bearable. William had many regrets. There was so much he had wanted to do with his father. He was devastated that his father wouldn't see his grandchild. He was devastated that his father wouldn't see the grand plans he had for the farm come to fruition.

William comforted his mother as best he could over the days following his father's death and suggested that it might be better if she came back to the farm for a few days. She agreed. William worked diligently on making the funeral arrangements. The townsfolk rallied around and helped William and his mother as much as was needed.

Since most of the family friends were located in the Hunterville District, William arranged for the church service to be held in Hunterville followed by a graveside service at the Hunterville Cemetery. William's father had left instructions that he wanted to be buried nearby his parents and close to the family farm.

Funeral at Hunterville Cemetery

The day of the funeral arrived. William gave himself a pep talk when he had a private moment alone. He was determined to try and be brave and composed at his father's funeral service. He knew it was going to be one of the hardest things he had ever done in his life.

Aoife supported both William and his mother in a dignified and loving manner. All three were dressed for the funeral entirely in traditional black. William's mother and Aoife both wore a single white rose on their lapels.

It was standing room only at the church service in Hunterville which was testament that the Thomson family was held in high regard in the district. William delivered an emotional and respectful eulogy, led the prayers and selected the music to be played at this father's service. It was traditional and conservative. The congregation which was intergenerational were all moved by his loving tribute. William was living proof that there is nothing more moving than a devoted son paying tribute to a lost father.

The funeral procession from the church in town to the Hunterville Cemetery was long. The farmer who owned the paddock close by the cemetery had opened it up for parking. William and his mother were holding up, but only just. Aoife knew that the burial itself was going to be particularly hard for William and his mother she was determined to be right at their side throughout.

The funeral hearse made its way inside the cemetery gates and up towards the plot where William's father was going to be buried. It was directly opposite where his parents, William's grandparents, were buried. William waited until the large crowd attending had gathered around the grave site and then he moved to the back of the hearse. William, Joseph and four of his father's closest friends carried the coffin over to the grave site. Aoife and William's mother followed closely behind the coffin. Aoife was keeping a close eye on William knowing that he was in a very fragile state. The coffin of John William Thomson was lowered slowly into its final resting place.

Ever thoughtful William had insisted that some music be played at the grave site before his father's coffin was covered with soil. His wish had been arranged by Joseph and the first tribute song to his father began. The crowd listened in respectful and approving silence as the song 'You Raise Me Up' was sung. It signified William's appreciation of the guidance, support and sound advice his father had always given him.

William's grief couldn't be suppressed any longer and he fell to his knees with tears of immeasurable sadness rolling off his cheeks and tumbling down onto his father's coffin. It was a fitting tribute from a son to his father. William's mother and Aoife were standing either side of him and each put a hand down on his shoulder to offer support. William stood up and moved to the side to gather a wreath which one of the craftspeople in Hunterville had made for him. It was made of intertwined branches and twigs of flowering Mānuka and red bead cotoneaster collected from the local area. The contrast of small white flowers, small bright red berries and green foliage was a simple but meaningful final gesture. William dropped the wreath down onto the top of his father's coffin and then with his bare hands, he pushed several handfuls of dirt down also. He stood up and moved away and bowed his head towards his father's gravesite.

Joseph made an announcement for him.

"Family and friends…William, Aoife and Mrs Thomson thank you all for paying your respects. Your kindness has been overwhelming and they are humbled by your support. It's time to say our final goodbye. If anybody would like to join the family up the road at the farm for repast please make your way there now."

To the emotionally charged song 'Time to Say Goodbye' sung by Andrea Bocelli and Sarah Brightman all the grieving persons at and around the gravesite started to slowly file away out of the cemetery grounds. Joseph and Suzie let William and Aoife know that they would accompany Mrs Thomson back to the farm.

The graveside service had been a little bit unconventional especially with the music but William would have it no other way. After twenty minutes all the people attending the burial service had departed. William and Aoife were the only ones remaining at the cemetery.

"Thanks for all your love and support today Aoife."

William didn't want to leave his father alone. Aoife smiled and leaned over and tenderly kissed him on the head. She waited until he was ready and when he was, they held hands and walked towards the cemetery gates. As they did, Aoife spoke softly to William.

The Old Woman by the Giant Macrocarpa Tree

"William, see that old woman over there by the giant macrocarpa tree across the paddock fence. Well, she was there when we arrived for your dad's burial service. She hasn't spoken to anybody or moved the whole time. It's a bit strange."

"Yes, I can see her. This is going to sound weird Aoife, but I feel like I know her even though I don't recognise her. I feel like I've been in her presence several times before today."

"I'll stay here but I think you should go over and ask her who she is and what she wants now that everybody has left."

"Maybe I should leave it until another time."

"Up to you but who knows if there'll be another time. I really think you should go over and talk to her. Something tells me that it's important."

"I think you're right. I will."

William carefully climbed across the wire fence separating the Hunterville Cemetery from the adjacent grassed paddock and started walking over towards the old woman who was forty metres away and standing directly beside the giant macrocarpa tree. A peaceful calm descended over him as he approached the woman. He felt drawn towards the old lady.

When he got closer, he could see that she was very pale skinned, was dressed in strange woven clothing and had a crown of vines and leaves on her head. In her right hand she was holding some kind of a wooden musical instrument. It looked like a flute. She had a reassuring and commanding presence. William sensed that she had great mana.

"Hello, I'm William. Do I know you? Have we met before?"

"We haven't met formally but we have been in each other's presence several times. I have been observing you."

"I'm sorry, I don't understand. Why?"

William sensed that this was not a normal situation or a normal encounter. The woman standing before him had a warm smile and spoke with a gentle voice.

"I know that today has been a difficult one for you especially, and your wife Aoife and your mother. Your father is safe so please don't worry. You'll meet him again soon. My search is over. I need your help. I have little time left."

"How would I be able to help you?"

Standing directly in front of William, she held him by both hands and spoke his name.

William.

He immediately knew who she was.

The old lady who had been standing by the giant macrocarpa tree started to explain to William how he could help her.